Blowback '63

Blowback '63

When the Only Way Forward Is Back

Brian Meehl

Summary: Teen twins, Arky and Iris, are at it again, clashing over the Jongler family fate and the ancient woodwind (a cor anglais) left to Iris by their missing mother. This time, when Iris unleashes the time-travel powers of the cor anglais, it launches Arky and Danny, a pitching ace on the brink of disaster, to 1863, where baseball was being played in the middle of the Civil War. Danny is thrust into a baseball world he never imagined. Arky stumbles on clues leading to his mother. And Iris, in the present, plays a risky game of cat and mouse with her first victim and beneficiary of time travel, Matt Grinnell.

ISBN-13: 9781974358717
ISBN-10: 1974358712
Library of Congress Control Number: 2017913434
CreateSpace Independent Publishing Platform
North Charleston, South Carolina

Edited by Gerri Brioso
Cover Design by Elizabeth Mihaltse Lindy
Cor Anglais and Map Drawings by Torsten Muehl

Printed in the United States of America

First Edition

Also by Brian Meehl

Blowback '07

Out of Patience

Suck It Up

Suck It Up and Die

You Don't Know About Me

Pastime

blowback
when things travel in a direction opposite to the usual one: unintended consequences

It's the past that tells us who we are.
—Stephen Hawking

Part I

Ensemble

1

Time-Travel Agent

With a lap to go, Arky Jongler-Jinks had a good lead on the one runner with a chance to catch him. As he churned past the stands, a smattering of students and parents cheered him on.

In the year he'd become a winning distance runner, Arky had learned to muffle the bleacher-bleaters and the pain screaming in his legs. He was locked on hitting his splits and answering challengers with a final kick that turned his lungs inside out. His race plan for the 2 mile and for life was the same: leave nothing on the field.

As he hit the turn, Matt Grinnell and Danny Bender watched from the stands. Slouched on the bleachers, they wore dirty baseball uniforms. Matt was big and muscular with thick black hair. Danny was long and lean with a blond buzz cut and jug ears. Having finished baseball practice, they were there to cheer on their small and fiery buddy. The trio—Matt, Danny, Arky—were known as the "two and a half musketeers."

"Hey, Ark!" Danny yelled. "One's gainin' on ya!"

Matt cupped his hands. "And she looks like Iris!"

Danny laughed at the reference to Arky's nemesis: his twin sister Iris.

The taunt pierced Arky's focus. He used it. The image of Iris catching him fired his afterburners. Answering his buddies, he flipped middle fingers from pumping fists.

After Arky won the race, the three friends grabbed showers and headed for the parking lot. The last Friday in April had delivered a warm day that made the end of school feel around the corner.

Arky was finishing his junior year. His plan to get into Harvard or Yale, become a Rhodes scholar, rock the universe, and make everyone in Belleplain wish they'd been nicer to him still felt a long way off. Matt and Danny were seniors. Matt had nailed a full-boat scholarship to a Division I football powerhouse, the next step in his dream of Big Ten stardom and becoming an NFL quarterback. Danny had to get through the baseball season for his shot at pitching in the Majors. If it didn't work out, Danny had plan B: become a Navy SEAL and strike out bad guys.

Danny's obsession with being a warrior had begun long before. Captain America had been his go-to superhero since his first *Captain America* comic book. Danny had seen every *Captain America* movie countless times. Even his pickup truck, a beat-up old Dodge, displayed his devotion to "Cap." He'd painted the hubcaps to resemble Captain America's go-to weapon, a shield with a blue star surrounded by red and white rings.

Reaching Danny's pickup, the boys split up; Arky followed Matt to catch a ride with him. Danny's expletive turned them around. His pickup was dead. Danny didn't have to pop the hood to know the problem—the starter was shot. It wasn't the first time his old beater had gone on the disabled list.

Watching Danny get out and slam the door, Arky turned to Matt. "Someday Captain America's gonna figure out he's driving Captain Junker."

Matt piled on. "Yep, all hubcaps, no horsepower."

Danny moved past them toward Matt's shiny Ford 150. "If *my* dad owned a dealership," he snarled, "I wouldn't drive a can of shit."

Matt slid Arky a look. It wasn't like Danny to play the poor-kid-rich-kid card.

"What's eating him?" Arky asked.

Danny moved to Matt's black pickup, with its custom gold trim, matching the colors of the North High Cyclones.

Matt thumbed his keys and beeped the truck. "He didn't throw his best stuff in practice. Probably nervous about Monday's game."

After school on Fridays, Iris Jongler-Jinks went to North High's Media Library Center and helped the librarian, Mrs. Doogan. Being Arky's twin, Iris shared her brother's slight frame and dark hair. Except for sharing the same parents and the same house, that's all they had in common. They were more like antitwins.

As Iris grabbed a cart of books that needed shelving, Mrs. Doogan looked up from her desk. "Iris, the note on top of those books is for you." Iris glanced down at a memo slip as Mrs. Doogan continued, "It's a note for your brother. Please give it to him so he can give it to Matt Grinnell."

Iris arched an eyebrow. "Why not just give it to Matt?"

"First, he rarely comes in the library," Mrs. Doogan explained. "Also, I know he and Arky are friends, and I trust Arky to impress on Matt the importance of the note."

Iris was tempted to say Matt was her friend, too, but she didn't want Doogan getting any weird ideas. Not that Matt, the top jock at North, would ever look at Iris as anything but Arky's skinny, music-geek sister. "Is Matt in trouble?" Iris asked.

"No," Mrs. Doogan said. "He needs to know that before he finishes high school he must return to North what belongs to North."

Iris acknowledged the librarian's dry wit with a quick smile and pushed the cart into the stacks. As soon as she was out of sight, Iris unfolded the note and read it.

Arky,

Would you please remind Matt Grinnell that he checked out two books in December, and he needs to return them to the library sooner than later. The honor and reputation of the "musketeers" is at stake. Not to mention a diploma, a scholarship, and the bright, shining future of our star quarterback.

Sincerely,

Mrs. Doogan

One word made Iris's heart jump: *December.* Even five months later, the wild events of late November into early December tingled under her skin every day. It was when the heartbreaking fact of her mother's disappearance a year before had been shot through a prism that refracted Iris's grief into hope. It was the week Iris and Arky had discovered that their mom, Dr. Octavia Jongler, might not be gone forever, but lost in the *past.* The reality-warping discovery had happened when Iris—the geeky girl who couldn't throw a ball more than forty yards—had accidently hurled Matt to 1907 and the Carlisle Indian School in Carlisle, Pennsylvania. She had not acted alone.

Blowing Matt to the past had been accomplished with an ancient musical instrument her mother had left Iris: a cor anglais. Most people translate "cor anglais" as "English horn." Another meaning is "horn of angels." It was the ancient woodwind's hidden powers that had transported Matt to another spacetime, where, after being treated to the healing effects of the past, he was able to "play his way home." Fortunately for Iris and Arky, shortly after Matt had returned in December, the cor anglais had buried his memories of 1907 so that he had no more sense of having time traveled than someone with glimmers of a "past life." Unfortunately for the twins, their mother's journey to the past had not ended with the same homecoming.

The fact that Matt had two unreturned library books going back to December aroused Iris's suspicion that Matt might not be as time-travel memory-free as she and Arky had assumed. *Why had he kept the books so long? What was in them?* The answers might reveal the disturbing yet tantalizing possibility that the veil between Matt's conscious and subconscious memory had begun to fray.

You would think someone with the power to hurl people to the past, and allegedly bury their time-travel memories when they returned, would know the answers to such questions. But there is one other fact that should be known. Matt was a first for Iris. As a time-travel agent, Iris was still a newbie.

2

Family Jongler-Jinks

MATT TURNED HIS F-150 into the driveway fronting the Jongler-Jinkses' two-story house. Arky rode shotgun while Danny sprawled in the extended cab, working his handheld device and racking up kills in a version of *Tour of Duty.*

Matt cut the engine.

"You coming in?" Arky asked him.

"Yeah. I got a new move I wanna show Iris."

Arky frowned at a line he'd heard too many times. Matt was referring to a *juggling* move. Over the winter, Iris had become Matt's juggling mentor. Arky accepted the unfortunate relationship as part of the deal he'd made with Iris to keep the lid on the disastrous week five months before. Arky also tolerated the Iris-Matt juggling thing because it kept another set of eyes, his sister's, on Matt in case of the ultimate disaster: Matt recalling his freaky time warp to 1907, where he played football at the Carlisle Indian School with Jim Thorpe and got coached by the famous Pop Warner. As universe shattering as that was to Arky on one level, the freaky events of that week were also a ball and chain on the brilliant future Arky had planned for himself. Time travel was not a skeleton Arky wanted out of the family closet.

As Matt opened the console between the seats and pulled out three lacrosse balls, Arky weighed in. "Lemme guess. Is it the move that's gonna get you into AP Juggling?"

Matt feigned elation. "If Iris teaches AP Juggling, screw college; I'm doing a gap year: twenty-four-seven juggling with your sister."

As Danny laughed and the boys got out of the pickup, Arky couldn't let Matt have the last word. "Really? Didn't you hear about the study that showed jugglers have more concussions than football players?"

Matt came back. "Ark, you're clairvoyant. That's my move!" He started juggling the balls, threw one high, bounced it off his head, and juggled on.

"Cool," Danny acknowledged.

Arky smirked. "Knock yourself out."

While Matt had acquired juggling skills over the winter, he had lost a defining feature: his long black hair. Most of it had been cut off in 1907. After his return to the present in time to win the state football championship, Matt considered his tousled but high 'n' tight haircut part of his luck and his new look.

After going into the house and into the kitchen, Arky didn't need to offer his friends something to eat or drink. Arky's casa was their casa. Danny grabbed a soda from the fridge.

Learning that Iris wasn't home yet, Matt went to the living room, swapped his lacrosse balls for bean bags from the basket Iris kept there, and juggled the bean bags over the couch. Howard Jinks, the twins' father, had banned ball juggling in the living room to protect the countless historical objects in the room.

As well as a free pass to a fridge, Danny liked coming to the Jongler-Jinkses' house because of the weapons hanging on the walls. Granted they were over 150-year-old muskets, pistols and swords from the Civil War, but Danny admired weapons and warriors from any era, from Captain America in World War II, to the first warrior ever. While Danny was unsure who that might be, he imagined the first soldier to be a caveman who recruited other cavemen into an army and marched them off to war with their clubs on their shoulders. Danny took his soda into the front hall, and looked for any new weapons that might have been added to the collection.

A singing voice came from the back of the house. "Goin' home, goin' home, I'm a goin' home." Danny recognized the voice of Arky and Iris's dad as his singing drew closer. "Quietlike, some still day, I'm jes' goin' home." Howard Jinks appeared. He carried a gray uniform in a dry-cleaning bag. When not being a history professor at the University of Belleplain, Howard was a passionate Civil War reenactor.

Danny recognized the uniform. "What's up with the Confederate uniform, Mr. Jinks? I thought you always went Yankee."

"I usually do, but the reenactment this weekend is special." He pointed to a framed photo hanging on the wall. "I'm playing Thomas Jinks."

Danny studied the ancient-looking photo, a daguerreotype of a young Confederate soldier with a full beard. On his forehead, a thick scar jagged into his hairline. It contrasted with the regal way he tucked his left hand into his uniform, Napoleon style. "That's a relative?" Danny asked. "I always thought he was just some Johnny Reb."

"No," Howard said, delighted to share the history. "Thomas Jinks is Arky's great-great-great-great grandfather."

Danny turned toward the kitchen where Arky was making a sandwich. "Arky, why didn't you tell me your greaty-great was a Johnny Reb?"

Arky called back, "Maybe 'cause he was a loser."

Danny returned to the daguerreotype. "Did this guy survive the war?"

Howard smiled. "If he didn't, the Jinks family line would have ended."

"How'd he get the gnarly scar on his head?"

Howard couldn't have asked for a better cue. "In the spring of 1863, Thomas fought in the Second Battle of Fredericksburg. He was left for dead with a bloody head wound. That's how he got the scar, and that's why I'm playing Thomas in Fredericksburg this weekend. I'm surprised Arky didn't tell you. He's going with me."

Arky entered the hallway, chewing on a bite from an overflowing sandwich.

"Ark, what are you goin' as?" Danny asked. "A drummer boy?"

"Not goin' as anything," Arky scoffed. "Haven't figured out my college essay, and I'm thinking maybe I'll get an idea from watching a bunch of middle-aged fat guys line up and shoot blanks at each other."

Danny pointed out the obvious. "Your dad's not fat."

"Thank you, Danny," Howard said with a smile, then tapped Danny's arm. "Hey, why don't you come with us? It would be refreshing to have someone who appreciates the history of a war that divided a nation and pitted brother against brother."

Arky answered with a full mouth. "I appreciate the Civil War. Me and Iris live it every day."

Ignoring the quip, Danny turned to Howard. "I'd like to go, Mr. Jinks, but I gotta work."

"Well, if you can get the weekend off," Howard announced as he headed for the front door, "the Civil War Express leaves at nineteen hundred tonight."

At the same time Danny was learning about the Confederate in the Jongler-Jinks family tree, Matt heard a car pull into the garage. He took his juggling balls and headed through the kitchen and the mudroom leading into the garage.

Finding Iris getting out of the Subaru wagon the twins shared—it used to belong to their mother—Matt insisted on showing off his new juggling move. Out on the driveway, he performed the head-bounce trick flawlessly and got Iris's applause. "Keep it up," she said, "and you're going to be a better juggler than me."

"Never." He caught the three balls. "After baseball season and graduation, it's gonna be all training and football. If I'm gonna be a freshman starter in the Big Ten, my juggling goes on a shelf."

Iris couldn't sit on her curiosity any longer. "Speaking of graduating," she said casually, "I heard you can't if you have overdue library books."

Matt frowned. "No way. They can't hold your diploma over a book."

"Doogan says they can. She says you have two overdue books from December."

He put on an incredulous look. "December? Why would I sit on books that long?"

Iris cocked her head and asked innocently, "I don't know. Why would you?"

Matt started to juggle. "Hey, if it's so important, I'll look around and see if—" He dropped a ball, tried to catch it on the rebound, but knocked it farther away.

Iris wasn't sure if he had fumbled it intentionally to avoid further questions or if something was making him nervous. Either way, it fueled her suspicion: he wasn't telling the whole truth. And *that* was fascinating.

The chance to continue interrogating Matt was cut off by Danny coming out of the house, followed by Arky eating the last of his sandwich. Matt and Danny left to drop Danny at his father's excavation business.

As they drove away, Arky turned to Iris. "So now you're teaching Matt to hit himself in the head with a juggling ball so that he'll what, bang open the door to all his memories of 1907 and put the Jongler family freak show on the six o'clock news?"

She answered his caustic question with her own. "Now you're spying on us?"

"Is there a reason I should be?"

Iris laughed. If there was one thing she was certain of, it was that she was the last girl Matt would be interested in. She ignored his question. "For whatever reason, if Matt *did* remember everything from 1907 and it helped us find Mom, that would be a good thing."

Not waiting for his next snide comment, Iris turned and headed into the house.

3

Music Maker

After Matt and Danny left, Howard corralled Arky for a trip to the store. They needed supplies for the long drive and the two days they would spend in the reenactors' camp near Fredericksburg, Virginia. Arky had his own grocery list that would save him from eating the Civil War grub reenactors delighted in: hardtack and beans.

Iris grabbed the opportunity to do what she tried to do whenever the house was empty. She pulled a battered wooden music case from under her bed. She lifted the case and headed up to the attic office.

It was the room their mother had set up and soundproofed for a yearlong sabbatical from teaching and research at the University of Belleplain. The attic office was where Dr. Octavia Jongler had claimed she was using her sabbatical to learn to play the English horn, a woodwind in the oboe family that's larger than a standard oboe and deeper in pitch. Octavia had also claimed she was writing a book about the experience, *A Year of Magical Playing: An Astrophysicist Explores Inner Space through Music*. Instead, as Iris and Arky had discovered five months earlier, their mother learning to play a modern English horn had been a cover. Her real purpose had been to master playing a four-hundred-year-old English horn, a cor anglais, at the center of a Jongler family legend about time travel. And it turned her hiatus from the university into a hiatus from everything when Octavia vanished seventeen months earlier, on the Monday after Thanksgiving.

As Iris climbed the narrow stairs to the attic room, she felt a pang of guilt for not sticking to her normal after-school schedule. For an hour, she was supposed to practice her oboe audition pieces for a summer program at the Oberlin Conservatory of Music. She had made it through the first round of tryouts and was two weeks away from a callback that could put her in the summer program. The program would be a big step toward getting into a top-notch music school for college.

In the attic office, Iris opened the old wooden music case and assembled the dark and ancient cor anglais. Longer than a standard oboe, the cor anglais was curved like a crescent. The Jongler cor anglais was made even stranger by a bas-relief decoration carved on the bell-end of the instrument: a large spider. Continuing the spider motif, the back, inside arc of the instrument was decorated with delicate inlay suggesting a spiderweb.

Iris inserted a double reed in the crook at the top of the cor anglais. As she moistened the reed with her mouth, her eyes fell on the opposite wall framed by the gabled roof and ceiling.

On the wall, their mother had built an assemblage that combined a huge spiderweb and her scientific passion for the cosmos. The deep-blue wall held a wide circle of large photos of galaxies and supernovas gyrating and exploding in colorful brilliance. At the center of this orbiting cosmos was a black "sun" housed in Plexiglas. The foot-wide disk of wood was a crosscut from the trunk of a grenadilla tree, the wood used to make fine woodwind instruments. Laid over the entire planetary-like display was a spiderweb of white silk. Octavia's cosmos of photos seemed to be caught in the web, with the black disk, like a spider, motionless in the center.

Iris began to play the old cor anglais. Strangely, she found it easier to play than her modern oboe. Maybe it was because the pressure of playing her oboe for the Oberlin callback was getting to her. Or maybe it was because playing the curved cor anglais filled her with pleasure and expectation. The pleasure came from knowing her mother's breath had flowed through the instrument, and her hands had fingered the same keys. The expectation came from knowing the cor anglais was the key to the past that might, one day, open a door to finding their mother.

Iris also harbored the hope that playing the cor anglais might trigger one of the music-induced visions she experienced when her synesthesia kicked in. Synesthesia is a harmless neurological disorder that cross-wires the senses. A synesthete might *see* music, or *hear* colors, or *taste* words. Iris's musical visions ranged from abstract shapes to scenes as vivid as dreams. The ultimate vision, of course, would be one of her mom. To invite that possibility, Iris often played her mother's favorite English horn solo, opening the second movement of Dvorak's 9th Symphony, *From the New World.* *

As Iris played the lamenting and poignant solo, she kept waiting for a hint of a vision to appear. During the winter and spring, except for occasional geometric shapes appearing in her visual field, she had not had a significant music-induced vision. The lack of such a vision fueled Iris's greatest fear: the hidden powers within the cor anglais, which she had spectacularly witnessed before, had gone dead.

Iris held the last note, and let it fade to silence. The moment she pulled the reed away, the door to the attic office began to open. She jumped, fearing someone was there. As the door slowly opened, no one appeared. Was it a draft? The old bones of the house stretching with the humidity of spring? A ghost? Or was it a sign? The vision she'd been waiting for? *Can't be,* she told herself. *My visions come with music, not silence.*

---

* The famous solo for the English horn, in what is popularly known as *The New World Symphony,* can be heard at https://www.youtube.com/watch?v=uCydQm83cJQ about forty-five seconds in.

Iris quickly stood to ensure it was real. The door was certainly open. So what had opened it? She laughed at a wild notion. She wasn't supposed to be in the attic playing the cor anglais. She was supposed to be in her room practicing her oboe for her Oberlin audition. Maybe her jealous oboe had summoned her.

Returning from their supply run, Howard pulled the car into the driveway and cut the engine. Oboe music drifted down from Iris's bedroom window on the second floor. Iris was practicing excerpts from Handel's *Sonata for Oboe and Basso Continuo in F Major*.

As Arky opened the passenger-side door, Howard stopped him. "She's sounding pretty good, don't you think?"

Arky looked toward the source of the music. "Yeah, sounds okay, but she's playing the wrong piece."

Howard gave him a puzzled look; he was the nonmusical one in the family. Iris and Arky were the experts. Because Octavia Jongler had played the oboe when she was young, she had insisted that her twins learn to play the oboe as well. While Arky had played through junior high, he had convinced his mother that being a science geek *and* a music geek was too much to endure for a postpubescent boy going into ninth grade. It could scar him for life. He'd won the argument, and Octavia was satisfied that Arky would continue as a budding scientist, while Iris carried the family torch for music.

"What do you mean 'the wrong piece'?" Howard asked.

Arky answered with a dismissive shrug. "She can play something more challenging than the Handel in F Major. She's gone totally chicken. When she goes to the callback, they're gonna go"—he faked a yawn—"'Boring.'"

"Have you told her this?"

"Of course." Arky frowned. "She never listens to me."

"Maybe what Iris needs is some support and praise," Howard suggested, "not criticism. Whatever her choice, we should make her feel like a virtuoso."

Arky flipped a hand at the music. "That'll never be virtuoso."

"That's not the point," Howard retorted. "I'm asking you to be supportive of your sister."

"Okay," Arky conceded. "I'll give her a pat on the head."

Howard's jaw tensed at his son's endless sarcasm. "Look, Mom's absence has been tough on all of us. But a girl losing her mother"—he let out breath to fight the welling in his eyes—"it cuts deeper than we'll ever know." He abruptly opened the car door. "Let's get the groceries. I'll put them away; you go tell Iris, in a *nice* way, that we brought home takeout."

As Arky grabbed grocery bags from the back, he reminded himself of the good news. Their dad still believed their mother's disappearance was from real causes. She'd either walked out on them, or been abducted by a psycho. Arky knew that the truth about Octavia's fate was something their father would never be able to handle. Octavia had played with fire. She'd not only learned to play the Jongler family cor anglais, she'd awakened its demonic powers. She'd blown herself to the past. She'd committed suicide by time travel.

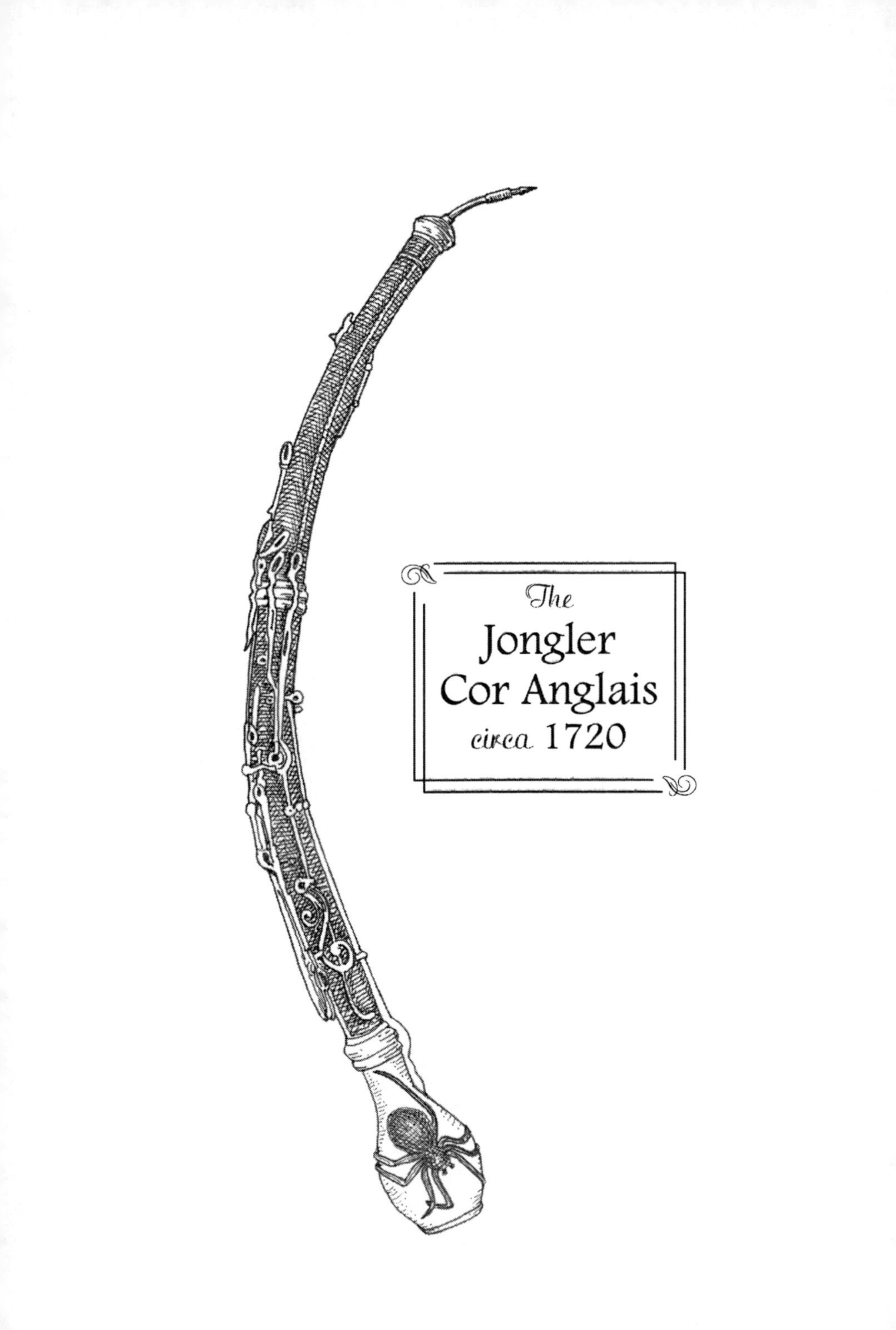
The
Jongler
Cor Anglais
circa 1720

4

Casting Lines

After Matt dropped Danny at Bender Excavation, his dad's company out on the edge of town, Danny wasn't surprised to find it closed up for the three-day Labor Day weekend. He used his key to the office to open it up and search the keyboard for a vehicle he could borrow for the weekend until he got his truck fixed. He plucked the keys to an old company van and headed out into the yard.

The vehicle yard at Bender's was a labyrinth of steel: a vast sprawl of heavy equipment, company trucks and a sea of junked cars that had been there since Ray Bender bought the place decades before. Danny found the van with Bender Excavation in peeling paint on the side panels. He hopped in and drove off.

Danny eased the van along a rutted dirt track leading down a tree-lined slope. He hoped the van didn't get stuck in one of the water-filled holes from recent rain.

Coming around a stand of trees, he spotted a white panel van parked near the edge of the lake. It confirmed his suspicion. His dad had come out to his favorite fishing spot after work. Danny liked not calling ahead and going with his gut to see if his dad would be there or not. He parked behind the van and walked out on the dock jutting into the lake.

Ray Bender sat in a wheelchair at the end of the dock and cast his line. Ray had been the main operator of all the equipment at Bender Excavation until a backhoe had done a nosedive off a flatbed and turned him into a paraplegic. He still ran the business with help from a crew, including Danny whenever he wasn't in school or playing ball.

Over the ratchet of reeling in his line, Ray heard the footfalls coming along the dock. He turned and acknowledged Danny with a smile.

"They bitin'?" Danny asked as he drew closer.

"Not as good as the bugs, Cap."

"Since when does Rambo complain about bugs?"

Ray and Danny had used the names of their boyhood heroes for years. It was their way of bonding and dismissing life's disappointments, from disability to divorce.

As Danny stopped next to his father's wheelchair, Ray cast his line again and answered Danny's question. "Since Rambo's tending the rod, his legs can't go Taekwondo on a mo-squito."

Danny chuckled.

Ray glanced back at the company van parked behind his own. "Your truck on the fritz again?"

Danny nodded and told him about the starter. "I was hoping to get an advance on my pay so I could fix it and not rely on Matt for my ride." He added the last part hoping to stir his dad's sense of pride over keeping up with richer families like the Grinnells.

Ray grunted, pulled up his lure, and cast it again. "Or you could take your newest video game to the auto parts store and trade it for a starter. You know, I don't pay workers, son or not, for work not done."

"Okay, fine." Danny interjected before he got a lecture about saving money for an emergency. "I'll wait till after the weekend."

When Danny had been younger, and his parents were still together, his father hadn't been so tough. His accident and long recovery, which led to his parents' divorce, had done more than leave his dad in a wheelchair. It had made the world a harsher place. There was nothing but hard work. There were no shortcuts.

Whether Danny became a ballplayer or a Navy SEAL was less important than if he *earned* it.

Ray lifted his lure and hooked it on the rod. "I can still help. Take the tow truck, and get your pickup to the yard before someone steals your Captain America hubcaps."

"Thanks, Dad," Danny said, trying to sound sincere.

Ray gestured to the small ice chest at Danny's feet. "Now take a peek in there."

Danny lifted the ice chest's lid. A nice bass lay on top of two unopened bottles of beer on ice. "Really? Now you're putting beer and fish on the same ice?"

"It's beer-battered fish without the batter." Ray chortled. "Now pop me a longneck, and let's get outta here."

Danny had to smile as he pulled a beer from under the fish, twisted off the cap, and handed it to his dad.

"Here's the good part," Ray said.

"You're gonna give me a beer?" Danny said.

"No way." Ray turned his wheelchair around. 'You got the big game Monday. The good part is I'm cookin' that fish up for dinner after you take it home."

Danny placed the ice chest on his father's lap and began pushing him back along the dock. "Why am I taking it?"

"I gotta do a couple of things at the office before I throw on my apron."

At the Jongler-Jinkses' house, Arky knocked on Iris's bedroom door. When she stopped playing her oboe, he told her dinner was ready.

"Come in," she said.

The invitation surprised him. Her room was usually off-limits. "You decent?" he asked.

Her exasperated voice came back. "Like I'd ask you in if I was naked."

He still didn't open the door. "For all I know, you decided to spice up your callback by playing naked so the committee would shift from audio to visual."

The door opened, and Iris pulled him into the room. "Don't be an idiot."

"What's up?"

"Why are you going with Dad to that reenactment?" she demanded. "You hate those things."

"I do. But I might get a college essay out of it." Even though Arky's admission deadline was six months away, he was on a quest to find a slam-dunk subject for his essay. It had to trigger a scholarship bidding war between Harvard and Yale.

Iris tossed her hands. "What could the Civil War possibly have to do with going to college?"

"Dunno," he shrugged. "Maybe something about how great American stories never die. About how reliving the only war fought on American soil is as timeless as the tradition of a midwestern kid going Ivy League and joining the one percent."

"Besides being a crappy idea for an essay," Iris retorted, "the Civil War wasn't the only war fought on American soil."

"Yes, it was."

"No. The Revolutionary War."

"Doesn't count," he parried. "It wasn't America till *after* the War of Independence."

Iris eye-rolled. "Whatever, the point is you should stay here this weekend."

"I thought you loved having the house to yourself."

She pushed the door shut so as not to be overheard by their father. "I had a weird thing happen this afternoon while playing the cor anglais."

"Okay," he said warily. Arky knew too well about her synesthesia, her visions, and the part they'd played when Matt's kidnapping by time travel had almost destroyed Arky's future. "What's the 'weird thing'?"

She wasn't going to tell him about the attic door opening; he'd explain it away with science. But nothing could take away the feeling she had about it. "What it was doesn't matter," she said. "What matters is that I saw something, and I think it's a sign."

"Of what?" he asked with a frown. "An earthquake? A plague of locusts?" His eyes popped wide. "The prom being cancelled?"

She ignored his mocking. "I've got a feeling the next time I play the cor anglais I'm going to get something about Mom."

"Oh, really?" he asked insincerely. "Is it the same feeling you had the dozen times we holed up in the attic this winter, and you playing the cor anglais was supposed to get it spitting mists again till the boomerang with a spider on it blew you, me, or both of us, to another era so we could find Mom? I mean, if we're gonna"—he air quoted—"'rescue' her from the past, shouldn't we get a Mom-sniffing dog and blow the dog back with us?"

Her jaw tightened. "That's not funny."

"Hey, it's not like I said *body*-sniffing dog. Like it or not, Sis, Mom is gone for good. Whether she's buried in the rubble of time, or buried somewhere here and now, we don't know where she is, and we're never gonna find out."

"You can't say that."

He shrugged. "Have it your way; you *imagined* I said it."

Iris fought back. "We didn't imagine sending Matt back to 1907 and him coming back."

He jabbed a finger at her. "*You* sent him back, not me. And yeah, we didn't imagine it. But the universe is filled with freak accidents that never happen again."

"Like what?"

"Like the big bang that started it all. Like the freak accident of no two snowflakes being the same. We've tried for months to repeat the anomaly that boomeranged Matt to the past, and we got zippo."

"But I know Mom's still alive. I can feel it."

Arky stared at his sister. "Look, Iris, I'm not blind, and I'm not stupid. I'm the first to admit that physics isn't airtight. In physics, there's slippage. Chance plays a part: accidents can happen. But that's all we've got: *accidents*. What happened to Matt isn't gonna happen again. As for Mom, for whatever reason—dead or alive—she hasn't been able to get back in *seventeen* months. See"—he set a hand on his chest—"I've got a heart; you're not the only one counting. But it was *Mom's* choice, not ours. I'm not gonna let her choice ruin my future. Which means, even if the time-travel freak show *could* happen again, I'm not gonna let it." He turned toward the door.

Iris let it go. His mind was set; his heart had hardened against hope.

Before opening the door, Arky turned back. "Has it ever occurred to you, Sis, that the reason you're struggling to get into a summer music program is that the oboe isn't your instrument anymore?"

"Meaning what?" she replied. "I should drop it and play the cor anglais?"

"Why not? It's playing you." He opened the door and left.

Iris fought the pressure in her chest, pushing a lump in her throat. She hated it when one of his barbs made her want to cry. She hated him for it. There was only one way to fight back. Prove him wrong.

For the moment, she settled for less. She snatched the library note she was supposed to give him off her desk and ripped it to shreds.

5

Seal and Fish

DANNY DROVE THE old van to the Belleplain Mall. His father's ice chest rested on the passenger seat. The beer had been removed, but the cooler still held a bass with enough ice to keep it chilled for an hour. Danny wanted to see someone at the mall before he went home. He found a parking spot at the end of a long row.

Walking up the aisle of cars, Danny saw four guys come out of the mall. Drawing closer, he recognized the Latino guys as some of the baseball players he'd be facing in the Monday game against City High. One of the guys was an old friend: Rafael Santeiro.

Danny and Rafael had played on the same Little League team and made it to the Little League World Series. They'd stayed buddies through Babe Ruth, but come high school, Rafael had decided to go across town to the more Latino school. Danny thought it was a dumb move because losing Rafael's power hitting to City High weakened North High's chances of winning State. Danny didn't buy Rafael's excuse at the time; the Latina girls at City High were more plentiful and prettier. Their friendship faded away after that, especially since they were now cross-town rivals.

"Hey, superhero" —Rafael called to Danny as the guys narrowed the gap—"I hope you got your shield on Monday 'cause we're gonna rock you."

Danny answered. "Cap don't need a shield when he's throwin' fire, and you guys are choppin' at it like a piñata." Seeing a couple of their faces tense, Danny wondered if "piñata" had been the best choice.

Passing each other, one of the guys, a tough named Hector, fired back. "The only piñata I'll be swinging at is your cup."

Danny kept on going as the laughing guys threw another taunt. "And you can bet he paints that just like his hubcaps."

As they hooted with laughter, Danny squashed the anger ballooning in his chest. Answering with fists wasn't an option. He disappeared into the mall.

Rafael had gotten into his own car when he noticed that his friends had walked past their car and were headed toward a van with Bender Excavation on it.

Rafael jumped out of his car. "Hey, what's up?"

Hector called back. "Checkin' Bender's ride."

Rafael's face pinched as he followed after them.

Reaching the van, Hector went to the passenger side and looked through the window. "What do ya know? He's got an ice chest." He opened the door.

"C'mon, Hector," Rafael urged, "save it for the game."

"How do we know he's not packin' human growth hormone or some other illegal shit." He opened the cooler. "Whoa! Check it out!" He lifted the fish out of the chest.

"So he went and caught a fish. Put it back," Rafael ordered.

"But, Raffy"—he thrust the fish high—"is no pescado." He flung it toward the others. "Is piñata!"

As all but Rafael laughed, the fish flopped out of the catcher's hands and hit the pavement with a *thwack*.

"Hector," Rafael implored, "you're makin' it worse."

Hector pulled a large jackknife out of his pocket. Opening it, he grinned at Rafael. "Not if it gives Bender's little brain more to think about when he's throwing at us."

Inside the mall, Danny went to the Navy Recruiting Office. It was his deterrent to getting in fights. He didn't want anything on his record to spoil becoming a SEAL. The contradiction didn't escape him. Not fighting was a requirement for being a fighter.

Danny spotted the familiar face of Lieutenant Feldman, the recruiter he'd talked to the most.

Feldman greeted him with a friendly smile. "Hey, Danny. What's up?"

"Got sumthin to show you, Lieutenant." Danny pulled out a scrap of paper and dropped it on the desk. "My latest PST times and scores." PST was the Physical Screening Test that candidates had to pass to get into the Basic Underwater Demolition/SEAL training program. Neither was for the faint of heart or slight of muscle.

Feldman gave the paper a look. "Pretty good." He handed it back. "But we can't do anymore till you walk in with that diploma."

Danny slid into the chair next to the lieutenant's desk. "You could at least set me up with a Naval Special Warfare Mentor. I mean, I could be talking to him, right?"

Feldman chuckled and leaned back. "If I were in your shoes, Danny—and this is off the record—I'd be more focused on finishing the baseball season with hot stats and talking to baseball scouts than talking to a mentor."

"Yeah, but the Majors is more of a pipe dream than the SEALs," Danny said. "I mean, you've seen me pitch. I've got major-league location but minor-league speed."

"Don't underestimate yourself," Feldman assured him. "Your arm's still developing."

"You wouldn't say that if you saw me practice today," Danny scoffed. "I'm just saying, Lieutenant, I can do both at the same time: chase baseball, chase the SEALs, and see who wins the race."

"Maybe you can," Feldman acknowledged as he leaned forward. "But let me ask you, what do you think the number-one cause for candidates washing out of SEAL training is?"

Danny shrugged. "It's gotta be their bodies can't take it."

"Nope." Feldman tapped his head. "It's up here. It's called second-guessing. Anyone suffering the pain and agony of SEAL training who starts thinking, 'Damn, it'd be easier being something else,' never makes it. If you don't chase your baseball dream first, it'll wash you out. 'Damn, I shoulda been a ballplayer.'"

Danny went to his go-to place when he wanted to think things over: the mall roof. It wasn't just a roof; it was a green roof. The sprawling expanse was a park in the sky, planted with native grasses that grew high and had once fed wild buffalo herds. While the prairie roof lacked Indian trails and wagon ruts, it had paths that curved through the high brown grasses greening up with spring.

Near a service shed that jutted from a picnic deck, Danny pulled a baseball from a hiding spot in the grass. He moved to the shed, where a rectangle was crudely etched on the concrete wall. Markings left by a baseball were visible inside and around the improvised strike zone. Using a coin, Danny marked an *X* in the lower-right corner of the rectangle. He walked back through an aisle of picnic tables to a point he knew to be sixty feet six inches, the distance from pitching rubber to home plate. He set up.

Danny didn't throw like most pitchers; he was a "submariner." He dipped into a bow, his left leg strode forward as his arm swung back and low, then his hand almost scraped the ground as he powered through, and released the ball at the tip of a cracking whip.

The ball struck the wall and bounced off. Danny jogged forward and checked the *X* in the strike zone. There was a fresh ball mark on it. He smiled. It was the sign he was looking for. He would have his stuff for Monday's game.

Danny climbed the service ladder on the other side of the shed up to its roof. From there he took in the entire view of the prairie roof covering the mall. The high grasses waved with the wind and stretched around him like a giant flying carpet hovering above the rest of Belleplain. Being up there made Danny feel like he was from another time, an avenging Indian riding a great swath of prairie about to descend on the town and cover everything in its path, starting with the parking lot and the Bass Sports fishing pond, and not stopping till Belleplain, and everything that had happened there, was buried and returned to the wild grassland it once was.

Danny's fantasy triggered a memory of the song he'd heard Arky's dad singing earlier. Danny sang it with a slight twist on the lyrics. "Goin' home, goin' home, it's a goin' home. Quietlike, some still day, it's jes' goin'—"

He stopped as something down in the parking lot caught his eye. His van didn't look right. It looked like something was smeared across the windshield.

Returning to the parking lot and his van, Danny discovered what it was. The windshield was slimed with blood and fish guts. More chunks of fish and guts littered the front seats. The skeleton hung from the steering wheel.

Danny grabbed the skeleton and flung it away. "Pricks!"

After dinner, Howard and Arky finished loading Howard's Subaru, and the "Civil War Express" headed for Fredericksburg, Virginia. They hoped to make it halfway there before stopping for the night and then finishing the journey early the next morning to make it in time for the first battle reenactment of the weekend.

When Danny drove the van down the entrance road to Bender Excavation, his bad mood wasn't helped by seeing that his father was still there. He had hoped to make up a story about the fish being stolen and not have to deal with the van being trashed.

When his father saw the van, he wanted to know what happened. Danny didn't finger Rafael and his crew for doing the damage, although he was certain it was them. But he didn't need anyone else to settle his scores. He told his dad he didn't know. Danny was surprised when his dad bought it and said he'd pick up barbecue for dinner.

Before wheeling up the ramp into his handicap van, Ray added, "With your ride smelling like that, you'll want your truck back sooner than later." He pointed to the labyrinth of junked cars. "There's gotta be a decent starter in one of those wrecks."

After his dad left, Danny put off cleaning the stinky van. He hopped in the tow truck and headed to the school to get his pickup. Besides, if he had any luck, a raccoon might come by overnight and start the cleaning job for him.

6

Fog of War

SHORTLY AFTER SUNRISE, Danny was back at Bender Excavation. The other workers had the Labor Day weekend off, but Danny wasn't going to miss racking up some hours. He couldn't punch his timecard for cleaning the van or fixing his pickup, but he did have company work. The forms were already in place for a new concrete ramp to replace the deteriorating wooden one giving wheelchair access to the office.

Danny used a bucket mixer attached to a Bobcat to mix the concrete, dumped the wet concrete in the first section of form, then smoothed out the gentle slope. After hosing out the mixer, he turned the hose on the van, inside and out. The vehicle was so old, water in the interior wasn't a problem. No raccoon had shown up to help, and it took brush-scrubbing to make it fishless. By the time he was done, the van didn't smell any worse than a fish delivery truck. It would do until he found a working starter in the junkyard and installed it in his pickup. Captain America would be cruising again.

In Fredericksburg, Arky watched his father, in his Confederate uniform, march off with a squad of rebels toward a mass of soldiers assembling behind a stone wall. Unlike the onlookers around him, Arky wasn't there to enjoy the drama of a Civil War battle with a few thousand reenactors. He was there for the eureka moment to spark a college essay that would make admissions officers shout, "Bring me the brain of Arky Jongler-Jinks!"

As Howard marched into the Second Battle of Fredericksburg with his muzzle-loading rifle, Arky was armed with his smartphone. So far, he'd only entered a few notes about a different "war between the states": the war between reality and reenactment. Behind the rebel troops, a high terrace of ground held Civil War cannons along with a row of Porta Potties. Arky noted it was a good thing that it was the cannons being readied for firing, not the Porta Potties. *Not exactly slam-dunk essay material*, he told himself, *but Rome wasn't built in a day.*

A Confederate officer, mounted on a horse and wearing a flashy uniform, galloped up to the throng of Johnny Rebs behind the stone wall and began shouting orders. Somewhere in the mass of rebels, Howard Jinks had become Thomas Jinks.

The officer's voice rose over the noisy excitement. "Besides the standard rules of engagement, I now charge you with an order never issued to the heroes who fought and died on this bloody day of May third, 1863! Anyone who hasn't turned off his cell phone, and announces his presence with a ringtone, will be executed on the spot!"

The soldiers let out a piercing rebel yell that would make zombies turn and run.

The officer continued his orders. "To your positions, sons of the South! Defend this wall till the Yankee aggressors are potted and salted in the field below!"

Arky entered "potted and salted" in his smartphone. Sprinkling an essay with archaic language would make admissions readers think, *Wise beyond his years.*

The mass of about two hundred Confederates spread like a giant bird opening its wings against the long wall. The wings bristled with fixed bayonets. The leading edge of soldiers against the wall lowered their rifles, aiming them down a long-sloping field. At the bottom of the field were at least a couple thousand soldiers in blue, backed by mounted officers. The Yankees had begun their attack and were marching up the field. The rebel cannons fired with great booms. Some advancing Yankees responded by flinging their arms wildly and flopping on the ground.

On their drive there, Arky had learned the reenactment rule for who got shot and who didn't. The commanding officer selected a month; anyone with a birthday in that month had to, at some point in the battle, take a bullet. It was the first note Arky had added to his phone: "The odds of dying in a Civil War reenactment are one in twelve."

The mock battle raged for an hour, with the Confederates repelling several Yankee charges. At one point, the Yankees waved a white flag so they could come up the field and collect their "wounded." The time-out gave the battlefield a chance to clear of smoke and several soldiers the chance to pull out cell phones and take a selfie.

The climax came when a storm of Yankees rushed up the field in a hail of popping muskets, went over the wall, and faked bayonet fighting with the Confederates until all the rebels had fallen or had run off to reenact another day. Arky was surprised to see his father, that is, Thomas Jinks, still standing and making a hasty retreat.

After an air horn signaled that the fall of Marye's Heights was over, Arky ducked under the yellow tape separating warriors from voyeurs and found his dad.

Howard met him with a beaming smile. "Pretty cool, huh?"

"Yeah," Arky said, "except you never got shot. You always told us Thomas Jinks was left for dead from a head wound. Did you get spared because you're not in the Born-in-January-Gotta-Drop Club, or did you decide to rewrite history?"

Howard gave him a shocked look. "Arky, a history professor never tinkers with the truth. Thomas wasn't shot on Marye's Heights."

Arky blinked in confusion. "Was he even here?"
"Most likely not."
"So where was he shot and left for dead?"

Howard and Arky drove through downtown Fredericksburg, a history-rich town built on the rising hills overlooking the Rappahannock River. Still wearing his Confederate outfit, Howard was hardly out of place; the town had been invaded by reenactors.

The sight of rebels and Yankees window-shopping together might have been another note for Arky's essay, but he was distracted by his dad refusing to tell the story of Thomas Jinks's fate until they reached a certain location.

Howard used the delay to turn the Subaru's dashboard into a lectern for his favorite subject. "Have you ever wondered why tens of thousands of people show up, year after year, to recreate the great battles of the Civil War?"

"Keeps me up every night," Arky deadpanned.

Howard proceeded, undeterred. "The reason so many Americans are enthralled with a war that ended long ago is simple. A struggle that sets countryman against countryman, brother against brother, taps the truth of all wars: It's Cain and Abel all over again. And brother-on-brother killing will always be ghoulishly fascinating."

Arky couldn't resist. "If that's the case, thank God me and Iris weren't twin boys. We would've gone Cain and Abel years ago."

They drove along a street descending toward bottomlands stretching to the Rappahannock River. Before reaching a riverside park, Howard turned the car onto a side street, pulled over, and got out.

Arky followed and looked around the commonplace spot. They were in a slight depression of land with a view of the riverside park. The wide, shallow bowl of land contained a neighborhood of small suburban houses that gently rose away from the park.

"This is it," Howard announced.

"This is what?" Arky asked, unimpressed.

From his Confederate jacket, Howard pulled out the framed daguerreotype of Thomas Jinks. His voice lowered as if imparting a sacred truth. "Here, or somewhere close by, your great-great-great-great grandfather was wounded and left for dead."

Arky looked around, trying to figure out why his father was acting so spooky and weird. "So you don't know for sure?"

"No, but history and family lore point to here and *how* it happened."

Arky shifted to attentive. "You've never told us how he was wounded."

His father smiled. "I've been saving it for when we were standing on the ground where it happened. I only wish Iris were here."

"No worries, Dad," Arky said, pressing fingers to his head. "I'm linked to the Twin Telepathy Center; we've got Iris on conference call."

It drew a smile from Howard before returning to his reverential mood. "Somewhere within shouting distance of this spot Thomas was felled. But his head wound was so traumatic he never remembered the exact events *before* his wounding."

"That's it?" Arky asked, disappointed. "The story is that there's no story?"

"No," Howard assured him. "Piecemeal accounts fill in some details. At dawn, on May third"—he swept an arm around them—"this ground was shrouded in fog. A small group of forward skirmishers from each side was probing the fog in search of the enemy. At some point, the enemy squads of about a dozen men each collided. All but one of them died from stab wounds, slashes and gunshots at close range in a hand-to-hand fight. One strange twist was that no evidence of their weapons or effects were found. It's believed the dead and dying soldiers were picked clean by slaves from the plantation that occupied this land. Later in the day, Thomas Jinks, lying among the dead, regained consciousness, stumbled to the Confederate lines and got medical attention."

Arky was mesmerized, a look he tried to avoid. "That's pretty cool. I can't believe you never told us this before."

Howard met his son's gaze. "I wanted you to hear it on the soil where the life of Thomas Jinks and all his descendants hung in the balance between coming into being or never having been."

Arky sparked with another idea for an essay: how the smallest moment can multiply to a major event—how the flap of a butterfly's wing in the Amazon can domino to a hurricane in America. *It's the Butterfly Effect from Chaos Theory,*" he told himself, *but in a* family. *I'll start with the tiny moment of Thomas surviving, which leads to the sprawl of the Jinks family tree, which comes full circle to the ultimate micromega moment. Opening my acceptance letter to Harvard!*

Howard continued, "There's one last twist that has nothing to do with Thomas, but it's a perfect example of how history is in the details." He pointed toward the river. "One of the Union soldiers who was wounded in the skirmish tried to make it back to the Union lines on the other side of the river. He only made it to the riverbank. He died there and was buried where he fell. His grave was marked with a wooden cross. Nailed on top of the cross was a harmonica that played in the wind."

Arky was thrilled, not with his father's footnote to the story of Thomas Jinks, but with another potential title for his essay: "From Head Wound to Harvard."

7

Intrigue

LATER THAT AFTERNOON, in Belleplain, Matt Grinnell stopped his pickup in front of the Jongler-Jinkses' house. When he killed the engine, the music blaring from his speakers was replaced by classical oboe music coming from a second-story window. Iris was practicing. But it wasn't as pretty as when he'd heard her play the oboe before. The music kept starting and stopping, like Iris was struggling with it.

Matt went to the front door and rang the bell.

A few moments later, Iris opened the door.

"Hey," Matt said. "I didn't mean to interrupt your practice."

"Believe me," she said, "you did the neighbors a favor."

Matt knew about her rejection from summer school at Juilliard, and that she had a callback coming up for a music school in Ohio. "It didn't sound so bad to me."

She frowned. "It was perfect if my audition piece was Handel's *Sonata for Oboe and Butterfingers.*"

He laughed. "Maybe you're thinking too much, trying too hard. I don't know about playing music, but when I play football and get in the zone, I'm not really thinking."

She wasn't in the mood for a comparison of the body-crashing sport of football to the art of transforming breath and fingerings into music that soared from the soul. "What's up?" she asked. "Do we have a juggling thing I forgot about?"

"No. I was hoping to pick up Arky for the party out at the lake," he explained.

She gave him a puzzled look. "You didn't text him or call him?"

Matt shrugged. "Decided not to. Figured I'd go old school and just show."

Hearing him say "Old school" made Iris want to say, *You mean like the Carlisle Indian old school?* She squashed the urge. It was part of her deal with Arky. She didn't risk prodding Matt into a full-on recall of 1907, if Arky didn't give up on the cor anglais helping them find their mother. *But then*, she reminded herself, *Arky had reneged on his part of the deal and given up on the cor anglais.* "Arky went to a reenactment in Virginia with our dad," she reminded Matt. They'll be back Sunday night."

"Right!" Matt slapped his forehead. "Totally slipped my mind."

"Uh-huh," Iris nodded, pretending to go along with his unconvincing excuse.

He perked up with an idea. "Hey, why don't you go to the party with me?" He quickly covered for any misreading of the invitation. "You know, as juggling buddies."

She laughed at his fumbling invite. "Does that mean it's a juggling party?"

He flashed his crush-inducing smile. "Nobody has juggling parties. It'd just be fun."

Going to a party with Matt's jock friends might be fun, she thought, *being treated like his token music geek not so much.* But Iris wasn't ready to answer. "If it's a party-party, shouldn't you be cruising for a new girlfriend?"

"I've got one, and she's not into parties."

His reveal caught her by surprise. Everyone knew Matt had broken up with Kelly, his old girlfriend, back in January. It was the first Iris had heard about a newbie. "You've got a new girlfriend?"

He jogged his head. "Yeah, sort of."

"Who?"

"It's kind of a secret, and nobody really knows her."

His dodge fueled her curiosity. "Sooo, are you going to introduce her to everyone at the prom?"

Avoiding her inquisition, he looked skyward. "Ah, haven't asked her yet."

Iris kept pressing. "I hate to go sister on you, Matt, but the prom is a month away. You better ask her soon."

"It's complicated."

"I'll say."

He tossed his hands. "So you wanna go or not?"

She bit her tongue not to say *To the prom or the party?* He looked uncomfortable enough. "You mean, as friends?"

"Of course."

"What if your new girlfriend shows up?" Iris shifted her slight figure into a pose. "I mean, how can any girl compete with *all* this?"

Matt laughed at her self-deprecation. "You'd be surprised how many can't."

His comeback threw Iris. It was more than a "friend" would say.

Matt filled the silence. "I'm just saying there's no way she'll show up."

Iris reclaimed her footing. "How can you be so sure?"

Matt gazed at Iris. "I get the feeling you don't wanna go to this party."

She hesitated.

He took it as an answer. "Rain check?"

Iris kicked herself for letting her curiosity override her crazy impulse to think of Matt in a different way. "Sure. Rain check."

He turned and headed for his truck.

She followed down the walkway. "By the way, did you look for those overdue library books?"

He moved around the pickup. "Forgot, but I will. If they were a trophy or a sports thing, finding 'em in my house would be impossible. But a *book* in my house, it'll stick out like a sore thumb."

As he got in the truck's cab, Iris rested her arms in the passenger-side window. "If they're so obvious, why have you been sitting on them since December?"

He shook his head at her doggedness. "I dunno. Since when did you become Inspector Gadget of Book World?"

"Just curious," she said casually. "I've spent so many years trying to figure out how my twisted brother thinks, I'd like to know how a normal guy thinks."

"It's pretty simple, Iris. Normal guys try *not* to think. That's what I love about football, and that's why I'm going to a party."

As he turned the ignition, she pulled away. "Have fun not thinking."

He grinned. "I plan to." He put the truck in gear. "Maybe someday I'll give you a lesson in not thinking."

Her insides ballooned at the second time he seemed to be hinting at something else. To hide the blush rising in her cheeks, she answered back. "I'll think about it."

Matt's laughter revved along with the truck.

Iris watched him drive away. She didn't know if he was flirting with her just to flirt, like getting in his daily workout, or if he was flirting to throw her off the overdue books, or if he was flirting with her to *really* flirt. Whatever, they all made her wish she'd said yes to the party.

8

Eureeka Moment

AFTER A CAMPFIRE breakfast in the reenactors' camp, Howard and Arky drove across the Rappahannock to Falmouth, the town on the other side of the river from Fredericksburg. Crossing the narrow river that had divided the Confederate and Union armies in the winter of 1863, Howard told Arky about the "picket truce" that existed in the months leading up to the major battle in the spring and how enemy soldiers would wade across the river and trade with each other, exchanging everything from newspapers to tobacco.

Arky was too tired after a bad night of sleep on hard ground to get excited even if his dad had told him about the Yankees and rebels meeting in the river for water aerobics.

Falmouth had been the hub of the Union encampment on the east side of the river in 1862–63. Howard wanted to show Arky a "followers' camp" that had been set up in a park. Not only did Civil War buffs recreate the camps of opposing armies, they also recreated the equivalent of Civil War groupies: peddlers, preachers and prostitutes who followed the armies to provide them with things Uncle Sam didn't.

Howard and Arky explored the rows of tents and wagons offering everything Civil War wonks craved, from hardtack to hoopskirts. Touring the camp, they heard music. Arky thought it might be a live band. When they turned into the next row of tents, he realized the lively tune was coming from a merchant selling music instruments. Fiddles, banjos, dulcimers and harmonicas were displayed in front of the tent.

The source of the music was an early record player heralding the music seller's inventory of CDs devoted to the tunes of the 1860s. The old record player was a fancy wooden box with a flared megaphone rising above it to broadcast music. The box held a turntable, where a bulky needle arm rode the groves of a plate-sized record.

Howard strode toward it. "That's a Victor Talking Machine!" he protested.

Arky followed with a gibe. "Is that how you and Mom played music when you were kids?"

Howard continued his protest. "It first came out in *1901*."

"Okay," Arky conceded, "it was before your time."

"That's forty years *after* the Civil War. It doesn't belong here."

Arky pointed to reenactors carrying shopping bags. "Dad, plastic bags don't belong here either."

"That's not the point." Howard thrust a finger at the Victor Talking Machine. "It's the kind of anachronism that cheapens history. History isn't a game of Mr. Potato Head, where you create whatever hodgepodge you want." He turned and hustled toward the tent's entrance.

Arky felt for the music seller, who was about to be slapped with a ticket for reckless endangerment of historical accuracy. Whenever his dad became History Cop, it reminded Arky why he and Iris could *never* tell him about Iris blasting Matt back to 1907. It would decimate Howard's belief in history as written in stone.

Arky's focus returned to the Victor Talking Machine, spinning its black record and delivering old-time fiddle music. Arky noticed that the machine sat on a tree stump, creating a table. As he took in the odd sight of an old record player on a tree stump, the fiddle music began to slow. It wasn't a tempo change; the notes began to elongate and distort. Seeing the crank on the side of the wooden box, he realized the hand-cranked machine was running down.

The last scratchy note groaned to silence as the record stopped. Arky's focus sharpened. Despite the weird juxtaposition of a record player on a tree stump, they had something in common. They both had *rings*. The stump's tree rings were a visual echo of the circular grooves visible on the now still record.

Arky's eyes widened with the punch of a eureka moment. *A tree, a record, both have* rings. *One plays the other doesn't. What if they* both *played?* "Holy shit!" he blurted. *What if the wooden disk hanging in Mom's office is more than a crosscut of a tree she brought back from Africa? What if it's a* record? *What if it's the clue we looked for all winter and never found?*

Arky's interest in trolling a Civil War reenactment for college essay material vanished like a puff of musket smoke. He wanted to get home so he could check out the wooden disk in the attic office. He thought about calling Iris to do the detective work, but she was like the four-year-old who climbs into a time-travel machine and starts hitting buttons and flipping switches to see what happens. The disk would have to wait.

His wish to get home ASAP caught a break after they drove a few miles north of Fredericksburg and toured the Chancellorsville Battlefield Visitor Center. Howard was ready to go home a day early. Having given Arky the overview of the battles in and around Fredericksburg in late April, early May of 1863, and having taken him to the spot where Thomas Jinks had almost died, Howard had accomplished the trip's major mission: to pass down what was known about Thomas Jinks to the next generation.

In Belleplain, Danny's dead pickup sporting Captain American hubcaps sat in the service yard. Wearing grungy coveralls with a Bender Excavation patch on the chest, Danny finished installing the starter he'd cannibalized from a junked car. He hopped in the truck and turned the key. Nothing. He turned it again.

Silence. His fist flew up as he punched the cab roof. The loud bang signaled that the upholstery was long gone.

Danny slid from the truck and shook the pain from his hand. He grabbed a big screwdriver from a toolbox, knelt down to one of the wheels and pried off its Captain America hubcap. He spun the hubcap toward the old Bender Excavation van he'd been using. The hubcap skidded in the dust. He moved to the next wheel and hubcap. If Captain American was stuck with a backup ride, his shields were going with him.

By the time Howard and Arky got back to Belleplain, it was raining. As Howard unpacked the car in the garage, Arky fought the urge to go to the attic office and check out the clue he'd discovered at the Followers Camp. For distraction, he followed another lead he'd thought of on the drive home.

He went to Iris's room. Sitting at her desk doing homework, Iris glanced up at her brother. "Why'd you come home early? Was Dad kicked out of the army for showing up with a weapon of mass cynicism?"

He smiled at her dig. "How long did it take you to come up with that one?"

She went back to her homework. "I'm not really doing homework; I'm just working on my snarkyisms."

Arky gave her an approving nod. "Keep up the good work."

Expecting him to go, she was surprised when he shut the door without leaving.

"I wanna take a look at Mom's journal," he told her.

It got Iris's attention. Two days before, he'd called Matt's trip to the past a "freak accident." Now he suddenly wanted to reopen their mother's secret journal. "What happened?" she asked.

Arky couldn't repress a teasing smile. "Oh, just something I wanna check out. But first, I need to see the journal."

Iris was the keeper of the journal. The twins had discovered it right after Matt had been launched into the past. Its red leather cover was embossed with *The Book of Twins*. Inside the front cover, Octavia had written the subtitle, *Sphere of Music*. The journal was a daily record of Octavia's secret practice sessions on the Jongler cor anglais, and the visions she'd had while playing the four-hundred-year-old instrument. Iris wasn't the only one in the family to have music-induced visions; she had inherited her synesthesia from her mother. The journal also held Octavia's thoughts and speculations on the "Jongler family legend." That is, that the ancient cor anglais with a spider on its bell was an instrument of time travel. The twins had scoured the journal's entries for anything and everything that would explain the disappearance of Matt, their mom, and any clues that might help them rescue the two "time voyagers" from the past.

Iris wasn't about to give it to him without more info. "You haven't looked at Mom's journal in months. What changed?"

Arky realized he had to give her more. "I saw something at the reenactment, and it might connect to something Mom wrote."

Iris's eyes lit up. "What?"

"It's probably nothing," he said dismissively. "I promise to tell you about it after Dad goes to bed, and I get a look at the journal?"

Her eyes narrowed at his maddening secrecy. "I hate you."

Arky smiled. "I missed you too, Sis. Now, let's have it."

Moments later, Arky was in his room with the door shut. At his desk, he leafed through the leather-bound journal, looking for a passage. It was a mysterious passage he vaguely remembered from when he'd first read it five months before. But now, after his discovery in Fredericksburg, it had haunted him on the drive home.

He found the entry and stared down at his mother's elegant longhand:

> How many times have I heard the hidden music of grenadilla? But when will I hear the hidden music of my cor anglais?

Each time he read it, he fought a greater urge to race up to the attic and test his theory.

9

Tempus Ludendi

After Howard had gone to bed, Arky and Iris quietly climbed the stairs to the attic office. Arky carried the journal, *The Book of Twins: Sphere of Music*, but had told Iris nothing about the passage from it that had inflamed his curiosity.

Inside the office, Arky moved to the wall holding their mother's strange assemblage: the galaxies and supernovas encircling the black disk of grenadilla wood, overlaid with the silky spiderweb. He lifted the Plexiglas shell protecting the disk. It came away, exposing the black disk mounted on the wall.

Fearing what he might do, Iris moved toward him. "What're you doing?"

"Shush," he said as he set the Plexiglas on the floor. He placed his fingers on each side of the crosscut of wood and gently pulled. It came away from the wall, leaving a small black peg—the innermost ring of the tree—which it had been hanging on. With the peg missing from the center of the disk, it resembled an old vinyl record.

"Holy shit!" Iris exclaimed.

"That's what I said."

She gaped at the discovery. "How did you know?"

He told her about the followers' camp and the Victor Talking Machine on the tree stump. He set the wooden disk on the table holding their mother's old record player. "If it looks like a record, maybe it is a record."

Iris shot him a dubious look. "How can a slice of tree trunk be a record of anything but a tree's growth?"

He raised the lid covering the record player and placed the wooden disk on the turntable. The hole in the middle of the disk fit perfectly over the stub at the turntable's center. "If the cor anglais can blow people to another era," he replied, "for all we know, a disk of wood could be a spaceship filled with micro-aliens."

She ignored his comment. "If we turn it on, and put the needle on it, do you think it'll play?"

"Doubtful, and I don't want to scratch the wood trying. Mom wasn't that dumb." Arky reached down and gently pulled on the base of the record player's tonearm. It lifted out of the post supporting it. "A wooden disk with rings instead of grooves would need something else to play it."

"How are we going to figure that out?"

Arky detached the wires connecting the tonearm to the turntable. "I'm guessing Mom already did. We're going to search this room like never before." He pointed at the disk on the turntable. "If she did such a good job hiding that, I'm sure she did a better job hiding whatever tonearm might play it."

The twins checked every board in the room, from floor to ceiling, in search of one that was loose or could be opened in some way to reveal a hiding place.

On the verge of giving up, Iris spotted something. Below one of the dormer windows, the paint between the windowsill and the trim board underneath had either cracked along the seam or been cut. She pushed on the board. It moved slightly. She fingered the bottom of the board and pulled. It slid out from under the sill, revealing a small drawer. In the drawer was a clunky device made of what seemed to be electronic components. It was about the same length as a tonearm, but thicker.

"Arky," Iris exhaled, "come here."

The moment he lifted it out, he had an idea what it might be: some kind of optical reader, like a handheld scanner. He tried to connect it to the turntable. The wiring matched; it fit neatly into the support post. Switching on the turntable, the disk of tree rings began to turn. He moved the new tonearm to the edge of the record and flipped the switch on top of the arm.

They watched breathlessly. Unlike a normal tonearm that traveled across a record as the needle was *pulled* by the grooves spiraling toward the center, the tonearm moved almost imperceptibly over the turning disk. It had a small motor to move on its own.

They heard a sound, an atonal note like the eerie call of a whale. As the tonearm crept across the revolving tree rings, the sounds grew stranger and more varied. Arky spoke under it. "It *is* an optical reader. Mom built it to translate tree rings into sound."

Iris hardly heard him. She was stunned by the distorted, haunting music. It was otherworldly music she had heard before: the music that came from the cor anglais when it took over her fingers, possessed her, and began to emit tendrils of mist. "Arky," she whispered, "it's like the music the cor anglais plays when it comes to life."

"What do you mean?"

"When it sent Matt to the past. And when it buried what happened to him in 1907 beyond his conscious memory."

Arky recalled the only time he had heard and seen the powers of the cor anglais come to life. It was right after Matt had come back. Iris had played the cor anglais in the locker room at school, the mists had wrapped Matt in a cocoon, and buried his memory. "Right," he said. "In her journal, Mom called it 'the hidden music of grenadilla.'"

Still in the thrall of the bizarre music, Iris jumped at the sight of something on her mother's desk. The computer keyboard on the desk was playing like a player piano, matching the dissonant music filling the room.

Grabbing Arky's arm, she pointed at the keyboard. "Do you see that?"

"See what?"

"Are the keys moving?"

Arky frowned. "No."

The moment Iris realized it was a vision triggered by her synesthesia, the keys stopped. So did the otherworldly music. Her eyes darted to the turntable. The tonearm had travelled across the wooden disk. She quickly told him her vision. "What does it mean? Is there any way for Mom's computer and the wooden record to be linked?"

"One way to find out." Arky stepped to the desk and hit the computer's boot-up button. "Turn both of them on and see if they talk to each other."

After the screen's desktop finished loading, he played the wooden record again. Halfway through the eerie music, an image materialized on the computer screen. It showed a red leather surface. A title emerged on the leather surface.

The Book of Twins:

Iris didn't know if it was another vision. "Are you seeing that?"

"Yeah," Arky breathed.

The title faded away as another title rose from the red leather.

Sphere of Science

"The music from the wooden record is an audio password," Arky explained as he yanked back the desk chair and sat. "It's opening the hidden cache we looked for all winter."

"The companion volume to *Sphere of Music*," Iris declared as she grabbed Octavia's practice chair and joined Arky at the desk.

"Exactly. It's Mom's scientific research on the cor anglais." He clicked on *Sphere of Science*. A list of documents filled the screen."

Iris sucked in a breath and read the top one on the list. "'*Tempus ludendi.*'"

"A time for playing," Arky translated.

"Just like she wrote at the beginning of her journal."

Arky clicked on the file.

It mushroomed to a screen of their mother behind a play icon. Her long auburn hair cascaded over and past the pulled-down hood of a Belleplain University sweatshirt. Unlike her twins, with their fine and precise features inherited from their father, Octavia had a generous face with full lips and large blue-gray eyes.

The sight froze Arky.

Iris grabbed his hand on the mouse and forced a click on the play button.

Their mother, sitting in her practice chair in the attic office, came to life. She greeted them with a warm smile. "Hello, Iris, and, I assume, Arky."

Hearing her say their names left the twins motionless.

"If you found this," Octavia continued, "it's probable that I finally learned to play the Jongler family cor anglais to its fullest, and one of my attempts at time travel was successful. Iris, don't feel slighted, but the technical difficulty of opening this cache is why I assume Arky is watching with you. If Arky *is* watching, well, the cat's out of the bag, and perhaps your father should know too."

Arky flinched at the insanity of telling their father anything.

Octavia's expression knitted to serious. "I'm sure you want to know what happened to me, where I am. I only know this. I've done what scientists have been known to do. I've thrown myself, and my family, into the unknown. But in that unknown, I am certain there is something beautiful...for all of us. And should the journey I've embarked on never end, and we are never reunited, words cannot express how much I love you. The only thing that comes close is music." A smile played on her lips. "*Tempus ludendi.*" From below frame, she lifted the curved cor anglais.

She wetted the reed, took a breath, and began playing the solo from Dvorak's 9th Symphony, *From the New World. Daa-da-daaa, daa, da, daaa...*

Iris choked back a sob as Arky stared at the screen, trying to compute what he was seeing and hearing.

In the pause after the opening measure, the faint thud of a closing door came up through the attic's floorboards.

Arky jumped at the sound, clicked the video to pause, freezing their mother and silencing the music.

"What are you doing?" Iris demanded.

"Didn't you hear that?"

"Yeah," Iris said as she stood, "and we gotta get Dad."

Arky grabbed her arm, yanked her back down, and whispered harshly, "No way! We don't do anything till we get Dad out of the house, see the rest of this, and see what else is in the cache. We have no idea what's in there."

She jerked her arm free of his grasp, and stared at him. "You're terrified, aren't you?"

"Of course, I am," Arky admitted as he stood and dissembled the optical reader from the record player. "Anyone who lives with a bunch of time-travel freaks would be terrified." He opened the hidden drawer under the windowsill and put the optical reader back in it. "I thought protecting Dad from you was hard enough, but now I gotta protect him from you"—he thrust a hand at the computer—"and Mom." He grabbed the wooden disk off the record player and replaced it on its peg on the display wall.

As Iris watched him set the Plexiglas cover back over the disk, she was whipsawed with emotions. She was elated by the sight and sound of her mother, thrilled by how the music flowed through them like shared blood, but dumbfounded at Arky's fear of their father knowing the truth.

Arky crossed back to Iris and stood over her. "We wait till Dad leaves tomorrow, then we check out rest of the file. Agreed?"

Tossed in her sea of excitement, Iris didn't want to spoil it by fighting with her insanely practical brother, drawing their father upstairs, and possibly leading to a worse scene. "Yeah," she conceded. "For now."

10

No-Hitter

MONDAY MORNING, WITH school out for Labor Day, Danny was back at Bender Excavation adding another section of concrete to the new wheelchair ramp. As he used a shovel to push the ingredients toward the auger in the bucket mixer, his hand still hurt from throwing a fist into his truck roof. He clenched and unclenched it to ease the pain.

After pouring and smoothing the concrete, he was washing out the mixer when he heard his cell phone in the van. He jogged over and took the call from Matt. Matt was in the high-school parking lot wanting to know where Danny was; the team bus was leaving in a few minutes for the game at City High. Danny whacked himself in the head for loosing track of time. Matt told him the coach wasn't waiting, Danny had to get to the game himself, and Matt would bring Danny's uniform.

Danny finished his clean up, hopped in the old van, and headed for City High.

At the Jongler-Jinkses' house, Arky and Iris's plan to wait for their dad to leave before they reopened the discovery in the attic office was stalled. Howard had spent the morning grading papers at home instead of at his university office where he usually worked.

After a near sleepless night of imagining what they might find in *Sphere of Science*, Iris worried that their dad's change of routine might be because he *had* heard them in the attic the night before. But her fretting was only a tremor compared to the earthquake of their midnight find. There was no more doubt about it: their mom was somewhere in the past.

Arky was also eager to dive into the new treasure trove. It would finally reveal all the scientific research their mother had done on time travel instead of the visions and conjecture she had filled her *Sphere of Music* journal with. But his fear of their dad catching them and discovering the time-travel skeleton in the family closet was greater than Arky's curiosity. They had waited five months to find the other *Book of Twins: Sphere of Science*; they could wait till it was safe to open it.

Arky went to Iris's room and found her doing homework.

She looked up and noticed his Cyclones baseball hat. "Where are you going?"

"Just because we discovered book two in the Jongler family library," he said, "doesn't mean reality stops. I'm supposed to be at a ball game; what's upstairs can wait."

"Maybe for you," Iris said. "I'll start without you."

"It's science," Arky countered. "You probably won't get it."

"It's not 'science,'" Iris came back. "It's Mom."

He realized, short of putting a lock on Iris's door and throwing away the key, he couldn't stop her. "Okay, but promise you'll wait till Dad leaves."

"Do I look like a moron?"

He shook his head in amused disbelief. "Why do you set me up like that?"

She answered with a moony look. "Because I love you."

"Now I know you're a moron. Be back after the game."

The City High baseball facility was packed with fans who had come for a spring ritual: the cross-town rivalry between Belleplain's two high schools, the City High Banditos and the North High Cyclones. As the Cyclones warmed up on the field,

Ray Bender watched from his wheelchair, on a stair landing at the visitors' end of the stands.

Arky had arrived early enough to claim a seat overlooking the visitors' dugout on the third-base side. It put him across the field from Matt, playing first base, and gave him the chance to keep an eye on Danny. Knowing about Danny's shaky practice on Friday wasn't Arky's only concern. Between missing the team bus and having to suit up inside the bus, Danny had little time to warm up. In the dozen pitches he threw, Arky noticed he kept clenching and unclenching his throwing hand. Danny getting nervous and twitchy before a game wasn't a good sign.

As Danny threw a last pitch, the Cyclones' heavyset coach, Mr. Costello, approached. "How you feeling?" he asked.

Danny had his game face on. "Good to go, Coach. Sorry about the bus screw-up."

"Over and done," Costello said. "What you don't wanna screw up is your big chance."

"I know, big game, gotta win."

"*Your* big game," Costello emphasized.

Danny gave him a puzzled look. "What do you mean?"

Costello turned to the crowded stands behind home. "See the guy in the red Cardinals hat?"

"Yeah," Danny said. "What's he doing here? There's no Cardinal fans around here."

"He's not a fan. He's a scout. He's here for you."

Danny's eyes widened. "Really?"

"Really. Give 'im control, don't worry about speed, and paint me some corners." Costello walked away.

Danny muttered to himself, "Yes, sir."

After the game started, it evolved into a pitchers' duel. Both Danny and the Banditos' pitcher were throwing terrific stuff. While the Cyclones scratched out a couple of singles, the runners were stranded. The Banditos had nothing to show but strikeouts, groundouts, and one blast to the outfield that had been caught on the warning track. Danny had a no-hitter going.

It didn't surprise Danny. His location had never been better. He wasn't just painting the corners of the strike zone, he was gilding them. Another advantage was his submarine delivery being every hitter's nightmare. His bizarre bow-down windup and knuckle-scrapping release from down under baffled hitters. Seeing a pitch shoot from the ground more like a golf ball than a baseball put batters on their heels. It was the reason Danny was being scouted. His delivery and the sinker it produced was a freak show that could give Major Leaguers vertigo.

So far, his pitching performance had also delivered a sensation Danny had only felt a few times on the mound. It was as if the batter wasn't there. All Danny saw was the zone. In the moment he set before beginning his windup, he saw the pitch he was about to throw hit its spot, then disappear in the dusty leather of the catcher's mitt. When he actually began his dipping windup, it was like the pitch had already been thrown. Danny had given the rare sensation a name. Whatever the pitch—sinker, slider, changeup—if he saw it before he threw it, he called it his "déjà vu ball."

Arky could see Danny had something going. The twitches and fist-clenching were gone. He looked totally relaxed, almost serene. The only thing keeping Arky from thinking about a no-hitter, or a perfect game, was one pitch Danny had thrown that had been as wild as his others had been perfect. It had barely gotten off the ground from Danny's low, snapping release. The pitch had hit the dirt ten feet in front of the plate.

In the bottom of the 5th inning it happened again. Danny dropped a sinker in the dirt well before the plate. It wasn't even close to the déjà vu pitch he'd seen before his windup.

The City High fans responded. A kid yelled, "Hey, Pescado! If you wanna get it up, try Viagra!" It provoked a chant from the Bandito fans, "Vi-ag-ra! Vi-ag-ra!"

The ball-busting didn't get to Danny; it was standard issue. Hearing "Pescado" wasn't. It meant his van getting fish slimed had gone viral. He brushed it aside and tried to see his next pitch. The batter invaded his focus. It was Hector, one of the guys who'd done the sliming. Hector bulged his eyes and puckered his mouth like a fish at Danny.

Danny answered by hurling a brush-back that sent Hector reeling out of the box. Despite the booing from the stands, Danny followed with three strikes, struck out Hector, and retired the side.

Heading for the dugout, Danny traded eye contact with Arky in the front bleacher. Arky threw him a low fist pump, urging him to stay cool, stay controlled. Danny's nod of affirmation was eclipsed by a Latino kid moving along the walkway behind the dugout roof. The kid flapped open an iPad and flashed it at Danny. "Yo, Pescado, nice fish wax!"

Danny glimpsed the iPad showing a picture of his van slimed with fish guts. As Cyclones fans yelled and threw food at the troublemaker on their side of the stands, Danny ducked into the dugout. The nickname pissed him off. Sitting on the bench, he clenched and reclenched his hand against the creeping soreness. His teammates didn't help as the Cyclones went three up, three down.

The bottom of the 6th started with the Cyclones getting the first two Banditos on groundouts. Danny kept his no-hitter alive. Then he walked his first batter, bringing Rafael to the plate. In Rafael's two prior at-bats, Danny had bottled his rage for his former friend; he was certain Rafael had taken part in the fish sliming. Danny had the edge in the grudge match. He had struck out Rafael in his first at bat. On his second trip to the plate, Rafael had been the one who'd blasted the shot that was luckily caught on the warning track.

Danny started with a chest-high brush-back to let Rafael know the plate wasn't his. Danny's next two pitches missed the corners—at least the ump thought so. Danny was behind in the count, three balls, no strikes. In the years Danny had played with and against Rafael, one thing was certain: his ex-friend liked to sit back and watch a pitcher who *had* to throw a strike. Danny swooped down low and threw a sinking fastball.

His scouting report on Rafael needed updating. Rafael went down for it and blasted the ball into centerfield. The sound off the bat confirmed Danny's worst fear. One thing in his report would never change: when Rafael caught it on the barrel, it was gone.

The Bandito fans went crazy as Rafael trotted the bases. First blood had been drawn; the Banditos led 2–0. Danny's no-hitter was history.

Danny glared at the ground and tried to calm himself. After his catcher, Miguel Guzman, one of the few Latinos at North High, paid a visit to the mound, Danny tightened focus, and got the next batter on a groundout, ending the inning.

11

Bad Pitch

IN THE TOP of the 7th, Matt led off for North. He was one of the few Cyclones with a hit against the Banditos' ace. Matt took two balls and then got hit in the ribs with an inside pitch. It wasn't clear if the City High pitcher was losing his stuff or if he plunked Matt to avoid what had happened to Danny: giving up a home run. Regardless, the Cyclones now had Matt on first base, with the tying run coming to the plate, no outs.

The Cyclones took advantage. Danny managed a single. Then Miguel blasted a home run, making it clear he didn't give a rip about whatever ethnic tensions infused the game. He was there to win. The Cyclones took the lead 3–2.

City High answered in the bottom half with a rally, putting several Banditos on base. But they lost two of them trying to steal and a third getting tagged at home. Even though they failed to tie the game, Danny was looking vulnerable. No one was more worried than Arky. Danny's shoulder jerks, twitches and hand clenching had returned.

In the dugout, the coach asked Danny, "Do you wanna finish this or not?"

Danny knew there was a chance he'd face Rafael again. "I wanna finish it."

The Cyclones did nothing in the top of the 8th, which brought the Banditos to the bottom half and another chance to retake the lead.

While Danny's déjà vu ball was history, and his sinker had stopped diving, he still had a decent mix of speeds. It didn't stop a Bandito from getting lucky with a bloop single and getting to first. It brought Rafael to bat. Danny's first pitch, a slider to make Rafael reach, dropped too low, hit the dirt and got away from the catcher. The runner on first dashed to second. City High fans took up their mocking chant: "Vi-ag-ra! Vi-ag-ra!"

With one ball on Rafael and two outs, Danny looked to Costello in front of the dugout. He figured the coach would give him the sign to walk Rafael to avoid the risk of him driving in the game-tying run. That way, Danny's next batter would either be a City High player in a bad slump or a pinch hitter who had yet to face him. Both options were better than pitching to Rafael.

Danny got the sign from Costello. At first he thought he'd misread it. Costello repeated the sign. Danny wasn't misreading anything; the coach wanted him to hit Rafael in retaliation for Matt. Danny liked it. It would settle a score with Rafael and then he'd finish the game by striking out the next batter. Danny gave Costello a head jerk.

Miguel jogged to the mound as City High fans booed the delay. Reaching Danny, Miguel said, "You can't hit 'im."

"Why not?" Danny shrugged. "They hit Matt."

Miguel yanked off his mask. "Open your eyes, man. We're on enemy turf, and people are itching for a fight. If you hit Rafael, the place'll go apeshit."

Danny set his jaw. "Coach told me to hit 'im."

"Forget Costello," Miguel snapped. "Walk Rafael or pitch to him, and I *know* you can pitch to him. If you hit 'im, don't look to me for backup."

Costello joined the conference. "What's going on?"

Danny answered. "Miguel wants me to walk 'im or pitch to 'im."

Costello glared at his catcher. "No one made you coach, Guzman."

As Miguel flushed with anger, Costello turned to Danny. "Do what I say. The last thing"—he jogged his head toward the scout in the red hat—"a scout wants to see is a player who can't follow orders." He turned and walked away.

The umpire was almost to the mound. "That's enough. Let's get goin'."

Danny took in his catcher. "No worries. I'll just graze 'im."

As Miguel returned to the plate, Danny looked away from the taunts coming from the City High side of the stands. He spotted his dad at the end of the bleachers. Ray shook his head. Danny knew what it meant. *Don't do it.*

Danny set, stared at the strike zone, and saw a sinking fastball drill into Rafael's hip: his déjà vu ball was back.

Danny checked the runner on second, wound up and hurled his speed sinker. The instant he released it, he knew it was off. Fear shot threw him twice the speed of the pitch. He wished Captain America would throw his shield to stop the ball.

Rafael tried to turn. Too slow. The ball hit him between the brim of his helmet and the ear protector. The shot to the side of his head dropped him in the dirt.

Danny rushed forward as his insides ballooned with nausea. The Banditos' bench exploded out of their dugout. The Cyclones answered in kind. Within seconds, the infield turned into a melee of red-white-black-gold, swinging fists and cursing players. The roiling fight was joined by bellicose fans from both sides.

As the brawl spread into the stands, Arky tried to escape but was pulled down by a City High kid who pummeled his head. Arky's attempt to go turtle and curl into a ball between the benches earned him body punches and kicks.

While the school's security officers couldn't stop the brawl, the wail of approaching sirens thinned the fighting to the most hardcore venting their fury.

Arky's beating ended when he heard the squishy blow of a gut punch. He looked up in time to see the face of the Latino kid who was beating him, contort, puff, and hurl. Just as Rafael was unable to turn and avoid Danny's bean ball, Arky couldn't dodge the gush of vomit.

Matt pushed away the retching kid and pulled his sputtering and grossed-out friend to his feet.

"Jesus!" Arky shouted as he sleeve-wiped his face and head. "Why'd you punch him in the gut?"

"Be happy I saved your ass!" Matt came back.

Arky tried not to throw up himself. "Where's Danny?"

Beyond the bleachers, Matt took in the lot of parked cars. People continued to fight with their horns as they tried to escape, while several police cruisers, sirens and flashers going, raced onto the scene. In the midst of the chaos, something caught Matt's eye. He saw Danny running through the parked cars. He was being chased by three City High players.

Arky stood in time to see Danny hop in his van and burn rubber. To avoid the jam of traffic clogging the lot's exit, the van turned sharply and lurched over the curb onto school grounds.

Matt and Arky watched the three ballplayers running after Danny give up the chase as one of them screamed. "You better run! We're gonna gut you like a pescado!"

12

Shit Storm

DANNY RACED THE van away from the school. He'd seen the ambulance that had sped away with Rafael in it. As sick and horrible as he felt about hitting Rafael, there was nothing he could do. It was too late. There was no taking the pitch back. He could only hope and pray Rafael would be okay.

Danny's face was marred with cuts and bruises from the punches he'd taken; one eye was puffy and almost swollen shut. He'd gotten more than he gave because of his split focus during the melee between the fists coming at him and two men leaving the game: his father and the scout from the St. Louis Cardinals. His father had left immediately, and Danny had spotted the scout leaving and getting into a white sedan.

As Danny accelerated onto the two-lane highway going west, he hoped his hunch was right: the scout was headed back toward St. Louis. He raced along the highway until his instinct proved right. He spotted the white sedan. He floored it and caught the sedan. The man at the wheel was still wearing his red baseball cap.

With the oncoming lane open ahead, Danny swung out, pulled alongside the car, and gestured for the startled scout to pull over. Spotting an oncoming semitruck, Danny gestured to the scout again. The oncoming truck hit its horn. The scout hit his breaks and yanked the sedan onto the shoulder. Danny whipped by him and pulled back into the right lane as the truck barreled by with its horn blaring.

Danny jumped out of the van as the scout leaped out of his car. "What the hell are you doing?" the scout screamed.

"I just wanted to tell ya that last pitch wasn't me." Danny implored. "It got away, and I'm torn up about it. That was my friend. I'd take it back in a heartbeat if I could. But everything you saw up till then is how I deal. I got control to spare."

The scout got in Danny's face. "If you had control to spare, you wouldn't have thrown a headshot! If you had control to spare, you wouldn't have chased me down and almost gotten us killed! You're way out of line! I'll tell you what the Majors have to spare. Hot heads. And we sure as hell don't need another!"

The scout dropped back behind the wheel and reached for the door, but Danny held the door. "I'm sorry," Danny apologized. "I just wanted you to know."

The scout stood back up, glared at Danny for a moment, then softened his tone. "Look, son, people get hit in baseball. It happens. And sometimes it's bad. But here's the knock on you. I'm not driving away and leaving you in the rearview 'cause you let a pitch get away and hit someone. I'm driving away 'cause I saw your stuff, *all* of it, and it doesn't add up. You're not big league material."

The words hit Danny like a sucker punch.

The scout slid back into his seat, shut the door, and drove away.

Danny stood there, unable to move.

At the Jongler-Jinkses' house, Howard finally left to do errands and get in a swim at the university pool.

Iris went straight to the attic office and followed the steps Arky had taken to set up the record player and play the wooden disk of grenadilla and its hidden music. No sooner had she opened the secret cache on their mother's computer, then the screech of tires pulled her to the dormer window facing the front of the house.

Down below in the driveway, she saw Arky get out of their car. Matt got out too, wearing his baseball uniform. She knew enough about Cyclones baseball to know that the team traveled to and from games in a bus. Matt coming home with Arky was odd.

She quickly put the computer to sleep, lifted the black disk of grenadilla wood off the turntable, and returned it to its place on the wall under the Plexiglas case.

By the time Iris reached the second floor hallway, Arky was coming up the stairs. He looked like he'd been in a food fight, and his face was bruised. He smelled even worse. "What happened to you?" she asked plugging her nose.

"Don't ask," he answered as he headed for a shower.

Iris went downstairs and found Matt in the kitchen. He held a dishtowel of ice to a lump on his forehead.

"Are you all right?"

He nodded. "Better than some other guys."

While Arky showered, Matt told Iris how the game had turned into a brawl when Danny beaned one of the City High players and knocked him out.

Iris flipped on the TV and changed it to a local channel. A reporter was on the screen in front of the Belleplain Hospital. She reported that Rafael Santeiro, the player who'd been hit in the head during the baseball game had been put into a medically induced coma to reduce brain-swelling and prevent life-threatening complications.

"Shit," Matt muttered as he pulled out his phone and tried to call Danny.

Iris took the opportunity to slip upstairs to Arky's room. She knocked on the closed door. "Are you dressed yet."

"Enough," came his answer.

She entered and told Arky the bad news.

Arky pulled on a shirt. "Even more reason why we gotta find Danny before City High kids do."

Iris shut the door behind her. "Arky, I got a feeling."

Arky slipped into a tennis shoe. "That's more than the guy in a coma can say."

"I'm talking about the signs," she continued.

While tying the shoe, Arky shot her a skeptical look. "What 'signs'?"

The thoughts that had kept her tossing and turning the night before tumbled out. "Friday afternoon I saw the door open in Mom's attic office, and no one was there. At my craziest, I thought it might be a sign of Mom coming back. Yesterday you found the key unlocking Mom's computer and her *Sphere of Science*, and last night we saw and heard Mom playing for us. All I can think of is that seeing her might be the vision, the horizon event, of her coming back. And now, all this stuff is happening with Danny."

Arky finished tying the second shoe and straightened up. "Besides leapfrogging all over the place like a demented cricket, what are you saying?"

"I've got a feeling the cor anglais is waking up. Something's gonna happen."

He gave her a hard look. "All I know is some Latino guys wanna kick Danny's ass, or worse." He brushed past her and out the door.

She followed, unable to say anymore without Matt overhearing.

Down in the kitchen, Matt told them what else the local news had reported. "A gang of City High kids showed up at North with a truckload of manure, broke some windows, and dumped it inside the school."

"Better they break windows than break Danny," Arky said.

"I tried Danny's phone again," Matt added. "He's still not answering."

Arky started back toward the front door. "We gotta find him."

Iris followed. "I'm going too."

"Not a chance." Arky wheeled on her. "I got my ass kicked once and I'll risk it again for Danny, but Dad will kill me if anything happens to you."

"But—"

"No!" Arky shouted. "Since you've got all sorts of woo-woo feeling about what's about to go down"—he searched for the right words to keep Matt in the dark—"why don't you go blow your horn till you have one of your crazy visions?"

Iris knew she was in a losing fight.

After Arky and Matt drove away, Iris went back to the attic and reopened their mother's secret cache on the computer. Iris read through the list of files under the first one, "*Tempus Ludendi.*" They all had scientific names that didn't make much sense to her. It really was their mom's *Sphere of Science*. Iris's focus wasn't helped by her nagging fears of where Danny might be, and why he couldn't answer his phone.

At the mall, Danny stood in front of Lieutenant Feldman's desk in the Navy Recruiting Office. Danny had already told the lieutenant how his shot at baseball was over, and he wanted to know if getting his GED before the end of the school year would fast-track him into the SEALs sooner than later.

Feldman studied Danny's battered face and spirit. "SEAL candidates with a diploma rather than a GED have a higher success rate at getting through the program and becoming a SEAL."

Danny shifted impatiently. "I'm not worried about my chances—it's all I got left—I just wanna know if I can do it sooner than later."

"I think you should finish school," Feldman said.

"If I wanted," Danny blurted, "I could get my GED in a week, and be in the *army* a week later!"

"You could." Feldman held on Danny with a steady gaze. "Did you know that the guy you beaned is in a medically induced coma?"

Danny blanched. He turned and rushed out of the office.

Arky and Matt drove to Danny's house. His dad's white panel van was parked out front but not the old Bender Excavation van they'd seen Danny leave the game in. They decided to drive out to the lake where Danny sometimes went fishing.

13

Signs

On the mall roof, Danny stood in the prairie grass with his arms on the parapet overlooking the sprawling parking lot and the Bass fishing pond. He yanked out his phone, turned it back on, and dialed Rafael's house. Rafael's father answered the phone. As soon as Danny identified himself, Rafael's dad cursed Danny and hung up.

Danny moved back through the high grass and found the baseball in its hiding spot. Returning to the parapet, he told himself, *Gonna throw the ball as far as I can. If it makes the pond, I finish school and go SEAL. If it falls short, I go army.*

He took a few steps back, wound up, and threw the ball as far and hard as he could. The white ball arced over the parking lot. Where it came to rest would fix his future. The ball hit the parking lot, bounced onto the grass perimeter surrounding the pond, and rolled to a stop short of the water.

Danny stared at the white speck lying in the grass. "Army."

In the attic office, Iris was buffeted between worst-case scenarios of what might be happening to Danny, and the dead-ends she kept finding in the computer cache where Octavia had hidden her science research on the cor anglais and time travel.

Whenever Iris was troubled and the house was empty, there was one thing that soothed her: playing the cor anglais. She finished assembling the instrument and inserted a reed. She began playing the solo from Dvorak's *New World Symphony.*

As she played, she hoped the lamenting music would yield a vision, especially now that when she played it she couldn't stop seeing and hearing her mother play it so soulfully on the file she'd left in her computer. The feeling was so strong, it felt like she wasn't playing alone. It felt like she was playing with her mother.

Reaching the lake, Arky and Matt saw that the double-ruts leading down to the lake's edge were slick and puddled from the rain the night before. Worried that the Subaru might not make it back up, Arky parked the car at the top of the hill. He and Matt walked down to the lake.

While playing the solo on the cor anglais, Iris felt a sensation she had wished for all winter. Her fingers became weightless, as if the keys were working her fingers as much as her fingers were working the keys. The hidden powers of the cor anglais were stirring to life. Her fear that its full powers might be awakening was overridden by her excitement. She had to play on.

Iris waited for the instrument to take control, to possess her hands, her arms, her lungs, and for the music to turn strange and otherworldly. But the music didn't shift. She kept playing Dvorak's beautiful solo in the perfect harmony of player and instrument being one.

Then she noticed something across the room. The black disk of wood hanging at the center of her mother's spidery cosmos was moving, not in any direction, but churning like it was no longer wood, but molten. Iris played on, prompting the vision to develop.

The black stirring circle lightened to gray and then like a peephole opening wider, the vision expanded around it. The churning gray grew to include the blade of a shovel working the mix. Iris recognized it as concrete being blended in some kind of tub or mixer with a corkscrew auger working the cement batter. The vision dilated further to include the arms and body of whoever was working the shovel. It was Danny.

As soon as she began the reprise of the opening melody—*Daa-da-daaa, daa-da-daaa*—the vision pushed toward her… then…on the peak of a note, something shot out of the viscous concrete—a grasping hand. The frightening shock knocked the reed from her mouth, killing the music and the vision.

Iris breathed sharply, her heart pounding. She didn't know if the grasping hand had been reaching to grab her or reaching for help.

At the lake, Arky and Matt didn't find Danny fishing on the dock.

Arky's cell phone rang. He saw it was Iris.

"Is it Danny?" Matt asked.

"I wish," Arky said, taking the call.

Hearing Iris launch into her vision of Danny, Arky moved away, not wanting Matt to hear.

Matt headed along the shore toward a duck blind Danny might have holed up in.

When Iris got to the part about Danny mixing cement, Arky cut her off. "He's at Benders," he blurted, struggling not to shout. "That the first place they'll look for him!"

In the attic, the cor anglais lay across Iris's legs. With her phone to her ear, she stared, wide eyed, at something across the room. "I gotta go," she said into the phone.

Arky yelled into his phone. "No-no-no! You stay there! Don't go anywhere!" Iris didn't hear him. She'd hung up. "Shit," Arky cursed as he saw Matt disappear into the duck blind. Arky dashed up the rutted road.

Coming out of the blind, Matt saw Arky sprinting up the road. "What happened?"

Reaching the top of the hill and the car, Arky jumped in the Subaru and sped away. He didn't like ditching Matt, but he had to.

Back in the attic, Iris gaped across the room.

In the doorway, stood her father.

With the cor anglais still across her legs, she couldn't speak.

Howard's eyes scanned the curved woodwind and the bas-relief spider on the bell. His gaze lifted to the spidery cosmos decorating the opposite wall, then returned to the ancient instrument. "How long have you had it?" he asked with disarming calm.

His question—not *What is it?* or *Who gave it to you?*—heightened Iris's shock. It hinted at him knowing more than she'd ever imagined. Iris answered with the truth. "Since the day Mom left."

"Left?"

Iris's shock was swept away by relief. She'd never been so thankful to be busted. The secret she'd denied him for so long was over. "Mom's out there somewhere, Dad," she blurted. "I know it."

"Where?"

She lifted the cor anglais. "Only this knows."

Her puzzling answer didn't faze him. He fixed on her with unblinking eyes. "What have you been doing with it?"

She wasn't ready to tell him everything, especially about sending Matt to the past. "I've been playing it ever since Mom disappeared, and she left it to me."

Surprisingly, he didn't ask about that day and how she'd gotten the instrument. Instead he stepped forward and reached out for the instrument. After she handed it to him, he turned it in his hands, studying the spiderweb inlay worked into the back of curved body and the spider on the bell. "Did Mom play it a lot?"

"All the time," Iris said, "when the house was empty."

"The only cor anglais I ever heard her play was her modern one. I never got to hear her play this one."

"I'm sorry."

He handed the instrument back to Iris. "Play it for me."

"Now?"

"Yes." Howard sat in a straight-backed chair against the wall.

Iris wet the reed and took a breath.

14

Chase

ARKY RACED THE Subaru wagon along the country road leading to Bender Excavation. Closing on a car up ahead, he pulled out to pass it. Going by, he recognized the three guys in the car: the same guys who had chased Danny in the City High parking lot. They had changed out of their baseball uniforms but wore Banditos hats. Arky quickly looked away, hoping they wouldn't recognize him. The bad news was his hunch had been right: they were headed to Bender's. Arky sped ahead and was relieved to see in the rearview that they didn't race after him.

Arky turned down the long entrance road to Bender Excavation and spotted Danny's van parked in the yard. Iris's vision had been right. Pulling into the service yard, Arky saw Danny, in his coveralls, hosing out the front-loading bucket on a Bobcat.

Danny watched as Arky skidded the Subaru to a stop and jumped out. Arky threw a hand at the fresh section of concrete added to the access ramp. "What are you doing?"

"Finishing something before I'm outta here."

There was no time to ask what he meant. "Three City High guys are coming for you," Arky exclaimed. "We gotta leave, now."

Danny's gaze shifted to the entrance gate. A sedan turned off the road, passed through the gate and proceeded down the narrow entrance road. "Too late."

Arky whipped around to see the sedan. "C'mon!" he urged as he grabbed Danny's arm and pulled him toward the labyrinth of junked cars and trucks.

The sedan pulled into the yard. Hector and his two buddies got out.

Hiding in the graveyard of cars, Arky and Danny watched as Hector reached back into his car, lifted a handgun, and stuck it in his waistband.

"Shit," Arky whispered. "You see that?"

"Yeah," Danny whispered back.

Hector walked to the bucket mixer and checked out the corkscrew auger at the bottom of the bucket. "You know, Pescado," he announced loudly, "we were gonna do a little Tommy John surgery on your arm, but this is better. After your 'accident,' you can collect workman's comp." He got a laugh from his buddies before he threw the switch on the mixer, and the auger began to rumble and turn. Over the noise, Hector ordered his friends, "Let's find 'im."

Arky and Danny used the noise to move deeper into the scrapyard of cars. Hector and his two-man crew fanned out and started into the labyrinth.

In the attic office, Iris played the lamenting solo from Dvorak's *New World Symphony.*

Her father was transfixed. The music coming from the ancient cor anglais cut to his soul. He hadn't heard it since the last time Octavia had played it on her modern English horn before she had disappeared.

Iris couldn't see the tears on her father's cheeks. She was in the grip of another vision. Like the previous one of the mixer and Danny, this one felt hyperreal too. She was looking down at a maze of junked vehicles as if from a helicopter. Two boys dodged through the narrow alleyways between the rusted cars and trucks. She recognized Arky and Danny. They weren't alone. Three other boys moved through the labyrinth as well, darting this way and that, hunting for Arky and Danny.

Clinging to the vision, and the music that was fueling it, Iris felt her fingering grow light. The cor anglais was once again stirring to life, taking control.

As Howard remained hypnotized by Iris's playing, the music began to segue from Dvorak's melody to something stranger. It grew in energy and pace, unlike anything he'd ever heard.

The chase at Bender's also intensified. Hector's voice rose from the junkyard. "C'mon, Pescado! The harder you are to reel in, the harder we're gonna be on you."

Arky and Danny ran down an aisle of junkers, away from the guys shouting to each other.

Inside the labyrinth, Hector stopped and peered through a gauntlet of busted-out windshields. He saw a movement. "I see him!"

In the attic, the music was now wild and frenetic. Iris looked like someone wrestling a black serpent.

Howard jumped from his chair to stop it. As he rushed forward, a ribbon of mist shot from the end of the cor anglais. He recoiled and gasped as the curling mist snaked along the floor. Another strand slithered from the instrument's bell.

As wild sound poured from the cor anglais possessing Iris, she and her father were spellbound by the mists pouring from the woodwind's bell. They slithered across the floor and climbed the wall displaying the spidery cosmos. The leading snake of mist slid under the Plexiglas case protecting the black disk of wood. The Plexiglas fell away. The thick cord of mist pulled back and plunged into the wheel of black wood, pulling the trailing stream of mists behind it like anchor ropes snaking through a ship's portal.

While Howard stared in dumbfounded shock, the cor anglais wailed on, disgorging mists that shot across the room and plunged through the black portal.

The only thing Iris controlled were her thoughts. She was terrified. She had no idea what was happening. This wasn't like the first time the cor anglais had come to life in her hands, wrapped Matt in a cocoon of mist in front of her, and vaulted him to the past. This was something different.

Running through the junkyard maze, Arky and Danny came to an abrupt stop. They'd reached the edge of the junkyard and the cover of the metal carcasses. An overgrown field stretched in front of them.

Danny squinted against the setting sun and pointed to the silhouette of an old barn a hundred yards across the field. "If we can make it there—" He sprinted onto the field. Arky raced after.

In the attic, Iris could no longer see the mists pouring from the cor anglais as it played her. She was blinded by another vision.

At first, all Iris could discern was darkness streaked with bars of light. The darkness slowly bloomed with light, letting shapes emerge. She was seeing the inside of a structure pierced by sunlight. Leaning against thick wooden posts were four-legged creatures. She made out a horse, a tiger, a dragon.

Hector and his two accomplices reached the edge of the junkyard at the same instant Danny and Arky, on the far side of the field, disappeared into the barn. Hector broke a smile. "Got 'em."

Inside the old barn, Danny and Arky darted through the pinstripes of light and dark, dodging around wooden animals set free from a merry-go-round. Rushing toward a ladder rising to a hayloft. Danny stepped on something and yelped as he fell with an ankle twist. Arky gave him a hand up and helped him toward the ladder.

Hector led his buddies jogging across the field; he pulled the gun from his waistband.

Arky pushed Danny up the ladder as he struggled and hissed from his ankle twist. Reaching the loft, they flopped on remnants of seed sacks and hay.

The cor anglais wailed, having locked Iris and Howard in its thrall.

Iris's vision pushed close to the wooden dragon. Its head displayed a gaping mouth with a tongue of fire. Suddenly, a snake of mist shot from the dragon's mouth. Pulling its endless body behind it, it coiled upward. Another serpentine mist quickly followed. The twin mists slithered along the underside of the hayloft floor.

Arky and Danny hadn't caught their breath when a bar of sunlight painting the floor between them dimmed. It didn't seem right. Arky turned and saw the first serpent of mist rising through a hole in the planking. Before he could scream, the mist shot forward and enveloped his throat. Danny thrust a hand at whatever the thing was. His hand was stopped as another mist whipped around Danny's arm.

In the attic, as Iris and the cor anglais scaled to a crescendo of sound, the mists no longer poured from the end of the instrument.

In the hayloft, the twisting mists enclosed Arky and Danny in two pearlescent cocoons painted with jagged slashes of light.

Almost to the barn, with the blazing sunset behind it, Hector and his buddies were startled by a double flash of light. It pulled them to a stop. Hector wrote it off as the sunset playing tricks on them and led his cohorts into the barn to grab their prize.

Stepping into the silence, Hector noticed the swirl of dust in a shaft of light. Someone had stirred it up. He smiled in triumph. "Hello, Pescado."

The only answer he got were the motes of dust evaporating into nothing.

In the attic, Iris gasped for air.

Howard—his face ashen from what he'd seen and heard—found his voice. "What happened?"

Iris grabbed a breath. The last thing she'd seen in her vision were two flashes of light. *Why two?* her mind grappled. *What happened at Bender's? Was it a vision or real?*

She stood and set the cor anglais aside. "We gotta find out."

15

Aftermath

On their way to Bender's, Iris drove her dad's Subaru sedan so that he wouldn't drive off the road in shock or excitement as Iris made good on her promise to tell him "everything." She started at the beginning. She told him about finding the ancient cor anglais in her room the day Octavia had vanished, the note her mother had left with it explaining her disappearance, and Octavia's request to keep it all a secret. Iris also told him about Octavia's journal, *The Book of Twins: Sphere of Music*. Iris stretched out her confession to avoid telling him two things she wasn't ready to reveal: that Arky also knew about the cor anglais and the reason he did was because Iris and the cor anglais had previously sent Matt Grinnell to 1907.

To stall further, she handed her phone to her dad and asked him to call Arky. When Howard only got his voice mail, Iris's fears mushroomed. What if the boys chasing Arky and Danny had got to them? She didn't know which was worse, that or the nagging questions she couldn't shake. *Why two flashes? Was it a vision or not?*

When they arrived at Bender Excavation, the dying sunset illuminated the scene. Arky's Subaru wagon and Danny's old company van were parked in the yard. The bucket mixer was still running. Howard went to shut it off.

Iris checked out what had been spray painted on the side of the van: You Can Run but Not Hide. Danny's Captain American hubcaps had been X-ed over.

Howard stepped next to her and touched the spray-painted message. The paint was still tacky. "What's this mean?"

"Good news," Iris said. "Whoever wanted to get Danny didn't. It looks like Arky and Danny got away." She didn't share the bad news. While she'd never been to Bender Excavation, it looked exactly like she'd seen it in her visions. Beyond the junkyard, she spotted a sagging barn silhouetted in the dimming light.

Moving through the field to the barn, Iris nervously explained to her father what she'd seen in her last vision: a structure pierced by light and mists pouring from a wooden dragon.

Getting to the barn and looking into the darkness, her stomach clenched. A merry-go-round dragon stared back at her. "Arky? Danny?" she called. No answer.

Howard looked confused. "Why would they be here?"

Iris didn't say. She pulled out her phone, turned on the flashlight app, and moved inside the barn. Howard followed.

Seeing the ladder to the hayloft, Iris climbed it and shined the light on the plank floor. Scraps of burlap and hay had been shoved around, showing fresh marks in the dust, like there'd been a struggle. The disturbance covered a wide area. The sight added weight to Iris's biggest fear. She had hoped—if her mother's "drifting soul" theory was right—that only Danny had been taken to the past. But the two flashes of light most likely meant *two* cocoons.

"What are you looking at?"

Too choked with emotion to answer, Iris scrambled down the ladder. She raced across the field along with the madly dancing phone light.

"Iris!" Howard called after her.

Getting to the service yard, despite the tears she was barely holding in, she forced herself to think. One certainty flashed through her: the cover-up had to begin.

She ran to Arky's Subaru and shone the phone light inside. Seeing his phone in the drink cup holder, she reached in and grabbed it. As her father jogged across the field toward her, she went to Danny's van. His phone and wallet were on the console. She opened the door to get them. She saw the keys in the ignition. Another thought fired.

As Howard, reached the yard, Iris sped away in the old Bender Excavation van. He stared after her, mystified and upset.

Iris swerved the van off the entrance road and onto the two-lane highway. As she sucked in breaths, her mind was in hyperdrive. The thing she and Arky had been trying to do all winter, the thing she had wished for—to reawaken the powers of the cor anglais and blow one or both of them back to the past to rescue their mother—had happened. The cor anglais had double dipped, but not with any time-travel *twins* she'd ever imaged—Arky and Danny.

16

Awakening

ARKY WAS HAVING a nightmare. He was trapped inside a long box. Sharp swords kept piercing the box, which he barely escaped by wiggling out of the way. Each sword knifing through the box gave him less space. He had no idea how some killer magician had locked him in there. With no wiggle room left, another sword knifed toward his chest. He screamed.

Arky came to with a start. The nightmare felt like it was still going on. Bright blades pressed him against a wooden floor. Coming fully awake, Arky realized they weren't swords; they were shafts of light coming through chinked walls. He remembered climbing into the hayloft of the old barn, the serpentine mist coming at him, followed by more snaking mists binding him and Danny.

Arky sat up, breaking the shafts of light. Beside him, Danny lay on the dusty hay-strewn floor, still not awake. To confirm his worst fear, Arky swung onto the ladder leading down from the hayloft.

Danny came to. He looked as clueless as a newborn. "What happened?"

Not answering, Arky scrambled down the ladder. The first heart-stopping clue was not seeing the merry-go-round animals.

He ran out of the barn and looked across a field greening up with new hay. The only thing rising beyond it was a thick forest lit by the rising sun. There wasn't any sign of Bender Excavation. "Shit!" he screamed. "I can't believe it!"

Danny limped out of the barn and joined Arky. He stared at the unfamiliar landscape. "What's going on?"

"Not talking about it!" Arky fired as he took off across the field.

Danny limped after him. "Wait up. What's the hurry? Where are you going?"

"To find out where the hell she sent us!"

"Where *who* sent us?" Danny called after him.

"My evil twin!"

Arky broke into a jog to try and think without getting battered with questions.

Danny called after him. "Oh sure, leave the wounded guy behind. Some marine you'd be! I'd call nine-one-one, but I left my phone in the van!"

Hearing him reminded Arky he was phoneless too. He'd left it in the Subaru.

Reaching the edge of the thick forest, Arky was struck by the size of the trees. This wasn't some second-growth forest. This was old growth. His skin crawled with fear. What if Iris had blown them back to the pre-European America, and they were about to be the first white guys to be slaughtered by Indians?

Danny had almost caught up to him. "I'm thinking they were just trying to scare us," he guessed. "They knocked us out, dragged our asses to the country, and dumped us out here to scare the crap out of us."

As he joined Arky, Arky hit him with a question. "What do you remember last?"

Danny squinted. "I dunno. Some kind of gas coming through the floor at us." He sparked with a notion. "That's what they did, they gassed us."

Arky started into the woods. "Think what you wanna think."

Danny followed as he checked out the massive trees. His ankle had loosened a little, and he could almost keep up with Arky. "Look, Ark, all I know is we don't know where we are, which means we're lost, and when you're lost you're supposed to stay put instead of getting more lost."

"Trust me," Arky answered with a rueful scoff. "You can't get any more lost than we are right now."

"What's that mean?"

"Stop asking questions I can't answer."

"Since when did you *not* have the answer to everything?"

Arky wheeled on Danny. "Okay, have it your way; I've got all the answers. You're in a dream, and you're stuck with me."

"Sounds more like a nightmare."

"Oh, it's a nightmare all right." Arky resumed walking. "Now shut up and limp."

"Okay, crabby." Danny took a few steps before exclaiming, "Hey! I got another idea. They superglued virtual-reality goggles to our faces to screw with our heads." He stopped and felt his face. "But I can't feel anything on my face." He limped after Arky. "Now *that* would be cool: VR goggles you didn't know you were wearing!"

Arky fought the urge to turn and slap him with the truth. *My sister just blew your ass back in time! And she blew you back in time with an innocent bystander*—me!

17

Confessions

IRIS DROVE DANNY's van into one of the empty bays in the Jongler-Jinkses' garage and killed the engine. She took Danny's phone off the console, shut it off, then shoved it and his wallet under the passenger seat. She slipped Arky's phone into her pocket.

When Iris got out and shut the bay's garage door to hide the van, Howard pulled his Subaru into the other bay.

Howard jumped out. "Why you brought that van here is the least of my questions. What the hell is going on?"

"Danny and Arky are gone," Iris answered, willing herself not to succumb to her emotions. She had to be tough. As much as she hated it, she had to be like Arky.

"To where?" Howard demanded.

"To another spacetime." She hit the other garage door button, closing the door to Howard's bay to totally mask the van. "But we can't tell people that, so we have to have a cover story until they get back, and the van—"

He grabbed her shoulders. "Stop and look at me!"

She wrestled with the tension gripping her. She hated upsetting her dad, even worse, she hated disappointing him. She met his eyes.

Seeing her distress, he tried to calm himself. "Even if what you're saying is true, how do you know Danny and Arky are coming back? Mom hasn't. What makes you so sure of anything you've told me?"

Iris realized by acting in control, by trying to be the "adult," she'd painted herself into a corner. She wanted to say, *Because I've done this before.* She was on the verge *of* spilling it all, of telling him about Matt and everything she knew, when she realized she had one more option. "Because Mom prepared me for this."

"How?" he demanded, his voice rising again. "Were you in cahoots with her *before* she disappeared?"

Iris swallowed the bitter arrow of his accusation. "No, Dad. Her disappearing was as hard on me as anyone."

Howard reached out and hugged her in contrition. "I'm sorry."

Iris welcomed his arms and said. "Mom can explain it better than me."

He drew back, his eyes wide. "How?"

"Come with me."

Upstairs in the attic office, Iris didn't need to play the black wooden disk to open her mother's cache on the computer. In the chaos of the last hours, Iris had forgotten about shutting it down. She sat her dad in her mom's chair at the desk, opened the cache, *The Book of Twins: Sphere of Science*, and opened the first file, "*Tempus Ludendi.*"

Iris sat in her mother's practice chair and silently watched her father watch the video of Octavia's message to her twins. As she played the solo from Dvorak's *New World Symphony*, she watched her dad's back spasm with sobs.

When Octavia finished playing, she looked out from the computer with a bittersweet smile. The video faded to black. It took a minute for Howard to collect himself and turn to Iris.

She was ready for the thousand questions he was sure to ask. He didn't.

"You've told me and shown me so much," he began. "It's time I share something with you."

Howard then revealed the first time he had heard of the Jongler cor anglais. It was early in his marriage, before the twins were born, on a night Octavia had had too much to drink. In her tipsy state, she'd told her husband about a family legend. Supposedly, there was a woodwind instrument, a cor anglais, that had been in the family for four hundred years. Legend had it that this ancient curved cor anglais was imbued with powers that could send people across the divide of time. When he had heard Octavia tell the story—which she never mentioned again—he assumed it was a drunken reverie or that it was an apocryphal family legend. After hearing it, he had joked that if he wasn't a good husband, Octavia would get rid of him by blowing him to the past. She had laughed at his joke. When Octavia had sobered up and Howard reminded her of the story, she had dismissed it as "one of those weird skeletons in every family's closet."

"Little did I know," Howard told Iris, "it was a real skeleton."

Iris had listened with rapt attention. "But if you'd heard the legend from Mom and then she took a sabbatical from work to learn how to play a modern cor anglais, didn't you suspect there might be more to it than she was saying?"

"Of course I suspected," he said. "But she assured me it was no different than someone who gets into genealogy and tracks their family tree to its earliest roots. Instead of tracking her genetic roots, she claimed she was attempting to track the family *legend* back to its origin and that learning to play the cor anglais was part of that pursuit."

"Dad, if you would've told me what you knew about the legend right after Mom disappeared, I would've spilled everything."

Howard's eyes filled with regret. "I wish I had. But I'm a Jinks, and you're a Jongler and a Jinks. We *know* how to keep secrets."

"And we've kept too many." Iris got up and headed for the door. "Don't move."

A minute later, she was back with the journal she had told him about earlier: *The Book of Twins: Sphere of Music*. Tucked inside was the note Octavia had left with it the day she'd disappeared. "If you want to know what Mom was thinking and seeing in her visions during the months she was playing the cor anglais, it's in here." She handed him the journal.

He held it reverently then looked up. During her trip to her room, Howard's unflagging optimism had triggered a question. "Now that we know what we know, that Mom is in the past, do you think Arky has been sent back to find her?"

Iris answered his hope with a smile. "I hope so."

Back in her room, having left her father to pour through the journal, Iris was overcome by a wave of exhaustion. She lay down on her bed and was drifting off when a ringtone jerked her back to consciousness. Someone was calling Arky's phone.

Scooping the phone off her desk, she saw the call was from Matt. She didn't know how Matt and Arky had become separated, but she suspected Arky had done the smart thing and ditched him before he'd gone to Bender's. She now had to do the smart thing and work the cover-up.

Instead of taking the call, she waited a minute, then texted Matt back on Arky's phone, pretending to be Arky. "Found Danny. Best to get outta town for a while. Gone fishing."

18

The Peddler

ARKY AND DANNY moved through deep woods.

While Danny's twisted ankle still bothered him, it was Arky's furious pace and refusal to slow down that was more irritating. "You got any idea where you're going?" he shouted ahead to Arky.

Arky ignored him.

Danny stopped and looked up at the monster trees. "I've never seen trees like this around Belleplain. Have you?" Getting only silence, he started up again. "You know, if things get nasty in here, you're gonna regret not being nicer. I've done survival training!"

Up ahead, Arky climbed a slight rise and stopped.

In a small clearing below was a covered wagon with dirty canvas. A big mule grazed in a stand of grass. Near the wagon was a campfire. A bulky man in a long coat and full beard sat on a wooden box and fussed with a pan on the fire.

Hearing Danny closing the gap behind him, Arky backed up and stopped Danny with a harsh whisper. "Keep it down."

Danny saw the scene in the clearing. "What the hell is that?"

"It's not an Uber driver," Arky snarled. Stumbling on a man with a wagon was better than cannibals cooking people, but it didn't calm the fear in his gut. Arky turned to Danny, grabbed the Bender Excavation patch on his coveralls and ripped it off.

"What'd you do that for?" Danny protested.

"Survival training." Arky tossed the patch away and started down the slope. "Morning!" he announced, hoping it didn't startle the man into drawing two six-guns and mowing them down.

As Arky approached the campfire, the man echoed, "Mornin'." He took in their appearance: a tall boy with grungy coveralls and a limp and a slight boy in Levi's and an untucked button-down. The man's eyes settled on the slight boy's shoes. "Never seen a pair of shoes like that."

Arky tugged his jeans lower to try and hide his Nikes. "My mother made 'em."

Danny scoffed. "Your mother doesn't make Nikes."

"Shut up," Arky ordered.

A smile broke through the man's beard. "Where are you boys from?"

"Not from around here," Arky answered, trying to get more info than he gave.

"Neither am I," the man replied, then jabbed a spoon at his wagon. "I'm a peddler." The man stood. He was taller than they'd expected. "And I can tell you this, it's a good time and place *not* to be from around here."

Danny had held his tongue long enough. "What do you mean?"

The peddler jogged his beard toward a steep hill. "Over the rise. See for yourself."

Arky started up the hill. Danny limped after him.

The climb ended on a bluff with a view across a river. On the other side, treeless hills rolled to the horizon. The hills were covered with a sprawling army encampment. Flying above the sea of white tents were countless flags. A few of them displayed a blue *X* with white stars over a field of red: the Confederate flag.

The sight sucked the color from Arky's face.

Danny looked perplexed. "It's a reenactment, right?"

Arky gaped at the unwavering nightmare. "No."

Danny gestured at the panorama. "It's gotta be."

"I know what they look like," Arky snapped. "If there's no RVs and Porta Potties, it's not a reenactment."

"If it's not," Danny said, "I bet you're right. This is a dream, one of those that goes on forever, like you're in a movie."

Arky had stopped listening. His attention was riveted on another piece of the panorama in front of them. The encampment over the river encompassed a town with a steepled skyline that he recognized: Fredericksburg, Virginia. There was more. Below them, and downriver on their side of the river, was another sea of tents. Rising from the rolling waves of tents was a different flag: the Union's stars and stripes.

Full comprehension nearly dropped Arky to his knees. Iris and the cor anglais had sent them to the Civil War! "Why'd she do this?" Arky yelled. "Why me! I get why the goddamned spider stick blew your ass outta Belleplain, but *me*? All I did was try and save your butt, and this is what I get! If I get home, I'm gonna break that stick over her head! If I don't, I hope she blows herself Jurassic and gets torn to shreds by a *T. rex*!"

Danny had watched Arky's tirade with blinking confusion. His expression opened with a realization. "Hey, maybe that proves it."

Arky flailed his arms. "Proves what?"

"That you talking such crazy shit could only happen in a dream."

Before Arky could calm down enough to rip Danny's dream theory to pieces, he saw the peddler climbing the hill toward them. Arky shot a warning to Danny. "Shut up, and let me do the talking."

Joining them, the peddler pointed across the river to the town. "The Johnny Rebs wintered around Fredericksburg." He pointed downriver to a tiny town engulfed by the Union camp. "On this side of the Rappahannock, the Yanks wintered around

Falmouth. For a fortnight now, both armies have been coming out of hibernation and getting ready to turn the river red."

From his visit to Fredericksburg, Arky remembered that the Battle of Chancellorsville, after several days of troop movements, began April 30, and the Second Battle of Fredericksburg, began May 3. "What's today's date?" he asked the peddler.

"I believe it's April twenty-third," he answered.

"The fighting starts in a week!" Arky shouted.

The peddler gave Arky a look. "I didn't realize you were a fortune-teller."

"You don't know the half of it," Arky said before turning to Danny. "We gotta get outta here."

The peddler raised a finger. "I could help with that."

Arky shot him a doubtful look. "How?"

"I'll show you in my camp." He started down from the bluff.

"C'mon, Ark," Danny said as he started after the peddler. "This dream gets weirder and weirder."

Arky followed, but there was something about the peddler he didn't trust.

Reaching the camp, the peddler said, "The first thing you boys will need is some different clothes. Those outfits will get you the kind of attention you don't want."

"What kind of attention?" Arky demanded.

"If you don't look like a local—and sometimes even that doesn't help—young men are easy pickings for whichever army sees you first and turns you into a soldier. I'd be happy to give you some clothes that'll help you pass for locals."

Arky eyed him. Something about the man kept bugging him. He might be a "peddler," but Arky wasn't sure what he was selling. "What do you want in return?"

"Nothing." The peddler grinned. "We're traveling men, boys. If a traveling man can't rely on the kindness of another traveling man, the world would just spin apart."

Inside the covered wagon, Arky and Danny changed into the simple wool clothing the peddler had offered them.

Removing his wallet from his jeans reminded Arky there were things in it that would give them away, like a driver's license and money with twenty-first-century dates. "Don't forget your wallet," he reminded Danny.

"Why?" Danny asked. "It's not like I've ever needed money in a dream."

"There's always a first," Arky countered. "Besides, if this is a dream, it's *my* dream, and in my dream I get to tell you what to do."

"Doesn't matter," Danny came back, "I left my wallet in the van. But here's the deal. Next time we get to something I wanna do, it's gonna be *my* dream."

His ridiculous logic made Arky want to tell him the truth then and there. But he couldn't do it with someone else around. There's no telling how Danny might flip out when he realized he was in 1863.

After they climbed out of the wagon, Arky asked the peddler what he meant by helping them to get out of there.

"The surest way out of here is to get up to Aquia Landing on the Potomac," the peddler explained, "and get a boat to Washington, DC."

"How far is Aquia Landing?" Arky asked.

"How far doesn't matter if you don't have the money to book passage on a riverboat. I've got a job for one of you boys, and I'm willing to pay for it."

"What kind of job?" Danny asked.

"I need something taken across the river to a general in the Confederate camp."

"No way," Arky declared.

"Is the river swimmable?" Danny asked.

"You can wade it."

Danny brightened. "Cool. I'm your guy."

Arky whacked him on the shoulder. "What the hell are you doing?"

"Hey"—Danny waved at their surroundings—"whatever all this is, we might as well go along to get along."

The peddler weighed in. "I like this boy's outlook."

"There's no way we're going over to the rebel camp," Arky protested.

"Who said anything about we? I'm doing the delivery"—Danny grinned at Arky—"'cause it's *my* dream now."

Despite the peddler's presence, Arky couldn't hide his exasperation. "Are you insane?" He gestured at the peddler. "For all you know he's a spy, and you could be running secret intel or battle plans over there that'll get you killed."

The peddler enjoyed a laugh. "The only danger in what I want delivered is if you drink it." He pulled two dark bottles from his pockets. "It's hair dye."

Arky's face knitted. "You want us to risk our lives for hair dye?"

The peddler looked hurt. "Do I look like a man who'd send anyone on a dangerous mission?" He didn't give them a chance to answer. "For months, there's been a truce between the two armies."

"You just said they were getting ready to fight," Arky reminded him.

"They are, but the Army of the Potomac and the Army of Northern Virginia move like cold molasses. In the meantime, General William Mahone won't ride into battle unless his prodigious beard is black as night."

Arky threw a hand toward the river. "So let him buy hair dye in Fredericksburg."

The peddler explained how the Union blockade of the Confederate states had been successful in denying the rebels all sorts of goods, from horseshoes to hair dye.

Arky wasn't done arguing. "If it's so safe to cross enemy lines, why don't *you* deliver it?"

"All the bridges are out," the peddler explained, "and I can't swim."

Arky leapt at his illogic. "You said we could *wade* the river!"

"You can." The peddler looked embarrassed. "I'm terrified of water even if it's ankle deep."

Danny had heard enough. "Stop buggin' the guy," he scolded Arky. "I said I'll do it." He reached out to the peddler. "Give 'em to me. I'll deliver your stuff."

The peddler started to handover the bottles, but Arky grabbed them. "I'll do it!"

"I took the job!" Danny protested.

Arky knew the peddler was right. There was a picket truce between the enemy armies, at least until the battle began. And the sooner they had money to buy two boat tickets and get far away from the battle, the better. "You got a bum ankle," Arky told Danny. "If things get ugly you're gonna need to run."

Danny didn't buy it. "It was my idea to go, and now you're putting me on the DL?"

The peddler shot him quizzical look. "The DL?"

Arky covered for the future-speak by pointing at Danny's head. "It's short for dumb"—he pointed at Danny's ankle—"and lame. If you wanna get this stuff to the general pronto, I'm your runner."

The peddler gave Danny a sympathetic look. "Your friend has a point. He's the best man for the job."

After Arky persuaded Danny to stay put, rest his ankle, and grab some sleep, he asked the peddler about his fee. While "four greenbacks"—two to be paid in advance, two to be paid after delivery—seemed like nothing for risking a trip to the Confederate camp, Arky figured 1863 dollars went a lot further than the useless ones in his wallet.

Watching Arky jog toward the river, a thought struck Danny. He turned to the peddler. "Do you think you can fall asleep while you're dreaming?"

The peddler answered with a wry smile. "Traveling man that I am, I believe anything is possible."

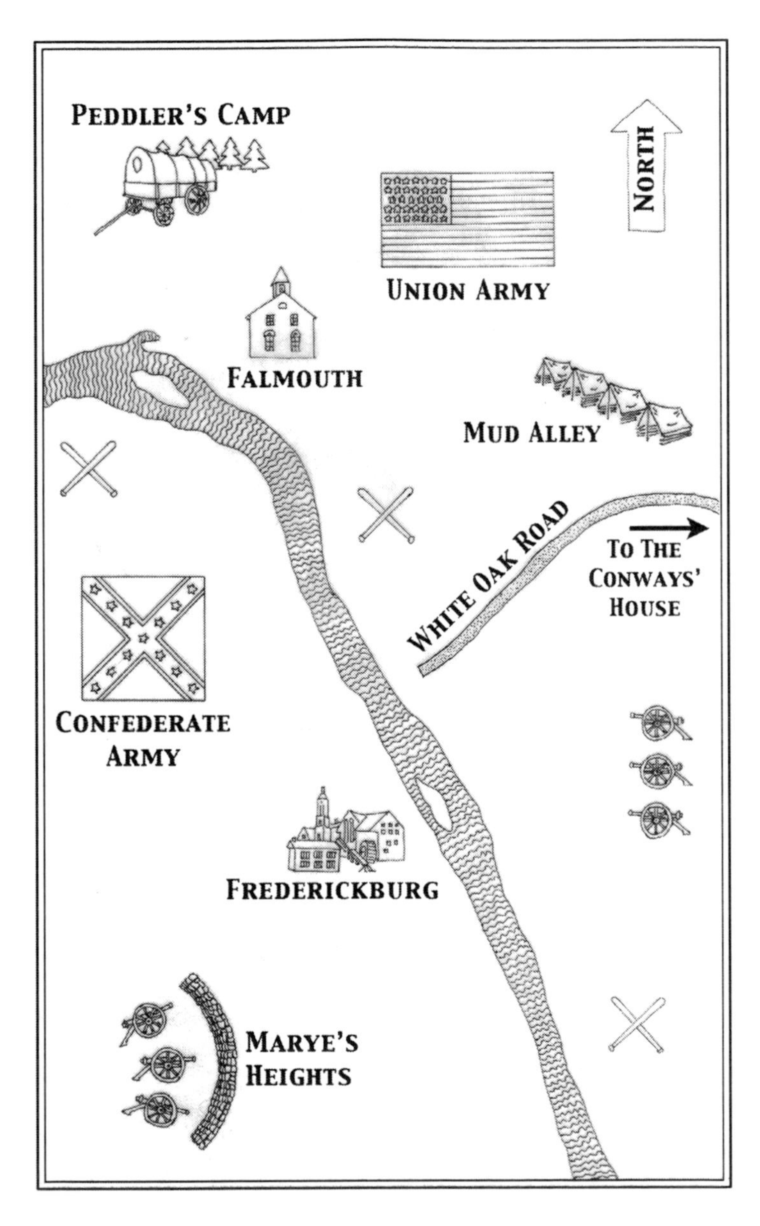

The Rappahannock River valley around Fredericksburg, VA, late April 1863.

19

Delivery Boy

REACHING THE BANKS of the Rappahannock, Arky gripped the two bottles and waded into the knee-high water. Having lost the cover of the woods, the fear clutching his chest felt as cold as the water. He was crossing a no-man's land between two armies with no protection but his father's grasp of history and the peddler's word. To fight his heart-pounding dread, over the rush of the shallow rapids, he spewed curses at Iris.

Halfway across, the *crack* of a musket made Arky slip and nearly sprawl in the rapids.

"Who comes there?" a voice shouted. On the opposite bank, two soldiers in gray uniforms were pointing their muskets at him.

Arky threw his arms in the air, holding the bottles aloft. "A delivery guy! I've got two bottles of product for General William Mahone!"

One of the puzzled soldiers called back, "You sound as strange as a Yankee."

"An' you look a-scared enough to be harmless," the other added.

After being invited to keep coming, Arky scrambled up the riverbank. The soldiers had a laugh over what he was carrying: hair dye for "Little Billy" Mahone. The soldiers roused a drowsy picket from a nearby campfire, told him to take over their post, and informed Arky they would escort him to General Mahone's field headquarters.

If meeting real-life rebels wasn't enough, whatever doubts Arky clung to about landing in the Civil War were erased by the Confederate camp. The reenactment he had visited was a toy-soldier picnic compared to the endless sprawl he moved through. The camp was acre after acre of soot-stained tents, dirty cookware, scattered furniture, busted boxes, hanging laundry, piles of garbage, and the occasional animal carcass readied for butchering and wrapped in flies. Amid the squalor was a steady parade of rebel soldiers. Unlike the ruddy, chubby-cheeked weekend soldiers he'd seen in his first visit to Fredericksburg, these soldiers stared out from gaunt masks of darkened hide or unruly whiskers that veiled the face-carving effects of war. Adding to Arky's shock was the assault of smells, from wood smoke to sewage with the occasional waft of coffee.

To mute the bombardment on his senses, Arky entertained a wild thought. *What if, among all the war-torn faces, I see the one soldier I might recognize: my great-great-great-great grandfather, Thomas Jinks?* Seizing on the ancestor scavenger hunt for distraction, Arky's eyes darted from rebel to rebel, looking for the full beard and familiar face that would soon be gouged in battle.

Back on the other side of the river, around the dying campfire, Danny finished a plate of fried cornmeal mush the peddler had made for him. Danny had earned breakfast by helping pack up the peddler's wagon and hitching up his mule.

The mundane activity of helping the peddler and eating had put Danny in a quandary. He'd never been in a dream that had lasted so long and that was so normal and kind of boring. A thought occurred to him. *Maybe it's not a dream. Maybe Hector and his crew found me in the barn, clocked me on the head, and I'm in a coma, just like Rafael.* The thought brought the regret of what he'd done to his old friend flooding back. *My shot at baseball deserves to be over*, he told himself, *but not Rafael's.*

The peddler returned to the campfire and sat on his box. "Not many folks run into the thick of enemy lines. Wherever you boys are from, it must be a powerful thing you're running from."

Danny was struck by how close the peddler's words came to his dark thoughts. He took it as a sign to talk about it. "I might've killed a buddy playing baseball."

The peddler absorbed it. "What are you gonna do about it?"

"Nuthin I can do"—Danny looked around—"till I get outta this dream, or whatever it is."

The peddler answered with sympathetic eyes. "*Tempus omnia revelat.*"

Danny's face creased. "What's that mean?"

"Time reveals all things."

Arky's escorts delivered him to a large tent: the headquarters of General Mahone. Besides being big enough to shelter a pickup, the tent was surrounded by chickens pecking at the stubbled ground. One of soldiers stepped inside the tent while the other minded Arky.

Having seen mostly dead animals and a few scrawny dogs, the chickens stirred Arky's curiosity. "Is 'Little Billy' Mahone also 'Little Billy' chicken farmer?"

Disliking Arky's attitude, the soldier flashed a threatening look. "Are you a Yankee sympathizer?"

Remembering he was talking to a guy with a loaded rifle, Arky ditched smartass and raised a hand. "No-no, I'm neutral. May the best team win."

Somewhat appeased, the soldier waved at the chickens. "Yer lookin' at the general's favorite regiment, the Tenth Virginia Flockers."

"What's so special about chickens?"

"Last I checked, soldiers don't lay eggs," the soldier deadpanned. "The general needs 'em for his bad digestion."

A prodigious belch brought their attention to an officer exiting the tent. General Mahone held a white napkin, which he must have been using for something else as his beard was caked with egg. Not just any beard, his two-foot whisker waterfall fell under a horseshoe-sized moustache. Both were streaked with gray. The facial-hair complex looked even bigger on the general's slight frame. He reminded Arky of an emaciated lawn gnome.

The little general let loose another belch. "Speak up, boy," he ordered. "What do you have for me?"

Arky raised the bottles of hair dye. "A peddler asked me to deliver these—"

Mahone let out a napkin-tossing whoop that scattered the 10th Virginia flockers in a squawking flurry. The commotion brought several more officers out of the tent. Mahone grabbed the bottles and presented them triumphantly. "Gentlemen, now that our colors are complete, the full brigade is ready for battle!"

The officers let loose a wild high-pitched yell that raised the hair on Arky's neck. The chickens shot into the tent.

Having given Arky a onceover, one of the officers turned to Mahone. "Now you mention it, sah, I could use a boy in my color guard."

Arky didn't like the sound of it.

"There'll be no pressing today," Mahone decreed. "This boy has exercised his duty to deliver material essential to the fighting ability of the Army of Northern Virginia. He has proved himself to be a son of the South and will better serve the cause as a spy on the enemy side of the water." The general handed the bottles to an officer and slapped a hand on Arky's shoulder. "I grant you safe passage back to the Yankee side, and when you gain something else of esteemed value"—his horseshoe moustache bent with a smile—"y'all come back now."

20

Silent Pleas

THE RISING SUN of the present century had climbed well into the sky above Belleplain.

The night before, Iris had given her father Octavia's parting note and her journal, *The Book of Twins: Sphere of Music.* Howard had spent most of the night devouring the journal. Reading of his wife's obsession with the cor anglais flooded him with hope and bolstered the conviction he now shared with Iris: Octavia was trapped in the past.

Iris was in the attic office digging further into the cache on her mother's computer, *The Book of Twins: Sphere of Science.* Despite the scientific nature of the files, including tests and precise measurements of the cor anglais, Iris was looking for any clue that would shed more light on the ancient instrument's powers. Octavia had run the cor anglais through a CAT scan and other tests to see if anything within the wood itself revealed something. All the scientific terminology made Iris realize that Arky had been partially right: most of the science was beyond her. But it didn't make her regret blowing him to the past, especially if he was there to rescue their mom.

The cell phone on the desk sounded an alert. It was Arky's phone, which Iris now carried with her. It was Matt responding to her Arky text about him and Danny getting out of town and claiming they had "Gone fishing."

Matt's text read, "Glad you found Cap. Why'd you ditch me at the lake? Had to hitchhike. School's shut from the manure hazard. Where are you? Musketeers fish together!"

It confirmed Iris's suspicion that Arky had ditched Matt at the lake because Arky hadn't completely dismissed her warning of the cor anglais coming to life. It reassured her that something she'd told her brother had actually sunk in; he didn't think she was *totally* nuts. But then, wherever he was, he knew that by now.

Iris texted Matt back on Arky's phone in Arky-speak. "Sorry about ditching you. I got an SOS from Cap, and there wasn't a moment to spare. You need you to stay, keep an eye on things, and keep us posted on Rafael." Iris sent it, then added another text. "That includes keeping an eye on Iris. She loses it over stuff like this."

Her smile was interrupted by hearing the doorknob turn. She shut off the phone.

Howard entered. He was carrying the cor anglais case that he'd retrieved from Iris's room. He also carried Octavia's journal, with her note to Iris.

Iris wasn't surprised he'd found the case—there was no longer any point in hiding it under her bed—but she didn't know why he'd brought it to the attic.

He set the case down and sat in Octavia's practice chair. After asking Iris several things about passages in the journal, Howard said, "Octavia talks about her synesthesia getting more active, her visions more powerful. Last night, you said the same has been happening to you. How do you feel about playing the cor anglais again to see if it sparks a vision?"

Iris felt like she was in a plunging elevator. She fought off the panic. "Dad, last time I played it, Danny and Arky got blown away. Aren't you scared of it happening again?"

Howard stayed eerily calm. "I've lost half my family to the past. If Mom's any precedent, there's no telling when we'll see Arky and Danny again. I'm less scared of the cor anglais blowing me away than I am of time travel being a one-way ticket. I'd rather see Mom and Arky in the past, than never see them again in the present."

Hearing the resolve in his voice made Iris want to tell him about how Matt's journey to the past had only lasted about a week in present time. But she checked herself. She didn't want to plant the seed in his mind that Matt's journey had been normal and that Octavia's had gone terribly wrong, that she might never return.

Sensing Iris's hesitation, Howard held up the note Octavia had left Iris and read the poem written on the back of it.

Wind in the wood
Tips on the keys
Add drifting soul
With silent pleas
Makes the music
A Jongler sees

He looked up at Iris with wet eyes. "I'm a drifting soul without her. Until yesterday, my silent pleas were unanswered. But now, the cor anglais makes the music I want to see: hope."

Iris had never heard her father talk like this, to articulate his grief. She couldn't say no.

Moments later, she stood in the middle of the room and held the assembled cor anglais. She couldn't play the Dvorak solo; that would be too scary after the last time she'd played it. Hoping the cor anglais would do nothing more than give her a vision, she chose another English horn solo she knew from Wagner's *Tristan and Isolde.*

As Iris played, and her fingers began to feel light on the keys, her stomach flopped. She fought off the urge to stop; she had to trust in the cor anglais always doing the right thing at the right time. Playing on, the keys didn't take over: it went no further than her fingers and the keys reaching perfect balance, feeling one and the same. As the music continued, a vision began to dance into view. Watching the vision take shape, she expected to see her mom or Danny or Arky. What materialized took her by surprise.

On a bed, lying on his back, Matt floated before her. He was awake. As Matt stared upward, he twirled a football in one hand. It was an old-fashioned football, bulbous and dark, like the ones she had seen in pictures from the early nineteen hundreds. When he tossed the football in the air, the vision disappeared.

She stopped playing. Silence crowded back into the room.

"So?" Howard asked. "Did you see anything?"

As much as Iris wanted to answer her father's openness with her own and tell him about the vision of Matt, she was too thrown by it. If her mother's poem was right, and "...silent pleas/Makes the music/A Jongler sees," why was she seeing *Matt*? Whose "silent pleas" was it answering? Her confusion only fortified her impulse to keep the vision to herself.

"I didn't get anything," she said, disliking the taste of the lie. She held up the instrument and tried to appease the disappointment in her dad's eyes. "The cor anglais has this annoying way of working on a need-to-know basis."

21

Two Good Men

ARKY WASTED NO time taking advantage of his safe passage back to the river. As he waded through the shallow water, he realized that whatever Yankee pickets might spot him knew nothing about his safe passage. To boost his chances of being taken as friend not foe, he sang what he could remember of "Yankee Doodle Mind Your Step." Fortunately, no Union picket shot him for being a rebel, or for singing out of tune.

As he ran back to the clearing, he went over the plan. With the money he collected from the peddler, he and Danny would head up to Aquia Landing and take a boat up the Potomac to Washington DC. Once there, they'd start looking for the one person who could get them home. Given what Arky had learned from Matt's time travel and his mother's journal, the only way back to the present was by finding a Jongler ancestor who possessed the ancient cor anglais.

When Arky reached the clearing, his plan did a face-plant. Except for a smoldering fire, the campsite was empty. Danny was gone. Thinking the peddler had skipped out on his final payment, and Danny might be sleeping nearby, Arky called his name. The only answer he got was squirrel chatter.

Arky's panic fueled a worst-case scenario. Danny had given up thinking it was a dream and had told the peddler he was a traveler from the future. The peddler, hustler that he was, had put Danny in shackles and was hauling him to the nearest freak show to hawk him as "Future Boy: the Sensation from Another Century!"

When Arky found wagon tracks in a wide trail cutting through the woods, he took off after them. As he ran, he blasted himself for being so stupid as to leave Danny on his own. He wondered if he'd ever see him again. The fear stopped Arky in his tracks.

What had yanked him to a bone-chilling stop wasn't losing Danny; it was the thought of his mother. In the mind-blowing events since he and Danny had come to in the barn, Arky had been so consumed with hating Iris he'd forgotten *why* he and Iris had tried over the winter to reawaken the powers of the cor anglais and send one or both of them to the past. He was flooded with questions. *What if that's why I'm here? What if the cor anglais wanted to send* me *here and* Danny *was the innocent bystander? What if I'm here to find Mom?*

A sound cut his brain-tumble short. The sound grew louder. Recognition dawned—the beat of pounding hooves. He shot off the trail.

The Union officer leading a dozen mounted soldiers spotted the figure dashing up the hillside. "Halt!" he shouted as he reined to a stop. The riders behind him obeyed.

Arky didn't. He only had forty yards to the crest of the hill, where he could disappear into the woods.

The officer drew his revolver and fired.

The bullet hissed over Arky's head before hitting a tree and peppering him with bark shrapnel. He dove to ground and raised his hands. "Okay-okay! I give up!"

After being ordered to come down the hill, Arky noticed the soldiers wore Yankee blue. He looked on the upside: they were the good guys. His optimism was misguided.

Because Arky had run, the officer took him for a rebel spy. They bound his hands, tied a rope to him, and led Arky back in the direction they'd come. Arky didn't wait to hear his Miranda rights. Nor were his captors bothered by his silence as they pulled him along and tossed insults at him. While their trash talk sounded old fashioned and quaint, Arky didn't fire back. Not only was he practicing a survival skill he might need in 1863—don't talk smack with guys who can whack—his mind was still burning with the notion that Iris and the cor anglais had blown him to the Civil War to find their mother and bring her home.

Passing through the outer ring of the Union camp and the sentries guarding it, Arky probed the scene with new eyes. But looking for a woman was almost a fool's errand. He only spotted a few—wives or laundresses outside some of the officers' tents—and none of them resembled his mother. He also noticed differences between the Union camp and the rebel camp he'd visited. Instead of two-man tents staked to the ground, the Yankee tents were raised by log walls, making them higher, roomier, and probably warmer as most of them had small brick and stone chimneys. The Yankee camp was also dotted with stacks of unopened crates and boxes. While the rebels might have better lungs for burping and battle cries, the Yankees had more supplies. Despite their differences, both camps had the overall look of a Boy Scout camp gone feral.

Arky's long walk on a leash ended in front of the field headquarters of a Union general. Arky didn't catch the general's name because something else had caught his eye: a nearby wagon and mule looked familiar. His suspicion was confirmed when a civilian came out of the general's tent. Even though his head was down as he counted greenbacks, there was no mistaking the peddler's bulky build and bushy beard.

"Two of those are mine," Arky declared.

The peddler looked up. Seeing Arky didn't surprise him. "Everything go well?"

"Product delivered," Arky snapped. "Where's Danny?"

The cavalry officer dismounted. "You two know each other?"

"Better than you might imagine," the peddler answered with a bent smile.

As the officer went into the tent, the peddler stepped forward and lifted two greenbacks. "This will make our transaction complete." He pulled on Arky's shirt and dropped the folded dollars down his front.

With his hands tied, Arky had no recourse. "What'd you do with my friend?"

"He has been pressed into the Union army," the peddler replied.

"Meaning you delivered him for a price."

"It's called a bounty."

The peddler's hypocrisy of warning them about being "easy pickings" for either army flushed Arky with anger.

The peddler offered an excuse. "Take it from me, son, the army's the safest place for your friend, Daniel. Three squares a day, a place to sleep, and no shortage of company."

"What about getting shot at?" Arky fired back.

The peddler lifted a helpless shrug. "When his time comes, his time comes."

Arky's urge to spit in the man's face was interrupted as a general came out of the tent with the cavalry officer who had nabbed Arky. As the mounted troopers saluted the general, the peddler sidled toward his wagon.

General John Gibbon was a handsome man in his midthirties with short-cropped dark hair. His stubbly beard was contrasted by a drooping Viking moustache. Arky was struck by the general's gaze. Gibbon's eyes glistened with calm intensity. They looked like the eyes of a warrior. The horrors they had probably witnessed fueled Arky's urge to get out of 1863 ASAP.

"What's your name, son?" Gibbon asked in a low Southern drawl.

A Union general with a Southern accent was as surprising to Arky as a Confederate general with a hair-dye fixation. "Arky Jongler-Jinks," he answered.

The peddler, still within earshot, turned. His eyes narrowed. Getting back to his wagon could wait.

"Not a name I've heard 'round here," Gibbon said to Arky.

"I'm not from around here," Arky declared.

Gibbon's forehead wrinkled at his prisoner's gumption. "Where are you from?"

"A long way from home. Where are you from?"

His captive's boldness heightened Gibbon's curiosity. "North Carolina," he answered with his rolling drawl.

Arky's audacity grew. "Aren't you on the wrong side?"

"I have three brothers on the wrong side," Gibbon replied. "I'm on the right side. What about you?"

Arky gave the right answer a twist. "I'm a Yankee fan."

The general arched his brow. "If you are indeed a 'Yankee fan,' let's test your bona fides. Sing me the first and second verse of 'The Star-Spangled Banner.'"

Arky swallowed. "How 'bout 'Yankee Doodle Mind Your Step'?"

"No," Gibbon ordered. "That's a nursery rhyme."

"No, really," Arky insisted, "it's a song too." He started to sing. "Yankee Doodle mind your step, Yankee doodle dandy—"

Gibbon yanked a revolver from his holster and fired a shot into the dirt in front of Arky.

Arky jumped and yelped. The scare was compounded by a shock. An officer brought Danny out of the tent. Arky's throat was too tight to speak.

"Ark!" Danny exclaimed before noticing the rope tethering his friend to a horse. "What got you tied up?"

Arky recovered enough to say, "Trying to find you."

"Well, here I am, and can you believe it?" Danny thumped his chest. "The Captain's been demoted to private."

"Enough," Gibbon ordered, waving his pistol at Danny. He turned back to Arky. "We're waiting for this cocky little songbird to sing 'The Star-Spangled Banner.'"

Arky cleared his throat. "How's it start again?"

Danny jumped in. "O-oh say can you see, by the dawn's early light—"

The officer next to him barked, "Dry up!"

Danny got the point.

Gibbon fixed on Arky. "Go on."

Arky took the tune up where Danny had left off. "What so proudly we hailed at the twilight's last gleaming. Whose broad stripes and big stars thru the"—he faltered—"something-something fight."

Gibbon turned to the officer who had silenced Danny. "Sully, detail a firing squad and have Mr. Jongler-Jinks shot as a Confederate spy."

"Okay, I don't know the song!" Arky confessed. "But I can tell you who wins the war!"

Gibbon's stony expression didn't change. "Worse, he's a fortune-teller." He turned to Sully. "Hang him."

Danny protested with his own logic. "But, General, sir, this is my dream, not his. If anyone should be shot it should be me."

The absurdity of the request caught everyone off guard but Gibbon. "Son, I don't want to shoot you?"

"Why not?" Danny demanded.

Gibbon's moustache twitched. "Because if we shot all the lunatics in the army, there'd be no army." The general took the laugh from his troops before waving a hand at Arky. "Take him away."

"General!" a voice boomed. It was the peddler striding back toward the group. "If I may intercede on behalf of the young man, I can attest to his northern sympathies. While his ignorance of 'The Star-Spangled Banner' may be attributed to a poor education, if you shoot him, you'll be wasting the fine legs of good runner."

"How do you know this?" Gibbon asked as the peddler reached them.

"I recently employed him, and he can run like a rabbit."

Gibbon looked at Arky then back at the peddler. "On your word, I'll spare him and hope he runs into battle and not from it."

"Excellent," the peddler acknowledged and clapped his hands. "Now, since I've collected one bounty"—he gestured at Danny—"on this fresh recruit"—he gestured at Arky—"and I've doubled my contribution to the Union cause, it only seems fair to collect another bounty."

Gibbon was no stranger to horse trading. He gestured at Arky. "This fresh fish is half the size."

The peddler nodded. "And for that reason he will cost you nothing but a favor."

"What favor is that?" Gibbon asked, intrigued by the unexpected offer.

"Let his God-given talents flourish by making him a foot courier."

"Done," Gibbon agreed. "But why give me a soldier at such a low price?"

The peddler's beard parted with a smile. "Because it would give me pleasure to see a boy named 'Arky' live up to the origin of his name. 'Arke' was the messenger of the Titans in their war with the Olympians."

Watching the peddler turn and move toward his wagon, Arky was torn between hating him for pressing them into the army and being thankful for being spared from a firing squad. But the latest wrinkle was the weirdest. Arky didn't expect a peddler to be familiar with Greek mythology, much less the origin of Arky's name.

22

Suiting Up

ARKY AND DANNY were taken to a quartermaster's tent. After learning they'd been conscripted into General Gibbon's Second Division of the Second Corps, they were issued uniforms. Then the jovial quartermaster told them he was going to give them something they wouldn't see again in three years of service: "Your last moment of privacy." He left the tent to let the recruits put on their new undergarments and uniforms.

"Quartermaster jokes," Arky groused as he wrestled out of his shirt. "We're gonna have plenty of privacy after we sneak out of camp and get outta here."

Danny pulled off his woolen shirt. "Ark, in every army that ever existed, they execute deserters."

Arky shook open the white shirt the quartermaster had called a "blouse." "And in every Civil War battle ever fought, they died by the thousands."

"We're not gonna make it to the battle," Danny claimed.

"Yeah, 'cause we're deserting," Arky said, pulling the blouse over his head.

"No, 'cause you said it's a week away."

Arky slid him a confounded look. "What's that got to do with anything?"

"No dream lasts a week." Danny legged out of his pants. "But here's the weird part. Just when I think it's gonna go nightmare, like you getting shot, it goes back to dream." He stood there stark naked. "And when I think it's a cool dream, it goes back to nightmare."

As Arky pulled on a pair of baggy undershorts, he was too stressed to keep holding back the truth. "It's not a dream or a nightmare."

"Of course it is. It all adds up," Danny insisted as he legged into his trousers.

"What adds up?" Arky echoed as he fumbled with the oddity of buttons on the fly of his pants instead of a zipper.

"After the baseball game blew up," Danny explained, "and I went to the recruiting office to try and go SEAL sooner than later, I went to the mall roof and asked for a sign."

It was the first Arky had heard of it. He stabbed an arm into a blue jacket. "What sign?"

"To see if I should go navy or army. The sign I got was go army. And since dreams are always some twisted version of real life, here I am in the *Union* army."

Danny's convoluted logic and blind refusal to accept their reality finally pushed Arky over the edge. He grabbed a long-barreled revolver lying on a table, and pointed it at Danny's chest.

Danny froze. "What're you doing?"

"Shut up, pay real close attention, and answer my questions." Arky kept pointing the revolver at Danny. "Now, what just happened?"

Danny swallowed. "You just pointed a weapon at me."

"Do you feel like you might get shot?"

"Yeah."

"Do you feel you might die?"

"Yeah."

"So, your 'dream' just turned into a nightmare. And what happens when you're about to get killed in a nightmare?"

The moment stretched as Danny thought about it. "You wake up."

"Are you waking up?"

Danny shook his head.

"Then we're not dreaming."

Danny's eyes widened. "No shit?"

Arky lowered the revolver. "No shit."

The quartermaster stepped back in the tent. He jumped at the sight of the pistol in Arky's hand. "Whoa, yer gettin' ahead of yourself, private." He crossed and took the gun from Arky. "You gotta learn how to handle a rifle before you get a sidearm." He noticed Danny's pale face. "What's the matter, son?"

Arky grabbed Danny and pulled him toward the entrance. "He needs some air."

Outside, Arky led Danny away from the tent to a dirt road cutting across the hillside. It commanded a view of the river valley.

Danny gaped at the Union encampment surrounding them. The hills, stripped of timber, were covered with blockaded tents up and down the Rappahannock River. The only ground lacking tents were two ribbons of bottomland running along both sides of the river. Beyond the bottomlands on the other side, the tent-covered hills surrounding Fredericksburg created a diorama of human anthills.

Danny let out a long breath. "Okay."

"Okay, what?" Arky echoed.

"It's not a dream. It's all too real for me to make up."

"It's more twisted than that," Arky said.

"What do you mean?"

Danny finally looked ready to listen. "You remember the ropey mists in the barn?" Arky asked.

"Yeah," Danny acknowledged. "I thought it was some kinda gas."

"It was something else. It came from my sister blowing on a woodwind instrument that's been in the Jongler family for hundreds of years. The instrument does more than play music. It blows people back in time."

Taking in Arky's unflinching expression, Danny struggled to comprehend. "How can an instrument do that?"

"I wish I knew. All I know for sure"—Arky gestured at the view—"is if it looks, feels, and smells like the Civil War, it *is* the Civil War."

Danny surveyed the scene for a long moment. "How're we gonna get back?"

"The same way we came," Arky said. "We find one of my ancestors with the Jongler cor anglais, and we get him to blow us back to Belleplain before we get killed."

Staring at Arky, Danny asked, "We could die here?"

"All I know," Arky answered, "is I'm not dying here to find out."

Danny pondered his meaning, then gave up. "I always thought your family was weird, but you really are freaks."

Arky frowned. "You don't know the half of it."

The sound of rattling wagons and creaking leather got their attention. A train of supply wagons was making its way along the road and coming toward them. Arky and Danny stepped up off the road to get out of the way.

23

Hot

In Belleplain, Howard had reluctantly accepted Iris's explanation that the cor anglais worked on a need-to-know basis. He had gone to the kitchen to make lunch.

Iris lifted Arky's phone off the desk and turned it back on. There was a text from Matt. He had responded to her Arky text discouraging Matt from joining them "fishing" and asking him to keep an eye on things, including Iris. Matt's text read, "Okay, be that way. Will hold down fort and keep eye on Iris. Have I ever told you I think she's HOT?"

It raised Iris's eyebrows and pulse. She told herself Matt had written it to goad Arky and that's all there was to it.

After reading the text several times, Iris decided to play the cor anglais again. Given the vision she'd had of Matt lying in bed and twirling an old fashioned football, who knows, maybe she'd call it back up and see more. She also wanted to rid her mind of a word no one had *ever* attributed to her: "hot." She picked up the cor anglais to calm the feeling thrumming inside her.

As she played the solo from Dvorak's *New World Symphony*, the music coming from the curved instrument did deliver another vision. But it had nothing to do with Matt.

The vision started when her room began to flicker with shards of white. The shards grew larger, obscuring her room, wavering and dancing to the rhythm of the music, until the room had been swallowed in white. The whiteness seemed like a riffling sheet hanging on a line or a sail wafting on a mast. Then the white field slid to the side, out of view, revealing the torsos of two boys wearing open jackets of some kind over white shirts. She recognized Arky and Danny. She only glimpsed them for a moment. Another white sail pulled across them like a sliding curtain. When this second sheet of white passed out of view, the boys were gone. So was the vision. Her room was back.

Iris went downstairs. Her knees felt weak. The vision had also deleted her notion that Arky and Danny might have been sent to *different* spacetimes. Iris was reassured by it. At least, they had each other.

Sitting at the kitchen island and eating lunch with her father, she asked if he had read the part in Octavia's journal about "horizon events."

"Yes," he said. "If I understand it correctly, it's a kind of vision Mom would have when she was playing the cor anglais. She would see someone, a 'time voyager,' who seemed out of place and out of time, and they would go around a corner, or disappear behind something, and she would know that the time voyager had gone over the horizon, beyond even the reach of her visions and the cor anglais."

"Exactly," Iris said.

"Octavia called it 'going solo,'" Howard added.

Iris told him about her vision of Arky and Danny.

When she finished, Howard asked, "Do you think that was their horizon event?"

"Yes." Iris nodded. "I think they've gone solo."

"Even though there's two of them," Howard questioned, trying to squash the emotion tugging at him.

"Yes."

Howard pushed his plate away, his appetite gone. "So all we can do is wait and hope, just like we've been waiting all this time for Mom?"

Iris nodded again. "Sorry, Dad."

"I'm not buying it. There's gotta be something we can do," he declared as his voice rose with frustration. "If I have to sit here and do nothing, I'll go crazy."

The *ring* of the doorbell made Iris jump. "I'll get it."

Howard saw the white panel van outside with Bender Excavation on the side. He got up and followed.

Iris opened the front door to find Ray Bender in his wheelchair. When he asked where they thought Danny might be, she told Mr. Bender that Danny had gone fishing with Arky to a location Arky wouldn't divulge in order to protect Danny from harm.

"How do you know that?" Ray demanded.

Iris shrugged. "Arky texted me."

Ray scowled. "If they wanted to be so secret, why'd they make their getaway in one of my company vans? If they had half a brain between the two of 'em, they would've taken the Subaru Arky left in my service yard."

Howard joined the cover-up. "They're teenagers, Ray. Half a brain between the two of 'em might be optimistic."

Ray's eyes narrowed. "No one would accuse your son of having anything less than a brain and a half."

Howard managed a smile. "I'll give you that, but book smart isn't street smart."

"We'll get Arky's car out of your service yard this afternoon," Iris offered.

Ray tossed his hands. "That's the least of my worries." With nothing else to go on, he asked them to let him know if they heard from Danny or Arky, and he left.

Returning to the kitchen, Iris said, "Dad, there is something we not only can do but *have* to do."

"What?" Howard asked.

Iris took Octavia's journal off the counter and opened it to the later pages. "I know you've already read this—"

"Cover to cover," he interjected, "and I'll do it again."

She continued, "One of the most important things Mom says is toward the end"—she looked at her father to emphasize the point—"right before she disappeared." She found a passage, handed him the journal, and pointed to the passage. "Read that to me."

He read. "'Everyone knows that tending to the present yields the future. But a Jongler knows the opposite is also true. Tending to the present yields the past.'"

"'Tending to the present yields the past,'" Iris repeated. "Mom went one step further. Tending to the present—taking a sabbatical to play the Jongler cor anglais—*took* her to the past. But it's the first meaning that's gotten me through so much since Mom went away. If we tend to the present, it will yield what we've lost to the past: Mom, Arky, and Danny."

Howard absorbed it for a moment. "My little philosopher."

"That's me," Iris said with a loving smile.

"I sure hope you're right"—he kissed her on the forehead—"and Mom's right."

After Iris went to her room, she lay on her bed and tried not to think about anything. It didn't work. She kept thinking of Arky's phone lying on her desk. She wanted to respond to Matt's "hot" text, but it felt so wrong. *Arky and Danny have gone solo,* she scolded herself, *and there's no way of knowing* what *might happen to them, just like Mom. They might never come back. None of them. And I'm obsessing over one word in a text, going boy crazy over Arky's best friend. I'm such a traitor.*

She turned on her side and gazed at Arky's phone. *Or,* she told herself, *is going a little boy crazy on Matt tending to the present to yield the past?*

She swung off the bed, picked up her brother's phone, and texted in her Arky-voice. "If you ever call my sister HOT again, I will kick your ass! So far, fishing sucks." She hit Send.

Less than a minute later, a text came back from Matt. "Bring it, lil man. She's HOT HOT HOT!"

Iris laughed and felt the flush of cheek-heat.

Part II

Duo

1

Company K

Danny and Arky watched the last supply wagon rattle away from them.

Walking against the plodding progress of the wagons, a black man strode toward them. Neatly dressed in civilian clothes, he sported a shock of white hair. Reaching Danny and Arky, the man took the young soldiers in. "Are you Daniel Bender and Arky Jongler-Jinks?"

"Yeah, we are," Arky replied.

"No doubt," the man said curtly. "Only fresh fish would stand around with their coats flapping like they stepped out of a whorehouse. Now button up before we march."

The boys exchanged a look. Danny gave Arky a surrendering shrug. "We're in the army now."

As the boys began buttoning the row of brass buttons fronting their jackets, the man introduced himself. "My name is Dabney."

Danny extended his hand. "Nice to meet you, Dabney. Danny Bender."

Rather than reciprocate, Dabney continued in his direct manner. "I'm the orderly for Company K of the Thirty-Fourth New York." He looked at Arky. "As for your name, I'd suggest we trim it to 'Jongler' or 'Jinks.' 'Jongler-Jinks' sounds like you've got trouble in your britches."

Danny chuckled as Arky censored a retort. Given that his Confederate ancestor, Thomas Jinks, was somewhere on the other side of the river, the last thing Arky wanted was someone labeling him as a rebel in Yankee clothing. "Fine, make it Jongler."

"Private Jongler, Private Bender, follow me." Dabney took off at a brisk pace.

The boys followed far enough behind to converse. Danny muttered to Arky. "Why doesn't he sound like a slave?"

Arky eye-rolled. "Because he's not a slave. There were free and educated blacks during the Civil War."

"Oh," Danny said.

Dabney led the boys through the "avenues" and "streets" of the Union camp. While they were no more than dirt byways separating companies and regiments, there was no shortage of street signs painted on wooden slats and staked in the ground, with names such as Hardtack Hill, Weevil Welcome and Home Shite Home.

Turning down a row of tents with a sign announcing, Mud Alley, Dabney pointed to a blue flag heralding a regiment. "This is your company street, home to Company K of the Thirty-Fourth New York Volunteer Infantry Regiment."

"We didn't volunteer," Arky pointed out.

Danny's focus was elsewhere. "Where is everybody?"

"Mostly on foraging detail," Dabney answered.

"What are they foraging for?"

"Anything other than the daily ration of salt pork, beans and hardtack."

Before Danny could ask another question, Dabney stopped at a makeshift table with several soldiers playing cards. "Sergeant Talcott, I've got some fresh fish."

The men looked up, including a man with a neatly trimmed moustache. James Talcott's uniform displayed the chevron of his rank. "From the river?" he asked.

"No, sir," Dabney replied with a smile. "Fresh from the waters of their mamas' loins."

The soldiers laughed as Talcott stood. "Then it's best I show 'em to their crib."

As the sergeant and Dabney led the boys to the end of Company K's tent-lined "alley," Talcott asked where they were from. Danny answered. "We're drifters, sir. We don't have a home."

Arky was impressed. Not only had Danny gotten out of dream mode, he seemed to be rolling with the punches.

"You're drifters no more," Talcott said. "And I'm going to make soldiers out of ya even if it kills ya."

Dabney laughed at the joke, and Danny managed a chuckle. Arky wasn't amused.

They stopped at the last tent on Mud Alley. Like the others, the shelter's low log walls raised a tent off the ground. A small brick chimney jutted up from the back wall. "Here it is, boys," Talcott announced, "home sweet home."

Arky peered through the tent's open flaps. As well as being empty, the floor was sunk two feet into the clay. "If we get killed," Arky asked, "does it double as our grave?"

"If that's how it worked," Talcott said, "its last two occupants would be lying there still."

The implication got Arky's attention. "What happened to them?"

"Dysentery."

"That's highly infectious," Arky waved at the tent. "Has it been disinfected?"

Talcott gave him a skewed look. "It's not a latrine, unless you shit where you sleep."

"What do you mean, it's not a latrine?" Danny asked.

"The shitter's the only thing that gets disinfected 'round here," Talcott replied. "It keeps the smell down."

Arky recalled basic science: Germs and bacteria had yet to be discovered. In 1863 people thought disease was carried by sewer gas. After his request for another tent was denied, Arky asked for some of the latrine disinfectant to clean the tent.

Talcott gave him a skewed look. "For a couple of drifters, you boys sure are persnickety."

"Maybe," Dabney added, "they're sisters scared to get their petticoats dirty."

Danny frowned at Arky. "Great. Now we're gonna get pegged as sissies."

"It's better than death by diarrhea," Arky retorted.

"If you'd like," Talcott offered Danny, "you can bivouac with someone else."

Danny covered for Arky. "We'll be fine, sir. When it comes to fightin' for cleanliness, or the Union, my buddy's a monster."

Mollified, Talcott told them they could find the supplies to "disinfect" their tent at the latrine. Talcott and Dabney began to leave, then the sergeant turned back to his new recruits. "If dyin' slow and miserable is what worries you, there's always a faster way."

"What's that?" Danny asked.

"Every deserter meets the same fate. Firing squad."

Once they were beyond earshot, Danny turned to Arky. "Didn't I tell ya?"

"He's just trying to scare us," Arky asserted, not ready to jettison the only plan he had. To avoid the subject, he changed it. "What made you think to call us drifters?"

"For all we know, there might be soldiers around here from Belleplain," Danny said. "If we told 'em our hometown and then got busted for being strangers to Belleplain, they might think we were rebel spies and shoot us for that. Besides, the way I see it, we *are* drifters. We drifted in from another time."

"Yeah," Arky said, impressed by Danny's foresight, "and mission one is to drift back."

"But first we disinfect the tent," Danny reminded him.

Arky glared at their sunken quarters. "It still looks like a friggin' grave."

2

First Supper

LATER THAT AFTERNOON, Dabney took Arky and Danny back to the quartermaster to pick up the rest of their gear. Besides a nine-pound rifle musket with ammunition and bayonet, they each collected more clothing, a greatcoat, bedding, tin cookware, a canteen, a tin cup and plate, utensils, a haversack to wear on their chest to carry rations, and a large canvas knapsack to carry all their soldierly goods, which came to about fifty pounds, give or take a ton.

After hauling their tortoise shells of gear back to Mud Alley, Arky and Danny stowed their gear in their tent and each drank a bucket of water. Dabney then took them to Sergeant Talcott's tent for their company assignments.

Beginning the next morning, Danny was to start training in basic infantry. Fulfilling the peddler's request, Arky was made a foot courier for the 34th New York's commander, Brigadier General Sully, and to serve in the regiment's "color guard."

As they left Talcott's tent, Arky kicked himself for not paying more attention during the reenactments he'd gone to with his father. "I get the courier thing," he said to Dabney, "but what's the color guard?"

"Being in the color guard comes with two great honors," Dabney replied.

"Forget the honors," Arky said. "What's the job?"

Dabney ignored his bluntness. "The first honor is to carry one of our flags into battle: the colors of the regiment, division, corps, or even the Stars and Stripes."

Danny piped in. "If he's carrying a flag, how's he gonna carry a rifle?"

"He doesn't carry a rifle," Dabney said. "Which brings me to the second honor. The color guard gets shot at more than anyone else. No other unit has a higher chance of making the ultimate sacrifice."

Arky threw up his hands. "Fantastic! Instead of a Yankee firing squad, they're throwing me at a rebel firing squad."

Reaching their tent, Danny had a question. "Since we don't start our assignments till tomorrow," he asked Dabney, "does that mean we have the rest of the day off?"

"Not quite," Dabney said, "but it brings me to your D 'n' A."

Arky blinked. "DNA?" He knew for a fact that the first inkling of DNA didn't come until the 1870s, and it wasn't called "DNA" until well into the twentieth century.

"D 'n' A," Dabney explained, "is short for duties and amusements. Mornings are for drilling and training; afternoons, if you're not put on detail, are free."

It was the first good news Arky had heard. If deserting was too risky, having the afternoons off would give him more time for finding the Jongler who would blow them back home, and/or finding his mother. From what he'd learned of Matt's time travel to 1907 and the Carlisle Indian School, the Jongler who'd sent Matt home was right there at the school. Maybe the Jongler with the cor anglais was just as close.

Starting the scavenger hunt for either of two Jonglers was delayed when Dabney gave Arky and Danny another chore. They fetched a bale of hay and spent the late afternoon scattering hay on their tent's sunken floor and arranging their gear in their cramped quarters. After Dabney returned and inspected their work, he told the boys to grab their dinnerware and led them to a mess tent.

In the clearing outside the mess tent, a dozen soldiers were already eating around a campfire. Their banter ceased when they spotted the two new recruits.

Dabney introduced them. "This is Private Bender and Private Jongler. No use asking where they're from; they're drifters who drifted down the wrong river."

A few soldiers chuckled as a hard-looking soldier took them in. "I've never known a 'drifter' to scrub out a tent like the last man who lay there was worse than a nigger."

Along with the jolt of hearing the word, Danny and Arky were surprised that no one reacted, not even Dabney.

The soldiers turned back to their chow. Dabney led the boys to a mess table. A cook ladled beans and salt pork onto their plates, topped it off with a couple of fat-looking crackers, and filled their tin cups with coffee.

As Dabney left, Arky and Danny found a spot on the ground several yards from the campfire circle and the renewed talk of the soldiers.

Danny kept his voice low. "I knew scrubbing down the tent was a dumb idea. We disrespected the guys who died there, and these guys were probably tight with 'em."

Arky scowled at the greasy spill of beans on his plate. "I'd rather be hated by a racist and his yahoo buddies than die of dysentery."

Danny shoveled beans into his mouth. "Whatever, I know the drill. We're like punk freshman on the varsity team. We're invisible, unseen, and unheard till somebody says different."

Arky probed his beans for a bit of salt pork that wasn't a chunk of white fat.

Danny noticed his reluctance. "Eat. You're gonna need the fuel tomorrow."

Arky lifted one of the thick, palm-sized crackers and took a bite. He practically broke a tooth. "Geez! It's like concrete!"

The hard-looking soldier in the campfire circle stood and shot Arky a menacing look. "That's the finest hardtack Major General Hooker can get. Do you have a problem with that?"

Arky recalled "Hooker" was the name of the general commanding the Army of the Potomac in 1863. "No, sir," he assured the soldier. "I'm just glad to know that when we run out of ammo and our bayonets are stuck in rebel ribs, we'll still have blunt instruments"—he pretended to hurl the cracker like a ninja star—"to crack their skulls."

He got a laugh from the men around the fire.

The menacing soldier released a sneering smile. "Let's hope yer fightin's as good as yer yappin'."

Having noticed the stripes on the soldier's uniform, Danny jumped in. "It is, corporal. I've seen Private Jongler kill people with his bare hands." He refrained from saying it was barehanded at the controls of a video game.

"Good," the corporal said, "'cause I'm lookin' forward to showin' both of ya the elephant."

Rather than ask what he meant by "the elephant," Danny and Arky followed the lead of the soldiers returning their attention to their circle and retreated to their own bubble.

"Ark, what'd I tell you?" Danny cautioned. "Unseen, unheard."

Later, Arky and Danny sat in front of their tent and watched the sun set behind the hills on the other side of the river and the endless spread of the Confederate camp. As darkness set in, a thick blanket of stars appeared. The stars were mirrored by the flickering "red stars" of the campfires sprinkled over the hills. Despite being bone tired, they couldn't help but be awed.

Keeping his voice low so as not to be heard by nearby soldiers taking in the same view, Danny whispered, "You know the other reason I know this isn't a dream?"

"What?" Arky asked.

"I'm not smart enough to dream something this beautiful."

Arky chuffed a laugh. "You're plenty smart, Dan-O. You're smart enough to keep your eyes on the prize."

"What's that?"

Arky kept his voice low. "We've got six days to find a Jongler and get home."

"What happens after six days?" Danny asked.

Arky gestured at the view. "Beautiful turns to a bloodbath."

A bugle began playing taps, signaling the order to retire.

"What if we don't find a Jongler?" Danny asked. "Or if we find a Jongler, and he can't send us home?"

"Ask me that in six days."

3

Book Bombs

After Iris had gotten Matt's text on Arky's phone saying she was "HOT HOT HOT!" she'd spent a fitful night of sleep trying to come up with a response, in Arky's voice of course. The guilt she felt about fixating on Matt was eased by her mother's advice: "Tending to the present yields the past." More importantly, Iris's gut told her that keeping tabs on Matt, and the lingering effects his voyage to 1907 had had on him, might yield a clue to bringing Danny, Arky and their mother home.

In the early morning, Iris finally came up with a response to Matt's text, but she waited to send it. A too-early text from Arky on a nonschool day would raise suspicions when Arky never missed a chance to sleep in.

Iris also had to make sure her dad followed through on his own tending to the present. She made him an omelet and persuaded him to take a break from Octavia's leave-behinds: *The Book of Twins: Sphere of Music* and *Sphere of Science.* After all, she teased, going to his job at the university was the only way to put food in the fridge and guarantee a steady supply of omelets.

After Howard went to work, Iris pulled out Arky's phone and sent the text she had composed to Matt. It read "How dare you call my sis HOT HOT HOT? Her honor isn't worth defending, but it must be done. I will appear from nowhere. Arky the Avenger."

As she loaded the dishwasher, Arky's phone beeped an alert. She checked it. Matt had texted back. "Shakin' in my boots. Bring it, Pee-wee."

Her face quirked with an idea.

Iris parked her car in front of Matt's house, went to the front door, and rang the bell.

Normally, it would have been a school day for North High, but it was still being decontaminated from the "manure spreading" by the City High kids retaliating for Rafael.

Matt opened the front door. He gave Iris a befuddled look. "I was expecting someone else."

"Who?" Iris asked.

"Your brother."

"He's still off somewhere in hiding with Danny," she explained.

"I know," Matt said. "We've been texting."

Iris couldn't resist. "About what?"

Matt shrugged. "Nothing important."

Iris detected a smile teasing his mouth. "I bet you're wondering why I'm here."

"Lemme guess," he said. "You came to see my trophy collection."

She answered with a chuckle. "No. I'm headed to school for orchestra rehearsal, and I thought you might want me to return those overdue library books."

He looked puzzled. "Isn't school closed?"

"The media center is manure free, so we're having rehearsal there."

"Oh." He stepped back. "C'mon in. I'll see if I can find 'em."

She followed him inside. Having never been to his house—their juggling sessions had always been at hers—the first thing she noticed was that Matt wasn't kidding about the trophy collection. In the living room was a glass case covering an entire wall. She moved toward it. "Wow. You won all that stuff?"

"It's mostly my dad's from college and his short trip to the NFL," Matt explained, "but I'm making a dent." Matt was well on his way to following in his father's footsteps. "Gunner" Grinnell had been a big-time college quarterback, but a knee injury in his first NFL season had ended his short-lived career.

Iris's attention was drawn to a dozen game balls in the case. She looked for the old bulbous football she had seen in her vision of Matt lying on his bed and tossing the ball. But all the footballs were the more slim modern ball.

Matt hung back at the room's entrance. "Trust me, you don't wanna go on the Gunner and Matt Grinnell sports tour."

"Why not?"

"There's nothing more pathetic than a trophy case."

His answer surprised her. "What's pathetic about it?"

"You might as well hang a big sign on it that says, 'I am what I was.'"

Knowing he meant it as a negative didn't stop her insides from jumping to another meaning. Matt was who he was now because of things that had happened to him in 1907. The things that had changed him lived in a "trophy case" deep inside him.

She moved closer to a football in the case and studied it. It was the one Matt had won for being MVP in the State Championship game back in early December.

Matt moved into the room. "Really, Iris, it's just a bunch of has-been junk."

Iris read the score on the championship ball, Belleplain 15–Rockford 14, and recalled how Matt, without knowing it, had used the changes he'd brought from the past to win the championship. "I get what you're saying," she acknowledged.

"These things just symbolize an experience. A trophy isn't a win any more than a gravestone is a person." She turned to face him. "But when you look at a trophy or a gravestone, it opens a window to everything you want to remember about the win or the person."

Her words stilled him. "Yeah, that's true."

Iris was struck by how quiet he'd gotten, how much he seemed somewhere else. She wanted to know where that was.

He shifted uneasily. "Hey, let's save the heavy stuff for school. I know you're not here to check out the Grinnell family bling." He turned toward the entranceway and the stairs. "The books are probably up in my room."

As he glanced back to see if she was following, he read her hesitation. He stopped and faced the awkwardness head on. "Iris, when I visited *your* room last year, nothing happened, remember?"

She did remember. Nothing had happened in *that* way, but she knew too well what *had* happened. She and the cor anglais had bundled him in mist and shipped him to the Carlisle Indian School.

"And when you come to my room," he continued, "the same nothing is gonna happen."

The way he said "nothing" made Iris want to kick herself for thinking there was anything to "HOT HOT HOT!" but Matt sticking it to Arky. It made her feel like the music geek who should stay in her shell. But she also welcomed his assurance. It gave her the pass to see his room. "Right," she said brightly. "The Book Extraction Team is here to make you cough 'em up."

As they climbed the stairs, Iris reminded herself of the facts. She was Matt's juggling mentor, and he was Arky's jock buddy who tossed her bones of flirtation.

Her determination to keep the room-visit as blasé as picking up a pizza suffered a blow when she entered the room and spotted the bulbous old football on the bedside table. Her heart leapt as she realized that her vision of Matt on his bed tossing a retro football had been real. She pointed at the ball. "Where'd you get the old football?"

The question puzzled Matt. Not only did she know what it was, but it was the first thing she'd noticed. "What makes you think it's an old ball? Maybe it's a rugby ball."

"You don't play rugby." She moved toward the ball. "And I've seen pictures of old footballs."

Before she got there, he said, "Please don't touch it."

The request intrigued her more than her wish to pick up the ball. "Why not?"

"It's an antique, and the leather's begun to flake."

She thought it was an odd thing to say when she'd seen him twirling it, albeit in a vision. Either her vision was off, or he was lying. "If it's falling apart, why don't you put it in a safer place?"

"I've been planning to."

She knew she was pushing it but couldn't stop. "Why do you have an old football?"

The way she seemed to look through him made Matt regret bringing her to his room. He went to his desk and picked up a pair of books. "Here they are." He handed the hardcover books across the bed to Iris.

When she saw the cover of the top book, her resolve to stay cool collapsed. The title read *Carlisle vs. Army: Jim Thorpe, Dwight Eisenhower, Pop Warner, and the Forgotten Story of Football's Greatest Battle.* "You-you've been reading this?" she stammered.

Matt gave her a skewed look. "You've read it too?"

"No, not really." To cover her bumbling, she pulled aside the first book to see the second. The cover of *The Real All Americans* displayed a black/white photo of old-style football players running a play. The subtitle mentioned Jim Thorpe, Pop

Warner, and the Carlisle Indians. She took a calming breath. Her trip to his bedroom had exceeded all expectations, that is, on the investigation front. Which reminded her, standing on opposite sides of his bed and not keeping the conversation going might be taken the wrong way. "What's with you and old-style football?"

Matt shrugged. "I figured if I'm gonna play college ball, I should know about the history of college ball."

Iris wanted to believe he was telling the truth, but there was another possibility that made her stomach knot. Maybe Matt's memory of spending weeks at the Carlisle Indian School in 1907 was seeping back into his consciousness. Maybe the memory burying the cor anglais had done when he'd gotten back in December was wearing off. Maybe it only lasted so long, and the memory cure had to be repeated.

"Did you read 'em both?" she asked.

"Yeah." He was only telling half the truth. He had read both books several times. They were more than page-turners; they were mind-turners. He would read them, and they would take him to a different time and place, a place that seemed incredibly real.

Iris flipped through the *Carlisle vs. Army* book and noticed an occasional note scribbled in the margins. "All right, cool. I'll get 'em back to Mrs. Doogan." But there was no way she was going to return them before she had a chance to read all the penciled notes he had scribbled in them.

Having procured the books and tingling from her find, Iris headed out of the room.

What she had failed to discover, and Matt had lied about to protect, was what was *behind* the old football on the bedside table. It was a small glass frame. In the frame was a pencil drawing of a pretty Indian girl with long black hair. The note on the back of the drawing identified her as Pigskin. Her real name, that the cor anglais had buried beyond the reach of Matt's memory, was Tawny Owl. While he had fallen in love with Tawny in 1907, the only thing Matt retained was a drawing of a girl called Pigskin and the mysterious feeling the drawing gave him.

4

Stone's Throw

After an early breakfast serving the same meal of beans, salt pork, hardtack and coffee, Sergeant Talcott took Danny to his first infantry training. Dabney escorted Arky to the field headquarters of General Sully.

All morning, Arky learned the ropes of being a courier: delivering messages and orders from General Sully throughout the massive tent city that comprised Gibbon's Second Division of the Second Corps.

Danny's first morning of training was as basic as it gets. He was taught how to stand, face, and march without a weapon. When he finally got to take up his rifle musket, he didn't take another step. There were so many things to learn about moving the rifle from one position to another, with or without a bayonet, that he wondered if he was being trained to be a soldier or a baton twirler. Even though it wasn't the SEAL training he'd always dreamed of, he liked the repetition and precision. It reminded him of why he loved pitching. Whether he was holding a baseball or a rifle, he could spend hours perfecting slight variations of the same motion. It didn't feel like a duty, it was fun.

In the early afternoon, Danny indulged in the "amusements" part of D 'n' A. He took a walk down the river to check out the full scope of the Union camp and take in Fredericksburg's riverfront crowding the other side of the river.

Unlike the hills that were practically treeless, the strip of floodplain alongside the Yankee side of the Rappahannock was home to clusters of trees. The Union generals had ordered some trees to be saved for the day when they could be used by snipers to pick off rebels in Fredericksburg.

About a mile downriver, the wide, shallow rapids that Company K looked over narrowed and deepened to the gently moving water that fronted Fredericksburg on the other side. Rising from the jumble of riverfront buildings, Danny spotted a timber bridgehead. It was all that remained of a bridge that had once spanned the river before being destroyed. But the bridgehead wasn't useless. Three Confederate soldiers sat on top of it and dangled long fishing lines in the river.

Their fishing made Danny think of his dad and wonder how he was doing. He felt bad about the worry and trouble his disappearance might be giving him. He felt worse about having ignored his dad's silent advice in the game not to hit Rafael. There was no way of knowing how things were playing out, or stopping the gnawing questions. *What if Rafael dies? What if his family sues? What if Dad loses his business?*

Danny's fears pushed him farther downriver.

Reaching a trio of tall trees, Danny spotted a Yankee soldier skipping stones across the water. Wanting the distraction of company, Danny joined him. The soldier didn't look any older than Danny, maybe younger.

After returning Danny's nod of a greeting, the baby-faced soldier hurled another stone, sending it skittering across the river's glistening surface. As it disappeared, he extended his hand to Danny. "My name's Henry Fleming. What's yers?"

"Danny Bender." They shook hands.

"I'm from the Three Hundred and Fourth New York," Henry continued. "How 'bout yerself?"

"The Thirty-Fourth New York."

Henry gestured toward the surrounding floodplain. "Do ya know where yer standin'?"

Danny shrugged. "Looks like a riverbank."

"Not just any riverbank," Henry announced. "This here is Ferry Farm?"

"What's that?"

The soldier answered with a disbelieving look. "Ferry Farm is where George Washington grew up."

Danny chuckled. "So George Washington slept here, a lot."

"From the time he was six years old till he was all growed up."

Danny looked around. "Cool. So this must be where he chopped down a cherry tree, couldn't tell a lie, and threw a silver dollar across the river."

"He did all those things"—Henry raised a finger—"but one. He never threw a silver dollar across the river. He threw a rock."

His serious tone amused Danny. "Okay, how many times did he skip it?"

Henry frowned. "He didn't skip it. He threw it all the way across."

"Not bad," Danny admitted with a nod.

"Not bad?" Henry jabbed a finger. "Let's see *you* throw a rock across it!"

Danny eyed the river. It was about a hundred yards wide. On the other side was a sprawling garden rising toward a big brick house. Danny began to windmill his arm and warm it up. "Okay. I'll give it a shot."

Henry relished the comeuppance his acquaintance was about to get. "I've seen the best hurlers in the army try to boost one over the river. Not a-one of them could do it. What makes you think you're so different?"

Danny chuckled at the answer he could give as he picked up a good throwing stone. "You don't wanna know."

"No, I do," Henry insisted. "Let's see it."

Danny took a bounding start toward the riverbank and threw as hard as he could.

The rock sailed high and long out over the water, a tiny black missile visible against the blue sky. It reached its zenith, then began its downward arc.

Danny's and Henry's eyes were locked on it.

For a moment the rock disappeared against the backdrop of the garden on the other side. Then it bounced off hard-packed ground and struck a rowboat beached on the bank. A *thud* came across the water.

Danny turned to catch Henry's reaction. He was startled to find Henry gone. As he started toward the trees to flush Henry from his hiding spot, the sound of a horse turned him.

A mounted Yankee rode toward him. "Did ya jus' do what I think ya did?" the soldier asked in an Irish brogue.

Danny was still trying to find Henry. "What?"

"Toss a stone across the river." The soldier halted his horse. He was a big man, in his early thirties, and no beard on his broad ruddy face. He looked as Irish as he sounded. His uniform displayed a sergeant's chevron.

"Yeah, I did," Danny said. "If you don't believe me," he gestured toward the trees, "ask the guy who saw it."

"What guy?" the sergeant asked quizzically.

Danny called to the trees. "C'mon, Henry, give it up."

The sergeant gave Danny a dubious look. "There's no one here but you an' me, lad."

"Yeah, there is. His name's Henry, and he's from the Three Hundred and Fourth New York."

The sergeant laughed. "The Three Hundred an' Fourth New York?"

"What's so funny about that?"

"Never heard of it. An' I know my regiments, lad, 'specially from New York."

Danny moved to the trees and checked behind them. Henry was nowhere in sight. How he had performed his disappearing act baffled Danny.

"An' what's yer regiment?" the sergeant asked.

"Thirty-Fourth New York," Danny answered, as he looked up on the wild chance Henry had somehow shimmied up one of the tree trunks.

The sergeant lit up with a smile. "Faith an' begorra! It's me very own. Tell me this, do ya play baseball?"

The question added to Danny's bewilderment. "Baseball?"

"Do ya know what it is?"

"Of course," Danny answered before it hit him. "Wait, they have baseball here in the middle of the war?"

"Aye, we do," the sergeant answered with bright eyes. "But don't be takin' my word for it. Seein' is believin'."

"I saw Henry," Danny insisted. "He's the reason I threw a rock across the river."

The sergeant took Danny in like he'd discovered a pot of gold at the end of the rainbow. "If that's what it takes ta put the devil in yer arm, I'm seein' yer wee little friend as clear as day."

After the sergeant introduced himself as George Cambell, and Danny did the same, Cambell escorted Danny back upriver to their regiment. Danny kept quiet and tried to make sense of his encounter with the soldier on the riverbank. He wanted to believe Henry was as real as the stone he'd thrown across the river. He wanted to believe the sergeant was punking him. If he wasn't, Danny figured there was another explanation. Henry was the ghost of a dead soldier who haunted the riverbank.

5

Hardball

WHILE ARKY DELIVERED dispatches for General Sully, he asked everyone if they knew anyone named Jongler. He was particularly hopeful when he asked a Union bandmaster, thinking he might know a Jongler musician. When one of Sully's messages took Arky into the small town of Falmouth, he asked shopkeepers. He grilled the local pastor, hoping he would know everyone in the area. But no one had heard of any Jongler.

Arky was ready to give up the search for the day when the owner of a dry-goods store asked him, "Have you been up to the followers' camp?"

"The followers' camp?" Arky echoed as he sparked with the memory of visiting the followers' camp during the reenactment with his dad.

Moments later, Arky ran up the hill to the followers' camp. The camp was a far cry from the neat rows of white tents selling Civil War memorabilia he'd seen with his father. Besides peddlers selling all sorts of things soldiers didn't get from Uncle Sam, there were services too, from laundresses to ladies of the night.

While Arky moved through the labyrinth of sights, sounds and smells of the camp, he kept his nose to the trail for a Jongler. Reaching a mildew-stained tent that fronted a semicircle of smaller tents, he stopped in front of the buxom matron sitting in a plush chair under a sign. The sign's curlicue lettering announced, Madame Monique's Damsels de Dalliance.

"Bonjour, petite soldier boy," the woman said with a French accent and an alluring smile.

Arky returned the greeting and took a guess. "Bonjour, Madame Monique."

"You have come to complete your manhood, yes," she said more than asked. "First comes war, then comes love."

Arky ignored her solicitation and uttered his standard opening. "I'm looking for a man or woman named Jongler." As soon as he said it, a horrifying thought hit him: *Mom's here in one of the tents. She's a hooker!*

"A jongler?" she said pensively.

Arky nodded, no longer sure of wanting the answer.

She leaned forward, confiding a secret. "I know some jonglers."

"You do?" he exclaimed, half in hope, half in dread.

"*I* am a jongler!" Monique exclaimed. "All my girls are!"

His face knitted. "What?"

She spread her gloved hands. "'Jongler,' 'juggler,' it means the same. And that's what we do, juggle men's hearts and other parts."

Her boisterous laughter sent Arky hurrying away. His fear of what he might discover had made him forget the meaning of the Jongler name.

Danny and Sergeant Cambell moved along the wide bottomland fronting the river.

As they approached the stretch below the 34th New York's camp in the rising hills, Danny heard a familiar sound: the *crack* of ball-on-bat. Up ahead, he saw Yankee soldiers positioned on a stretch of flat ground as another Yankee dropped a baseball bat and ran toward first base. The surprises didn't stop. The baseball sailing through the air looked black. A fielder caught it on the fly barehanded. None of the players wore gloves. After getting the ball back, the pitcher threw underhand to the next batter. It wasn't windmill, fast-pitch underhand, it was straight-armed, lob-it-over-the-plate underhand.

"Well, Danny-boy," Cambell said, pointing to the scene, "how'd ya like ta get in the game?"

Danny was still absorbing the sight of Civil War soldiers playing ball. "I'm not big on softball," he said. "I play—" He stopped himself. He was done with baseball. He didn't have what it took—that's what the scout had said—end of story.

"You play what?" Cambell prompted.

"I used to play hardball," Danny said.

"Never heard of it." Cambell broke into a smile. "But we can turn it inta 'hardball'"—he snapped his fingers—"like that."

Cambell prodded his horse and cantered onto the makeshift ballfield. "Time ta switch ta Massachusetts rules, boys." He wheeled and pointed at Danny. "An' we've got a third-sacker ta try out. Private Danny Bender."

Danny's hesitation was answered by coaxing shouts and gestures from the players for him to join the game. He was torn. Part of him never wanted to throw a baseball again. But he wanted to see how the game was played in 1863. *Besides*, Danny told himself, *it's* softball, *not baseball.* He jogged forward, and the players cheered.

As Danny was welcomed, and the third baseman stepped aside to give Danny his position, he recognized several faces and figured most of the players were from the 34th New York. At third base, he noticed the pitcher's position was like softball too. It was about forty-five feet from home plate, instead of baseball's sixty feet, six inches.

Danny recognized the player who came to bat. It was the mean-ass corporal who'd given him and Arky a hard time the night before. The others called him "Piper." The next surprise was the pitcher's delivery. He switched to overhand and hurled a pitch. Piper took a big cut and missed.

Danny looked at Cambell, on the foul side of third. "I thought it was underhand."

"Not in Massachusetts rules," Cambell said. "You can pitch anyway ya want. Now pay attention 'fore ya take one in the teeth."

Danny took his advice but shook his head over throwing overhand from forty-five feet, a pitching distance Danny hadn't seen since Little League. At least their overhand pitching didn't have modern speed.

Cambell's warning proved prophetic as Piper's drilled a line shot at Danny. He caught it on one bounce. The sharp sting to his hands didn't override the fear clawing at him as he stepped into his throw. He couldn't escape the memory of his last pitch that had dropped Rafael. Fortunately, his sidearm from third to first was on target and wouldn't hit anyone in the head.

The first baseman was startled by the rocket coming at him, but caught the ball with two hands, then cursed Danny for throwing it so hard.

"There's no need for ya ta kill the batsman twice," Cambell announced.

While players laughed, Danny didn't miss the hateful look from Piper, who had stopped between home and first. "I was just throwing him out," Danny explained.

"Aye," Cambell said, "but jus' like everyone else, we play the bounder rule."

"What's the bounder rule?"

"Catchin' it on one bound kills the runner as sure as catchin' it on the fly."

Danny waved his hands. "Got it. Sorry," he shouted to the first basemen. Didn't know. I'm used to the 'fly rule.'"

While Danny was glad not to see any more action for the rest of the inning, he kept his eyes peeled for any other twists to the Massachusetts rules of baseball.

With the side retired, Danny got his first chance to bat. Lifting the long bat, its weight surprised him. He figured it was heavier because the dark brown baseball they played with was slightly larger and softer than a modern baseball. He was also surprised by how slow their overhand pitching was; every pitch looked like a changeup. After two unwieldy swings and getting teased for looking like a "windmill in a nor'easter," Danny laid into a pitch, driving a line shot in the gap between center and right field.

While the outfielders chased the ball down, Danny churned for second as he saw the second baseman, Piper, waving for the throw from the outfield. After rounding second, Danny was halfway to third when Piper got the throw, spun and hurled the ball. It struck Danny square in the back.

"That'll teach you to go for a three-sacker!" Piper proclaimed.

Danny wheeled and charged. He almost got to Piper before two players grabbed Danny. "I'm gonna kick his ass!" he shouted, struggling to break free.

The players threw Danny to the ground, pinning him down.

Cambell loomed over them. "Ya really don't know the rules, do ya?"

"What rules?" Danny shouted. "All you guys do is cheat!"

"Danny-boy," Cambell said calmly, "you've been plugged. By Massachusetts rules, when yer plugged between the bases, yer dead, yer out." The sergeant waved Danny's captors off and offered Danny a hand up. "If all yer knowin' is New York rules, with its soft game for city gents, yer gonna havta learn the rules o' 'hardball.'"

Hearing the word "plugged" fired a long-forgotten memory in Danny. When he was little and played backyard whiffle ball, they threw the whiffle ball at base runners and plugged them. The recollection didn't lessen the pain in his back. Refusing Cambell's hand, Danny jumped to his feet. "I play Midwest rules, not this bullshit."

He turned and stalked off. He tried to drown out the Herkimers' taunts and jeers and suck back the moisture in his eyes. He didn't know if it was from the burning pain in his back or the humiliation trailing after him. Bottom line, he told himself, it's what he deserved for playing baseball again.

6

Between the Covers

IRIS RETURNED HOME from rehearsal at the school. The two overdue books on Carlisle football she had gotten from Matt earlier in the day were still in her backpack. She was too excited to make lunch. She sat at the kitchen island and pulled out the books.

She was going to read them herself to learn more about the Carlisle Indian School in the nineteen hundreds. She knew Matt had been returned from 1907 to the present by Alfred Jongler, a music teacher at Carlisle at the time, who was Iris and Arky's great-great-great grandfather. If there was any chance that Matt's buried memories of time travel were beginning to seep back to consciousness, she needed to know what he knew from reading the books versus what he might have remembered from time travel.

She started by flipping through *Carlisle vs. Army* to check out the margin notes she had glimpsed in Matt's room. In the first few chapters, the notes were mostly one-word exclamations like "Wow" and "Cool." Halfway through, there was a note that stood out. Matt had written, "I've seen this before. Where?" Iris's heart raced as she read the two paragraphs he'd bracketed. It was an account of Jim Thorpe's first varsity touchdown run in a game against the University of Pennsylvania.

Was Matt having a déjà vu? Iris wondered. *Or was it more than that?*

She flipped pages, looking for more margin notes. The next one blew her away. The page displayed a picture of Jim Thorpe carrying a football and running toward the viewer. Matt had written, "I know him—like Pigskin."

The blunt and odd comment filled Iris with a mix of excitement and fear. What did it mean? Had Matt regained full memory of his time travel and wasn't telling anyone? And why "like Pigskin"? The questions fueled more. *What if Matt's holding on to what he knows until the perfect time to use it against me, Arky, or Dad? What if, having remembered everything from 1907, he learned something about where Mom is, but isn't telling?*

The sound of the front door opening startled her. She jumped off her stool and slid the two books onto the seat of the high-backed stool that was tucked under the counter. She moved to the fridge like she was making lunch in hopes that her father, coming into the kitchen, wouldn't see the books. "What are you doing home so early?" she asked, trying to sound casual.

He hung his backpack on a stool. "I canceled my last class. Teaching history isn't the same when you know its holding your wife hostage."

Iris stared into the open fridge, riveted on nothing but her mental scramble to come up with an excuse to get her father out of the kitchen.

"I'm much more interested in what you might have found—" Howard stopped.

Iris sucked in a breath as she turned.

He held the two books she had tried to hide, one in each hand, studying their covers. He looked up, perplexed. "Why do you have books on a Native American school that played football in the early nineteen hundreds?" Before Iris could concoct a believable lie, his face dawned with a realization. "My God, is that where they are?"

"I don't know where they are," Iris answered, trying to hide the fear in her voice.

He lifted the books. "Then why the sudden interest in football? Where did you get these?"

She couldn't escape. She wished Arky was there; he could lie his way out of a noose. The best she could do was delay the confession. "Matt gave them to me."

"Matt?"

She nodded.

"Why would he..." Howard's eyes darted back and forth between the books, then back to Iris. She watched his wheels turn. "My God," he finally said. "Last year, Matt disappeared for a week. Did he"—he held up the books.

Iris nodded again. She felt like a little kid caught red handed. She slid into a chair and confessed how Arky and Danny weren't the first. She and the cor anglais had sent Matt to the Carlisle Indian School in 1907 and, how, when he returned, she played the cor anglais to bury his memory of the experience.

Howard listened intently, not missing a word. "It's like Mom predicted in her journal," he said.

"Yeah," she concurred, "time-travel amnesia."

His eyes narrowed; he tapped his fingers on the books about Carlisle football. "If he's not supposed to remember, what was Matt doing with these?"

She heaved a breath. "That's what I'm trying to find out."

"There's only one thing to do. You and I are going twenty-four-seven on bringing back your brother, Danny, and Mom."

Iris knew that her dad cancelling one of his classes at the university was a slippery slope. She had to get him off it. "Dad, when Matt was gone, Arky had one thing right; he insisted we act normal. It's the only way we hid the truth. It's how we fooled everyone. You and I need to do it again. If we don't, the police, or someone like Mr. Bender, will figure out we know something, and they'll be all over us."

Howard thought about it. "You and Arky certainly fooled me."

"And now we have do the same: act normal and reveal nothing. It's the toughest part of what Mom said."

"'Tending to the present yields the past,'" he repeated.

"Yeah. I don't know how it works, but I know in my gut that somehow what we do here affects them in the past. Arky and I tended to the present, and somehow it helped 'yield' Matt. We have to do the same for Arky, Danny, and Mom."

Howard held her with a stern look. "Is there anyone *else* I need to know about?"

"No, I swear, Dad," Iris declared, "there was no one else. Matt was my first!" As soon as she said it, she felt her cheeks flush.

7

Agent

Danny and Arky delayed going to the mess tent so they could catch each other up on their day. Danny told Arky about his morning of drilling. While he also told the story of meeting Henry and equaling George Washington by throwing a rock across the river, he didn't mention Sergeant Cambell and playing baseball. He was still too pissed about it. It wasn't so much being mad at Piper and Cambell—they were just playing their weird baseball—Danny was angry at himself for getting suckered into it.

For his part, Arky skipped over the routine of running messages and related his efforts to find a Jongler, including his encounter with the madam of a whorehouse.

Danny grinned. "You didn't spend our boat-ticket money on a hooker, did you?"

"Yeah, right," Arky snarked. "That's why I'm here, to carry a nineteenth-century STD back to the twenty-first."

When they went to mess, Danny was glad to see that Piper and the other ballplayers had already eaten and left. He wasn't in the mood for any trash talk about leaving the game, or Arky knowing about it. The two of them soon had the campfire to themselves. The downside of eating late was getting the burnt scrapings of beans and salt pork from the bottom of the cook's pot.

As the mess tent closed up, they washed down their hardtack with coffee. In the dying light, two men came toward them. It was Sergeant Cambell and Dabney.

"Evenin', lads," Cambell said cheerfully. He seemed a little tipsy.

"Evenin', Sergeant," Danny replied warily, hoping they'd keep on moving.

"Danny-boy, I want ya ta meet my new manservant." He slapped Dabney on the back. "Dabney."

Arky had assumed that the Irishman might be Danny's drill sergeant but was surprised by his claim. "I thought Dabney was Sergeant Talcott's orderly."

"He was," Cambell proclaimed, "till I won him in a poker game."

Leaving Dabney to stand stoically in the background, Cambell sat on an empty box at the fire. He praised Danny for the baseball skills he had displayed that afternoon, particularly his cannon of an arm.

"Really?" Arky said, turning to Danny. "You didn't tell me you played baseball."

"Not surprisin'," Cambell said with a laugh. "It didn't end well." He turned back to Danny. "Now, I know ya marched off the field with yer steam up—"

"And with a monster bruise on my back," Danny interrupted.

"All part o' the game," Cambell said. "I've talked it o'er with the lads, an' we'd like ya ta be a Herkimer."

Having learned the nickname for the 34th New York—from Herkimer County—and highly intrigued by this development, Arky pointed out, "He already is a Herkimer."

"I'm talkin' 'bout a Herkimer who throws baseballs, not minié balls," Cambell clarified. He turned back to Danny. "We've got some big games lined up, an' I'm believin' we can take it all"—he paused for effect—"champions o' the entire Army o' the Potomac."

"How many baseball teams are there?" Arky asked.

Cambell's eyes gleamed. "When spring broke, baseball fever swept through camp. We got dozens o' teams." Sensing Danny's reluctance, he tried another tack. "I'm not sayin' you'd be one o' the first nine. But if ya were one of our reserves, it'd give ya chance ta learn our game, an' give ya somethin' ta brag about ta yer kinfolk back home."

Danny fought the urge to say that his kinfolk hadn't been born yet.

"So, wha' do ya say, Danny-boy?" Cambell pressed.

"I don't think so," Danny said. "From what I saw, it looks like you've got plenty of team without me."

Cambell leaned forward, having lost his jovial manner. "If ya know what's right for ya, you'll be down on the river tamorrow afternoon when we take on the Nineteenth Massachusetts."

Danny returned his hard gaze. "You're not my sergeant."

"Don't worry, Sarge," Arky interjected. "I'll make sure he's there."

Cambell turned to him. "Will ya now? Who are you?"

Arky smiled. "I'm his agent."

"His what?"

"Not important," Arky replied. "He'll be there."

Cambell stood, returning to his jovial self. "We'll be lookin' forward to it." As he strode off, Dabney silently followed him.

When they were out of earshot, Danny muttered, "Asshole."

"Him or me?" Arky asked.

"Both," Danny grumbled as he headed off to the latrine before calling it a night.

Arky chewed over the turn of events. It undercut his latest theory that Danny had been the one in the wrong place at the wrong time when they had been blown away. Danny had been blown to 1863 for a reason too, and it had to do with baseball. It also lowered the probability that Arky had been sent to 1863 to find his mother and swung the pendulum back to Arky being the innocent bystander.

After taps, Danny and Arky lay in their cramped quarters in the only way they could fit: head-to-feet, feet-to-head. They listened to the hoot of an owl coming up from the river.

Arky broke the silence. "Why don't you wanna play baseball?"

Danny let out a sour laugh. "All I've ever wanted to do was play baseball, but FYI, there was a scout at the game."

Arky didn't quite follow. "What game?"

"The only one that matters: when I hit Rafael. I chased the scout down. He told me I wasn't 'big league material.' That's good enough for me. One pitch, dream over."

Arky was struck by the bitterness in Danny's voice and that he hadn't told him about it before. It also bolstered Arky's notion that they were there because of Danny and baseball. And if Danny playing ball had some connection to their ticket home, Arky wasn't going to let him walk away from it. But Arky knew he couldn't force it. Luckily, Iris had given him some soft-selling woo-woo stuff that might work on Danny.

"Look, Dan-O," Arky began, "I don't know how and why the cor anglais that sent us here does what it does, but there's a hint in its name. 'Cor anglais' means 'horn of angels.'"

"Meaning what?" Danny asked.

"Angels help people. You totally screwed up playing baseball, and the cor anglais sent you back—coincidence of coincidences—to a time and a place no one would imagine baseball was ever played. And now you've got a chance to play. Call me crazy, but I think you were sent here to play ball."

"As some kind of torture?" Danny asked. "Is this God's twisted way of punishing me for almost killing a guy, if I didn't already?"

Arky realized soft sell wasn't going to work. He pivoted to what came easier. "The point is, if baseball has to do with why we're here, and how we're gonna get back, if you don't play, you're never gonna find out if you killed Rafael or not."

The silence stretched as Danny mulled it over. "Okay, if you think that's what I gotta do, I'll go on the stupid team as long as you answer a question."

"Sure," Arky said, surprised by how fast Danny had come around.

"If I'm here 'cause of baseball, why are *you* here?"

Arky was surprised by the perceptiveness of the question. But he still wasn't ready to tell Danny about his mother. "I haven't figured that out yet," Arky hedged. "Maybe it's to be your agent."

Danny grunted. "It's not like they're paying me."

"I didn't mean it literally. It's about protecting your interests."

"What interests?"

Arky thought for a moment. He didn't want to burden Danny with the whole "drifting soul" theory, and he certainly didn't want to tell him what the cor anglais had done to Matt. "Think of it this way," Arky said. "Let's say you just got kicked out of Major League Baseball. But I'm not giving up on you. We could've gone to some league in South America or the Japanese League, but no, lucky us, we got sent to the Civil War League. And your job is to play baseball here, while my job is to find the Jongler, the ticket home, that's gonna get us back to the Big Leagues. Do you follow what I'm saying?"

Danny answered with a ragged inhale.

Arky stared up into the blackness. They had five more days and counting before whatever "game" they'd been thrown into turned deadly.

8

Play Ball

THE NEXT AFTERNOON, Danny reported to the bottomlands along the river for the game between the 34th New York and the 19th Massachusetts. Arky would be there as soon as he finished his courier duties.

Danny was surprised to see a couple hundred soldiers gathered to watch the game. A few had climbed a big tree on the riverbank for a better view. The soldiers rooted for their favorite team by trading insults and making bets. Danny overheard one of them mention "the Second Corps Championship." He also saw Sergeant Cambell, the Herkimers' captain, negotiating with the captain of the Massachusetts team, a lieutenant named Robinson.

Given the ridicule the Herkimers had piled on Danny the day before, he stood off to the side with Dabney. Cambell's new manservant seemed to be overseeing the regiment's baseball equipment: three bats and one ball.

Danny asked him something he'd been wondering since the night before. "If you're a free man and not a slave, how can they add you to the pot in a poker game?"

Dabney answered with a rueful smile. "Freedom's not all it's cracked up to be."

Danny chuckled and felt a bond with Dabney. They were both stuck where they didn't want to be.

The negotiation between the two captains grew heated. Cambell wanted to play the game by New York rules: underhand pitching and no plugging. Robinson wanted to play by the more "manly game" of Massachusetts rules: overhand pitching and plugging. Before coming to blows, Cambell suggested a compromise: they would switch rules every inning—the odd innings would be played New York style, the even innings by the Massachusetts game.

Danny was glad he wasn't playing. Having made a fool of himself trying to decipher one set of rules, he didn't need two sets to pretzel his brain. He was even happier to be bench-riding—not that there were benches—when he heard the other team's name, the Pluggers.

Danny watched a ritual he hadn't seen since being a kid. Cambell tossed one of the long bats in the air, caught it with one hand and then he and Robinson fist-stacked up the handle until the last fist topped the bat: Cambell's. Having won the bat toss, he elected to take the field first so the Herkimers would bat in the bottom half of the innings.

As Herkimers jogged onto the field, Cambell strode toward Danny and Dabney. "Well, don't jus' stand there," he boomed with a smile, "be a scout!"

Danny looked at Dabney uncertain who Cambell was talking to. Dabney looked equally confused.

"Danny-boy," Cambell continued, "yer gonna be scoutin' the right field."

"I thought I was a reserve," Danny said.

"One o' our scouts took sick this marnin'." Cambell pulled Danny onto the infield. "No need ta worry, lad. With Piper at the pitchin' point, the only flies comin' yer way will all 'ave wings." Cambell pushed Danny past Piper, who seemed to be the Herkimers' regular pitcher.

As Danny headed to right field, Piper called after him. "An' remember the bounder rule; one-bound catch an' he's out. No need for double killin'!"

During the 1st inning, played by New York rules, Cambell's forecast of no fly balls didn't hold. Piper was a lefty, and despite his speedy underhand pitching the Pluggers belted fly balls into the outfield and pierced the infield with hard grounders.

Whatever butterflies Danny had about being put in the game mushroomed when he saw the first fly ball sail his way. He rushed forward to catch it on the fly, then remembered the bounder rule before trying a diving catch. He pulled up to take it on the bound. Given the rough ground, the ball took a wild high bounce. Danny felt like a bad gymnast as he flung his body in an off-balance, twisting leap, and snagged the ball. He earned cheers for his comical contortion. It gave him a shot of pride and relief. This was no groomed field, there was no pitcher's mound, or chalked lines. This was a sandlot game, the kind he hadn't played for a long time.

As the Pluggers kept blasting shots at the Herkimers, another feeling bubbled through Danny. He wanted the hits to keep coming. He didn't care about the score; he just wanted to run and catch and throw.

Which is what he did to finally stop the Pluggers' onslaught in the 1st inning. With two outs and a runner on second base, a fly ball was hit to Danny in deep right. As the ball sailed at him, he made a glove of his bare hands. Without gloves, making a one-handed catch with a dismissive glove-flip was not an option. Barehanded catching was about cushioning the blow and not breaking fingers. Danny's hands found the ball, but it bounced out. The runner on second base, who had to hold on the bag on any fly out, bolted for third. Danny scooped up the ball and fired. The ball rocketed like it had come off a bat, not an arm. The third basemen, Cambell, managed to stop the bullet of a throw and tag the stunned runner out. Even more astounded was the crowd of soldiers as they sucked in a gasp, then exploded with a roar. They had never seen a ball thrown so hard.

While Danny knew it was a good throw, he didn't get what the Herkimer fans were so excited about. It was only the 1st inning, and the Herkimers were behind 7–0.

Cambell watched Danny jog in and then chattered at his players as they came in. "C'mon, Herks, time ta answer fire with fire."

While Piper had thrown the Plugger batters a steady diet of quick, underhand pitches, the Massachusetts's pitcher had a wide variety of speeds and arcs. He used them to force the first three Herkimer batters to hit grounders and pop-ups that were easily caught. The top of the batting order's miserable three-up, three-down start wasn't the only thing Danny noticed. Whenever a foul ball was sprayed right or left, Dabney ran after it and brought it back. Apparently, he was equipment manager *and* ball boy.

The Herkimers retook the field for the 2nd inning, to be played by Massachusetts rules. As Piper returned to the pitching point, Danny hoped he had better stuff overhand than underhand. He didn't.

By the bottom of the 3rd inning, it was clear Piper couldn't silence the Pluggers' bats whether he was throwing underhand or overhand. They kept walloping the ball, adding another eight runs to their tally. The good news for Danny was that batting ninth he didn't come to bat until the bottom of the 3rd in which New York rules applied. If he got on base, he didn't have to worry about being nailed by a throw.

As he took easy swings getting ready to bat, a cheer erupted from the 34th New York fans when the Herkimer batter blooped a ball over the infield for a single, the Herkimers' first hit. Heading to the plate, Danny ignored his butterflies and told himself, *Avoid the double play; get it in the air.*

Underhand pitches were so foreign to him, Danny swung early at the first two, missing both. *Worse than a double play*, he thought, *striking out in softball!* The pitcher, testing how early

Danny might swing, tossed a high arcing pitch, hoping to drop it through the strike zone.

It was another weird thing Danny had learned about 1863 baseball. The umpire called strikes but not balls; balls weren't part of the game yet. And strikes were called in an odd way. For one, the umpire didn't stand behind the catcher, who stood a few steps back with no protective gear or glove. The ump stood off to the side. And he gave a batter a *warning* when the first pitch in the strike zone wasn't swung at: "Warning, striker," was the call. After a warning, the next pitch in the strike zone was a called strike.

Danny waited for the high lob of a pitch to come in and swung. He got under it, lifting the ball in a high long shot. During the roar from the Herkimer fans, Danny took off. Rounding first, he saw the ball sail over the centerfielder's head. With no fence or wall, he raced on. As he'd seen from the Pluggers' long hits, there was only one kind of home run: inside the park.

When Danny crossed the plate behind the runner ahead of him, the Herkimers had made their first dent in the Pluggers' lead, 15–2. Danny enjoyed the handshakes and backslaps from his teammates, even though Piper landed his backslap on Danny's bruise from his plugging the day before. He covered his wince of pain with a tight smile.

When Arky arrived at the game, the Herkimers had retaken the field to start the 4th inning. He was surprised to see Danny in the outfield: not only was he playing, he was in a position Arky had never seen him play. Arky took it as a good sign. If playing baseball in the Civil War had something to do with why they were there, Arky was for anything that might get them home sooner than later.

After Piper's pitching took another battering, and the Pluggers piled on more runs, the Herkimers finally retired the side. Danny trotted in and greeted Arky with a grin. "Hey, Ark."

"For someone who didn't wanna play," Arky said, "you don't look miserable."

"It's the outfield," Danny pointed out. "It's a blast."

"Yeah, a blast for the other team. What's the score, twenty to two?"

Danny shrugged. "You know what they say, it's not whether you win or lose, it's how you play the game." He sat on the ground. "As long as I don't get my ribs broken, I don't care if we lose a zillion to two. That's why I have a strategy."

Arky sat next to him. "What's that?"

"A home-run defense."

"Huh?"

"To not get plugged, soaked, drilled, killed, and whatever else they call it," Danny explained, "I'm swinging as hard as I can, hit a homer every time, and never get stuck on base."

After the next Herkimer batter hit a line drive to left center and hustled out a double, Cambell came over to Danny and Arky. "Our bats are finally heatin' up," he said, "but we gotta make a hurlin' change." He squatted next to Danny. "Startin' next innin', I want ya ta pitch."

Arky watched Danny tense before he said, "I don't throw slow, underhand stuff."

"All I know," Cambell added, "is that Piper hurlin' New York or Massachusetts style won't win the game. I need ya at the pitcher's point."

"I'm not a softball pitcher," Danny reiterated.

"I'm not asking ya ta be," Cambell clarified. "Jus' throw like ya do in the outfield with tha' low swoopin' toss o' yers."

"We call it a submarine pitch," Arky interjected.

Cambell stood up—"We'll call it whatever ya like if it works"—and walked away.

"Shit," Danny mumbled.

Arky took in Danny's tight expression. "I know you're thinking the worst, but it's not gonna happen again."

"Are you kiddin'?" Danny thrust an arm at the Massachusetts pitcher. "It's forty-five feet from pitcher to batter, not sixty feet plus. If I bean someone at that range I'll kill 'em" for sure!"

"Keep it down," Arky cautioned. "The reality is you can't kill anyone here; they've all been dead for ages. It'll be no worse than pitching to zombies."

The strange thought gave Danny pause.

Arky continued his coaching. "If you're here to play baseball, it's not like you're an outfielder. You're a pitcher. So, c'mon, Cap, all you gotta do is go out there and do what you always do. Throw your best stuff, one pitch at a time."

The *crack* of ball-on-bat snapped Danny to the field.

The Massachusetts player at second base caught the hit on one bounce, ending the inning. The player flipped the dark baseball to the middle of the infield.

Danny watched the ball roll to a stop in the worn and dusty spot of the pitcher's point. "One pitch at a time," he echoed as he rose and fought the dread gnawing at him.

9

Bending the Rules

DANNY PICKED UP the dark brown ball, stood at the pitcher's point, and oriented himself. Instead of placing his right foot against the rubber—there was none—he had to judge his stride so his left foot didn't cross a line scratched in the dirt. It was the "pitcher's point." Lifting his gaze to home plate, he hadn't seen it so close since Little League. It made him feel claustrophobic. Not only was the batter dangerously close, so was the pitcher to getting hit by a line shot.

The first batter for the Pluggers came to the square plate of iron lying in the worn grass. It was their captain, Lieutenant Robinson. *Great*, Danny thought, *if I hit this guy, he's an officer. He can have me shot.* It triggered the vivid memory of the ball striking Rafael's head and seeing him drop like a stone. Danny tried to shake it off, along with the scare of Robinson not wearing a helmet: another protection 1863 baseball lacked.

Danny fingered the ball into position, dropped into his bowing windup, powered through as his knuckles barely cleared the dirt, and released his submarine fastball.

Having never seen a pitch come at him so fast, Robinson jumped back. The Herkimers catcher yelped when his hands stopped the bullet from smashing his face.

The crowd froze. They'd never seen such a blistering pitch, much less the bowing contortion Danny had performed to throw it.

The wide-eyed umpire recovered enough to announce, "Warning, striker!"

As the Herkimer fans exploded with approval, Danny let out a nervous laugh: half from relief for not hitting the batter, half from the truth of the call. *Warning, Striker!*

Robinson turned and barked a protest at the umpire. "That's not a legal underhand pitch! He bent his elbow and jerked the ball!"

Cambell yelled from his position at third base. "It's legal as Lincoln! His arm was perpendicular ta the ground an' parallel ta his leg, like the rules call for!"

Robinson wasn't buying it. "He jerked the ball with his wrist!"

Cambell threw up his arms. "I didn't see a jerk. Did anyone see a jerk?"

A chorus of "No!" came from the Herkimers and their soldier fans.

"Let 'im throw it again," Cambell suggested to the ump, "an' see if ya see a jerk."

The ump agreed and motioned Danny to throw his next pitch.

Danny wound up and hurled a sinker past Robinson's late, slashing swing.

"Strike one!" the ump ruled.

The crowd of soldiers, delighted by Danny's speed and bizarre delivery, roared.

Robinson was livid. "He did it again! He jerked his wrist!"

Cambell started toward home and Robinson. "No, yer jerkin' yer eyes 'cause the truth is he's throwin' Jim Creighton style. No one ever said Creighton was a cheat!"

The mention of Creighton, the most famous player in baseball, added boisterous fuel to the soldiers rooting for the Herkimers.

Robinson bellowed at the ump. "Judgment! Legal or not?"

Before the ump ruled, a voice boomed across the field. "Judgment shall be made!" It came from a mounted officer approaching on a horse between the third-base line and the crowd. It was General Gibbon, the commander of both regiments playing the game. He continued in his Southern drawl. "If it was good enough for Creighton, it's good enough for us."

While the Herkimers and their fans cheered, the Pluggers and their rooters protested.

Gibbon called to the Pluggers' captain, "Lieutenant Robinson, what's the current tally in the Second Corps Championship?"

"Nineteen to two," Robinson answered, setting his anger aside long enough to boast. "Pluggers on top!"

"Nineteen to two!" Gibbon repeated. "Are my Herkimers waving the white flag?"

"No, sir!" the players in the field chorused back.

Gibbon wheeled his horse to the surrounding crowd. "Did you come to see one of our regiments turned into cannon fodder?"

"No, sir!" the soldier-fans bellowed.

Gibbon turned back to the Herkimers. "Then put your hearts into it, boys, and let's see some baseball!"

A cannonade of "Huzzah!"s erupted from the throng of soldiers.

Danny didn't disappoint. He struck out Robinson and tied the next two batters in knots as they flailed at Danny's sinker. During the bottom of the 5th inning, the Pluggers were so rattled they gave up six runs to the Herkimers.

Danny was surprised when Cambell told him to pitch the 6th inning as well. It was an even inning to be played by Massachusetts rules with overhand pitching. Cambell told Danny to let him worry about what was legal and what wasn't and sent him back to the pitching point.

The Pluggers saw Danny throw one pitch, the same submarine pitch they'd seen before, and Robinson stormed over to the ump. "It's Massachusetts rules now! He can't throw underhand, he has to throw overhand!"

Cambell trotted in from third base. "There's nothin' in Massachusetts rules that says ya have ta throw it underhand or overhand. Ya can toss it anyway ya like."

Robinson charged toward Cambell. "You can't have it both ways!"

Cambell didn't budge as they went chest to chest. "It's not our fault yer bats can't touch leather even if the cow was wearin' it!"

Robinson took a swing at Cambell, missed, and got popped in the face by Cambell. It triggered the 1863 equivalent of a bench clearing. The Pluggers surged forward to back up their captain; the Herkimers raced in from the field to even the fight. Before the two swarms collided, a gunshot ripped the air. Being soldiers first, baseball players second, everyone to a man snapped to the sound.

Still astride his horse and watching the game from back behind home plate, Gibbon held his smoking revolver aloft. "Gentlemen, in the excitement of the contest, you've overlooked a matter of import." He waved his revolver down the left field line to the furthest reach of the crowd. Under a parasol was a Southern belle in a fancy hoopskirt. With her was a well-suited gentleman. "There is a lady present," Gibbon announced. "We don't fight in the presence of ladies. We fight in the presence of secessionists."

The soldiers answered with a bellowing cheer.

As Arky stared out toward the pair of Southerners, his eyes brightened.

"Now," Gibbon resumed, "besides wanting the best nine to win the Second Corps Championship, I'm wanting the best nine to win the Army of the Potomac Championship. For this reason," he decclared, "I agree with Sergeant Cambell's interpretation. His pitcher is throwing in accordance with the rules of New York *and* Massachusetts."

In the Herkimer cheer that followed, the Pluggers bitterly accepted Gibbon's judgment.

With Danny's pitching, the game shifted. The Pluggers couldn't hit his sinker, slider, or anything else, and if they got bat-on-ball, they hit mostly grounders. With the Herkimer bats coming to life, the Pluggers made it worse when they vented their anger by trying to plug Herkimer base runners with bone-breaking throws that, more often than not, flew wild and added runs to the Herkimers' comeback.

Another result of Danny's speed was more foul balls. With only two game balls, all fouls had to be chased down. As Dabney had been running after the most errant fouls, Arky volunteered to chase down the ones on the left side of the field, while Dabney patrolled the right. Cambell accepted Arky's proposal, and Arky named him and Dabney "ball boys."

As the Herkimers chipped away at the Pluggers' lead, Cambell hit a towering foul down the left side. Arky ran it down and hurled the ball back to the Pluggers' third baseman. Arky's ball-boy duties had finally brought him close to the two Southerners watching the game. While Yankee soldiers were giving the Southern gentleman and belle under a parasol a wide berth, Arky wasn't so shy. He joined them and launched his investigation in a roundabout way. "Excuse me," he asked the gentleman. "Do you know who Jim Creighton is?"

The man, about thirty, with a refined Virginia accent, replied, "Jim Creighton is baseball's most famous player, that is, until he died in October of last year."

"Was he killed in the war?" Arky asked.

"No," the gentleman replied. "Creighton struck a home run with such might that he twisted his gut and died of the consequences."

"He was only twenty-one," the young woman, a petite blonde, added. "He was also the best pitcher in the game."

"Fascinating," Arky said, then got to the point before another foul ball came his way. "My name's Arky Jongler." He extended his hand and looked for signs of recognition.

He got none as the man shook Arky's hand and introduced himself. "I am Cuthbert Conway, and this is my young sister, Elizabeth Conway."

Elizabeth gave Arky a polite "Nice to make your acquaintance, Mr. Jongler."

"I am a great devotee of baseball, Mr. Jongler," Cuthbert added. "If you know this pitcher for the Herkimers, I would like to meet him after the game."

Despite Arky's disappointment of his Jongler search hitting another dead end, he obliged. "Sure, no problem. He's a friend of mine."

"What's his name?"

"Danny Bender," Arky answered. "I'll introduce you afterward."

10

Delay of Game

BY THE END of the 8th inning, Danny's dominant pitching had allowed the Herkimers' hot bats to tighten the game to 19–18, with the Pluggers clinging to a one-run lead.

In the top of the 9th, Danny worked the first Plugger batter. Taking his stance at the pitching point, he heard a sound he thought was distant thunder. But the rumble didn't stop. Danny turned toward the sound and saw a squad of mounted soldiers, about a dozen strong, galloping toward centerfield. He assumed they would stop, or veer off, but they kept charging right into centerfield, throwing up chunks of ground in their wake.

Watching from off the field, Arky gaped at the sight. His first fear was that it was terrorism circa 1863: What looked like Union cavalry were really Confederate terrorists in Yankee blue about to start lopping off heads with their sabers. Bolstering his fear was the soldier leading the charge. His Union jacket flapped open like wings.

As the Herkimer center fielder dodged the charging troopers, the second baseman and shortstop ran for safety. Refusing to be intimidated, Cambell strode into the narrowing gap between the cavalry charge and Danny at the pitching point. When the troopers bore down on him, Cambell didn't budge. At the last second, the lead soldier with the flying coat yanked his horse to a stop, bringing it up in a leg-kicking rear. The soldiers behind him hard-reined their mounts to a halt, tearing up ground.

Danny watched with wide eyes. Whatever comfort he'd found in the familiarity of baseball was disrupted by the reminder that it was a game in the middle of a warzone.

While the young, clean-shaven officer settled his horse, Arky saw why his jacket was open. It was a style thing. Under it was a brightly colored checkered shirt. More surprising were the bars with a star on his shoulders: the boyish-looking officer was some kind of general.

The second baseman, having retreated to first base, turned to Piper, now playing first. "Who is that?"

"Francis Barlow," Piper answered with admiration. "He's shot more skulkers and cowards than any general in the army. We could use more of him."

Despite Barlow's reputation, the crowd of soldiers jeered his intrusion.

Barlow eyed them with contempt, then issued a decree with a thin voice. "I order you to disband this frivolous assembly and return to preparing for the battle ahead."

Cambell had recognized the general by his signature plaid shirt. "But, General Barlow"—he began as Gibbon, on his horse, trotted up behind Cambell.

"If you must know, General," Gibbon interrupted, "they *are* preparing for battle."

Barlow straightened indignantly in his saddle. "A boy's game does not harden soldiers to a man's war."

"Baseball raises their morale," Gibbon countered, "gives them exercise, and, most importantly, builds a bond all men need when they face the enemy."

"All a soldier *needs*," Barlow fired back, "is a steeled will and plenty of lead."

The crowd held their breath, wondering how this confrontation would end.

"Soldiers aren't machines," Gibbon declared. "And until you can cut the hearts out of men and still lead them into battle, you and your interlopers have two choices. You can dismount and review the rest of our ball and bat drill or you can remove your pretty shirt from my drilling ground so I can prepare my men as I see fit."

The cheer that exploded from the ballplayers and soldier-fans startled Barlow's horse. He wheeled it dramatically. Unable to be heard over the shouting crowd, Barlow spat on the field.

As Barlow and his troopers galloped off, Gibbon turned his horse and walked it by Danny. "Do me a favor, son," he said under the noise. "Make my saving this game worth my while."

Amped by the request from what he considered a very cool general, Danny did his part. He dispatched the first three Plugger batters, giving the Herkimers the bottom of the 9th to tie or win the game.

While the Herkimer rooters were wild with excitement over the chance to win, no one was more intrigued by the young pitcher who had shutout the Pluggers than Cuthbert Conway. He had also seen Danny contribute with his bat, getting hits and driving in some of the Herkimers' comeback runs. Cuthbert turned to his sister, Elizabeth. "So, what do you think of Daniel Bender?"

"I'll admit he's a fine pitcher and hitter," Elizabeth conceded. "But there's a large difference between Mr. Creighton and Mr. Bender."

Cuthbert gave her a curious look. "What would that be?"

"Creighton swung at a pitch so hard that it tore up his insides and killed him. Mr. Bender's not playing baseball in New York City; he's in a war. If swinging hard or throwing hard doesn't kill him, most likely, something else will."

Cuthbert frowned at his sister's fatalism. "That's your problem, Liza Jane. You're always looking at the dark side of life."

In the bottom of the 9th, it wasn't Danny who played the hero. With two outs, the tying run on second, and the winning run at bat, Piper lifted a shot through the left-center gap and drove the tying run across the plate.

Piper didn't stop there. He rounded third and, seeing the chance to beat the throw home, went for it. The Pluggers' catcher, Robinson, blocked the plate and awaited the throw. Piper dove at Robinson as the catcher leaped for the high throw. Piper caught Robinson's legs, flipping him in the air like a pinwheel. He came down on Piper with the ball in hand, but too late. Piper was sprawled on the iron plate. The New York Herkimers had beaten the Massachusetts Pluggers, 20–19. They were the Second Corps champions.

In the bedlam that followed, the soldiers of the victorious 34th New York swamped their heroes and lifted Piper, Danny and Cambell aloft. Arky finally pulled Danny away from the celebrating players and soldier-fans to make good on his promise to the Conways.

When Arky introduced Danny to Cuthbert and Elizabeth, Cuthbert gave Danny a hardy handshake and bubbled with praise. "I've seen some of the greatest ball clubs play some of the greatest games, from the New York Knickerbockers to the Philadelphia Athletics, but I've never seen a baseball display like that!"

"It was a team effort," Danny said modestly.

Surprisingly, given Liza's bleak view of Danny's future, she joined in her brother's enthusiasm. "I must say, Mr. Bender, while Mr. Piper proved to be the hero of the eleventh hour, the Herkimers never would have reached that hour if it weren't for your pitching prowess."

As Cuthbert raised an eyebrow at her coming around to his point of view, Danny uttered another sports cliché. "We just took it one swing at a time."

Liza responded with a friendly smile. "That's a wise strategy, Mr. Bender, when there's no telling what may be hurled at you next, a baseball or a minié ball."

Danny answered with a grin and more than sports-speak. "Don't worry, Ms. Conway. I've already been plugged by a baseball, and a minié ball's gonna do the same"—he thumped his chest—"just bounce off this tough hide."

Surprised by Danny's jump from modest to macho, Arky made an excuse and pulled him away. Out of earshot, Arky warned, "Take it easy, Romeo. We're not here for the local talent."

"Hey, if you're gonna make me play baseball," Danny teased, "I can't ignore the benefits." He turned and threw a good-bye wave. "See you around, Ms. Conway!"

Arky gave him the last word. He knew Danny was just amped from the win, not to mention slaying his pitching demons. And Arky had no fears about Danny hooking up with a Southern belle. Danny's win-girl average was pathetic no matter what century he was in.

11

Pigskin

WHILE DANNY HAD overcome a shy attack with a Southern belle, in Belleplain, there was nothing shy about Iris's mission.

After seeing the cryptic notes Matt had written in the margins of the library books about the Carlisle Indians, including the mysterious entry next to a photo of Jim Thorpe, "I know him—like Pigskin," Iris was determined to find out what Matt had remembered, if anything, about his journey to 1907.

Iris parked in front of the Grinnell house and rang the bell.

Matt opened the door. He recognized the books Iris was holding but ignored that she hadn't returned them to the library. "Two visits in two days," he said, "is this how stalking begins?"

Iris had anticipated he might lead with an evasive comment. "No, didn't you hear about the school?"

His coolness flickered with concern. "No. What?"

"It's been declared a Superfund site. I'm collecting donations to have it cleaned up sooner than later, or none of us will ever graduate, and we'll spend our lives in the lowest percentile of the ninety-nine percent."

He chuckled; she was Arky's twin for sure. "Great," he said sardonically, "and we'll never get outta Belleplain."

Cutting to the chase, she held up the books. "I brought these back."

"Why?"

"I saw your notes in the margins." His uncomfortable reaction reminded her to take it slow. She didn't want to scare him into slamming the door. "Besides all the overdue fines you owe the library, I didn't want you to get hit for vandalizing them too."

"It's not like I threw manure in them. Are a few pencil marks a crime?"

"To Mrs. Doogan, yes." She handed him the books. "You can keep these. I ordered new ones for the library."

He took in the familiar covers: *Carlisle vs. Army* and *The Real All Americans*. "Thanks. I'll pay you for the new ones."

"That's okay," she said. "Consider it an early graduation present."

Her generosity didn't surprise him as much as her sensing his attachment to the books. "Why do you want me to have them?"

Iris looked up and blinked at the raindrops that had begun to fall. "I'll answer that if you invite me inside and tell me something I'd like to know."

"C'mon in," he said with a diffident shrug. "It's not like the playbook of Matt is all closed up."

Moving inside, she was intrigued by his comment. It was the second time he'd referred to himself in the third person; it was the kind of thing someone who was hiding something would say.

After getting her a glass of water from the kitchen, they went into the living room. "Okay," he said, sitting on the couch. "What's the big mystery bouncing around in Iris's head like a runaway juggling ball?"

While his cavalier attitude heightened her curiosity, she kept playing the cool hand. "You told me you wanted to know about the history of college football, and you showed me that antique football in your room."

He shrugged. "Yeah, so?"

She picked up the *Carlisle vs. Army* book he had left on the coffee table. She sat on the couch next to him, opened the book to a page, and pointed at the note he had written next to the photo of Jim Thorpe running with a football. "Why did you write, 'I know him—like Pigskin'?"

An awkward moment followed. Iris let it linger. She didn't care if Matt was squirming because he'd been busted for writing something weird in a book or if he was squirming because of the tension crackling between them.

He exhaled. "It was just a weird feeling."

His answer wouldn't do. She had to know more. "What if you *did* know him?"

The questions froze Matt. He wanted to tell her all about the weird, almost crazy feelings that visited him each time he'd read one of the books. "I dunno. I just got the weird sense that I knew him, you know, like in another life."

"But you didn't write 'like in another life.' You wrote, 'like Pigskin.' What's that mean? That you feel like you know Thorpe like something as familiar as the pigskin of a football?"

Matt shook his head. "Footballs are made of cowhide not pigskin."

"Even more reason not to write, 'like Pigskin.'"

He looked up at the ceiling. "I'll tell you if you promise not to laugh."

Knowing he was on the brink of confessing something, she tried to put him at ease. "I haven't laughed since my mother disappeared. Why should I start now?"

He answered with a nervous chuckle, then stood up. "Be right back," he announced as he left the room.

Iris listened to his solid footfalls going upstairs. A desire swelled in her like a wave. She wanted to follow. She checked it. If she did, it would become something else; she might never get the answer she wanted to *What does he know?* She wasn't there for whatever was dancing between her and Matt. She was there for her dad, her mom, Arky and Danny.

Matt came back downstairs. Entering the living room, he carried a small picture frame. He handed it to Iris and sat in the chair next to the couch.

While part of her wished he had returned to the couch, her heart raced just the same. In the picture frame was a fine drawing of a pretty Indian girl. Her long black hair fell down over an old-fashioned nightgown. "Who is it?"

"Turn it over," he said.

She did. The double-glass frame showed the front and the back. On the reverse was a note. She read it out loud. "For my warriors. From Pigskin. PS: I have one of you; you should have one of me." An arrow pointed to the other side. Iris turned the frame and took in the Indian girl again. She looked up at Matt. "'I know him...like Pigskin.'"

He nodded, reached out, and took the picture back.

As she watched him gaze down at the Indian girl, Iris had no doubt. Whoever she was, he was still in love with her. What Iris didn't know were the answers to the new questions searing her mind: *Where did he meet her? When did he meet her?* But she couldn't ask them. She had to settle for something less. "Where'd you get that?"

Matt was too embarrassed to tell the truth: he had found it in the side pocket of his sweatpants the day he'd returned from his week-long disappearance—a week he still couldn't recall—and he had no idea how the drawing got into his pocket. He went with a credible lie. "I was helping my mom pick up a dresser at an antique store, and I came across a box of old postcards and stuff. I found it there. I thought it was cool, so I bought it."

Iris studied him, trying to decipher if he was lying to cover up something he didn't understand or was lying to cover up something he knew all too well. She let him off the hook. "Are you taking Pigskin to college with you?"

Matt released a laugh. "Maybe." He looked at Iris. "Can I ask you something?"

"Shoot."

"This is the part I thought you were gonna laugh at."

She opened her hands. "Try me."

"It's stupid," he said with a sheepish look, "but do you believe in past lives?"

She weighed her answer. She wanted to tell him that what he had written in the book was true. He *did* know Jim Thorpe. He *did* fall in love with an Indian girl nicknamed Pigskin. And even if he didn't know her real name, or how he'd brought her image back from 1907, he knew one thing for sure. Love. It was that certainty that handed Iris her decision. Telling him the truth would be cruel. If he knew Pigskin had been real, he might never get over her. And him not getting over her fired a dark instinct in Iris: jealousy.

"No, I don't believe in past lives," Iris said. "I think people see things in pictures and drawings they want to believe."

12

Cross-River Rivals

WORD OF THE 34th New York's stunning victory over the 19th Massachusetts spread through the Second Corps. While Danny's name was buzzing through camp, he took pride in the attention that came with it. For the first time since he could remember, the praise wasn't just for his pitching. It was for hitting and fielding too.

To keep Danny mindful of being a soldier first, a ballplayer second, the next day Cambell took Danny and Arky to the river to train them in the basics of picket duty.

While they brought their rifles and followed Cambell to the river, Arky hid his fears about marching toward the enemy with a loaded weapon—an invitation to be shot at if there ever was one—by asking Cambell questions. "I heard there was a picket truce. Is the picket truce a full-time thing? Or are their picket truce *breaks* where, to remind the enemy they are the enemy, the pickets shoot at each other?"

Cambell laughed at his odd thinking. "Aren't you the squirrel on a hot skillet?"

To cover for Arky being a smartass, Danny asked, "What's a picket truce?"

"They don't shoot at us, we don't shoot at them," Cambell explained. "'Least till we get back ta the killin' part o' war. Till then, the river is full o' surprises?"

"What surprises?" Arky asked.

"Showin' is better than tellin'," the sergeant answered.

The reality of picket duty was less dangerous than they'd imagined. It was simply sitting around a fire, if wood could be found, and keeping an eye on the opposite riverbank where rebel pickets were doing the same. The only threats to watch for were rebel spies trying to sneak across the river.

While keeping a lookout, the boys couldn't help but notice another sight on the floodplain across the river. A bunch of rebels were playing baseball. With the river only a hundred yards across, they could hear the bat-cracks, cheers and shouts of the game.

"They play too?" Arky asked.

"Baseball fever isn't just for Yankees," Cambell said.

"If Yankees play by New York and Massachusetts rules," Danny asked, "what do rebels play by? Georgia rules?"

Cambell chuckled. "No, baseball spread ta the South well before the war. They're fightin' ta keep their slaves, not fightin' ta change the rules o' baseball." He walked toward the riverbank, motioning them to follow. Stopping at the water's edge, he pointed across at the game. "How many players do ya see?"

Arky swiftly counted. "Nine on each side; eighteen."

"Not by my calculation," Cambell said. "I see seventeen an' a half."

"You can't have half a player," Danny said.

"Aye, ya can." Cambell grinned. "He's comin' ta bat now."

They watched a batsman step up for his turn at bat. Two things made him stand out. He was dressed in civilian clothes and not wearing one of the Confederates' gray or butternut uniforms. When he swung at the first pitch and knifed a liner into left field, his other distinction stood out. He swung the bat with his right arm only. From across the river, they could see he was missing his left hand.

"That's not half a player," Danny quibbled.

Cambell turned to him. "You try ta catch, throw, an' bat with one hand. You'll be feelin' like half a player soon enough." He gazed back across the river. "His name is Jacko."

It took Arky by surprise. "You know him?"

Cambell frowned. "No, that's enemy ground o'er there. We named 'im after the Jack o' Diamonds."

Danny chuckled. "Diamond, baseball, got it."

"And all Jacks in a deck of cards only show one hand," Arky added.

Cambell looked impressed. "There ya go again, bein' the clever one?" He turned and yelled across the river's shallow rapids. "Ahoy, Jacko! That was a fine hit! Try that o'er here, an' we'd snare it on the bound!"

It got the rebels' attention, including Jacko's. A player shouted back, "I hear the only thing Johnny Yank catches is dysentery!"

After the rebels had their laugh, Cambell returned fire. "We'd be happy ta answer that in a match between our best nine an' yer best nine!"

Another rebel player joined the fray. "If you play baseball like you've been fightin' the war, you'd turn tail after four innings!"

Cambell answered the insult by starting to wade across the river, rifle in hand.

Several pickets on the rebel side stood up and grabbed their rifles. Danny and Arky watched in shock, convinced they were about to see the sergeant shot dead. But the pickets didn't take aim at the intruder crossing the watery no man's land. Instead, one of the rebels set his rifle down and moved to the bank to meet Cambell.

Danny and Arky watched with amazement as the two men shook hands, spoke to each other, and seemed to exchange items they pulled from their pockets. The rebel baseball players, seemingly used to Yankee visits from across the river, ignored him and went back to their game.

Even though Arky was witnessing something his father had told him about, it was striking to see it: enemy soldiers trading like guys in a flea market.

As Cambell waded back to the Union riverbank, Danny blurted, "Is that normal?"

"As long as the picket truce stays in place," Cambell answered and bounded up the low bank. He pulled a pipe from his jacket. "When men don't fight, they trade." He produced the pouch he'd gotten from the rebel and pulled out tobacco. "It's the way o' the world." He filled his pipe. "An' the only way ta get good tobacco 'round here."

"What did you give him?" Arky asked.

Cambell grinned. "I gave him the devil." Off the boys' puzzled looks, he extracted a small box of matches from a pocket, and read the brand name on the box. "Lucifers." He struck a match and lit his pipe. After exhaling a smoky plume, he added, "They give us smoke, we give 'em fire. It's a sign o' things ta come."

After their midday meal, and with no detail assignments from Sergeant Talcott, Arky tried to persuade Danny to join him to help search for a Jongler. Danny told Arky he wanted to check out the cannons and artillery regiments occupying the highest hills on the Union side of the river. They had a clear view of Confederate-occupied Fredericksburg, and the town was within range of the Union's biggest guns. Danny assured Arky that he'd look for a Jongler among the Yankee gunners. "Besides," he added, "we can cover more ground by splitting up."

Once Arky left, Danny started in the other direction.

At the end of Mud Alley, before he turned up the hill, Danny stopped and looked at the river valley below. Across the river, he was surprised to see another ball game being played by a couple of rebel teams. He changed his mind about checking out the Union cannons and started down to the river.

13

Tomboy

DANNY FOUND A large tree on the riverbank that had been spared for future use as a stand for Union snipers. He sat down in the shade of the tree with his back against the trunk.

Watching the rebel ball game across the water, he couldn't tell if they were the same players from the morning game. If they were, he wondered if they ever took time off for drilling and getting ready for the battle that Arky had told him about. *Maybe that's why they lose the war*, Danny thought. *They play too much baseball.* The only thing he could see for sure was that the same player he'd seen earlier, the one-handed civilian, "Jacko," was playing in his second game of the day.

Seeing the game from such a distance soon made Danny sleepy. As his head slowly nodded back against the trunk, a leaf fluttering down from above jerked him awake. He turned his attention back to the game.

After a minute, another leaf spiraled down. It didn't add up; what tree drops leaves in the spring? He looked up. He was startled to see a pair of trousered legs standing on a high branch in the tree. At first he thought it might be a Yankee picket keeping an eye on the other side. But the trousers weren't Union blue.

"Hey," Danny called up. No answer came back. A bolt of fear shot through him; he might have stumbled on a rebel spy who had crossed the river, was hiding in the tree, and might shoot whoever discovered him. With no weapon to defend himself, Danny jumped up.

The pair of legs bent and the person's torso appeared as a high voice commanded, "Shhh! Don't run."

The face that appeared behind the cover of leaves was even more startling. With her hair under a broad-brimmed hat, and her figure hidden by men's clothing, Danny recognized Elizabeth Conway. "It's you!" he croaked.

"Keep it down," she ordered. "We might be seen."

Danny glanced around at the empty riverbank. There was no one in sight, except the players across the river. He looked back up. "What are you doing?"

"Watching the baseball game."

"Not that," Danny said. "Why are you dressed as a guy?"

She started climbing down from the high branch. "Have you ever tried to climb a tree in a hoopskirt?"

Danny chuckled at the image. "No." As she continued down, he was struck by how agile she was. She may have been a Southern belle, but she was also a tomboy.

"The truth is, Mr. Bender"—she stopped on a branch about ten feet above him—"a lady can't walk through the Union camp without the accompaniment of a man to vouch for her purity."

The stark contrast of her looking like a boy and sounding as Southern as ever made Danny smile.

She sat on the branch. "From my perch up there, I recognized you, and I thought, 'What is Private Bender doing here?'" She answered her question with another. "Could he be thinking about crossing the river and playing for the rebels?"

"No way," he declared as he thought of a joke. "I'm signed with the Yankees." When she responded with a puzzled look, he wanted to explain. But he wasn't sure if the New York Yankees existed yet. Most likely not.

The lingering moment was relieved by the *crack* of a bat and shouts sounding from the game across the river.

She glanced toward it. "As you may have noticed, I do enjoy baseball."

"Yeah," Danny said. "But not many baseball fans cross-dress and climb trees to see a game."

Her brow knitted. "Cross-dress?"

"Never mind," he said, kicking himself for another foot-in-mouth. He told himself to stop trying so hard and got back to her blue eyes. They were fixed on him. He wished he knew what was going on behind them.

"I've met some strange Yankees, Mr. Bender," she said after a moment. "But you may be the strangest of them all."

He wasn't sure if she meant it as a compliment or not. "Can I ask you a favor?"

"You can try."

"Can we drop the mister and miss stuff? I'm Danny. I'd like to call you, what, Elizabeth?"

She considered it. "Since we both share an interest in baseball, we can certainly be friends, and my friends call me 'Liza.' But now it's my turn to ask you something."

"Shoot," he said, then shot up a hand. "Oh wait, that's not a great thing to say in a war zone." He finally got a smile for his efforts. He tried to build on it. "Yes, *Liza*, ask me anything."

"As an observer of the rebel baseball players, what do you think of the one civilian who plays with them?"

Along with the random question, he was struck by how being on a first-name basis hadn't exactly loosened her up. "You mean Jacko?" he asked.

"Jacko?"

"Yeah, Jacko, that's what we call 'im. For a guy with one hand, he's really good."

"I think so too."

Danny's curiosity fired. "If he's a Southerner, why isn't he a rebel?"

She chuckled at his naïveté. "Really, Mr. Bender, I mean, Daniel. If you can't load and fire a rifle musket with one hand, you can't be a soldier."

Danny thought about it. "I think I'd rather have two hands and be a warrior than have one hand and be a ballplayer."

She gave him a disapproving look. "I doubt he had a choice in the matter."

He realized his misstep. "Sorry." He hit his head, trying to make a joke of it. "Sometimes I say the stupidest things."

"Sometimes it's best to say nothing at all."

He took her advice and did just that.

Her gaze returned to the ball game. "Tell me, Daniel, do you have a sweetheart back home?"

The out-of-the-blue question quickened his pulse. "Nope," Danny answered. "I'm solo these days."

If "solo" was another future-speak, he didn't get the chance to find out. She stood up on the branch and started climbing back up through the branches.

"Where are you going?" he asked, wondering if he had said something wrong.

She kept climbing. "To see the rest of the ball game."

Her sudden exit baffled him. "Nice talkin' to ya."

He didn't get an answer.

As Danny walked back up the hill to camp, he replayed the "game film" of their surprise meeting. In some ways it was no different from his brushes with girls in Belleplain. He'd done his usual stumble through the booby-trapped maze of trading words. While smartass, zinger-throwing, twenty-first-century girls usually left him dazed and confused, his encounter with Liza couldn't have been more different. She'd left him pumped and fascinated. She wasn't some Southern belle out of the movies. She was a cross-dressing, baseball-loving, tree-climbing beauty who could turn her back on you in a heartbeat. There was no telling what other talents she had. Danny was infatuated.

14

Songbirds

Arky's search for a Jongler had taken him back to the followers' camp. The day before, he'd only scratched the surface when it came to searching the sea of tents, wagons and cluttered campsites for the Jongler who might be among them.

After an hour of getting nothing but headshakes and blank expressions, Arky heard a sound he thought was an audio mirage, a sound that couldn't be real, and had to be his stressed-out brain playing tricks on him. A female voice was singing "Goin' Home," the song inspired by Dvorak's *New World Symphony* and his mother's favorite music. Arky sprinted toward the sound.

> It's not far, jes' close by,
> Through an open door;
> Work all done, care laid by,
> Goin' to fear no more.

Arky's heart raced faster than his feet. And even though the singing voice changed to a man's baritone, Arky was dead certain he'd fly around a tent or wagon and see what the song promised.

> Mother's there 'spectin' me,
> Father's waitin' too;
> Lots o' folks gather'd there,
> All the friends I knew.

Bolting past a large tent, Arky saw the singing couple as they both sang the final lines.

All the friends I knew.
Home, I'm going home!

The shock of who they were—and who they weren't—brought Arky to a sharp stop in front of them and a familiar wagon. The woman was Madame Monique, the whorehouse madam, he'd met the day before. The man was the peddler, the same conman who'd delivered Danny and Arky to their present fate.

The peddler recognized Arky and turned to his singing partner. "Well, Madame, it seems our sirenlike singing has brought Odysseus to our shores."

Also recognizing Arky, Monique got in on the joke. "Bonjour, Monsieur Odysseus. What brings you to Followers' Island?"

Arky ignored their banter. "That song! How did you learn it?"

"I just learned it from this fine gentlemen," Monique replied, touching the peddler's arm.

Arky's eyes shot to the peddler. "Who taught it to *you*?"

He answered with a shrug. "I learned it from a woman—never got her name—who passed through camp."

"What woman?" Arky demanded.

"She worked briefly with a fortune-teller," the peddler replied.

"Where's the fortune-teller?" Arky fired back.

"She's no longer in camp," Monique explained. "She read her tarot cards, saw a terrible battle coming, and left a few days ago."

"Where did she go?"

"North," Monique said with a vague gesture. "Perhaps to Washington."

"We could only tell you where she went…" the peddler began and Monique finished his thought "…if *we* were fortune-tellers." They shared a laugh over their joke.

Arky answered by turning on his heels and marching away. He didn't give a rip about a couple of old fools having a laugh at his expense. And he had no need of asking what the woman who "passed through camp" looked like.

What he had just discovered completely rescrambled his ideas of why he had been launched to such a god-awful time and place. It wasn't an accident. And it wasn't to be Danny's "agent."

Hearing the song, "Goin' Home" pointed to the truth. It was 1863, but the song's melody, from the second movement of *The New World Symphony*, wasn't written until *1893*. And the lyrics had not been written until sometime in the 1920s. Only a time traveler from the future could have taught the peddler "Goin' Home." And that time traveler had to be Octavia Jongler.

As Arky continued to unpack his discovery, he couldn't avoid blaring questions. *Why would Mom do something so stupid as teach someone a song that wouldn't be written for another fifty years. Why would she threaten the future of history?* Only one answer made any sense to him. *She* is *in 1863! And leaving crumbs on a trail for me to follow!*

When Danny returned to Mud Alley, he found a surprise in their tent. Two full-dress uniforms hung from a hook on the ridgepole. A note was pinned to one of the uniforms. It was from Cambell. The sergeant had used the winnings from beating the 19th Massachusetts for a shopping trip to the quartermaster. He wanted the team, including their newest ball boy, to look their finest for the victory dinner they had been invited to. It would be at Cuthbert and Elizabeth Conway's house, where the team would be presented to "the female society of Falmouth."

Danny's inside jumped with a double realization. His wish to see Liza again had come true. But more bizarre, and mysterious, was why she had never mentioned the party in their tree encounter. He grinned at the thought that she had the double identity of a masked superhero. Wearing a hoopskirt, she was Elizabeth Conway. Disguised as a boy, she was Baseball Babe.

Indulging his good mood, Danny tried on the dress uniform. It fit perfectly. It sparked an idea. Danny grabbed the baseball bat Cambell had lent him, stepped out of the tent, and headed in the direction of Falmouth.

15

Say "Cheese"

IN TOWN, DANNY asked where he could find a photography studio. He was directed to the "daguerreian room" above the bank. Finding the Stafford County Bank, Danny spotted a sign jutting from the building: Falmouth Photographic Studio. He climbed the wooden stairs going up the side of the building, opened the door, and stepped inside.

The studio was lit by skylights in the roof. The photography equipment looked bulky. Except for the space where people posed for their pictures, the room was cluttered with props, from drums to huge daggers, and backdrops depicting idyllic country scenes untouched by war. On the wall was a list of fees. A single tintype was one dollar.

A man emerged from a backroom wearing an apron and drying his hands on a towel. Looking over his wire-frame glasses, the man eyed the baseball bat in Danny's hand and introduced himself as Mr. Snyder. After Danny said he wanted his picture taken, Snyder informed him he would need half a dollar before making the tintype and the other fifty cents when it was ready to be picked up.

Danny kicked himself for not borrowing a dollar of the four that Arky had earned for running the peddler's hair dye across the river. Danny stalled to figure out how he might put off the first payment. "Are you saying I can't take the picture with me?"

"Oh, you can take it with you," Snyder said with a droll look, "as long as you camp out here for a day."

Danny looked incredulous. "It takes that long to make a picture?"

"You're not the only likeness I've got to capture," Snyder explained. "But if you want to jump to the front of the line, I'm happy to charge you five dollars."

"How 'bout this?" Danny asked. "If you take my picture now, and let me pay the dollar when I pick it up, I promise to talk to the captain of the New York Herkimers and see if you can be the team photographer."

It was Snyder's turn to be surprised. "You're one of the Herkimers?"

"Yeah, I play for 'em."

"Is your name Daniel Bender?"

Danny nodded. "For a place that's only got newspapers and a telegraph, news travels fast."

As Snyder related how he'd heard about the Herkimers-Pluggers game from a soldier who'd come in to pick up his picture, he was all business. He set up his camera and posed Danny sitting on a chair, holding the bat like his weapon of choice. He told Danny to keep still and then ducked under the black cloth behind his camera.

Danny flashed a smile.

Snyder popped out from under the cloth with a puzzled look. "What are you doing?"

"Ah, saying cheeeeese." Danny elongated the word to a frozen smile.

The photographer looked more baffled. "Do you say 'cheese' all day long?"

"Well, not all day."

"Daniel, I am creating your *likeness*," Snyder instructed. "A likeness is what you look like most of the time. So if you want a likeness, you might want to look more serious."

"You mean, like, put my game face on?"

"What is a game face?"

Danny displayed his game face: a hard gaze right at the camera.

Snyder clapped his hands. "Now you look like a soldier!"

Danny returned to camp and found Arky in their tent. Arky also had found his new uniform and knew about the Conway party.

"This is our chance," Arky said excitedly, keeping his voice low.

Danny was nonplused. "For what?"

"If the Conways' house is outside the camp, when we're coming back at night, we hang back behind the others, slip away, head up to Aquia Landing, and catch a boat to DC." Arky was convinced that Washington was where they would find his mother.

"We could," Danny said, lacking Arky's enthusiasm. "But there's two problems."

"What?"

"We'll be in dress uniform and stick out like sore thumbs."

Arky considered his point. "What's the other problem?"

"I've been checking around," Danny said. "If you get caught without written orders, like you've got a leave to visit home, they arrest you and haul you back to camp."

Arky hadn't thought they might have to travel with orders. Disheartened, he backhanded his hanging uniform. "Great, we'll be all dressed up with nowhere to run."

"Look at the upside," Danny offered. "We're going to a party to check out the local talent *and* to see if any of the pretty ladies knows a Jongler."

Arky's disappointment turned to suspicion. "What put you in such a good mood? And why'd you put on the fancy threads so early?"

Danny answered with a grin. "Went to Falmouth and had my picture taken."

"What?" Arky exploded. "Are you insane?"

Danny pulled back, baffled. "What's the big deal?"

Arky reined in his voice but not his anger. "The last thing we need is photo evidence we were here. What if the picture survives and your dad or mom see it? Or your kids? No, wait, that assumes some woman is stupid enough to let you pollute the gene pool with a bunch of mini-Dannys."

"Hey," Danny protested, "it takes brains to play baseball."

"Yes, it does," a voice interrupted. It was Talcott, poking his head into their tent. Since the two privates had been granted leave to go to the banquet at the Conway house that night, Talcott gave them picket duty on the river for the rest of the afternoon.

Danny and Arky grabbed their rifles and headed down to the river. On the way they continued their argument.

"Look," Danny said, "it's been three days, and it's not like you've found a Jongler. I'm just trying to roll with the punches."

"I'm looking," Arky shot back and stopped himself from telling Danny what he'd discovered in the followers' camp. "And I'll be doing it tonight while you're preening like Captain America for a bunch of Southern babes."

Danny had yet to mention his encounter with the cross-dressing Elizabeth Conway. And he wasn't about to. He'd already been burned once for his honesty.

They walked in silence until Danny finally spoke again. "Ark, have you ever thought we might not be getting outta here for a while. I mean, we might be stuck here for weeks, a month, maybe more. We might be stuck in 1863 for years."

Arky scowled. "Jesus, Danny. Listen to yourself."

"What?"

"You can't be stuck in one year for *years*."

"I'm just saying," Danny resumed, despite the correction, "we should be thinking about a plan B."

"The only plan B," Arky declared, "is if we're not outta here by the time the battle starts, we do whatever it takes to not get killed."

They bottled their quibbling as they reached the picket post, where they relieved the two pickets on duty. After the soldiers left, Danny threw twigs on the bed of embers and restarted the fire.

Arky glared across the river at the Confederate encampment and struggled to tamp down his anger and frustration. If Danny was going stupid and having his picture taken, someone had to keep thinking straight. Which is what Arky tried to do. By the tally of days he had carved on a fireplace brick in their tent, it was April 26. With the battle on the 30th, their escape window was narrowing, and Danny *had* raised a point. *What if our exile to the past isn't like Matt's,* Arky fretted, *but more like Mom's? What if we're stuck in the Civil War for months? What if we're here even longer?* Arky pulled out of his dark spiral by returning to his discovery that afternoon: the "crumb" of "Goin' Home" that his mother had left. As he wondered about the other crumbs she might have dropped for him to discover, he gave it a name to lighten his mood: *Crumb theory.*

Arky's withdrawn silence didn't escape Danny. It was totally unlike him to kick back and not say a word. "I don't know what you're thinkin'," Danny finally said. "You wanna know what I'm thinkin'?"

Arky shrugged. "Hit me."

"Tonight, when we're hangin' with all those girls, maybe we'll meet the girls of our dreams."

"Yeah, right," Arky scoffed, then entertained a crazy thought. *Maybe I'll meet my mother.*

16

Dark Vision

In Belleplain, Iris was chasing a different woman. At her computer, Iris was searching the Internet for a girl nicknamed "Pigskin," who might have been at the Carlisle Indian School in 1907. It was the girl she was certain Matt was still in love with, even though all he had was a drawing, a note, and a feeling that he knew her in a "past life."

In all her searches of websites dealing with the Indian school, Iris had found nothing. Pigskin seemed to have fallen through the cracks of history.

Hearing the cor anglais solo from *The New World Symphony* drift down from the attic office reminded Iris that she needed to get in her practice session for her Oberlin callback. The music sounded particularly mournful because Iris knew who was playing it—her mother—and also because of who had taken to watching the video file countless times a day—her father.

To push down her concern about her dad's mental state, Iris assembled her oboe and shut her door against the music from above. Iris began practicing one of the excerpts from the Handel sonata for her Oberlin audition.

Since December, Iris's synesthesia had rarely kicked in while playing her oboe. Even when it did, her music-induced visions were more of the abstract-shapes variety. Her most fleshed-out visions had only come while playing the cor anglais.

After the first few measures, hints of a vision did begin to appear. Dark lines danced across her visual field. Except for noting them, Iris kept playing. The dark lines stretched and expanded, obscuring more and more of her room. She brushed aside the twinge of panic she was going blind—she knew it was simply a vision—and played on.

When the darkness had swallowed her room, Iris began to see shapes in the darkness. She made out a silhouette: the broad back of young man's torso and head. Something was sliding up and down his back. It came into focus. They were arms. A young woman's arms. A crescent of white loomed from behind the young man's back. More white slivers and patches appeared. Iris realized they belonged to the nightgown or nightshirt the girl was wearing. In a flash, Iris knew what she was seeing: a young couple making out.

The couple stopped and grew still. The girl pulled back. As she did, Iris realized who she was, who *they* were. It was Matt and the Indian girl from the drawing. Pigskin.

Iris almost stopped playing for lack of breath. She sucked in air and kept on, certain that the music was the only thing that would sustain the vision playing a scene that riveted and repelled her at the same time.

As Iris rode a passage of rising notes, she felt the weightless sensation of being lifted out of her chair and pulled higher, until she hovered above Matt and his Indian girl, with her long dark hair falling over her white nightshirt. Despite the weird sensation of being suspended in midair, Iris kept playing.

She looked down at the Indian girl cradling Matt's face in her hands. Slowly, the girl lay back onto a couch. Matt remained motionless. The girl's dark hands slid down the whiteness of her nightshirt, collected clutches of material and slowly drew the whiteness past her knees, up to midthigh. She paused. An unspoken invitation shone in her black eyes.

Iris yanked the reed from her mouth. The vision vanished as swiftly as the music. She pulled in sharp breaths as she struggled with what she'd seen. She swirled with confusion. She didn't know if she'd seen something that had actually happened in 1907, or if it was a vision of her own making: a vision triggered by green-eyed jealousy. Her only certainty was that she had stopped it at the right time. Real or not, she didn't want to see more.

Her breathing steadied. She collected herself. She had to keep her eyes on the prize. The vision and her consuming feelings about Matt—wanting him, being jealous of him for crushing out on an Indian girl from the past—wasn't what mattered. The only thing that mattered was reaching into the past and pulling Arky, Danny, and her mom back. It was a choice Iris faced. To tell Matt the truth, and awaken his full memory of 1907 so he might help in the quest, or keep him in the dark so his Indian Sleeping Beauty would remain forever locked in a pencil drawing.

Iris jumped at the sound of her bedroom door opening.

Her father stood in the doorway. He looked disheveled. "Why did you stop playing?" he asked.

Looking at him with his mussed hair, his clothing more rumbled than usual, and the eyes of a man dancing on the edge of a cliff, Iris's heart lurched. "It didn't sound right," she said, concocting a lie.

He stared at her. "I've heard you play the cor anglais more beautifully than anything else. Why don't you put your oboe down and play the same thing on the cor anglais?"

Iris shook her head at the crazy idea. "The Handel sonata wasn't written for English horn."

Howard's head jerked back with a loud laugh and then came back to Iris. "All the rules have been broken, Iris. Breaking another one isn't going to hurt anyone." He turned and left.

Listening to his retreat, Iris's worries and fears deepened.

17

Mixed Signals

THE CONWAYS' ESTATE was on the uplands east of Falmouth. While the house's Greek Revival facade gave it a grand appearance, it needed a paint job. The outbuildings and surrounding fields were being reclaimed by Mother Nature. The farmhands and slaves who used to work them had gone off to fight or had run away.

Despite the setbacks, Cuthbert and Elizabeth kept the place running with the help of three former slaves who had cashiered their freedom into paid jobs on the Conway farm. Cuthbert's business dealings in the North supported the property.

In the late afternoon, the New York Herkimers' two-mile march up White Oak Road to the Conways' house went without a hitch. Halfway there, when the dozen soldiers, resplendent in their dress blues, moved through the checkpoint protecting the perimeter of the Union camp, Sergeant Cambell loudly announced, "New York Herkimers, Second Corps champions, coming through!" Their fame was all they needed as the two sentries at the checkpoint sang their praises and let them pass.

Arky and Danny exchanged a look. Baseball notoriety had some perks.

At the Conways' house, Cambell, wearing a captain's sash of golden silk emboldened with green letters proclaiming "Herkimers" led their entrance. They were greeted by the applause of a dozen Southern belles dressed in the best finery the war allowed. Their beautiful faces, billowing hair, and soft shining dresses did nothing to disappoint the eyes and hearts of the young soldiers.

After introductions were made, the young women entertained the Yankees with music and poetry in the parlor. Then they moved to the dining room.

The bountiful dinner, complete with wine, was dominated by talk of baseball. Cuthbert, Cambell, and several other players knew the baseball scene in New York and Brooklyn. They regaled the table with stories of heroics and disasters on the ball fields of famous clubs.

Danny, thinking the ladies might be bored with a bunch of jocks talking baseball, waited for an opening. He got it after Cuthbert wrapped up an account of the latest baseball trend in New York City, "ice baseball," and how uproariously funny it was to see the ludicrous spills and collisions of men playing baseball in ice skates.

"That sounds wild and crazy," Danny interjected as eyes shifted to him. He pressed on despite the nervous wavering rise in his voice. "But, you know, we can talk baseball back in camp. Maybe, with all the ladies here who don't follow baseball, maybe we should talk about something else."

Liza turned to him with an appreciative smile. "Mr. Bender, thank you for speaking on behalf of the ladies and making a fine point. If we hear one more story about the exploits of baseball in the land of Billy Yank, I fear we will turn *blue* in the face."

As she garnered a laugh, Danny brightened. She was on his side.

"It is my suggestion," she continued, "that we alter our color, leap across the river, and change the subject to the baseball being played by Johnny Reb."

During the "hear-hears," Danny tinged with embarrassment from his effort being slapped aside. He wondered if she was any different from twenty-first-century girls: if she was just another mean girl in a hoop skirt.

Obeying Liza's wish, Cambell led the charge as the table launched into lively accounts of the rebel baseball they'd been seeing across the Rappahannock. It seemed everyone had a story about the baseball prowess of "Jacko," the one-handed player, and the only civilian. Everyone, especially Liza, seemed to delight in it.

Danny had retreated into silence.

When the party rose from the table and retired to the parlor for coffee, tea and cake, Danny went wallflower. Stopping by the corner Danny had retreated to, Arky reminded him that a few hours before he'd had been gung ho about cruising the Southern belles. Unable to pull Danny from his funk, Arky went back to mingling, and asking every young lady if they knew any Jonglers, especially a woman named Octavia.

As teacups emptied and plates rattled onto a waiter's tray, Liza paid a visit to Danny in his corner. "I owe you an apology," she said.

He played dumb. "There's nothing to be sorry for."

"Yes, there is. You wanted to talk about something other than baseball, and I didn't let you."

"It's your party."

"What did *you* want to talk about?" she asked.

"It's not like I had anything to say. I figured someone would come up with something."

"So you were"—she mimicked his submarine style of pitching—"throwing a pitch and hoping one of us would put it in play."

"Pretty much," he said, liking her imitation.

"A pitch such as"—she placed a finger on her chin—"hmm, let me see." She feigned inspiration. "So, Daniel Bender, where do you come from?"

He hesitated. Repeating that he was a "drifter" would sound creepy. "Not from around here," he said.

"That's obvious," she replied. "Virginia Yankees are a rare breed." Waiting for him to elaborate, she held his gaze.

He lost the staring contest.

She bobbed her head, chasing his eyes. "You really are mad at me for resisting your attempt to rescue me at the dinner table."

Since she wasn't dropping it, Danny followed her lead to blunt. "Yeah, it felt like a…" He stopped himself from saying *slam* but couldn't think of another word.

"A rude slap?" she provided.

"Yeah, a slap."

"Then let me ask, Mr. Bender. Do you believe human beings are part of the animal kingdom?"

Danny went with her bizarre leap. "Yeah, we're part of the animal kingdom."

"And are you a keen observer of the animal kingdom?"

"I think so."

She leaned in a little closer. "Then you must know that many animals begin their courtship with roughhousing, sometimes even biting."

A laugh popped from Danny. She was back to being full of surprises. "Do you want me to bite you?"

"Of course not," she said through a laugh, then fixed on him with her blue eyes. "But, in my experience, I've found that colliding conversations can sometimes lead to comingling hearts." She turned to go.

Whatever response he might have formulated was drowned by the *swish* of her hoopskirt.

It *swished* again as she turned back. "I'm looking forward to your play in the final championship game."

Danny was so dizzied by her hairpin turns—figurative and literal—all he managed was a nonsensical, "Me too."

He retreated to the quiet of the front porch to not let the chatter of the others snuff out the sparks that had flown between them.

A few moments, later Sergeant Cambell joined him. He took out his pipe and filled it with tobacco. "If ya ask me, I'd say ya've taken a shine ta Ms. Conway."

Danny frowned. "I didn't ask ya."

"Aye," he said with a chuckle, "but yer still in need o' some courtin' advice."

It was Danny's turn to laugh. "I'm not *courtin'* her."

"Ya might think yer not"—Cambell struck a match, and lit his pipe—"but I can see it in yer eyes, an' the eyes never lie."

Danny answered with an eye-roll.

Cambell didn't miss it. "See, yer tryin' to hide what's in 'em. Now, here's my advice. If ya want ta impress her, she's got ta know yer plans."

"What plans?" Danny asked incredulously.

"For after the war," Cambell said, as if stating the obvious. "When ya go ta New York, join one o' the great baseball clubs, an' become more famous than Jim Creighton." When Danny laughed at the ludicrous idea, Cambell pointed his pipe stem at him with a cautionary look. "But ya can't be tellin' her this directly."

"Why not?" Danny exclaimed. "Who else would I tell?"

Cambell puffed on his pipe. "It's not how a Southern gentlemen would do it."

"I'm not a Southern gentleman," Danny pointed out.

"Aye, but ta court a Southern lady, it's a Southern gentlemen ya got ta be. An' ya don't make yer case ta the lady herself. Ya make it ta the gentlemen in *charge* o' the lady. If ya do that, ya'll get her attention. But if ya make yer case ta her face, she'll want nothin' ta do with ya." He pointed his pipe again. "Do ya know why?"

"I give up."

"'Cause it'll make ya nothin' but a damn Yankee who invaded the South, an' didn't respect the law o' the land, an' the law o' the Southern heart."

The sound of everyone gathering in the entrance hall sent Cambell and Danny back inside.

Cuthbert and the Southern ladies had formed a line. The Herkimers had started to proceed through it to say good-night to their host, hostess, and the charming ladies who had so keenly reminded them of what they were missing from their lives back home.

Danny hung at the back of the line, hoping to buy some extra time with Liza. It gave him time to realize that some of Cambell's advice was dead-on. It's exactly what an 1863 girl would want to hear: what a rich hotshot you were going to be in the future. The other part—going through Cuthbert to get to Liza—seemed old fashioned and silly. Especially since, it wasn't like Danny wanted to marry her. He just wanted to hang out with her and see what happened.

Reaching Cuthbert, the first in the line, Danny shook his hand. "I had a great time. Thank you."

"No, thank *you*," Cuthbert said enthusiastically, "for the honor of one day being able to say, 'The great pitcher, Daniel Bender, dined here.'" He leaned in and confided, "In fact, visit anytime."

When Danny got to Liza at the end of the line, he resisted the urge to defy Cambell and blurt out all his "plans" about going to New York after the war. Instead, they exchanged good-nights, and Danny did what he'd seen the other soldiers do. He bent down and kissed her gloved hand.

"Good luck in the championship game," Liza added.

Straightening up, a response popped out of Danny's mouth. "The only luck I'll need is you being there."

It was unclear who was more surprised: Danny, by how effortlessly the words had come, or Liza, by his unexpected charm.

She withdrew her hand and gave him a smile. "I'll try not to disappoint you."

On the way back to camp, Arky got Danny to hang back from the others. Arky wanted to know what had brought Danny out of his shell to talk to Liza for a while.

Danny claimed they had only talked about baseball. He didn't want his good mood ruined by Arky busting his chops for crushing out on a Civil War girl. "Find any intel on Jonglers?" Danny asked, changing the subject.

"Not a stitch," Arky answered. While true of the party, it hadn't been true of his trip to the followers' camp. But Arky wasn't ready to share that his mother was somewhere in the spacetime vicinity. And he didn't think Danny could wrap his brain around the complication of Octavia dropping a 1920s song fifty years before its time as a crumb for Arky to follow. Arky wasn't sure *he* understood it.

Arky's silence was music to Danny's ears. It gave him the chance to sort out the feeling swirling through him. Replaying his interchange with Liza in the parlor, he tried to get a handle on her bundle of contradictions. She was a Southern belle and a tomboy. She slammed him and then practically asked him to bite her. She was Ms. Conway and Baseball Babe. He gave up after he heard his father's advice: *Here's the thing about girls*, his dad had told him. *Don't try to understand 'em, just enjoy 'em.*

18

Crazy Talk

THE NEXT DAY was hot. The midday heat caused Cambell to move the Herkimers' baseball practice to late afternoon. It gave Danny the chance to slip into town and pick up his photograph.

When Snyder handed Danny the tintype, neatly set in a fancy metal frame, Danny checked it out. The black and white photo showed him looking rugged and handsome in his Union uniform. The baseball bat, gripped at the handle, rested on his shoulder. The picture gave Danny a smile, along with knowing what he planned to do with it. He looked up at Snyder. "If my name was on it, it'd be a baseball card."

Behind his glasses, Snyder's eyes popped wide.

His reaction immediately told Danny he'd done it again: given up a futurism.

"A 'baseball card'!" Snyder exclaimed. "A photograph *and* a name!"

Danny tried to change the subject. "So, about paying for this, when do you wanna do the Herkimers team photo?"

Snyder ushered Danny toward the door and slapped him on the back. "Son, don't you worry about a team photo. You've just paid me a million times over!"

Approaching the checkpoint on White Oak Road, Danny saw two different guards from the day before. It wasn't going to stop him from testing the limits of the Herkimers' fame.

"Private Danny Bender," he announced to the soldiers, "pitcher for the New York Herkimers. Requesting permission to pass"—he pulled up his framed tintype and showed it to the guards—"and deliver this to my girl up at the Conway house."

The soldiers studied the tintype, then looked back at Danny. "We could throw ya in the stockade for courtin' the enemy," one of them said with a hard look.

The other grinned. "But a soldier's not a soldier if he don't got a heart."

Danny stepped onto the Conways' porch and clanked the iron door knocker. After being admitted by a black servant, he waited in the parlor for one or both of the Conways to appear.

With a night to sleep on it—interrupted several times by memories of Liza—Danny had decided to heed Cambell's advice on the long-shot chance that he and Arky might get stuck in the past longer than Arky had been predicting. Danny was ready to blow Cuthbert away with how he, Daniel Bender, was going to take the New York baseball world by storm. Sitting on the couch, Danny waited with the kind of nerves he only felt before big games.

Hearing footfalls in the hall, Danny was disappointed to see the servant appear again, carrying a tray. Danny noticed there were *two* glasses of water on it. "Who's the other glass for?" he asked as the servant set the tray on the table in front of the couch.

The servant didn't answer as he turned and left.

Danny kept his response to himself. *Dude, I'm a Yankee. I'm one of the good guys.*

A few moments later, hearing the *swish* of a hoopskirt revved his pulse.

After Liza greeted him, they exchanged some small talk about the weather and the success of the party the night before.

Danny was puzzled by how overly polite she was being after her racy talk the night before. He had to hand her that: she kept him guessing. Which was fine with him. He was used to it. You could compile all the stats and scouting reports on a batter and still not know when he was going to defy the predicted and do the totally unpredicted. Sometimes all the intel got in the way. Sometimes pitching to an unknown was easier to pitching to a known. It was one of the things he liked about Liza. She was the ultimate unknown.

Reminding himself he wasn't on the pitching mound, Danny asked the question that had been on his mind since she'd walked in the room. "Where's your brother?"

"He's gone to Washington on business," Liza explained.

"Hm," Danny grunted. "That's too bad. I wanted to talk to him."

Liza perked with interest. "About what?"

Even though he was defying Cambell's advice, Danny couldn't resist offering a bullet point. "I wanted to tell your brother about how, after the war, I'm gonna take the baseball world by storm. That was the plan, anyway."

"Plans do change"—she glanced out a window looking toward the river valley—"especially in war."

In the following silence, Danny told himself to drop the future-plans thing, and pull out the thing in his jacket. He reached for his water glass.

"Before my brother comes back," Liza said, "and you get another chance to speak to him—which could be days—it might be helpful to rehearse your presentation."

"Rehearse it?"

"Yes, present it to me, as if I'm Cuthbert, so that we can be sure it's sounding the right notes. Or, should I say, hitting all the bases?"

Danny told himself it was a win-win. He'd practice his talk and impress Liza at the same time. She couldn't disrespect him for being a "damn Yankee" if it was *her* idea. "Okay, I'll pretend you're Cuthbert." He took a swig of water.

She spread her arms into a manly bearing. "So, Mr. Bender, what are your plans after the war?"

Danny set the glass back on the tray. "Well, Mr. Conway, I'm gonna join the best baseball club in New York, and change the game forever."

Her head cocked with a dubious look. "Really, Mr. Bender? Why would you want to change a game that's perfect already?"

"Oh, you don't know what's coming," he answered. "For one"—he held up his left hand and splayed it wide—"gloves."

Liza looked aghast. "Gloves?"

"Yeah, players are gonna wear 'em."

"But, Mr. Bender," she continued sternly, "if baseball players wear *gloves*, does that mean ladies will play too?"

"No, they'll be big leather gloves to help 'em catch the ball."

"They can catch the ball already."

"Right," he acknowledged. "But when players start throwing the ball harder and faster, they'll need a glove. And when pitchers start throwing ninety miles per hour and up, catchers will need a big fat glove."

"A glove?" Liza exclaimed. "A catcher would need to dig in and build a breastwork against such cannonballs being hurled at him!"

Danny stifled a laugh at how seriously she was taking her role. "Okay, sir," he continued, "let's talk pitching."

"Let's do," she said encouragingly.

"Right now, pitchers have it too easy 'cause there's no penalty for *not* throwing strikes. But"—he raised a finger—"a pitcher will have to throw strikes if he faces the threat of *walking* a batter."

She looked more baffled than ever. "You mean, take him for a stroll?"

"No-no, if the pitcher doesn't throw the ball in the strike zone, we'll call it a 'ball.' Then, after four balls, the batter gets a free 'walk' to first base."

She crossed her arms over her chest and scowled. "You mean to tell me someone could get on base without ever swinging the bat?"

"Yeah, it's a base on balls."

Learning back in her chair, she treated Danny to a scornful look. "Tell me if I'm missing something, Mr. Bender, but it's my understanding that baseball is a *manly* game. No one should be rewarded for standing there and doing nothing. I believe in Christian charity, but idleness is a sin. From the way you see the future of baseball, you would have the pitcher throwing so hard and fast that no striker will be able to hit the ball. And if the only players who can get on base do so by standing there and never lifting the bat from their shoulders, why, the players in the field might as well lie down and take a nap. If this comes to pass, the game of baseball will be *ruined*!"

Danny stared at her and tried to decipher if her shooting him down was real or if she was just playing Cuthbert to the hilt. "So, Mr. Conway," he answered back, "are you saying I'd be an idiot to go to New York and change the game forever?"

She gave him an unyielding look. "Your fate, Mr. Bender, is in God's hands." She leaned forward. "But what impresses me is a young man who thinks for himself. While I am certain that your wild thinking about baseball's future will not come to pass, if you apply your inventive mind to the future of industry, I'm certain you will become a master of your own fate. *That* is the kind of man who deserves to marry a fine young woman like my sister."

Danny broke into a big grin. "So you bought it?"

She cocked an eyebrow. "Bought what?"

"C'mon," Danny beseeched, "Go back to being Liza?"

She dropped her attitude and rewarded him with a smile. "That was fun."

"Maybe for you," Danny said playfully. "You almost had me ready to throw myself on a bayonet."

Liza stood. "Please, don't do that."

He rose too, and announced, "I brought you something." After a brief struggle with his jacket, he pulled the framed photo from his pocket. He handed it to her.

She took in the tintype of Danny in uniform, shouldering a bat. "Don't you look handsome?"

"I want you to keep it."

She looked up. "Don't you have family to send it to?"

"Even if I did, there's no mail service that could get it to them."

Her head tilted. "Why not?"

"That's another story. Please keep it."

She handed it back to him. "I can't. Good day, Mr. Bender." She turned and walked out of the room.

Danny stood there, confused. It was the second time she'd turned her back on him so abruptly. It didn't make sense. And she'd thrown him another contradiction. They'd just had a blast, but she wouldn't take something as small as his picture. It made him want to yell out, to make her come back.

He had a better idea. He set the framed tintype on a side table and left.

After Liza heard the front door shut, she returned to the parlor to fetch the tray and glasses of water. She saw the tintype on the side table. She crossed to it, opened the side table's drawer, and shoved the tintype into the drawer.

19

Jacko

On the way back to camp, Danny felt guilty about leaving the tintype. It felt good at the time, but, after thinking about it, he began to feel like, in a weird way, he was forcing himself on her. *It is what it is*, he finally told himself. *Besides, leaving it with Liza was the lesser of two evils. If I kept it, and Arky saw it, he'd do something crazy like make me eat it.*

Having some time before baseball practice, Danny went to his tent, stretched out, and tried to catch a nap. He was interrupted when Arky came through the flaps.

"Where have you been all afternoon?" Arky asked.

"I went up and visited Liza at her house," Danny admitted casually.

Arky stared down at him. "That's outside the camp perimeter. How'd you get past the guards?"

"I told 'em I was Danny Bender, the pitcher for the New York Herkimers." He segued from fact to fiction. "I told 'em there's no way I would desert 'cause I gotta be here for the Army of the Potomac Championship."

"That worked?"

Danny shrugged. "Wouldn't have seen Liza if it didn't."

Arky wanted to grill Danny about the perimeter thing, but his gut told him Danny was holding out. "Why'd you go see her?"

"They invited me."

"Who invited you?"

Danny clasped his hands behind his head. "Cuthbert said visit anytime."

"What about Liza?"

"She's cool. She's a big baseball fan."

"We know that," Arky said, irritated by Danny's evasiveness. "And we know they have a big estate that's falling down around them? As far as I can see, Cuthbert's biggest asset is Liza, whom he'd be happy to marry off to a guy they think is gonna make a lot of money after the war being a baseball player."

Danny wondered if Cambell had been talking to Arky. "You know that's not gonna happen."

"*They* don't know that," Arky snapped. "As far as they know, you're fair game."

"I don't think they're as poor as you think."

"How do you know that?"

"They just threw a big party, and Cuthbert's in DC on business."

"He's wasn't there at the house?" Arky demanded. Danny shook his head. "It was just you and Liza?"

Tired of the interrogation, Danny raised up on his elbows. "What's the big deal?"

"Jesus, Danny, it's friggin' 1863, where unmarried guys and girls aren't supposed to be in the same room together without a chaperone."

"There was a servant."

"Servants aren't chaperones," Arky shot back. "I wouldn't be surprised if you took that picture you had made and gave it to her."

"No," Danny lied, then followed with a half-truth. "I took your advice and got rid of it."

"At least you got that right. But you gotta cool your jets with this girl," Arky implored, "or you're gonna end up in a shotgun wedding."

Danny dropped back down on his back. "I don't see it that way."

"Oh? How do you see it?"

"You know how you told me I can't kill anyone here 'cause they've all been dead for ages."

"It was a pep talk to get you to pitch."

"Whatever, I figure the same goes for Liza. Whether we hook up or not doesn't matter."

Arky blew up. "Using that logic makes you a necrophiliac!"

Danny scrunched his face. "That's sick."

"No, *you're* sick!"

Danny popped back up on his elbows. "If you ask me, what's sick is being stuck somewhere and not making the best of it."

"Okay, don't listen to me!" Arky flailed his arms. "Tomcat around all you want. But when it's time to go, we go. Got it?"

"Danny-boy!" a voice yelled from outside the tent. The tent flap pulled aside, revealing Cambell in the tent opening. If he'd heard any of their argument, he didn't show it. "Private," he said to Danny. "Yer needed for picket duty."

Danny scrambled to his feet and stepped out of the tent. Turning back, he gave Arky a thumbs up. "Cap's got it."

At the river, Cambell and Danny relieved the pickets that had been on duty and sat on the ground to keep an eye on the rebels across the water. The rebel pickets doing the same on the other side were far less interesting than the regular bunch of rebel baseball players in the middle of a game. Jacko, the one-handed civilian, was playing as well.

It was an uneventful game of grounders, dashing men, and boisterous shouts until a stocky player stepped to the plate. On the first pitch, he launched a bomb over the leftfield scout, Jacko himself. Jacko turned to chase it down. When the ball came down, it hit a rock and took a huge bound into the river. To cries of dismay, Jacko plunged into the river and went after the ball, bobbing downstream.

Cambell leapt to his feet and charged into the shallow river. He splashed through the shallows, then dove into the deeper water to join the rescue.

As the two men swam furiously to save the ball, rebels and Yankees on both banks cheered them on. Despite not having a left hand, Jacko was a decent swimmer. However, the river won the race when the ball was sucked into a stretch of rapids and disappeared. Groans sounded from both banks.

Danny took it all in with delight, especially when the hitter, who'd been rounding the bases to claim his home run, was ruled "Out!" for hitting into "Foul ground!" and "Foul water!" He suffered more ridicule for ending the game. It was the rebels' only ball.

While the ball was lost, an opportunity wasn't. Cambell swam across the deep water to the shallows and joined Jacko, trudging out of the river. Jacko's dejected look prompted Cambell's sympathy. "Nothin' worse than losin' a good ball."

"It weren't a good ball," Jacko drawled. "It was homemade. We haven't seen a good baseball since we took one from you Yanks at Manassas."

Cambell wasn't surprised by the dig of a Union loss or Jacko's Confederate sympathies. Cambell answered with a jab of his own. "The spoils o' war are only as good as the hands holdin' 'em." When Jacko answered with a hard look, Cambell extended his hand. "The name's George Cambell. Sorry about the loss of your ball, Jacko."

While Jacko shook Cambell's hand, he didn't correct the name the Yankee sergeant had used. "I'm the captain of the Alabama Brawlers," he said.

Cambell jogged his head toward the rebels arguing about who had won the game. "What are the Alabama Brawlers doin' with a captain who's not in Lee's army?"

"'Cause I'm the best player," Jacko answered.

Cambell chuckled at his bravado and, from what he'd seen of the Brawlers, couldn't disagree. "Speakin' of best, have ya ever imagined a contest between yer best nine an' our best nine?"

Jacko tapped his head. "Reckon I've seen it up here a dozen times."

"An' how are the Billy Yanks doin'?" Cambell asked.

Jacko grinned. "No better than you're doin' in the war."

"If that's the case," Cambell said, "we ought ta get that contest outta yer head, an' onta the field."

Across the river, Danny was riveted by the two men talking in the distant shallows. He wished he could hear them over the chatter of the rapids. He watched as Cambell turned and started back across the river.

That evening, Danny and Arky were invited to eat the standard-issue slop of beans, salt pork, and hardtack at the mess tent of Cambell's Company G. The sergeant had assembled the Herkimer ball team for a meeting. While they ate, Cambell, with Danny chiming in, regaled the team with the story of trying to rescue the rebel baseball hit into the river. He told them about meeting Jacko, the one-handed player and captain of the Alabama Brawlers. However, he left out their ribbing exchange about the Yankees' best nine taking on the rebels' best nine.

When Cambell finished, Piper asked, "What about the Army of the Potomac Championship? We gonna get the game in before we go back to killin' secessionists?"

Cambell answered with a wry smile. "Don't ya worry 'bout the final game. Yer captain's workin' on it."

Arky stared at Danny on the other side of the fire, his face illuminated in the flickering light. Arky didn't like what he'd heard—the animated way Danny had added bits to the ball-rescue story—and what he saw in his face. Danny had the blissful look of someone who was at the baseball camp of his dreams. If that wasn't bad enough, Arky had no idea how deep Liza had her hooks into him.

After dinner, on their way back to Mud Alley, Arky broke the uneasy silence. "You know what scares me more than anything?"

"Dunno," Danny said. "What?"

"You getting too comfortable here."

Danny laughed. "Ark, we're sleepin' on hard ground and eating pig slop. I'm just grabbin' what's okay about the place till you find a Jongler and get us outta here."

Arky wished he could believe him.

20

Jongler Found

THE NEXT MORNING, Sergeant Talcott sent Arky to General Gibbon's headquarters. Gibbon needed a dispatch taken to the commander of the Army of the Potomac, headquartered a few miles inland from the river at the top of White Oak Road. Unlike Danny, who had used his celebrity to get past the sentries guarding the camp perimeter, Arky was given an order from General Gibbon to get him through the checkpoint on White Oak Road. It didn't stop Arky from testing the limits of Herkimer fame.

When he got within sight of the checkpoint, he ran the rest of the way to it. Still running in place, he told the guards he was on the Herkimers baseball team, on a training run before the Army of the Potomac Championship game, and he needed to keep running up White Oak Road.

The two guards doubled over in laughter. "Well, stop yer running right now," one of them shouted between guffaws. "Yer gonna wear yerself out!"

Arky glowered at their amusement, pulled out his order to get him through the checkpoint, and told them they were lucky they'd passed their "checkpoint inspection," or he would have reported them, and they would have been thrown in the stockade.

Past the checkpoint, on the way up White Oak Road, the sight of the Conways' farm only worsened Arky's mood. It was a spider's web waiting to snare Danny.

Major General Hooker's headquarters was a sprawl of big tents on a place called Cannon Ridge. It had an impressive view of the hills billowing down to the river, Fredericksburg, and the opposing Confederate encampment. While Arky didn't get a glimpse of "Fighting Joe" Hooker, he delivered the dispatch and headed back to camp.

On the way, Arky passed the Conway farm again. Coming up White Oak Road, he spotted a rider on a horse trotting toward him. Drawing closer, Arky noticed how the rider, a civilian in a suit, casually handled the reins with one hand. The man looked vaguely familiar. When he raised his free arm and gave Arky a handless wave, Arky realized who he was: Jacko, the baseball player from the rebel side of the river.

Swinging around to watch him, Arky was surprised to see Jacko turn his horse onto the Conways' entrance road and slow to a walk. Frozen with curiosity, Arky watched as Jacko tied the horse to a hitching rail in front of the house and strode up the steps to the porch. The door opened and he was admitted without knocking.

Unable to contain his curiosity, Arky cut across the overgrown field toward the house. Reaching the house, he stooped below window level, and moved around till he heard voices. Liza and Jacko were in the dining room.

Arky didn't rise up and peek through the open window for fear of being seen. He stayed low and listened. Jacko seemed to be delivering letters to her, which was confirmed each time Liza enthusiastically read the names of the senders on the envelopes. As Liza uttered the Conway name a few times, Arky made two assumptions. One, they were letters from relatives on the rebel side of the river and, two, Jacko was not only a one-handed ballplayer, he was also a one-handed mailman. When Jacko said he had to go into Falmouth to pick up some supplies and medicine before heading back across the river, Liza protested. A long silence followed.

Unable to resist, Arky rose up just enough to peek through the window. Jacko and Liza were locked in an embrace and kissing passionately.

Arky shot back down. *Holy shit*, he mouthed as his mind seared with an image: Jacko's handless arm clutching Liza's back.

Hearing Liza utter a beseeching and tearful good-bye as she and Jacko moved back toward the front of the house, Arky's mind resounded with dot-slamming. Liza and Jacko were lovers—she was major into Yankee baseball *and* rebel baseball—she was a baseball groupie—and if Cuthbert Conway wanted to pull Danny into the family using his sister as bait, then Liza was using Danny as the bright shiny object to distract Cuthbert and cover for her real lover: *Jacko*.

Arky didn't give a rip about a Southern belle doing her best Scarlett O'Hara, but he wasn't about to let Danny get sucked into a Southern gothic quagmire. As soon as Jacko turned his horse down White Oak Road, Arky moved around the house and banged on the door.

Liza opened it. She was surprised to see the ball boy from the Herkimers.

Arky noticed her cheeks were still flushed. He didn't mince words. "So Jacko is your boyfriend."

"Jacko?" she demurred despite the deepening flush of her face. "I don't know whom you're speaking of."

"That's what we call the one-handed guy who plays for the rebels," Arky said. "The guy you just had serious lip-lock with."

His accusation and bizarre language didn't stop her from pivoting to umbrage. "You've been spying on me!"

"Call it what you want. You're leading Danny on when you and Jacko are tight."

She gave him a baffled look. "You talk in the strangest ways."

"You know what I mean."

"I do," she admitted with a cold look. "You've discovered my secret." She stepped back. "Why don't you come in and let's discuss it?"

He didn't budge. "What's to discuss? You're busted." Off her blank look, he rephrased and tested his theory of her endgame. "You're done leading Danny on to placate your brother. Or would you rather I told Cuthbert about Jacko?"

She answered the threat with a steely gaze. "I will not speak about such serious matters on my veranda. Please come inside."

Arky didn't move.

"Please, I think I deserve the chance to explain my curious ways."

Figuring it might lead to gathering more ammo to kill Danny's crush, Arky followed Liza into the parlor where they sat in opposite chairs.

She began by negotiating terms. "Since you have breached my privacy, why don't we extend the intimacy and address each other in more familiar terms."

"Fine with me, Liza."

She smiled. "Thank you, Arky. Your insinuation is correct; my brother wants me to marry a man of means or at least a man with the *promise* of wealth. I chose Danny to appease Cuthbert for good reason. Danny is an exceptional baseball player, my brother admires him, and that admiration may buy me some time. Cuthbert is also determined that I marry a Yankee and not a man sympathetic to the Confederate cause."

"Meaning Jacko."

"You call him Jacko, I call him Thomas. And if my brother were to learn of my association with Thomas, he would send me away from Falmouth and the man I love."

"Whatever, it's a double lie," Arky fired back. "You're deceiving your brother and Danny."

The accusation made her stiffen. "I am not deceiving Danny. I am not the master of his affections. I am only the master of mine, and, while I admit I admire your friend as a baseball player, the war for my heart has been decidedly won by Thomas Jinks."

Arky's jaw dropped. "Thomas Jinks!"

"Yes." She took in Arky's stunned expression. "His name seems to have robbed your face of color."

Arky flashed on the daguerreotype of Thomas Jinks hanging in his house: a bearded Confederate soldier with an ugly scar on his head and his "hand" tucked inside his jacket. The one-handed Jacko was his great-great-great-great grandfather! "B-but," he stammered, "Thomas Jinks ends up—I mean, what if he joins the rebel army?"

She let out a fluttering laugh. "Don't be silly. General Lee has no use for one-handed soldiers."

Arky was dumbfounded by another possibility. Elizabeth Conway was his great-great-great-great *grandmother*. The consequences of that and the possibility of Danny screwing up his family tree, not to mention Arky's very own existence, made him feel sick. Liza blurred out of focus. The room began to spin.

"Arky," he heard her say as if hearing it from the bottom of a well. "Are you ill?"

He saw her swimming shape rise from the chair. Thinking he was about to faint, he folded between his knees and sucked in breaths. When he straightened up, Liza was gone.

She returned carrying a tray with two glasses of water and a pint bottle. If it was liquor, Arky wanted to skip the water and chug the bottle.

"It seems we have both suffered shocks," Liza said as she poured a dose of what was in the bottle into one of the glasses. The water swirled dark. "I don't want to imagine Thomas in any uniform, rebel or Yankee, and something has greatly upset you. When I'm overwhelmed, I find comfort in a strong tonic." She placed the tray on the table between them, sat, and handed the glass of darkened liquid to Arky.

Arky swigged a gulp of the tonic. The bitterness made his face prune.

Liza chuckled as she poured a dose of the tonic into her own glass. "I made the same face when I first tried it, but it does calm the fires of agitation."

Whatever relief it might have delivered was swept away when she set the bottle of tonic on the tray in front of Arky. The label read, Jongler's Rejuva-Nation—for the Wars Within. "Where'd you get that?"

Liza sipped her tonic. "My brother procured it."

"Where did *he* get it?" Arky demanded.

"I don't know," she answered, struck by his intensity. "It's the kind of thing you might find in the followers' camp."

"Where's your brother?"

"In Washington. What's so important about a tonic?"

Arky ignored the question as he grabbed the bottle and scanned the label. At the bottom, in small print, it read, Jongler Apothecary, Trenton, New Jersey. His head snapped up. "Can I keep this?"

Liza studied his wild expression. "I'll be happy to give it to you, provided you agree to not compromise the delicacy of my situation."

Arky's mind was elsewhere. "Which is?"

"That neither my brother nor Danny can know about the one you call Jacko."

Arky had every intention of telling Danny that the girl he was crushing on was his and Iris's great-great-great-great grandmother. Then he reminded himself that none of it mattered if they could get to New Jersey, find the Jongler who made the gnarly tonic, and get the hell out of 1863. "Deal!"

21

Request To Play

IRIS WAS IN a dead sleep. The dilemma she'd been wrestling with had kept her up long into the night: to tell Matt about the girl he loved from 1907, and make him suffer the pangs of unrequited love, or not tell him about the girl he loved in the past, and free him to love a girl in the present.

The chime of a doorbell invaded her sleep. She escaped her tangle of bedding and squinted against the sunlight flooding her open window. Looking outside, she saw Matt on the front stoop, dressed in his disjointed outfit of letter jacket, cargo shorts and flip-flops. Seeing him fired a fact in her groggy brain: her father now knew about Matt's trip to the past. A bolt of panic shot through her. If her dad answered the door, he might start interrogating Matt, and throw open the Pandora's box of Matt's full-on memory. Even though she had impressed on her dad that dealing with Matt was *her* job, especially given her dad's semi-unhinged state these days, there was no telling what he might do.

Her eyes darted to the driveway in front of the garage. The sight of only one car eased her panic. Howard had most likely torn himself away from the attic office and gotten himself together enough to go teach one of his classes at the university.

Another doorbell ring pulled her back to Matt. She lifted the window screen and leaned out. "You can stop now."

He looked up and grinned. "Hey, Iris."

"What do you want?" she asked. "It's so early."

"It's almost ten," he corrected.

She had no idea she'd slept so late.

He spread his arms. "You gonna come down and talk to me, or are we gonna do the Romeo and Juliet balcony thing?"

While she was impressed by his reference, it was spoiled by a memory: the image of Matt and Pigskin about to make love. Sweeping it aside, she answered banter with banter. "The balcony thing worked for them. So, c'mon, Romeo, whacha got?"

Matt laughed. He pulled a square of paper from his jacket pocket. "I brought my drawing of Pigskin."

Iris covered her mix of disappointment and intrigue with bravado. "You let her out of the house?"

"Yeah." He held up the drawing. "I was hoping to hook Pigskin up with your oboe. You know, you could play something and, who knows, maybe you'd have one of the visions you told me about and have a vision of her."

Iris instantly regretted having told Matt about her synesthesia during one of their winter juggling sessions. She also swallowed a response that came to mind: *I already had a vision of Pigskin, and you, and it's not a movie I wanna see again.* Fighting the jealously clawing at her, she said, "Okay, Romeo, lemme get this straight. You've come to my balcony to pine for another girl?"

He gave her an innocent shrug. "I'm just trying to figure out if this girl is from a past life or not."

"I told you I don't believe in past lives." Realizing it might've sounded bitchy, she tried again. "Arky says past lives are for those who can't handle the present."

"Yeah, well," Matt replied, "part of handling the present is figuring out the past." The words surprised him. It was a weird thing he had gotten used to: things popping out of his mouth that seemed to come from someone else. He cut to the chase. "Do you wanna fire up your oboe and give it a try, or not?"

Iris wanted to play something all right. She wanted to play the cor anglais and blow him back to 1907 so that he and Pigskin could live happily ever after, and she could stop her fantasizing about something between her and Matt. "Actually, Matt," she said, "I've got a fever blister coming on, so my lips are on the disabled list."

"Sorry to hear that." He strained to spot the blister. "Don't you have a concert coming up soon?"

"Yeah."

"Well, I hope your lips get off the DL before then." He turned and headed toward his pickup.

Watching him go, Iris felt guilty for lying and, worse, for being so petty. All the poor guy wanted was to get his heart straightened out, and she'd gotten all moody. Her mental search for something to stop him from leaving on a sour note was ended by a Subaru pulling into the driveway. It was her dad. Iris prayed for Matt to get in his truck and drive away.

Matt stopped beside his F-150, placed the Pigskin drawing in the front seat, and watched Howard get out of the car.

Howard looked rumpled and exhausted as he pulled a bag of groceries from the backseat.

"Hey, Mr. Jinks," Matt greeted him. "Can I help you with those?"

"I'm not an old man yet," Howard answered. "But I may be by the time Arky gets home."

"Dad," Iris intervened, "I could've done the shopping."

Spotting her leaning out the window, Howard ignored her comment, and looked back at Matt. "I see Iris didn't invite you in for some coffee."

"It's okay," Matt said. "I just wanted to ask her something."

"I thought you kids did everything by text or phone."

"It wasn't a text or phone thing," Matt said as he fished for a lie if needed.

Despite his fatigue, Howard's curiosity sparked. "Oh, what was it?"

Iris tensed. The last thing she needed was for her dad to hear about Matt's obsession with Pigskin.

Matt delivered his lie. "I wanted to know what she thought of a new juggling move I've been working on."

Iris breathed a sigh of relief and wanted to blow Matt a kiss.

"I see," Howard said, sounding a bit disappointed. "It must be easier to juggle now that your long hair is out of the way."

"Dad, would you leave him alone?" Iris admonished as Matt opened the door of his truck. "He's got better things to do than worry about hair hazards in juggling."

"I never thought about it, Mr. Jinks," Matt said, "but you're probably right."

Howard kept pressing. "You ever think you're going to grow your hair long again? You know, like an Indian?"

Before Iris could protest, Matt answered. "Nah. Been there, done that." He slid into the pickup and started it.

After Matt drove away, Iris confronted her father down in the kitchen. "I can't believe you asked him that!"

"Did you hear what he said? 'Been there, done that.' Does he remember it all, or not?"

"No, he doesn't, but if you keep grilling him, there's no telling what he might remember! I'm sorry I told you about it."

Howard jigged his head. "Sorry, Iris. I'm tired; it slipped out."

"You gotta be more careful," she urged. "If something triggers Matt's memory, we're screwed. He'll blow the whistle on the cor anglais, and us, and there's no telling what could happen. Is that what you think Mom would want? For the whole world to know about the cor anglais and the Jongler family to be turned into a freak show?" As much as Iris hated sounding like her brother, she had to knock some sense into her dad.

Howard slumped into a counter stool. "I only want two things. Everyone to come home and for the cor anglais to go back in its case."

"Right. But until then," she reminded him, "we gotta keep it normal, like you keeping to your schedule at school."

He gave a half-hearted fist pump. "Right. Tend to the present."

After her father retreated to his bedroom, Iris made breakfast and took it to her room. On top of her dad's near disastrous brush with Matt, she couldn't stop stewing over Matt showing up and wanting to use her to get to Pigskin. The more she thought about it, the more she wanted to throw a dart back at him.

She got out Arky's phone and read the text string. In the last text from Matt, he'd called Arky "Pee-wee." In Arky-speak, she texted back. "Goliath, prepare to be smitten. David."

After a bite of toast, Iris got a return text. Matt wrote, "I already am."

Iris was certain he was alluding to Pigskin. But her jealousy couldn't repress a crazy thought. Maybe he was referring to her.

22

Deduction

WHEN ARKY GOT back to Mud Alley, he looked for Danny. Talcott told him he'd gone on "pitching detail" at Company G. Arky headed down the hill to Cambell's company street.

Getting there, he saw Danny surrounded by a few Herkimer players. He was throwing pitches down the middle of the dirt lane to another player-soldier. Seeing Danny throw a pitch, Arky saw the ball sink and bounce before the catcher snagged it. Getting the ball back, Danny showed the Herkimers how he was gripping the ball.

As Arky closed in on the catcher, Danny threw again. Arky jumped in front of the catcher, knocked the ball down, and snatched it up.

"Hey, Ark," Danny protested, "what're you doin'?"

Arky kept coming toward him. "What are *you* doing?"

"I'm teachin' 'em how to throw a breaking ball."

Arky threw the ball off to the side, grabbed Danny's arm, and pulled him away.

"Geez, Ark," Danny protested, "what's your problem?"

A Herkimer called after them. "Hey, ball boy, you're supposed to fetch it, not fling it!"

Hustling Danny away from the laughter, Arky laid into him in a harsh whisper. "Chances are breaking pitches haven't been invented yet."

"How do you know?" Danny objected.

"It's called deduction, dumbshit! If we haven't seen anyone *throw* a breaking ball—curveball, slider, sinker, whatever—it means it hasn't been invented. And that's not the point. You don't do shit that's gonna change history!"

"What's it matter if they get to breaking pitches now or next year?" Danny objected.

Reaching the end of the tent row, Arky pulled Danny onto the lane leading down to the river. "I'm not talking about pitches!" he snapped. "I'm talking about my life!"

Danny's face knitted. "What do you mean?"

An approaching soldier took them in. Arky hissed, "Shut up and walk."

Reaching the deserted bottomlands between camp and the river, Arky spilled what he'd seen and heard at the Conways' house. Liza and Jacko were lovers; Jacko wasn't some one-handed ball player, he was none other than Thomas Jinks, Arky's great-great-great-great grandfather, the same man whose daguerreotype Danny had seen back in Belleplain. As Danny struggled to follow the tumble of revelations, Arky brought down the hammer. "If Thomas and Liza are hooked up, that means they're gonna get married, making Elizabeth Conway my great-great-great-great grandmother!"

Danny was still catching up. "Which means—"

"You gotta stop messing with her!"

Danny kept thinking out loud. "I get that Jacko is your supergreat granddad, but how do you know Liza is your supergreat grandma? It's not like her last name is Jinks."

"'Cause they're not married yet," Arky fired back. "It'll become Jinks when she marries him."

It didn't settle Danny's doubt. "Do you have a picture of Liza in your house? Have you ever heard of Elizabeth Conway?"

"No!" Arky shouted. "But there's not a lot of picture taking these days. When's the last time you saw someone here take a selfie?"

Danny knitted his brow. "All I'm sayin' is that I'm not so sure about your 'deduction.'"

"My deduction?" Arky echoed.

"Yeah, that Thomas marries Liza. He could marry anyone, and Liza could end up marrying someone else."

"We don't have time for this bullshit!" Arky lambasted him as he yanked the bottle of tonic from his pocket. "I also got this from her."

Danny took in the Jongler's Rejuva-Nation label. "Wow."

"Exactly," Arky declared. "I'm going to the followers' camp to see if I can find who sells it. He might be our Jongler. You gotta come with me."

Hearing a shout up the hill, they turned and saw Cambell, a bat on his shoulder, leading the Herkimer players down the slope. "Danny-boy!" he called, "you've been holdin' out on me! I want ta be seein' this pitch o' yers ya call a 'bender'!"

Arky wheeled on Danny. "A 'bender'? You gotta be kiddin'."

Danny answered with a sheepish shrug. "Looks like we got practice."

"Right," Arky almost spat. "You've got better things to do than go home." He turned and starting running up the hill, taking an oblique path to avoid the Herkimers.

As he ran, Arky's fury with Danny for screwing up in so many ways had his brain boiling. He didn't know what would make him feel better, breaking the bottle of tonic over Danny's head or chugging it to see if it really calmed "the wars within."

Arky let the steady pace of churning up the hill empty his mind. It opened the door to a doubt that he'd brushed aside. What if Danny was right? What if, for whatever reason, Elizabeth Conway *didn't* marry Thomas Jinks, and *didn't* produce a branch of the Jinks family tree?

Arky quickly slammed the door on his doubts. The evidence was too strong against it. He knew Liza had to be his great-great-great-great grandmother because she was a cold calculating manipulator. And it was from Elizabeth Conway that Arky had inherited the cold-calculating-manipulator gene.

23

Siren Call

On his run to the followers' camp, Arky's mind spun possible scenarios. If he did find the Jongler who sold the tonic, and if the Jongler possessed the cor anglais, it's not like Arky could tell him to fire it up and send him home. If he went home solo and left Danny, Danny could screw up the courtship between Thomas and Elizabeth and vaporize a 150 years of Jinkses, including Arky and Iris. As much as Arky relished the annihilation of Iris, it was blown away by finally getting *why* he'd been blown back to 1863 with Danny. It wasn't to find his mother. It wasn't to be Danny's agent. It was to stop Danny, like a clueless squirrel, from eating the acorn of the Jinks family tree.

Arky's brain fever took a break as he ran up a rise toward a group of soldiers. Reaching them, he realized they were watching something.

In a sunken road, a steady ribbon of marching soldiers, rolling cannons and supply wagons moved north. Arky knew exactly what it meant from his trip with his dad to the Chancellorsville battle site. A huge chunk of the Union army had begun its move north to go upriver, cross it, and attack the left flank of Lee's Army of Northern Virginia. At any moment, Arky and Danny could be swept into the surge of troops moving north, or held in Falmouth until May 3 and flung across the river into Fredericksburg. No matter which, time was running out.

Seeing a gap in the juggernaut of blue, Arky dashed through it.

Reaching the vast field of the followers' camp, Arky was startled by the scene. The camp was breaking up. Tents were coming down; wagons were being loaded. Some were already on the move, heading toward Washington.

Plunging into the sea of activity, Arky asked the first person he met what was going on. He got a frank answer. Between big battles, camp followers were happy to help soldiers part with their money. Come the first sign of soldiers about to part with life and limb, the followers became leavers.

Arky hurried through the chaotic decamping, looking for any wagon that advertised tonics, potions, or elixirs. He was stopped by a sound filtering through the clamor of shouting voices, clattering wagons and braying mules. The sound didn't belong. He realized what it was—some kind of music. From what, he couldn't tell.

He dashed toward the music, trying to identify what was playing it. Dodging through mules, merchants and mayhem, the music grew closer, louder. He recognized the sound of a woodwind. Whether it was a clarinet or some kind of oboe, he couldn't tell.

Like everything else, the music was on the move. Even though he ran toward it, the vexing tune shifted from faint to loud and pulled him this way and that. Then he heard the music sound a passage, low and melancholic, that could only come from one woodwind, a cor anglais. The instant Arky recognized it, the music stopped.

So did he. He strained to hear the cor anglais again, to resume its siren call. It didn't. He wondered if he had imagined it.

Refusing to give up, Arky dashed through the camp, looking for anyone who might be the seller of Jongler's Rejuva-Nation. No one had heard of it. But what they *had* heard was the music. It was a blessing and a curse. It was real, but he'd lost it.

Watching the wagons move toward the perimeter of the Union encampment, Arky was tempted to stow away in one of them, get past the sentries, continue his search for the cor anglais and its player, and, when he found them, come back for Danny. But leaving without Danny wasn't an option, he told himself. Even if Arky found a Jongler and the cor anglais, coming back into camp, he might be nailed as a deserter. It only stirred up his rage at Danny. If he had only come to the followers' camp, they could've stowed away together and chased after the cor anglais.

Returning to camp, Arky forged his fury into a strategy: Danny was on a strictly need-to-know basis. Getting to Mud Alley, Arky found Danny sitting on a box in front of their tent. He was holding his right hand in a bucket of water.

"What did you do now?" Arky asked.

"Shoulda gone with you," Danny said. "Tried to stop a line shot without a glove." He pulled his swollen hand out of the water. "Hope it doesn't swell to the size of a mitt."

"Did you tell Cambell?"

Danny shook his head. "Nah." He stuck his hand back in the water. "It'll be better in a couple of days."

Arky's stony expression didn't change. "We could be dead in a couple of days."

That evening, Arky didn't say a word about what he'd heard and seen at the followers' camp. He had other things on his mind. Like how to kill the Danny-Liza thing.

Arky figured there were two ways to torpedo it, either via Danny or Liza. Since Danny was more like a big bulky battleship that was too dense to torpedo, Liza was the better target. Arky entertained everything from letting her know that Danny was infected with every venereal disease known to 1863, to telling her that the reason they'd been on the run, and had stumbled into the Union army was because Danny had killed a baseball player with a pitch to the head, was wanted for murder, and would be caught and hanged if he ever became a famous baseball player.

Danny wasn't sure what to make of Arky's sullen silence. He was just glad he still hadn't told Arky about giving his tintype to Liza. If he knew, Danny was sure Arky's head would explode, or he'd grab a rifle and shoot him. But Danny did feel bad about one thing.

After taps, as they lay in their tent, Danny brought it up. "I just want you to know that, even though I showed some of the players how to throw a breaking ball, and called it a 'bender,' it's not 'cause I wanted to change history and have a breaking pitch named after me."

"Oh, really," Arky said dryly. "Why was it?"

"I figured if I called it a 'bender,' it wouldn't stick and whoever comes along and invents the curveball, the sinker, the slider, and all the others will get credit for giving 'em the right names."

Arky didn't' even try to decipher his convoluted logic. "If we get back to Belleplain and there's a pitch called a 'bender,' we'll know your thinking is full of shit."

Danny chuckled. "Yeah, and it would be kinda cool."

"About as cool as me not being born," Arky added. "Now shut up so I can escape this nightmare and maybe dream something nice."

24

Signs of War

As DAWN GRAYED the sky, the river was buried in thick fog. The silence enveloping Mud Alley was broken by the crackle of distant musket fire. The soldiers of Company K, including Arky and Danny, scrambled out of their tents in everything from long johns to birthday suits. The gunfire was coming from downriver. Arky's face was as white as the whitest birthday suit.

"What day is it?" Danny asked.

"The twenty-ninth," Arky stammered.

Danny lowered his voice. "I thought you said nuthin started till the thirtieth."

"It doesn't," Arky said unconvincingly.

Danny tossed a hand downriver toward the rattling gunfire. "Then what's that, someone making popcorn in the fog?"

Sergeant Talcott emerged from his tent in full uniform and bellowed, "Company K! Fall in for roll call whether you're wearin' knickers or nuthin!"

As the one-hundred-odd men of the company scrambled into rank, they could hear the surrounding companies of the 34th New York getting similar orders.

With his ragtag company assembled, Talcott acknowledged the distant musket fire. "For you fresh fish that is the sweet sound of battle. And we're gonna march into it!"

The company responded with a full-throated "Huzzah!"

Arky used it to cover his expletive, "Shit!"

Talcott ordered the men to get dressed, gather their weapons, pack one day's supply of rations, and "eat breakfast on the double-quick."

When Arky and Danny reached the privacy of their tent, Danny said, "Seems like we're gonna see the elephant sooner than later."

"Elephant?" Arky barked. "What elephant?"

Danny was surprised he hadn't heard the expression. "'Seeing the elephant' means going into combat."

"I don't wanna see the friggin' elephant!" Arky spat.

Gesturing for him to keep it down, Danny said, "Okay, okay. It's that or plan B, desert."

"It's too late!"

At breakfast around a campfire, soldiers wolfed down beans and hardtack, and talked excitedly about finally getting back into the fight. Danny scarfed down his food along with the others.

Arky, a ball of nerves, didn't touch a thing. He was trying to solve a mystery. Stymied by it, he blurted it to the others. "Why are we only taking one day of rations if the battle that's starting might go on for days?"

Piper, one of the soldiers at the fire provided an answer. "It's usually 'cause the generals know something we don't."

"What?" Arky demanded.

"If I had to guess," Piper said, "either they know we're gonna whop the Rebs in one day, or they're throwin' us at the enemy like sacrificial lambs, and they don't wanna waste the rations."

For some reason the other soldiers thought this was hysterical.

Under the laughter, Arky turned to Danny. "How can you eat?"

"How can you not eat?" Danny answered, stuffing a last piece of bean-soaked hardtack in his mouth. "It might be the last time we ever taste food."

"That helps!" Arky tossed his plate of beans and salt pork into the fire.

The soldiers stared at him.

Piper fixed on him with hard eyes. "Do that when you're carryin' the regiment's colors into the fight, and you might be the one who gets burned."

As Company K fell in, along with the ten other companies of the 34th New York, the musket fire to the south died down. Some soldiers speculated it had been saber rattling by one side or the other. Some guessed it had been a small skirmish that had succeeded or been repulsed.

When the regiment's thousand men were assembled, Arky held Company K's flag. Next to him, Danny shouldered his rifle. Trying to relieve the sickly expression on Arky's face, Danny said, "Don't worry, Ark. Where you go I go."

General Gibbon appeared, riding his horse down the alley of men. "Boys!" he proclaimed. "If you've got eyes and ears, you know General Hooker has been moving the bulk of the army north toward Chancellorsville, leaving us to look after Falmouth like a bunch of schoolmarms. Well, today, we're gonna throw off our dresses, march outta the schoolhouse, and take the battle to the south!"

The regiment bellowed its approval.

Gibbon waited for the huzzahs to finish. "And here are the men leading the charge!"

A strange sight caught their attention. Sergeant Cambell, riding a horse, led a column of ten men with Dabney bringing up the rear. They didn't shoulder rifles. They shouldered bats. It was the Herkimers baseball team.

Approaching Company K, Cambell pointed into its ranks. "Piper, Bender, Jongler, fall in! It's our day for the Army of the Potomac Championship!"

As the regiment hollered and tossed hats in the air, Danny exploded with laugher and whacked Arky on the back. "And you thought we were goners!"

Arky was relieved and livid. "Did you know about this?"

"Hell no!" Danny pulled Arky after Piper as they went to join the marching column of ballplayers. "The Cap rolls with the punches."

With the team leading the way, the 34th New York swung in behind them, cheering and rejoicing that the elephant had to wait another day.

As Arky marched, he breathed a sigh of relief, but he knew it was short-lived. He knew it was the last day before the "elephant" turned into a stampeding herd called the Battle of Chancellorsville. He and Danny had less than twenty-four hours to find a Jongler or take their chances at desertion.

25

Yankee Rules

By the time the 34th New York arrived downriver, a few Yankee troops from the Sixth Corps had crossed the river under the cover of morning fog, pushed back rebel defenders, and established a bridgehead on the opposite bank. That skirmish had been the source of the musket fire that had woken the regiment at dawn. Army engineers were now laying a pontoon bridge to move more troops across. The Confederates who had been pushed away from the river had retreated up a long slope to Marye's Heights.

Except for the Yankee storming party that had crossed, the mass of troops from the Sixth Corps were still on the Union side of the river. They were waiting for the order to cross and attack Fredericksburg. Given the morning's success, the Sixth Corps was in the mood for a baseball game, especially since the Army of the Potomac Championship had come down to the champions of the Sixth Corps, the 77th New York Saratogas, against the champions of the Second Corps, the 34th New York Herkimers.

The two teams gathered on an improvised ballfield on level ground that had been cut down to short grass. It was the best field the Herkimers had seen to date. While Cambell was pleased with the field, he wasn't pleased at seeing the general of the Sixth Corps, who, along with General Gibbon, was to oversee the game. The advocate for the Saratogas was Major General John Sedgwick. Being a major general, he outranked Gibbon by a star.

Sedgwick raised an arm to quiet the huge crowd of soldiers arcing the infield. He was an affable man with a full beard that jutted down like a cowcatcher on a locomotive. He spoke in a baritone that easily carried to the throng of fans. "Today," Sedgewick began, "we are gathered to play a game that will decide the champion of the Army of the Potomac."

The soldiers, whether rooting for the Saratogas or Herkimers, boomed a cheer.

Sedgwick resumed. "Last night, General Gibbon and I discussed the rules of the game. The good general and his Herkimers prefer the New York style of play."

The 34th Regiment erupted in support of New York rules.

"My Saratoga boys prefer the rough 'n' tumble Massachusetts rules."

The Saratoga fans, vastly outnumbering the Herkimers, thundered their approval.

Sedgewick waited for quiet. "While Gibbon and I entered our negotiation with strong differences, I brought a wet peacemaker to the table." He got a booming laugh. "For those of you unfamiliar with whiskey, it has a way of making your dearest friend your sworn enemy, and your sworn enemy your dearest friend."

The crowd answered in a chorus of "Hear-hear!"

"As our meeting progressed," Sedgwick resumed, "the general and I became less adversaries than allies. We realized that today's ball game is a small reflection of the war around us. Just as we are divided over the rules of baseball, our nation is divided over the rules of government. Shall we be one nation, or two? Shall all men be free, or some be slaves? And so is baseball divided. Shall we pitch underhand or over? Shall we tag a runner or plug him with a throw that can break his ribs? Last night, in the spirit of unity, we made a set of rules taking the best from the New York and Massachusetts games. In the name of peace and fraternity, there will be no plugging between the bases." He waited for the groans of disappointment to subside. "However, just as war must be fought with all we have to throw at the enemy, this game will not be played with the dainty toss of a New York pitcher in a petticoat." He magnified the cheers and laughter by miming a wimpy, underhand throw. "The ball shall be hurled overhand with the ferocity of a wood splitter bringing down his axe!"

Before the soldiers reacted, General Gibbon added, "And we shall call these rules, 'Yankee rules!'"

As the soldiers roared their approval, Danny and Arky, standing near the Herkimer players, stared at the generals. "Did they just invent modern baseball?" Danny asked.

Arky was struck by the possibility but was not in the mood to show it. "Maybe, maybe not. But we're not here to 'invent' anything else."

Danny shot him a puzzled look. "Like what?"

"Like the 'sinker,' 'slider,' or even the 'bender.'"

Danny lifted his hand and stared at his swollen palm and fingers. "I'll be lucky if I can throw it straight."

Cambell won the bat toss and opted to take the field first.

Danny's concern about his swollen hand was right. While he could get his fingers on the seams of the ball, they were too swollen and sore to put spin on it. Fortunately, the Saratoga batters had never seen pitches coming at them so fast, and even though the ball shot over the middle of the plate, the first two batters struck out swinging, and the third grounded out. The contingent of Herkimer fans loved it, but Danny knew better. If all he could throw was grapefruits down the middle, it was only a matter of time before they adjusted to his speed and became grapefruit pickers.

In the bottom of the 1st, the Herkimers followed up Danny's seemingly great start with hot bats. They put four runs on the board. In his first at bat, Danny even managed to spare his right hand from more punishment by chasing a pitch low and outside and left-arm steering it over the third baseman for a single.

In the next two innings, Danny's worries came to pass. His hand, somewhat loosened up, still couldn't get the ball to break; the Saratogas adjusted to his speed, and the grapefruit harvest began. By the bottom of the 3rd, with the Herkimer bats taking a breather, the Saratogas took the lead for the first time, 7–6.

When Arky wasn't chasing down foul balls to the left side, he was keeping an eye on Danny. He understood why Danny's sinker was hanging in the zone, and nothing was tailing inside or out. What Arky didn't get was a nervous tick he'd never seen Danny display. Between pitches, he kept eyeballing the crowd. Before Danny went out for the top of the 4th, Arky called him on it. "When you're not watching balls fly out of the infield, your eyes are all over the place."

Danny played dumb. "Really?"

"Really. It's like you're wearing a pair of glasses with eyeballs on springs. What are you looking for?"

Danny answered with a casual shrug. "I just thought maybe Liza would've heard about the game and showed up."

Arky had suspected as much. "Well, she's not here, and even if she heard about it, her brother is probably still in DC, and there's no way she'd come here"—he waved at the rowdy mass of soldiers—"without an escort."

"Yeah," Danny said, "right."

Arky changed the subject. "Have you told Cambell about your hand yet?"

Danny shook his head. "Why should I?"

Arky shot him an exasperated look. "I'm not the one who cares about this game, but if you keep feeding 'em home-run balls, Cambell or even Gibbon might think someone got to you and you're throwing the game."

"No way," Danny scoffed.

"Yes way," Arky came back. "If Gibbon will shoot someone for not knowing 'The Star-Spangled Banner,' what'll you think he'll do to an early version of Shoeless Joe Jackson. I didn't come here to see you become Headless Danny Bender."

"Dude," Danny said with a frown, "your paranoia is worse than my pitching."

"Oh right," Arky retorted. "We're trapped in the Civil War. Why would I be paranoid?"

Seeing a Herkimer hitter ground out to first, ending the inning, Danny forced a smile. "Thanks for the pep talk."

As Danny pitched, Arky's ball-boy duties sent him after a towering foul ball down the left side that flew to the furthest sprinkling of fans watching the game. When Arky reached the thinning fans and waited for a local civilian who had chased the ball into the weeds to throw it to him, Arky noticed a boy standing alone, also in civilian clothes. Arky might have ignored the soft-faced "boy," but he looked strikingly familiar. Arky realized it was Liza dressed as a boy.

Pretending not to recognize Arky, Liza looked away, and watched the ball being relayed to Arky. After throwing the ball to the third baseman, Arky jogged back in and weighed a decision. If he told Danny that Liza was there, it might pick him up, along with his pitching, and save him the humiliation of losing the game. But the downside of telling Danny and potentially inspiring him to win the game was worse. *If it works*, Arky speculated, *Liza might go cheerleader and get so smitten with jock-hero Danny that she dumps Thomas.* Arky didn't have to debate his future existence being more important than some forgotten baseball game. Liza being there would stay a secret between Arky and his great-great-great-great grandmother.

26

Foul Ball

THE 5TH INNING proved decisive, on and off the field. Danny and the Herkimers gave up several hits to load the bases with no outs. The Saratogas were threatening to pile up an insurmountable lead. And the Saratoga batter was swinging for a grand slam when he rifled a line drive foul to the left side.

Arky dashed after it as Cambell used the pause to visit his morose-looking pitcher. "Tell me somethin', Danny-boy," Cambell said, "are ya pitchin' from another era?"

Danny was startled by the question, unsure if he'd tipped his hand in some way, and Cambell had figured out he was from the future. "I dunno, whata ya mean?"

"The days o' tossin' the ball over the plate so they can put it in play are over," Cambell explained. "It's no longer a game o' who's better at fieldin'. That's why the strike was invented, ta make it a game o' strike 'em out too."

Danny brushed aside the history lesson. "I'm throwin' strikes."

"Aye." Cambell nodded. "An' everyone of 'em is gettin' served up like breakfast, lunch an' supper."

"I'm trying to paint the corners," Danny protested.

Cambell gave him a cockeyed look. "I da-know what 'corners' yer talking about, but the only ones I see ya paintin' are the corners o' the Herkimers' coffin."

As Arky chased down the long foul, he hoped Liza had written Danny off as a one-game wonder and gone home. Unfortunately, the only one who'd left was the local who had helped Arky collect the ball earlier. Liza was still there, standing alone. About to jog past her to get the ball, she looked down to hide her face under her hat brim. Arky answered her lame attempt with a jibe. "Nuthin to see here, Miss. The Herks are goin' down." He didn't slow down for her response.

As Arky reached down and scooped up the baseball, his head was jerked up by a sound: music. He instantly recognized the woodwind music that had eluded him in the followers' camp. This time it was more than sound. On the hillside, rising from bottomland of the ball field, was a man on a horse. The long, curved instrument in his hands was visible as it moved with the music coming from it. Arky had no doubt; it was the ancient cor anglais. The man playing it had to be a Jongler.

The restless crowd sounded over the music as they yelled and booed Arky's delay getting the ball back to the game. He barely heard it. Dropping the ball, he took off at a dead sprint toward the rider on the hillside. Arky was deaf to the boos and shouts of protest behind him.

At the pitching point, Danny, still hanging his head in dejection, was oblivious to Arky's desertion. Cambell waved Piper in from right field. While Piper couldn't throw with Danny's speed, he could mix up his location and speed enough to keep the Saratoga hitters guessing, which had to be better than the all-you-can-hit buffet Danny was serving.

As Arky dashed over the ground, the rider, still playing the instrument, turned his horse, and started up the hillside. "No-no-no!" Arky shouted.

With Piper jogging in from right field, a cheer went up from the crowd. While Danny stared at the ground, Cambell turned to see a boy running the ball in from foul territory, as the crowd celebrated their new ball "boy." Liza's running didn't betray her, but she didn't dare throw the ball in; that was a skill she hadn't mastered.

Having reached the bottom of the hillside, Arky churned up the hill after the rider with the cor anglais, still playing as his horse ambled toward the top of the hill. "Stop!" Arky shouted. The rider, immersed in his playing, kept going.

At the pitching point, Cambell said to Danny, "Well, don't jus' stand there. Go be scoutin' right field."

Before Danny could obey, the baseball was thrust under his nose. He looked up from the small hand clutching the ball and found the red-faced panting kid with blue eyes who had delivered it. He recognized her instantly.

"I'll be takin' that," Cambell ordered, oblivious to Liza's disguise.

Before he could take it, she flipped the ball to Danny. He caught it. She gave him an encouraging look.

Cambell was taken aback by the kid's defiance. When she turned and ran back toward foul territory, it dawned on Cambell who it was. "I'll be damned," he muttered.

Arky's legs and lungs churned. He kept narrowing the gap on the rider-musician, playing as he crested the hill. Another eighty yards and Arky would catch him.

Piper arrived at the pitching point and demanded the ball from Danny. "Give it."

Danny turned to Cambell. "Lemme finish this batter. If I don't, and they score one more run, I'll give it up."

Cambell fixed on Danny as the mass of soldiers vented their impatience. The sergeant ignored their loud protests as he spotted a fire rekindling in Danny's eyes.

The umpire made the protest official. "Let's play ball!"

"Now that you've fattened 'em up," Cambell said to Danny with a gesture to the loaded bases, "let's see if ya can throw 'em some poison."

Heaving for breath, Arky reached the crest of the hill where, moments before he had seen the rider sink over the hill's horizon.

He pulled up short with a sharp gasp. The rider, the Jongler playing the cor anglais, was gone, nowhere in sight. In his place, a vast camp of Union soldiers busied themselves with pitching tents.

Arky stared wildly, trying to decipher the rider having disappeared like a mirage. There was only one explanation. He had imagined it: the horse, the rider, the cor anglais, the music. Arky screamed an f-bomb. Not only had it been a hallucination, it was damning evidence he'd taken a step closer to being like Iris. His synesthesia gene, and the visions that came with it, had just fired for the first time.

Down on the ball field, there was nothing imaginary about Danny's first pitch after Cambell's visit. The four-seam fastball Danny threw from his down-under delivery did something it hadn't done all day: break, sink, and baffle the hitter.

27

Connectivity

In Belleplain, Iris shared Arky's agony, but for other reasons. All morning, after denying Matt's request to play her oboe in hopes of triggering a vision of Pigskin, she had been tormented by guilt. *C'mon*, a voice kept nagging, *the poor guy has no memory of what he went through in 1907; he's just trying to figure it out.* The voice was magnified by temptation. The last words Matt had texted Arky in reference to smitten—"I already am"—couldn't be silenced. She wanted to test them.

Iris arrived at the front door of Matt's house. She held her backpack with a music case tucked in it. She rang the bell.

Matt answered the door. He was surprised by her showing up, even more so when she told him she had changed her mind: she was there to play the oboe for him. As pleased as he was, he couldn't hold back a little shot. He studied her face. "What happened to your fever blister?"

"False alarm," she decreed.

After inviting her in, Iris asked, "So where's the drawing of Pigskin?"

"Up in my room," he answered.

She shouldered her backpack. "Then let's go."

He was impressed with her boldness.

In his room, Iris sat in his desk chair. "Okay, here's the thing," she said, placing her backpack on the floor. "When I play, I might have a vision, but, who knows, maybe you'll be the one who has the vision."

"That'd be cool," he said. "But I don't have that thing you have."

"Synesthesia," Iris filled in as she got up and plucked the framed drawing of the Indian girl off his bedside table. "You may not have it, but you've got a thing for this girl"—she handed him the drawing—"and if you're holding her picture while I'm playing, there's no telling what might happen."

Iris returned to the chair and lifted her backpack. "Now, sit on the bed."

Holding the framed drawing, Matt obeyed. "Okay, coach."

She unzipped a pocket on her backpack, pulled out a length of black material, and tossed it to him. "Put it on."

He held it up. "A blindfold?"

"Yep. Not being distracted by things around you might help a vision come."

"This is getting weirder by the minute, but hey"—he shrugged—"what's to lose?"

Once he had the blindfold on, Iris pulled the music case from the backpack. It wasn't her oboe case; it was the old wooden case. She'd brought the cor anglais. While she worried that doing the right thing for Matt might turn into a mega-wrong thing—like totally restoring his memory of 1907, or blowing him to the past for the second time—a stronger feeling overshadowed her concerns. Everything was going to be okay; the cor anglais wouldn't let anything happen that wasn't meant to be.

She began to assemble the ancient instrument. "Everything's black, right?"

He nodded. "Yeah."

"Try to make your mind just as black and empty."

Matt tried to stop the sounds of her assembling the instrument from putting pictures in his head of what her hands were doing. He heard her mouth wet the reed.

She began to play the piece that triggered her richest visions: the solo from Dvorak's *New World Symphony. Daa-da-daaa, daa-da-daaa...*

Matt was stuck by how much lower and mournful the music sounded compared to when he'd heard her play the oboe. It didn't matter. The music was beautiful; he let it wash over him. It sent images flickering through his mind. He became hyper aware of his fingertips holding the picture frame. In his mind's eye, he could see the framed drawing. It turned into a shallow pan, like the one miners use to pan for gold. Pigskin was still visible in the bottom of the pan. The image was so strong it made him gently circle the "pan," as if the music swirling through him was water washing away the dust of the pencil drawing and out of it would rise the treasure of his Indian girl in the flesh.

Iris was so caught up in playing, she didn't see Matt gently rocking the frame in his hands. She swelled with the emotion the piece always filled her with when she played it on the cor anglais. And she thrilled with the sense of her and the instrument performing a perfect dance between fingers and keys. The music flowed as effortlessly as water from a spring.

Halfway through, the first hints of a vision began to appear. The scene of Matt's room, with him sitting on the bed and holding the picture frame, began to saturate with blue. It kept bleeding to dark blue until that was all Iris could see.

Playing on, the solid field of blue began to show motion, like a surface shifting in the wind. Then the riffling surface moved away from Iris, yielding some kind of frame around the blue. As Iris played several rising notes, she realized what she was seeing. A person in a dark blue shirt was walking away from her. When she saw the back of his head and torso, she recognized who it was. Arky. A moment later, she realized he was walking down some kind of slope. Arky stopped. Iris played on. He turned his head, looking back at something up the slope from where he'd come.

It felt like he was looking right through her. Then he turned his head away and proceeded down the slope.

As the vision began to fade with the last notes of the solo, Iris pulled one more detail from the vision. Beyond and below Arky, in a distant field, there were men in dark clothing playing at what looked like baseball. Letting the last note fade to silence, the vision faded with it, and she closed her eyes.

When Iris opened them again, Matt and his room returned as it had been. Lowering the cor anglais, she felt an incredible peace. Not only had she played flawlessly, she had seen her brother. "Anything?" she whispered to Matt.

Matt knew the image of him "panning for gold," for the real Pigskin, was more like a daydream than a vision. He shook his head, still blindfolded. "No. You?"

She couldn't tell him about what she'd seen. She was still trying to decipher it. "Nothing but the pleasure of playing," she said with a small smile.

He didn't have to see her smile to sense it. "And the pleasure of hearing." He lifted a hand to the blindfold.

"Don't take it off."

His hand stopped. "Why?"

"You'll see."

He recognized the sound of the instrument being taken apart. Despite his puzzlement, he didn't move. He wasn't done basking in what the music had given him.

With the cor anglais back in its case, Iris stood, lifting the case and the backpack in each hand. She moved across the space between them. "We didn't see Pigskin," she said. "But there's other ways to find her." Iris bent down and kissed Matt on the mouth.

His surprise lasted a second before he gave into her kiss. Fully.

Iris enjoyed it as long as she could without dropping the things in her hands and giving more.

She pulled away and slipped out of the room.

Matt didn't move.

As Iris made her way home, she drove extra slow. Her mind was so riveted on the vision of Arky, she worried it would blind her to something on the road. And then there was the torrent of feeling from the kiss. The twin distractions made driving feel as dangerous as the day she took her driver's test. She struggled to focus on just *one* distraction.

If the vision of Arky was anything like the horizon event she'd had of Matt the day before *he* had returned in December, seeing Arky might mean he was on his way back too. But, in the vision of Arky, there was something about the expression on his face when he looked back toward her that haunted Iris. *Why did it feel like he was looking right at me*, she wondered, *or through me. What had he turned around to see?* The questions kept tumbling. *Why was he alone? Why wasn't Danny with him, like the first vision she'd had of them? And why was he walking toward some kind of ball game?*

Her questions, with no answers, lost the battle to the tugging memory of the kiss. She sloshed around in the giddy rush of it like a kid playing in warm rain.

When Iris almost ran a stop sign, she berated herself for letting the kiss blind her. She forced herself to focus on the encounter she was driving toward: her father.

Do I tell him about the vision? she wondered. Her gut told her no. There were too many things she didn't understand about it, too many x factors. *Why was he dressed all in blue? Why did it seem like all the men in the field below Arky were wearing blue?*

The answers came as she flashed on a painting in their house: men in a field, all in blue. *They were Union soldiers!* The revelation burst out. "They're in the Civil War!"

28

Nail-Biter

DANNY FELT LIKE a miracle had touched his hand. Whatever soreness had been in it was gone. Even though his fingers were still a bit swollen, he could get them on the seams, and snap the ball at release. He had his breaks back—down, away, in—they were all there. And the "angel" who had delivered the miracle was still watching the game from beyond left field.

With a mix of speeds, locations and breaks, and the Herkimers backing him up, Danny dispensed with the next three Saratoga batters. He escaped the jam of the bases loaded, no outs, and the Saratogas came up empty handed.

As Danny walked in from the pitching point to the cheers of the Herkimer fans, he only had eyes for one of them. He looked out past the left field line and tipped his hat to Baseball Babe. Liza answered with her own nod of recognition.

Danny was distracted by the sight of Arky running in. Danny had been so absorbed in the roller-coaster ride on the field he hadn't realized Arky had deserted the game.

As one of the Herkimers went to bat, and Arky reached him, Danny asked, "Where have you been?"

Arky wasn't about to tell him he'd just hallucinated a Jongler playing the cor anglais. "I had to take a piss," Arky claimed. "Can't a ball boy take a piss?" He waved a hand at the Herkimer players shouting encouragements to the Herkimer batter at the plate. "What's got them jacked up?"

The Herkimer batter seemed to answer by rifling a shot to centerfield and getting a thunderous cheer from the Herkimer fans.

Danny grinned. "We just got out of a big jam, and I got my stuff back."

"Why?" Arky asked. "What happened?"

Danny wanted to tell Arky about the surprising "ball boy" who'd run the ball in but checked himself. It was a superstition thing. Telling Arky about Liza being at the game, sharing the secret, might mess with the mojo. Danny just lifted his right hand and wiggled his fingers. "Fingers loosened up."

Any other day, Arky would have seen through Danny's lie and known exactly what had boosted Danny's spirits. But Arky's "encounter" on the hill had scrambled his radar. For all he knew, Danny was simply pumped by having his "stuff back."

While the two of them hoarded secrets, the Herkimer bats held back nothing. They went on a hitting streak, shredding the Saratoga defense with piercing grounders, rocketed line drives, and towering shots to where the scouts weren't scouting.

When the Herkimers finally put down their bats to retake the field, it wasn't for long. Danny's pitching was back to his A game. He even began to have flashes of his déjà vu ball, where he saw the pitch before he threw it, and throwing it was instant replay.

Arky's radar wasn't so weak he didn't begin to notice the one "twitch" Danny had developed while he was pitching, waiting to bat, or rounding the bases. He kept glancing out to where Liza was.

In the bottom of the 8th inning, with the Herkimers at bat and trying to build on their two-run lead of 13–11, it wasn't Arky who popped the lid on the secret. It was Danny. "Why didn't you tell me she was out there?" he asked Arky.

Arky played dumb. "Who's out there?"

"Liza," Danny said flatly. "You've been chasing foul balls out there all day. Don't tell me you didn't notice."

Arky hedged. "You didn't need me to figure it out."

Danny answered with a frown. "Thanks. You're a real pal."

"Look, Dan-O," Arky pushed back, "this game doesn't mean shit."

"It does to me," Danny shot back.

Arky continued, keeping his voice down. "The only thing that matters is getting out of here before we get shredded in a hail of minié balls."

They were interrupted as Cambell informed Danny it was time to shut down the Saratogas for the last time. The Herkimers' cushion building had fallen flat, but they still held a 13–11 lead going into the top of the 9th.

Danny's irritation at Arky not giving a rip about the game, even if there were bigger issues, gnawed on his focus. When he gave up several hits and a run, he cursed himself for sharing his secret about Liza, and screwing with his mojo. It got worse. Another batter got on base, putting Saratoga runners on first and third.

It brought the biggest Saratoga to the plate, a brute named Morrison. His oafish looks no longer fooled Danny. Morrison had studied Danny's every pitch like he was Sherlock Holmes. And with each at bat since Danny had started throwing his breaking stuff, Morrison had been getting better wood on the ball.

Using his sinker, Danny quickly got two strikes on Morrison's monster swings. He figured he'd put Morrison away with a slider and make him chase outside. Danny saw the déjà vu ball and threw exactly what he'd seen in his mind's eye. Morrison's long-armed swing reached for it and crushed the ball into the right-center gap.

The Saratoga fans answered the resounding crack with an explosion of sound.

Danny watched helplessly as the ball went so far that it bounced into the uncut grass. The two fielders chased after, bounding through the high grass. Morrison thundered around the bases like a bull driving runners through the streets of Pamplona. When he crossed the plate, the Saratogas had retaken the lead, 14–13.

During the cacophony that erupted from the Saratoga fans, Danny angrily told himself to forget Liza, forget Arky, and laser focus on the pitches that would get him out of the inning. When he saw Cambell coming toward him from third base, Danny shot up his hand. "I got it."

Cambell, trusting his ace at the pitching point, went back to third.

Danny did have it. He retired the next two batters to end the top half of the 9th and gave the Herkimers their last chance to answer fire with fire.

They started with a spark. The Herkimers' Piper led off with a hot grounder the second baseman mishandled and Piper hustled out a single.

Danny came to bat next, and sliced a shot into right field for another single. It put Piper on second as the tying run, with Danny on first as the winning run. The hoarse voices of the Herkimer fans filled the air. They smelled the blood of victory.

Standing on first, Danny looked out past third base to find Liza. She was gone. Thinking she might have moved closer to the game, closer to the throng of soldiers on the third-base side, he scoured the crowd. He couldn't find her small frame. It baffled him. *Why'd she leave the game* now?

The Herkimers' whiff of victory turned sour. The next two Herkimer batters grounded out without being able to advance the runners. It brought Cambell to bat.

The bellowing mass of soldiers, whether from the 34th New York or the 77th New York, were in a frenzy.

Behind home plate, generals Gibbon and Sedgwick watched with the nail-biting anguish of their rank. Victory on the battlefield was beyond their reach, it could only be seized by men of lesser rank.

Cambell stepped to the plate. With two outs, the entire game was on his shoulders. It was hardly dead weight; it was more like a rabid gorilla clawing at his back. He was so jacked he came out swinging with the strength of nine men. His massive cuts earned him two strikes.

From first base, Danny had seen it before: a player tangled in the web of trying, not doing, of letting the future blind him to the present and not trusting the simple things he'd done ten thousand times. "Hey, Sarge!" he yelled at Cambell. "We're not across the river yet. Save something for Johnny Reb!"

A burst of laughter and cheering erupted from the crowd as the electric tension exploded like a balloon. No one laughed harder than General Sedgwick.

As Arky stared out at Danny on first base, his reaction was different than anyone there. Of course, Arky's stubborn refusal to not get hooked into caring about the game had been weakened by the cliffhanger the game had become. As terrifying as being caged in the Civil War was, and knowing about the slaughter that was about to unfold, he wasn't a robot. He wasn't immune to the excitement around him. But that wasn't what had his attention. Danny's joke to dispel the crushing tension was the best "pitch" he'd thrown all day, maybe in his life. And seeing Danny answer the crowd's laughter with his faux innocent, *What did I say?* arms-spread gesture, gave Arky a chill. Danny looked *too* comfortable. Danny wasn't just in the moment, he was *of* it.

Cambell shouted back at Danny, "Aye-aye, Private!"

On the next pitch, Cambell swung a bit early, but the *crack* left no doubt as to how well he'd connected. The line shot hooked into left field threatening to go foul. Cambell took off for first base.

The sprinting left fielder couldn't reach it on the fly or the bound as the ball landed fair. Cambell barreled around the bases, driving the runners in front of him. The left fielder, dashing after the ball, hit a depression and sprawled face first in the grass.

Piper and Danny crossed the plate with Cambell bringing up the rear. With Cambell's walk-off home run, the contest was over. The 34th New York Herkimers, 16, the 77th New York Saratogas, 14. The Herkimers were the Army of the Potomac champions.

The Herkimer players leaped on the heroic trio followed by the rush of soldiers from their regiment. The stunned Saratogas stood in the field like pillars of stone.

The mass of soldiers from the Sixth Corps, having witnessed a great championship, turned the pig's ear of defeat into a silk purse. A chant, that began small, rose from the thousands of soldiers and rolled across the field. "Yan-kee rules! Yan-kee rules!"

While Danny was as jacked with adrenaline and as high on the euphoria of victory as all the Herkimers, he kept looking for the one person he wanted to share it with. But Liza, the Baseball Babe who had turned him into Captain America, was nowhere to be seen.

General Gibbon led a triumphant march back to camp, and Cambell announced that the team would host a celebration for the regiment that evening. Gibbon brought the 34th New York back to reality by reminding them that the celebration would be canceled if they were ordered to break camp and join the flow of troops upriver or lead an assault across the river on Fredericksburg.

29

Family Album

When Iris got home, she was surprised her father wasn't there. She was too excited to call him and tell him about her discovery: she knew where Arky and Danny were!

She moved through the house, looking at every photograph or painting that her father had hung related to the Civil War. She was looking for some clue, some sign, that might connect Arky to the war.

When she took in the most obvious connection, the daguerreotype of Thomas Jinks hanging in the hall, she scrutinized his uniform and the scar on his forehead. Another revelation struck. It wasn't a *Jinks* she should be looking for; it should be a Jongler. There had to be a Jongler in or around the Civil War who could send the boys back. She raced through the living room and upstairs.

Reaching the attic office, she pulled the Jongler family photo album off the shelf. It was the same one she'd poured through after Matt had returned from 1907 and had revealed the picture of the Jongler who had surely returned Matt from the Carlisle Indian School back to Belleplain: Alfred Jongler, the music teacher at the Indian school, and their great-great-great grandfather.

She flipped through the album's pages. All the photos were protected in plastic pockets. Reaching the section displaying Jonglers and their relatives from the late nineteenth century, one picture grabbed her attention. It was a daguerreotype of a large man, bearded, standing proudly in front of his business. The sign above the glass-fronted building announced, Jongler Apothecary.

Below, on the border of the photo, written in elegant longhand was Rufus Jongler, Trenton, New Jersey, 1865.

Iris wondered if Rufus, the father of Alfred Jongler, had anything to do with the exact where and when of Arky and Danny. Certainly, 1865 would put Rufus in the same time as the Civil War.

Despite the plastic pocket protecting the old photo, Iris noticed a strange defect in the picture. There seemed to be a ridge running up and down in the left and right sides of photo. The more she looked at it, the more she realized there were other hints of a ridge on the top and bottom of the picture, hinting at a rectangle.

It hit her. The ridges might have been caused by something. She reached into the plastic pocket and felt behind the picture. There was something there, hidden by the picture of Rufus Jongler. She carefully pulled it out.

Iris gasped when she saw the face staring back at her. It was a tintype of a young Yankee soldier holding a bat on his shoulder. He looked like Danny. The more she stared at it the more obvious it was. It *was* Danny. And the bat confirmed what she'd seen in her vision. In the distance, behind Arky when he'd walked away from her, were soldiers spread out in a field, playing baseball.

With shaking hands, she turned the tintype over. Written on the back, in elegant writing, was April, 1863. The writing matched the writing on Rufus's daguerreotype.

Iris yanked out her phone and speed-dialed her father. He answered. "Dad," she exclaimed, "I know where they are!"

30

Game Ball

For the party celebrating the Army of the Potomac Championship, the regiment's cooks served up a meal that fell short of a feast for kings, but exceeded the soldiers' daily fare of salt pork and beans. In a buoyant speech, Cambell lauded every Herkimer for their effort whether they played or cheered them on.

After taps sounded, and the throng of soldiers headed for their tents, Talcott allowed the team to party on and awarded them with a gift from Gibbon: two jugs of whiskey. The Herkimers and their ball boys wasted no time filling their tin cups and toasting their victory.

Several shots in, Cambell stood at the table. "Tanight," he announced, "we've got sumthin that'll last longer"—he raised his cup of whiskey—"than a bit o' the creature." Getting a boisterous laugh from his team, the sergeant pulled the game ball from his jacket. He held it in the lantern light and read what had been written on it with lye to bleach the brown leather: "'1863—Army of the Potomac Championship—34th New York—16, 77th New York—14.'"

The team gave a raucous cheer as Dabney moved the lantern in front of Danny and set an ink bottle on the table.

Cambell continued, turning the ball in the light. "As ya can see, all the players have signed it, but one." He handed the ball to Danny, looking stunned and tipsy. "With great pride, we present the ball ta our hurler who, after a rough beginnin', found the pitch that won the game, an' will take him ta the heights o' fame after the war."

Over shouts of "Hear-hear!" Piper proclaimed, "If he survives it!"

Cambell let the drunken laughter die as Dabney placed a pen on the table next to the ink bottle. "An' now, Daniel Bender, it's yer turn ta sign the ball with not only yer name, but the name o' the pitch that'll change the baseball world. The 'bender.'"

As the team took up a chant—"Ben-der! Ben-der!"—Danny shot Arky an uneasy look.

Arky returned it with an eye-roll. At least signing a baseball wasn't as bad as having his photo taken; a signature was less incriminating when Danny Bender wasn't the most unique name. There was also an upside to Cambell's prediction: the "bender" pitch would never make it to the future. That is, as far as Arky knew.

After taking up the pen and signing the ball with the bleaching ink, Danny rose unsteadily to his feet with the ball in hand. The whiskey had kicked in. "I dunno if this is a new tradition or not, but the person who should have this ball is the MV"—he checked himself—"the most valuable player of the game. And there's no doubt, after he hit the walk-off blast, that the game ball belongs to our great captain, Sergeant Cambell." Danny thrust the ball at Cambell as the other players shouted their approval.

Cambell didn't take it. "No, Danny-boy, I want you ta have the game ball." He took in his players with a mischievous smile. "'Cause I've got me eye on another."

Piper voiced the players' puzzlement. "Another what?"

"If the stars o' war align," Cambell announced with twinkling eyes, "we're not stoppin' at bein' champions o' the Union army; we're gonna be champions o' *both*."

In their whiskey-soaked state, the players struggled to absorb what he'd said.

One of them broke the confused silence. "Good one, Sarge! Yer tuggin' our legs!"

During the guffaws and drunken reactions, Cambell's expression didn't change.

Piper held him with wary eyes and made his own announcement. "The time for playin' is done. It's time we got back to fightin' and killin'."

Cambell answered the challenge with a sly smile. "We'll be seein' 'bout that." He turned, left the table, and headed toward his tent with a slight weave.

The Herkimers stared after him with whiskey-glazed eyes.

31

Bearing Gifts

THE NEXT MORNING, Danny and Arky had barely finished breakfast when Arky was sent on courier duty. Dabney appeared and told Danny to get his rifle and come with him.

Down at the river, Dabney delivered Danny to Cambell on picket duty next to a dying fire. Cambell was using a telescoping spyglass to look at Fredericksburg across the river.

As Dabney rekindled the fire, Cambell handed the spyglass to him. "Tell me if ya see what I see."

Dabney trained the spyglass on Fredericksburg. After a moment, he said, "General Wilcox is still in camp."

Cambell nodded with a smile. "Along with the Alabama Brawlers."

Although Danny recognized the name of the rebel baseball team that Jacko was the captain of, he was confused. He pointed upriver at the rebel encampment. "I thought the Brawlers were camped upriver. Did they move into Fredericksburg?"

"No," Cambell said. "If they moved anywhere, they would've moved farther upriver ta counter all the troops we've been sendin' up there."

Danny's confusion grew. "Then what're you spying on Fredericksburg for?"

Cambell handed him the spyglass and directed Danny to train it on a particular house. Danny found the house, with a long yard sloping down to the river. The yard had a clothesline festooned with clothes. "See the clothesline?" Cambell asked.

"Yeah." Danny was baffled by what laundry had to do with anything.

Cambell continued, "Each o' the colored shirts on the clothesline stands for a rebel general. The red one ya see is for General Wilcox. When it's hangin' on the line, it means he's still in camp. If there's no red shirt, it'd mean Wilcox moved out an' left camp."

"But how—" Danny began.

Cambell cut in. "See the negro woman hangin' laundry." Danny nodded. "That's Dabney's wife. She's the laundress for General Jubal Early, who's quartered in that house. The general's laundry tells us the whereabouts of all the rebel generals."

"You're kiddin'."

Dabney sat by the fire. "We don't kid when it comes to the Confederates. And my woman will keep doing the general's laundry till the rebel army is hung out to dry."

Cambell laughed as he jumped up and cast off his great coat. He walked down the riverbank and waded in.

Danny jumped up. "Sarge, the picket truce is over. You're gonna get shot!"

Cambell ignored him and kept wading.

Halfway across, a rebel picket raised his rifle and fired a warning shot. "If you keep comin' I'll shoot you. It's high time we got back to fightin' to settle this war and go home."

"I'm all fer that, Johnny Reb," Cambell yelled as he waded on. "But I've got a present for the Brawlers of Alabama, an' I'm not goin' back ta killin' till I give it ta a one-handed fella we know as Jacko, an' you know as the captain o' Brawlers baseball."

The rebel who had fired the shot said something to his fellow picket, who took off at a run. "All right, you've got safe passage. But after this, we go back to fightin'!"

Danny had no idea what Cambell was up to.

A few moments later, Cambell reached the other side and was joined on the riverbank by Thomas Jinks, whom the other picket had fetched.

Cambell reached into his jacket and pulled out a new baseball. It was made of deep brown leather with precise white stitching. He offered it to Thomas. "Every baseball team, even yer worst enemy, deserves a decent ball." When Thomas hesitated, Cambell added, "Take it, 'fore I change me mind."

Thomas didn't move. "I've got nuthin to give in kind."

Cambell flipped the ball, triggering Thomas to catch it before it fell in the water. "Sure ya do. My New York Herkimers jus' won the Army o' the Potomac Championship. We've got no one else ta play. It'd be a fine gift if yer Alabama Brawlers were willin' ta take us on in the Blue an' Gray Championship."

Thomas laughed at the wildly insane notion. "Both sides are on the brink of battle, and you wanna play baseball?"

Cambell assured him that both armies were dragging their feet before the big battle, and there was no telling when it would start. "Besides," he added with a devilish glint, "nobody's gonna know about the game, 'cause we'll be playin' it under the light o' the comin' full moon."

Thomas eyed Cambell. "I've known a few Irish in my time; you're the craziest one yet."

"An' I don't need an answer right off," Cambell added. "Talk it o'er with yer lads, an' if they agree ta play, I'll give ya a signal, an' ya'll signal me back."

When Thomas asked what signal to look for, Cambell reached into his jacket and pulled out another gift, a harmonica. "From my side o' the river, I'll play 'Dixie,'" Cambell said. "If yer Brawlers are in for the Blue an' Gray Championship, ya answer with 'Yankee Doodle.'"

Amused by Cambell's musical diplomacy, Thomas lifted the harmonica. "I'm not a soldier. How do you know I'll be anywhere around here to hear it?"

"If there's a chance o' you an' yer Brawlers takin' us on," Cambell answered with an impish smile, "you'll be listenin' with jackrabbit ears."

Thomas answered with his own smile. "I hear you have a candy of a pitcher."

Cambell cocked his head. "'Candy'? I don't speak rebel. What do ya mean?"

"The best."

Cambell's curiosity fired. "How do ya be knowin' that?"

Thomas's smile broadened. "My best nine have more than scouts in the outfield."

Cambell chuckled. "Hopefully, you'll be hearing from me." He turned to go.

"Sergeant," Thomas added. "If we're fool enough to play, where and when?"

On the other side of the river, Danny and Dabney had been taking turns watching the two men through the spyglass. Despite their view being obstructed by Cambell's back, it seemed he had given Thomas a couple of items.

After Cambell turned away, Danny watched through the glass as the sergeant turned back for another short exchange with Thomas. After that, Cambell started back across the river.

When the sergeant got back to the Union side, Danny hounded him with questions about what he and Thomas had talked about and wanted to know if it had anything to do with the crazy idea of being champions of both armies.

Cambell answered with a Cheshire-cat grin. "If a Blue an' Gray Championship is in the cards, it's a toss-up 'tween the gods o' war an' the gods o' baseball. But if the baseball gods win"—he pointed affectionately at Danny—"the ball will be in yer hands."

Arky's day was far less intriguing. With most of the Union army in motion around the hub of Falmouth, and with Gibbon's two brigades seemingly stuck in the eye of a blue hurricane, Arky was running messages from one headquarters to another like a scurrying rat. It was so exhausting he wished for another hallucination of the Jongler playing the cor anglais that he'd had at the ball game. Anything would be better than reality. But the only thing he saw out of the ordinary wasn't imagined and it laced his exhaustion with adrenaline and filled him with dread. The number of sentries stationed around the perimeter of the Union camp had doubled. It was strong evidence that the desertion rate before a battle spiked and the odds of any escape was narrowing to nada.

The afternoon delivered the most jarring harbinger of things to come. Downriver, where the Army of the Potomac Championship had been played only the day before, artillery batteries on both sides of the river opened up and lobbed cannon fire back and forth to announce the pending battle and soften up each other's positions.

The thunder of real cannons turned Arky into a running bag of Jell-O.

32

Surprise Visitors

BESIDES THE SMOKE rising downriver and signaling the start of a major battle, the other news still reverberating through the Union forces, whether lying in camp or on the move, was about the Herkimers' triumph in the army's championship game. As the story traveled via "grapevine dispatches," the exploits of the Herkimers' pitcher turned into a tall tale. As some soldiers heard it, Daniel Bender could throw the ball so hard and fast that he had been transferred to an artillery unit and was hurling cannonballs across the river along with the other twenty pounders.

With the afternoon off from picket duty or drilling, Danny tested his hero status. He walked to the checkpoint at White Oak Road and greeted the two sentries on guard. One of them was tall and lanky, the other was short and stout.

When he introduced himself as Daniel Bender, the guards laughed at his unlikely claim. Danny pulled the championship ball from his jacket and showed it to them. At the sight of the dark ball, and all that was written on it, the guards went bug eyed. They gushed over Danny's signature in white ink.

Having reduced them to starstruck awe, Danny made the offer he had concocted on his way there. "There's a girl up White Oak Road I want to see before I get thrown into the fight. If you let me pass it's a win-win for both of us."

The guards' awed expressions shifted to confused. "A 'win-win'?" the short one asked.

"Yeah," Danny explained. "If you let me pass"—he extended the ball to them—"you get to hold onto this till I get back. It guarantees I come back."

The tall guard eyed him suspiciously. "What if you don't?"

"It's my loss and your win," Danny answered. "You keep a ball that's worth more than you'll ever make in the army."

The soldiers quickly agreed that no one in their right mind would give up such a treasure and not come back for it. They accepted the ball as Danny's bond.

Danny's walk up White Oak Road was buoyed by a hope: that Cuthbert Conway had still not returned. Even if he had, Danny planned to proceed with his own plan B. After all, it's not like Arky had found a Jongler to get them home, and it was looking more and more like the only place they were going was into the fight. If it was true, and Arky *never* found a Jongler, Danny wasn't going to sit back and wait for life to happen to him. He was going to seize the day, even if it was in another century.

As Danny walked, a civilian, driving a one-horse buggy, rode by him, heading in the same direction. Danny thought nothing of it, except to wonder if it was local Southerner leaving Falmouth to escape the pending battle. It triggered a thought. *What if Liza had done the same? Or was about to?* Danny quickened his pace.

At the Conways' estate, the civilian in the buggy drove it down the entrance road. He reined the horse to a stop in front of the house. The man jumped out, came up onto the porch, and was met by Liza as she opened the door. He handed her a stack of letters.

She took them with a worried look. "Where's Thomas?"

"He couldn't make the delivery," the man said. He nodded at the letters in her hand. "One of them is from him."

After the man left, Liza went inside, and shuffled through the letters until she found the one with Thomas's handwriting.

She ripped it open. Between several pages of stationary, she found a daguerreotype. She took it in with a gasp.

Thomas stared out from the photo. He was wearing a Confederate uniform.

"You promised!" Liza shouted as she flung the picture to the floor.

By the time Danny arrived at the Conways' house, and Liza answered his knock on the door, Liza had things back in order and had removed any sign of tears she might have shed.

She seemed surprised and relieved to see Danny. "When I heard the cannons, I thought you had marched off to battle."

Danny shook his head. "Nope. The Thirty-Fourth New York is still in camp, protecting Falmouth."

Her eyes shifted to the horizon over Falmouth. "In a day or two, there may be nothing to protect."

"No way," Danny said. "There's you to protect."

She acknowledged his chivalry with a tight smile. "Don't worry about me, I can take care of myself. If the battle crosses the river, I have a carriage ready to take me to Washington."

He had hoped for a different response. "Are you going to invite me in?"

She fluttered a hand. "Forgive my distraction. The beginning of battle has my mind in a blur, but it's no excuse for a lady to forget her manners."

After inviting him in to the parlor, she went to the kitchen to fetch something to drink. Listening to her in the kitchen, Danny assumed his other hope had come to pass: Cuthbert was still away. He rehearsed in his mind what he planned to say.

Returning with two cups of tea on a tray, Liza scolded herself. "Shame on me for not having said it; congratulations on rallying your team to a stunning victory."

Danny was glad she had brought it up first. But he wasn't going to let her off so easy. "We were still behind when you left," he said. "How do you know we won?"

She didn't miss the shade of disapproval in his voice. She answered it with cool conviction. "I knew you would. It's called a woman's intuition. Sometimes we know things before men have a clue." She set the tray on the table.

Danny's expectation of her offering an excuse, an apology, or even regret at leaving the game at the climax caught him off guard, not to mention the hint that she could read his mind. It put him on his heels.

Liza sat in a straight-backed chair and poured tea.

He dropped to the divan opposite her.

Seeing his unease, she qualified her assertion. "Besides, you had already turned the game around with your pitching. The rest was clean up."

Danny tried to get back on track. "I only turned it around after I knew you were there."

"Oh, Daniel," she said dismissively, "you would have done just fine whether you knew I was there or not."

"No, you being there made the difference," he insisted. "That's what I wanna talk to you about."

"My land," she exclaimed, fluttering her hands. "I feel a blush coming on."

Danny felt his confidence coming back. "Look, I know Thomas Jinks is your boyfriend." He waited for her reaction. She lifted her cup and saucer. He continued, "But it's not like you and him are engaged, right?" He thought he saw her tense.

She took a sip of tea. "Now, that's quite a 'bender' you just threw me."

He bristled at her not answering. "I'm not pitching right now."

"Of course not," she conceded. "But you are tossing me things I'd rather not swing at."

"All right," he said, answering her dodge. "I'll throw you the wildest pitch I've got." He took a moment, gathered his resolve, and stood. "I'm pretty sure I love you."

She put her teacup down with a bemused expression. "'Pretty sure'?"

As much as she wasn't making it easy, Danny plunged on. "Yeah, if love means that I want to marry you and make a life with you after the war."

She fixed on him. "Daniel, I'm flattered. But what would you bring to a marriage?"

"How 'bout everything." Despite her not reacting the way he had imagined, he had to get it all out. "I really am gonna take the baseball world by storm. I know you believe all my baseball ideas are crazy, but yesterday, we won 'cause I saw you. It made me wanna win. You make me wanna do everything. And I'm not just talking winning other championships and setting records. I'm talking about making it America's game like no one can imagine. And all that's gonna make me rich. And *that's* what I can bring to a marriage!"

"Well," she said, countering his exhilaration with calm reserve, "I certainly admire a man with confidence. But tell me, of all your wild ideas about the future of baseball, what's the wildest of them all?"

He told himself not to fall for the trap of answering with crazy stuff like the World Series and Jumbotrons. He had to think of something wild *and* believable. He was surprised how easily it came. "The Herkimers might have one more game to play. Against a rebel team. Against Jacko, I mean Thomas Jinks, and the Alabama Brawlers."

Her face tightened as she stared at him. The notion was not only preposterous, it pulled on the wound rending her heart. "Daniel, the only 'game' left to play is the next battle in this awful war."

Danny had said what he'd come to say; he didn't have any more words. He stood, grabbed her by the shoulders, pulled her up from the chair, and kissed her.

For a moment, she surrendered to his passion and then pushed away.

Danny stepped back. He couldn't tell if her eyes blazed with anger or passion. He didn't know if she was going to slap him or answer with a kiss of her own.

The tense silence was broken by the bang of the knocker on the front door. They both jumped at the sound.

Liza bustled out of the parlor into the front hallway.

Danny didn't move. He didn't care if it was a military detail coming to take him away for going AWOL. He had declared his love. He had seized the day.

Liza opened the door. Standing outside was a burly man with a full beard. He held a wooden box under his arm. "Hello, sir," she greeted him. "May I help you?"

Seeing her flushed face and the young soldier in the parlor, the man took the situation in with a bemused smile. "Ms. Conway, I hope I'm not interrupting matters of great import."

"Not at all," she said touching her hair, ensuring it wasn't out of place.

When Danny turned and saw the man in the doorway, he froze. It was the peddler.

"Then I'll state my business," the peddler told Liza. "I've come at the request of your brother, Mr. Conway." He tapped the wooden box under his arm. "He asked that I deliver this before I headed north. He wanted another case of Jongler's Rejuva-Nation."

Danny gaped at the peddler.

The peddler threw a nod to Danny. "Hello, Daniel. Fancy meeting you here."

Recovering from the shock, but still in seize-the-day mode, Danny blurted, "Where's the man who makes that stuff?"

"I'm a middleman," the peddler replied. "I get it from a seller in Washington." After setting the case on a chair in the hallway, he took in the young people with a sly smile. "Like they say in the army, 'As you were.'"

After he disappeared onto the porch, Liza turned to Danny. "I must say, I'm feeling overwhelmed."

Danny moved into the hallway toward her. "Is that a good thing or a bad thing?"

"I don't know," she answered.

Danny waved his arms in frustration. "With all that woman's intuition, what *do* you know?"

She fixed on him like a teacher on a schoolboy. "I know two things. It's a woman's right to change her mind."

The words gave him a ray of hope; he looked for more in her eyes. They were unknowable.

"But before she does," she added, "it's her duty to think it over." Liza brushed past him, walked through the parlor, and disappeared.

Danny stared after her, flustered, heartsick, and wanting her more than ever.

The thump of cannons sounded from the distant horizon.

"Don't think too long," he muttered.

33

Proposal

Iris and Howard sat at the kitchen island. Danny's tintype lay on the counter. Iris had already shown her father where she'd found it—behind the daguerreotype of Rufus Jongler in the family album—and had told him about her vision of Arky and the distant ballplayers.

Howard was certain the tintype was authentic. While his mind swirled with questions—*How did it end up here? Who hid it behind the picture of Rufus? Was it Octavia?*—his heart pounded with excitement and fear. He knew too much about the Civil War.

Iris asked the question that had been bugging her. "Why is he holding a baseball bat?"

Howard told her how baseball was a burgeoning sport before the Civil War, and there were many accounts of soldiers playing baseball during the war, particularly on the Union side.

Hearing it triggered something she'd been unable to shake since seeing Danny's tintype. "If he's playing baseball back then, maybe it's connected to what happened between Danny and Rafael Santeiro."

"Why do you say that?" Howard asked as he turned the tintype over and reread the date penned on the back: April, 1863.

Iris reminded him of what Octavia had written about the cor anglais sending a "drifting soul" back in time to be healed by the past.

But Howard couldn't escape his darkest thoughts. "The spring of 1863 saw a lot more killing than healing." He turned the tintype back to Danny's image as he raised another question. "And why was Arky sent back to such a dangerous place if it wasn't to find Octavia?" He let out a caustic chuckle. "Hell, if the cor anglais is a horn of angels, it should've sent the only person to the Civil War who'd enjoy it: me."

Iris gave him a smile and pressed on. "Do you remember reading in Mom's journal about the 'horizon event'?"

Howard nodded. "Yeah."

"With Matt, right before he came back from 1907, I had a vision of him, a horizon event. My vision of Arky might be the same thing: a sign they're about to come back."

Howard turned to her. "Have you had a vision of Mom?"

"Not yet."

They were both startled by the jangle of the doorbell. Iris glanced out the window and saw Matt's pickup in front of the house. She left Howard at the island.

Opening the door, Iris found Matt. They hadn't seen each other since their kiss in Matt's room. Actually, Matt hadn't *seen* her since she'd asked him to put on a blindfold before she'd played the cor anglais for him.

Wanting to hide the drama in the kitchen, not to mention her surprise at seeing him again so soon, Iris tried to sound casual. "Hi, Matt."

"Hello, Iris," he said a bit formally.

Given the awkwardness of pretending nothing had changed, that they were still just friends, and not wanting her father to hear them, she stepped outside and shut the door. "For a second"—she looked up at Matt with a coy smile—"I didn't recognize you without your blindfold."

He chuckled and pulled the blindfold from a pocket. "Speaking of, you left it."

She took it. "Are you telling me it's my turn to wear it?"

He laughed nervously. "Don't tempt me. I just wanted to talk to you."

"Okay." She didn't move.

"Are you gonna invite me in?"

"Actually, no," she said with an apologetic shrug. "Me and my dad are in the middle of something."

"Oh."

She killed the urge to explain further. She didn't mind the awkward silence. After all, she had kissed him first; it was his turn to go first.

"Up in my room…" He looked skyward, then back down. "Even though neither of us had a vision of Pigskin, I sorted some things out about the girl in the drawing."

"Really?" Iris's curiosity raced on two tracks: Had he remembered something about his heartthrob from 1907? Or was he finally over her?

"Yeah." He nodded. "Pigskin is just a drawing of a girl who might have, for all I know, never existed. Thinking I might've known her from some past life is living in fantasy land. Past lives are stupid."

His confession twisted Iris. Having a wish fulfilled—Matt getting over the Indian girl—was music to her ears, music that ended in discord. She didn't want him to give up so easily on Pigskin. She couldn't stop herself from testing his resolve. "Some people really believe in past lives."

He shrugged. "Not me. I'm going back to the game of here and now. I'm gonna totally focus on college, football, and living in the present."

Iris wagged her head. "Hate to nitpick, but college and football are months away."

"Exactly."

Her brow knitted. "Okay, so what's 'living in the present'?"

"Asking you to the prom."

The declaration left Iris speechless. The silence was broken by the sound of her father's cell phone ringing in the kitchen. It made Iris flinch.

"So it's out there," Matt added. "Will you go to the prom with me?"

She was still off balance. "I don't know what to say."

"There's only two answers."

Iris wanted to blurt *Yes!* It was checked by a double wave of guilt. How could she be tingling over a stupid prom when her brother and Danny were in the Civil War, and her dad was probably on the brink of losing it. *If all that wasn't bad enough*, she scolded herself, *Matt is asking me to prom only because I convinced him that the love of his life, Pigskin, is a figment of his imagination, which, of course, she isn't.* She finally replied. "Ah, there's a third answer."

"Really? What?"

The front door swung open. Howard appeared, holding his cell phone and a jacket.

"Hey, Mr. Jinks," Matt said, taking in Howard's troubled look and disheveled appearance. "Everything okay?"

"No," Howard declared as he stabbed an arm into his jacket.

A bolt of fear shot through Iris as she tried to come up with something to override whatever was going to pop out of her dad's mouth.

Howard beat her to it. "My TA just called. I totally forgot my lecture today." He pulled on his jacket and lunged toward his car. "Gotta go tend to the present by *teaching* the past."

While Matt thought it was a weird thing to say, Iris grimaced at the statement.

As Howard got in his car, Matt turned to Iris. "'Tend to the present by teaching the past'? What's that mean?"

Iris scrambled. "It's his history-professor mantra, 'Tend to the present by teaching the past.' And a weird-dad thing." Watching Matt's reaction, she hoped he bought it.

Matt watched Howard drive away. "I wish my dad was as weird as yours."

Iris popped a laugh. "Believe me, that's not a wish you want to come true."

"Okay," he conceded. "Can we get back to the prom? Do you wanna go?"

She gave him an encouraging look. "I've got a lot going on right now. Can I think about it?"

Matt chuckled. "Right, the 'third answer'; hadn't thought of that one. But then," he added with a smile, "after that kiss you gave me, why would I?"

Iris blushed and wanted to kiss him again to see if it was as good without a blindfold. She told herself to get a grip.

Matt backed toward his truck. "Okay, I'm good with you thinking about it."

"I've already started," she said buoyantly.

"But don't think too long," he added. "The prom's in two weeks."

As he got in his truck, Iris debated his last words. *Was that a friendly reminder, or a threat? Does he have a backup girl? Am I on a deadline?*

34

Tent Talk

When Danny made it back to camp in time for supper, Arky demanded to know where he'd been. Danny twisted the truth. He pulled the championship baseball from his pocket, which he had collected from the two guards he had left it with, and told Arky that he'd taken it "on tour." He'd gone around camp, showing the ball to soldiers, and letting them hold it for good luck. After all, if it brought good luck to the Herkimers on the baseball field, it would bring good luck on the battlefield.

Danny was lying for the same reasons he'd lied before, but now he had a new excuse to withhold the truth. It was bad luck to tell a friend that you were in love with a girl when you weren't sure if the girl loved you back.

"Really?" Arky asked suspiciously. "We're hours away from maybe getting thrown into battle, and you're taking a victory lap with a stupid ball?"

"It was more than that," Danny said, bracing up his lie. "Everyone I met, I asked if they knew a Jongler."

"And?"

"No luck." Danny considered telling Arky about meeting the peddler again and discovering that he sold the Jongler tonic. But Danny kept it to himself for a couple of reasons. He had checked, and the peddler just sold the stuff. And Danny knew telling Arky about the peddler would lead to him getting busted about going to Liza's. Danny could only lie so much before it all fell apart.

Arky wasn't sure what was worse: If Danny was piling on lies or if he was just blindly indifferent to the slow-motion guillotine that was falling toward them. Arky didn't get if Danny's oblivion was because he was still walking on air from his stupid baseball victory or if he was just dumber than Arky ever imagined.

That night, in drizzling rain, Danny and Arky bedded down in their tent and fought off the cold with a fire in their small fireplace. To try and break Arky's dark mood, Danny told him about Cambell's trip across the river to give Thomas Jinks a baseball to replace the one the Brawlers had lost in the river. Danny didn't mention the potential baseball game with the rebels for good reason. He had sworn his secrecy to Cambell on that one. Of course, he'd broken that oath with Liza, but that was different. It was for a good cause, especially if this was it—1863 and nothing else.

For Arky, the bizarreness of hearing that his great-great-great-great grandfather had been given a baseball by a Union soldier, and the thought that his dad would've been ecstatic over such trivia, was snuffed by self-disgust. "If I hadn't wasted yesterday chasing fouls at that stupid game," he carped, "I could've gone off to whatever's left of the followers' camp and maybe found our Jongler."

"You could have," Danny conceded. "But if you hadn't gone off to take a piss, Liza never would've run the foul ball in and given me the jump juice to win the game."

"Shut up about baseball," Arky snapped. "It's over and done, and so are we if we don't figure out how to get outta here."

"You're the one who brought it up," Danny pointed out.

As Arky fumed, Danny tried to a think of a way to distract him. He rolled on his side, opening up a narrow space of ground between their blankets. "It's April thirtieth. Show me everything you remember about the coming battle."

Arky tried to dispel the blackness swallowing him. The sound of the rain on the tent didn't help. After a long moment, he pushed on his side.

Danny had already brushed aside the hay carpeting the floor. He handed Arky a knife to scratch in the clay floor. "Try not to stab me with it," he said, hoping to get Arky back to his good ol' sarcastic self.

Arky took the knife. "Don't give me any ideas."

"Impossible," Danny said with a slight smile. "You're the idea guy, not me."

In the firelight, Arky scratched a map in the clay of what he remembered. He showed Danny how the fighting would begin several miles west of them around Chancellorsville. He pointed out that all the fighting would be there until the Yankees crossed the river at dawn on May 3 and attacked Fredericksburg. "Sometime during that dawn," Arky reminded Danny, "Thomas Jinks will be wounded and left for dead."

Danny's brow knitted. "But if he's not a rebel soldier, how does he become one in the next two days?"

"If I knew that," Arky answered, "I'd be Nostradamus."

The only thing that stopped Danny from asking *Who's Nostradamus?* was the knife in Arky's hand.

"What matters," Arky continued, "is that Thomas comes to, survives, and goes on to marry my great-great-great-great grandmother, Liza Conway." To emphasize the point, he impaled the clay map with the knife. "You got that, Cap?"

Danny gave Arky a mini salute. "Aye-aye, Private."

35

"Dixie"

THE MOONLESS DARKNESS was broken by a bugle playing reveille.

Arky's eyes banged open. He and Danny scrambled out of their tent into darkness under a dome of stars and the spill of the Milky Way.

Sergeant Talcott's voice sounded over the grumbling chorus of men emerging from tents. He ordered Company K to "Tumble up and fall in!"

After assembling, Talcott informed them that the 34th and other regiments had received orders. They were to pack three days of rations and be ready to march upriver when the order came. Talcott dismissed them to gather up their gear.

Heading back to their tent, Arky could barely contain his panic. "That's it, we're screwed! We going to Chancellorsville and getting thrown into it!"

Danny kept his thoughts to himself. His worry that he might not see Liza again was proving true. Marching to Chancellorsville was going away from her, and there was no telling what waited for them on the other side of the river.

As they packed up, Arky struggled against the terrifying sense that the guillotine's blade had been cut loose. He racked his brain for a way he and Danny might slip away from the herd of human sheep packing up for a trip to the slaughterhouse.

Seeing Arky's agitation, Danny was struck by another feeling. Despite his regret over not being able to say good-bye to Liza, he felt strangely calm. He didn't know if it came from a skill he'd acquired on the pitching mound and in life: When everyone and everything around you spins out of control, be the eye of the hurricane. Go quiet. Watch it blow. Or, he wondered, was it a different feeling? Was his calm and sense of acceptance a sign that his plan B was more than a plan, it was his *fate*? And whatever happened—whether it be death, glory, a life lived out in the past—was meant to be.

As Danny watched Arky vent his fear on the supplies he was jamming into his backpack, he felt bad for him. Danny wished he could pour his sense of calm into a cup and hand it to Arky. "You know," Danny said quietly, "I just want you to know that it's nobody's fault that we're not getting outta here, that we haven't found a Jongler."

Arky stopped and glared at him. "What are you saying?"

"Maybe we're doin' what's meant to be," Danny said. "And I'm okay with that."

"The only thing that's 'meant to be'"—Arky shouted before squashing his voice—"is us getting outta here. And if *you* wanna die in a war that's already been won, go ahead. But I'm not!"

Danny didn't respond. A war of words with Arky was always a suicide mission.

Company K sat in Mud Alley and waited for the order to move. Come sunrise, they had heard nothing. By midmorning they still sat. They were getting restless.

Arky finally got the break he'd been hoping for. Talcott put him on courier duty and ordered him to run to General Gibbon's HQ. General Sully wanted to know what Gibbon knew and how soon the First Brigade would march.

Before Arky left, Danny said, "Hey, be sure to come back."

Arky bristled at the implication. "I may be a chickenshit, but I don't desert my friends."

As Arky started the run up to Gibbon's HQ, the big show began across the river in the distant hills around Chancellorsville. It opened with an overture of thumping cannons as both sides traded salvos. Then came the far-off staccato of musket fire, crackling with the rhythm of monkeys on snare drums. The percussion of battle raised a thick blanket of smoke on the western horizon.

Approaching Gibbon's HQ, Arky saw two soldiers sitting in chairs in front of the field tent. Drawing closer he recognized General Gibbon and a barrel-chested staff officer he'd seen before. While the lieutenant smoked a cigar, Gibbon split his attention between the rumble of cannons coming from the west and the stick he was vigorously whittling with a knife. He wasn't whittling as much as reducing it to shaving.

When Arky reported that General Sully wanted to know if there were further orders yet, Gibbon stopped whittling. His furious look made Arky think Gibbon was going to stab the messenger.

"We've been ready to move upriver or cross it since daybreak," Gibbon fumed, "but haven't heard a word from Hooker in Chancellorsville." He jabbed his knife skyward at a big hot-air balloon floating over the river that the Union army used to observe rebel troop movements. "Tell Sully if he's wants to know more, he should stick a cork in his bunghole, fill up with gas till he floats, and take a look for himself."

The lieutenant enjoyed a laugh.

"Yes, sir," Arky said. "I'll tell him exactly that."

With no news to report to General Sully, Arky figured he could stretch his courier run long enough to make one last trip to the followers' camp.

His wild hope that he might find a Jongler lingering there was dashed when he came over a rise and saw what was left of the camp: a vast field of trash and detritus. Whatever Jongler had been there had been as evasive and illusionary as the Jongler mirage he'd chased up the hillside at the championship game.

At the far edge of the deserted camp, he could see the staggered line of sentry posts guarding the perimeter of the Union encampment against deserters. He suddenly brimmed with temptation: to run the line, to escape the maw of war that was devouring life and limb across the river, to go it alone. *Besides*, Arky assured himself, *if Danny's right, and Liza* doesn't *marry Thomas, she won't be a Jinks, and Danny can chase her all she wants, right into his own miserable "meant to be."*

Arky heaved a breath to rid himself of the temptation. As much as he was pissed at Danny for his infuriating mix of idiocy and resignation, he couldn't desert him. They had come there together, they had to leave together.

In Mud Alley, Dabney appeared and told Danny that Sergeant Cambell wanted him down by the river.

When Danny and Dabney joined Cambell on picket duty, the sergeant had his spyglass trained across the river on the house with the rebel general's laundry hanging out to dry. "Fine news," Cambell said. "Wilcox's red shirt is still on the line. The Brawlers are in camp."

"So?" Danny said.

"That means, Danny-boy," Cambell said with a grin, "the Blue an' Gray Championship is in play."

"But, Sarge," Danny said, "we could march upriver any minute."

Cambell shut his spyglass. "Packin' up isn't marchin'. Nine times outta ten, packin' up turns inta stayin' put." Cambell pulled out his harmonica. "An' now it's time ta see if the Gray has turned white." He started to play "Dixie" on the harmonica.

Danny looked around to see if any Yankees were within earshot. Playing "Dixie" could be as dangerous as wading across the river when the picket truce was over. Relieved to see no one, Danny asked Dabney, "What's he's doing?"

Dabney shrugged unknowingly.

Cambell finished the tune and focused his attention on the opposite riverbank.

"Sarge—" Danny started.

Cambell cut him off. "Shut up, an' listen."

A few moments later, a harmonica sounded from the other side, playing the lively strains of "Yankee Doodle." Cambell let out a laugh.

Danny was mystified. "What's going on?"

Cambell turned to Danny with a triumphant smile. "Jus' firmin' up our plans."

Danny was wide eyed. "With Jacko and the Brawlers?" Cambell nodded. "When?" Danny stammered. "*Where?* In the middle of the river?"

Cambell answered with a wink. "Jus' leave the when an' where ta yer captain."

In the late afternoon, with Danny and Arky back in Mud Alley, two reports from the battle in Chancellorsville crossed the river and made their way to the "schoolmarms" guarding Falmouth. The first day of head-on collisions between the Army of the Potomac and the Army of Northern Virginia had ended in a draw. The second piece of information was a revised order from General Hooker. Gibbon's two brigades were to break camp, bivouac down by the river, and wait for the order to attack Fredericksburg.

When Arky heard the news, he breathed a tiny sigh of relief. It bought them another thirty-six more hours to wiggle out of the tightening noose before the 34th New York became part of the May 3 dawn attack on Fredericksburg.

36

Dust Up

By nightfall, the 34th New York and the other regiments of the First Brigade had left their stockaded tents on the hillside and moved to the bottomlands running along the river. They were bivouacked in small "dog tents" used when troops were on the move.

To the west, a nearly full orange-red moon rose from the smoke lingering above the day's fighting at Chancellorsville. The moonrise wasn't all that captivated the Yankees along the river. On the other side, rebel campfires gleamed in the hills like the hundred eyes of Argos, the Greek giant. Just as intriguing was the noise traveling across the river. The rebels were sounding off in waves of whooping and hollering.

Around a fire, Danny, Arky and Cambell were taking in the curious display.

"What are they so happy about?" Danny asked.

"If the first day o' fighting 'round Chancellorsville ended in a standstill," Cambell answered, "they're hootin' 'cause General Hooker spared 'em the lash, an' Johnny Reb counts a tie as a win. They can holler all they want, as long as they're not ginnin' up ta pour 'cross the river, an' bring the fight ta us."

Even though Arky was sure such an attack wasn't in the cards of history, he bolstered the sentiment. "I'm with you, Sarge."

"If they're heatin' up for a fight," Cambell added, "the first causality will be the game o' games."

Arky's curiosity fired. "What 'game of games'?"

Danny was startled that Cambell had let it slip.

"Can't say." Cambell stood and tapped the chevron on his uniform. "It's why I'm wearin' stripes an' yer not." He returned Arky's peeved look with a crafty smile. "Battle plans revealed are battle plans spoiled." He walked away, heading for his own company.

Arky spun on Danny. "What's he talking about?"

Danny shrugged. "We're outranked. He knows stuff we don't."

"And we know stuff *he* doesn't. What *game* is he talking about?"

Danny wanted to share the craziness of the Blue and Gray Championship, but he felt telling Liza about it had pressed his luck enough. "I've been sworn to secrecy."

"Secrecy? Are you shittin' me?" Arky struggled to keep his voice down. "The only secret that matters is that we don't belong here. Now tell me what you know, or I swear, if I get a chance to get outta here without you, I will."

Danny answered the threat with a bent smile. "'Leave no man behind.' Some soldier you turned out to be."

"That's because I'm not a soldier," Arky fired back.

Danny shrugged. "You are now."

Arky jumped to his feet.

Taking it as a threat, Danny shot up his hands. "Okay-okay, I'll tell you something I've been meanin' to."

Arky hovered over him.

Danny continued, "Yesterday afternoon, I snuck out to Liza's house."

It took Arky aback. "You got past the perimeter guards again?"

Danny nodded.

"How?"

"After winning the army championship," Danny answered, "I'm kinda a rock star around here."

Arky was stunned. He crouched back down and struggled to temper his anger so nearby soldiers wouldn't hear. "Jesus, Danny, if you'd told me yesterday, we might've slipped outta here."

"I didn't think they'd give both of us a pass."

"Everything's negotiable," Arky shot back. "Why'd you go to Liza's? What happened there?"

Danny knew he had to lie. "I just wanted to say good-bye."

"Oh, yeah," Arky said accusingly. "Did you?"

Danny nodded as he bit back a satisfied smile. "And after I did, a weird thing happened. The guy, you know, the peddler who turned us into the Yankees, he delivered a case of that tonic to the Conways' house."

Arky's jaw dropped. "Jongler's Rejuva-Nation?"

Danny nodded.

Arky's mind tumbled like a slot machine in hyper drive. The first man they'd met—a peddler who called himself a "traveling man"—the man who'd delivered Danny to the army—the man who'd known the origin of his name, "Arky"—the man who'd saved him from a firing squad—the man who'd claimed he'd learned "Goin' Home" from a woman "who passed through camp"—the man who'd delivered Jongler's Rejuva-Nation—had to be the Jongler he'd been looking for all this time! Arky couldn't believe he'd been so dumb and blind. "Did you ask him his name?" he demanded.

Looking puzzled, Danny shook his head. "No. He said he was a middleman and bought the Jongler tonic from a guy in DC."

Arky fired questions. "Did you think he might be lying? That he made the tonic? That his name was Jongler?"

"He just delivered the stuff and left. That doesn't mean he's a Jongler."

Arky waved his arms. "Did you think to ask him where he's camped?"

Danny's confusion only grew. "Why would I do that?"

"You moron!" Arky screamed as he dove at Danny. They sprawled on the ground, with Arky throwing punches and Danny fending them off.

Within seconds, soldiers jumped in, pulled Arky off Danny, and yanked him to his feet. They laughed at Arky's beet-red face.

One of them was Piper. "Leave it to the fresh fish to try the oldest trick in the book," he said with another laugh.

"What trick?" Danny asked, still stunned by Arky's attack.

Sergeant Talcott, having arrived to check on the commotion, answered. "To pick a fight the night before and sit out the real fight in the stockade."

"If I'd known that," Arky spat, "I would've kicked his ass days ago!"

He got another laugh from the soldiers.

After Danny reassured Talcott that the fight was over, Talcott told them that if they tried it again, their next cooling off would be in the river.

Once they were left alone, Danny wanted to be sure of one thing. "So, the peddler is Jongler?"

Arky answered with a venomous, "Duh."

When Company K was ordered to their tents for the night, Arky dragged his bedding out of the tent and slept outside. He still wanted to kill Danny.

As he curled in a ball under his blanket next to the fire, Arky didn't know who he hated more, himself or Danny. At least Danny had an excuse. He'd been stupid before he got to 1863. But 1863 had *made* Arky stupid. *And the stupidest thing,* he berated himself, *was not grabbing the chance to desert at the followers camp alone.*

In the blackness of his misery, Arky thought of his mother. And he realized that she hadn't taught "Goin' Home" to the "peddler" thinking he was a stranger. She must have known he was a relative, a Jongler. The song had been more than a "crumb"; it had been a flashing neon sign pointing to the peddler. And Arky had missed it.

The only thing that ended his black spiral was the blacker tomb of sleep.

A few miles upriver, from a fire-lit clearing, came the sound of a cor anglais playing a brooding melody. It was the same clearing where Arky and Danny had first stumbled on the peddler.

Sitting on a barrel by the fire, and playing an old cor anglais, was the peddler, Rufus Jongler. As he moved the curved instrument to the lamenting melody from Dvorak's symphony, *From the New World*, thc cnd of the woodwind caught the firelight. Rising from the bell was a spider carved in bas-relief.

37

Sign

THE MORNING WAS chilly, pulling coiling strands of mist off the Rappahannock. Arky and Danny shared a silent breakfast of cold beans and hardtack. The only thing hot was the coffee Danny had managed to brew over a tiny fire.

Arky warmed his fingers on his tin cup and watched the misty columns rising from the river. He wished they would snake across the water, wind around him, and send him home. His anger had been dampened by the cold night. And he refused to give up, to surrender to despair. He assessed the situation. He knew, despite the eerie silence across the river, that May 2 would bring a bloodier day of battle, more slaughter, and the actions that would finally throw the 34th New York over the river in the dawn of May 3. "We have less than twenty-four hours to get outta here," he said quietly.

"Does that mean we sit here all day?" Danny asked.

"Yeah," Arky nodded, "unless history has a way of rewriting itself."

Danny had done some thinking himself before he'd gone to sleep the night before. He pulled the signed baseball out of his pocket.

Arky scowled at the sight of it. "You should throw that in the river. The only 'game' left is the one that's gonna kill us."

"Look, I may have screwed up with the peddler, or Jongler, if that's who he is"—he turned the ball in his fingers—"but I'm thinkin' this might save us."

Arky looked at Danny for the first time. "How?"

Danny leaned close so as not to be heard by neighboring soldiers. "What if I traded it for two tickets outta here?" He pocketed the ball and began to rise.

Arky pulled him back down. "Where are you going?"

Danny smiled. "To see if any guards are interested in buying."

As Arky stood to go with him, Talcott approached. "Jongler," he said, "Sully wants you for a message."

Before Arky could object, Danny answered for him. "He's on it, Sarge." Danny waited for Talcott to leave, and turned to Arky. "I'll go do the trading, come back, then tonight, we're gone."

The cold in Arky's bones warmed with a glimmer of hope.

When Danny reached the checkpoint at the base of White Oak Road, he was glad to see the same two guards who, the day before, had held the ball as bond for Danny's return to camp. It would make his negotiation that much easier. But the negotiation was more complicated than what he'd pitched to Arky.

Danny began by telling them that he wanted to say good-bye to the girl he was courting, and they could again hold the ball as the promise of his return.

"The fight's already started," the short guard pointed out.

The lanky guard gestured toward the river. "And the Second Corps is down at the river ready to cross it."

"That's right," Danny conceded. "But we're not hittin' Fredericksburg till tomorrow at dawn."

"You can't know that," the tall one objected.

"Yeah," the short one jibed, "who made you a general?"

Danny let them have their laugh. "I've got my sources. Believe me, we don't go anywhere till dawn tomorrow." His confidence gave them pause. "And I'm not done sweetening the pot," Danny added. "If you two can do double duty and be on guard here tonight, you get to keep the ball."

The short one's eyes bugged. "How's that?"

"By letting me and a buddy through the line."

The tall one gave him a condemning look. "That's desertion."

"Maybe," Danny said with a shrug. "But it's also givin' you a ball that's money in the bank. And every day you keep it, it's gonna get worth more and more."

They paused, not wanting to be the first to open the door on aiding a deserter.

Danny eased their doubt. "Tell you what"—he flipped them the ball and the tall one caught it—"you keep it while I see my girl. When I come back, you let me know if we have a deal."

He walked past them and hoped he didn't get shot in the back. All he heard was the hushed voices of them starting a debate.

As he hiked up the gentle roller coaster of White Oak Road, Danny finalized his game plan. If Liza had an answer, and agreed to marry him, then that was it. He would retrieve the baseball and give it to Arky so he could escape on his own and find the Jongler who would get him home. Danny didn't plan on going anywhere. He would join the attack on Fredericksburg and take his chances at surviving the war. If he did, he'd make a life with Liza and do what he always wanted to do no matter what century he was in: play baseball in the bigs. *Bottom line*, he told himself, *if I don't have the pitching chops to make it back home, and I do here, why not stay where I can be a star?*

But, he continued, working through his options, *if Liza says no, that's different. I'll desert alongside Arky, find the Jongler who's been hiding in plain sight, get back to Belleplain, go Captain American, and become a Navy SEAL.*

By the time the Conways' house came into view on the crest of a hill, the thump of cannons signaled that the day's battle had begun to the west, along with a veil of smoke lifting in the direction of Chancellorsville. Coming up the entrance road, Danny saw Liza sitting on the verandah.

Climbing the steps onto the porch, he noticed her hooded eyes fixed on the distant battle. She acknowledged him with a lazy glance. On the table beside her was a bottle of Jongler's Rejuva-Nation and a cloudy glass of water. From her lackadaisical appearance, Danny wondered if the tonic contained some kind of drug.

He followed her gaze across the river valley. "Are you looking for something?"

"Yes," she answered, speaking for the first time. "A sign."

"A sign of what?"

"One doesn't know until the sign comes."

He tried to rouse her from the stupor she seemed to be in. "I know what you mean. Yesterday, me and Sergeant Cambell got a sign that the game against the Alabama Brawlers is on."

The surprise worked. She turned to him. "Really?"

"Yeah, but there's no way we're playin' it," he said. "The rebels sound pretty busy over there, and—" He checked himself from sharing the timing of the attack on Fredericksburg. He wasn't so crazy in love that he'd give intel to someone who, for all he knew, might be a rebel spy.

"And what?" she prodded, wanting him to finish his thought.

He kept it vague. "The time for baseball is over."

She straightened, enlivened by something. "'The time for baseball is over'?"

Seeing her perking up made him want to say more. "Yeah. The way I see it, until this Civil War thing gets settled, and the country is one country again, baseball is never gonna take off and become America's game. So, the sooner we get the fight over with, and get the whole country back to playing baseball, it'll be better for me, you, and the future. I don't mind puttin' down the bat and takin' up a rifle if it makes America a better place when I take up a bat again."

She stared at him, wide eyed.

He wondered if he'd overdone it. "Did that sound crazy?"

"No!" she blurted. "That's the sign!"

He was clueless. "What sign?"

"'To everything there is a season,'" she continued excitedly. "'A time to kill and a time to heal, a time to keep and time to cast away.'"

"Ah, yeah," he said uncertainly. "That's another way of putting it."

She pulled something from a pocket on her dress and thrust it at Danny.

He took it. It was her daguerreotype of Jacko in a Confederate uniform. Despite Danny's surprise, he didn't know what it meant. "Okay, Jacko joined the army."

"You mean Thomas Jinks," she corrected.

"Yeah," he said, resenting her bringing Jacko into it.

"Do you know why?"

Danny dropped the daguerreotype on the table. "Not a clue."

Liza never took her eyes off him. "He's willing to die to end our separation."

Something in Danny tightened.

She motioned to the empty chair flanking the table. "Please sit."

"Why?"

"I need to tell you something."

The words twisted his insides tighter. He reluctantly obeyed.

"Yesterday, you brought up the subject of marriage," Liza said, having become fully alert and clear eyed. "When you said you wanted to marry me, I kept something from you. I should have said, 'You're not the first to ask. I'm betrothed to Thomas.'"

Danny's confused look made her think he didn't understand.

"We're to be married. We've been engaged for months. I kept it a secret to avoid my brother's disapproval. I'm sorry if this hurts you, but you've known he is my beau, and you've known that you and I have been a distraction."

"A distraction?" Danny repeated. "You helped me win the game of my life."

"Maybe so, Daniel. But life isn't a game. It's what it is right now." She turned to the horizon. "War. It's North against South, you against us. I don't know who will win. All I know is that the war for my heart has been fought and won by Thomas Jinks."

Danny's insides twisted and seethed under his stunned expression.

Fearing what he might do to her daguerreotype of Thomas, Liza picked it up and slipped it back in the pocket of her dress.

"What did you do with my picture?" he demanded bitterly.

She pushed herself up from the chair and moved toward the front door.

The sound of her hoop skirt sounded like the shush of a broom sweeping him away like dirt. He jumped up. "Stop doing that! Stop turning your back on me!"

"I'm not," she tossed back, still moving. "I'm getting something." She went inside.

Danny stood motionless as his insides roiled. The thunder of cannons made him want to fly across the river and plunge into battle, delivering destruction and death. The creaking door brought him back to the porch.

Liza moved to him with something in her hand. She pushed it toward him. It was the metal frame holding Danny's tintype.

He fought the urge to slap it out of her hand.

"You're going to need this," she said.

"For what?"

"For the girl who will return your love."

"I don't want it."

She lowered the framed photo and kept her eyes on him. "I know you'll land on your feet and survive this war. And you,

Daniel Bender, will take the baseball world by storm just like you told me. It's what you want more than anything else. What Thomas wants more than anything else is me. I'm who he's fighting for."

In the cold silence, she tucked Danny's tintype into his jacket pocket.

He didn't resist, but it didn't stop him from releasing his anger. He turned, snatched the bottle of Jongler's Rejuva-Nation off the table, and took a slug of the bitter tonic. He brushed past her toward the steps, spun, and hurled the bottle at the front door.

Liza cowered.

The bottle shattered. A splash of brown stained the door. The dripping stain formed the shape of a great brown spider.

38

Crumbs

In Belleplain, as soon as Howard had dispensed with his teaching obligation at the university, he had rushed back home.

He was in the attic office with the Jongler family album in front of him. He was convinced that if there had been one picture—Danny's tintype—hidden behind a fronting picture, there might be another set of "twin" pictures. He was meticulously pulling each picture from its plastic sleeve in search of more buried treasure.

Having started at the beginning of the album, he had worked through almost all the photos dating from the twentieth century, when he came to the two facing pages displaying pictures of his and Octavia's wedding. He stopped and took in each picture, devouring the details of each one. His eyes welled with tears; the photos went blurry.

He scolded himself for being a nostalgic old fool, wiped his eyes, and got back to taking out each picture and checking for another. Reaching the top picture on the second page—his and Octavia's wedding photo—he pulled it out. His fingertips immediately sensed a different texture on the back of the photo.

He turned it over. A second before, youthful and beaming versions of him and Octavia had stared at him. Now, another photo, black and white, gazed at him: Octavia looking the age she was now. If that wasn't enough to make Howard's heart stop, the old photo exploded with details. She wore a long black dress and a bodice-gripping jacket. Her long hair was pulled up,

Victorian style. The detail that made Howard gasp was what she held in her hands. The curved, Jongler cor anglais.

"Iris!" Howard shouted.

With shaking hands he broke the slight grip that time had left between the two photos and turned the old, black-and-white one over. In elegant penmanship, someone had written, Paris, 1894.

"Iris!"

Footsteps sounded on the attic stairs; Iris burst into the room.

Howard thrust the photo at her.

She stepped forward, took it, and shouted, "Ohmigod!"

It's all the confirmation Howard needed. "On the back. She's in Paris, 1894!"

Iris burst into tears, from joy, from pain, from the pure unabashed relief that her instinct had been right. Her mother *was* lost in time!

Howard, unable to contain his own emotion, joined Iris in tears.

When they recovered enough to speak, Iris, in fits and starts, unpacked the full meaning of the discovery. Since the picture had been hidden behind their wedding photo, the person most likely to have put it there was Octavia herself. Where *she* had gotten it was a mystery. Perhaps she'd found it elsewhere in the album. Wherever it had come from, Octavia hiding her own photo behind her wedding photo meant she wasn't just chasing a wild dream that the Jongler cor anglais might transport people through time. The photo of herself in 1894 was the only evidence Octavia needed to prove she was destined to become a time voyager herself. For all the months she'd spent during her sabbatical claiming to be writing a book about learning to play the cor anglais, she knew one fact. Her time voyage wasn't a matter of *if*; it was a matter of *when*.

Iris went on to excitedly tell her father that the outfit Octavia was wearing in the photo, and her Victorian hairstyle, matched what Iris had seen in the music-induced vision she'd had of her mother five months before. The photo nailed the validity of that vision.

"It might even be a sign," Iris gushed, "like the horizon event of Mom coming home. Even if it's not, Mom hid her 1894 Paris photo in the Jongler family album for the same reason she left me the good-bye note on the day she disappeared, she hid her music journal inside the wooden music case, and she encrypted her scientific research on the cor anglais deep inside her computer."

"Why?" Howard asked.

"They're crumbs she left for us to follow."

39

Encounter

WHILE HOWARD AND Iris brimmed with new hope, Danny bore the burden of a broken heart.

Halfway down White Oak Road, Danny was stopped by a sound coming over a rise in the road. It was music from some kind of instrument. Its low, plaintive tone matched his brooding mood. Danny moved up the rise to find the source.

Down the road, he saw a man straddling a big mule. He was playing a long, woodwind instrument of some kind. Danny recognized the musician: the peddler.

As Danny approached, the peddler reached a pause in the melody and stopped.

"Is your name Jongler?" Danny demanded.

"Yes," he answered. "Rufus Jongler."

Danny stared at the strangely curved instrument. "What is that?"

"The music, or the instrument?" Rufus asked in return.

"That thing you're playing."

Rufus lifted the curved woodwind. "An English horn." Noticing Danny's disappointment, he added, "Also known as a cor anglais."

Danny's eyes jumped back and forth from Rufus to the strange decoration on the bottom end of the instrument: a carved black spider.

"I see you're intrigued by it," Rufus said. "Would you like me to keep playing?"

"I've gotta get Arky first." Danny started away. "Don't go anywhere, I'll be—"

"Perhaps," Rufus interrupted, "there's no time to fetch your friend."

Danny turned back. He understood the implication: *Save yourself before it's too late.* He fought the temptation. There's nothing he wanted more than to be gone, to be as far away as possible, to stuff Liza in the memory of a dream gone disaster.

Rufus studied the thoughts racing behind Danny's eyes. "Should I keep playing?"

Danny's eyes hardened. He could survive a broken heart, but not a broken spirit. *Leave no man behind*, sounded in his mind. "We've waited all this time for you to say who you are," he told Rufus. "You can sure as hell wait for us."

"And I will." Rufus raised a hand. "But I want you to know, while I was playing, the cor anglais gave me a strange vision."

"Of what? Me and Arky getting killed?"

Rufus didn't fault him for his petulance. Having been the guide for a handful of time voyagers, not only were Daniel Bender and Arky Jongler-Jinks his first *twosome*, it was also the roughest voyage Rufus had ever witnessed. He suspected that two drifting souls, especially when one was a Jongler, was the cor anglais stretching its powers to the limit. "No," Rufus said. "My vision was simply of a baseball glowing like the moon."

Danny frowned. "What's that mean?"

Rufus spread his hands with a bewildered look. "I have no idea." Taking the reins, he turned his mule and started up the road.

"Where are you going?" Danny called after him.

As his mule plodded on, Rufus answered without turning back. "I guide my mule"—he lifted the cor anglais—"the cor anglais guides me."

When Danny reached the checkpoint, the two guards were waiting for him.

"You've got a deal," the short one said as he flipped Danny the ball.

Danny caught it.

"But we don't wanna see you again till tonight," the tall one added.

40

Confession

ARKY HAD WAITED past noon for Danny's return. While it had turned into a bright sunny day, the longer Arky waited, the more he was plagued by dark scenarios. He imagined Danny might have negotiated with the wrong guards, been turned in for attempting desertion, and been locked up. Worse, what if Danny had double-crossed him, and deserted by himself?

His fears lifted when he saw Danny's lanky figure striding toward their dog tent. Arky waited for him to get close. "Where the hell have you been?"

Danny surveyed the sprawl of soldiers lounging, playing cards, and writing letters in anticipation of battle. "I'll explain, but we gotta find a place to talk."

The two of them found a spot on the riverbank where the rush of rapids would mask their conversation. They sat on a sliver of sand protected by the eroded riverbank.

"What happened?" Arky demanded impatiently.

After meeting Rufus Jongler, and during his return to camp, Danny knew Arky was going to grill him like a terrorist. "I got some shit to tell you, but you gotta let me talk, and not yell at me, and call me a dumbshit. And if you try to kick my ass again, I'll beat you within an inch of your puny life. Okay?"

Danny's rare assertiveness and threats had Arky's attention. "Okay, I missed you too."

"Don't be an asshole."

"Takes one—"

Danny shot up a finger. "Shut up."

Arky "zipped" his lips.

Danny started with the easy part. He told Arky how he'd negotiated their desertion for later that night. Then he confessed part of what had taken him so long. "I went to Liza's house and found out she's engaged to Thomas Jinks."

The only thing stopping Arky from ripping Danny's head off for his deception was Arky being proved right: Liza *was* his ancestor. But vindication didn't kill his curiosity. "You fell for her hook, line and sinker, didn't you?"

"Yeah," Danny admitted. "I even gave her my tintype."

"You did what!"

Danny shot up a hand. "Chill." He pulled the tintype from his pocket and handed it to Arky. As Arky shook his head over the pure idiocy of it, Danny kept the story of Liza dumping him to the basics. "I really liked her; she didn't feel the same. That's why she gave it back."

It didn't fool Arky. The waver in Danny's voice betrayed him. "Meaning she played T-ball with your heart."

"Yeah," Danny said bitterly.

Seeing Danny's twisted face, Arky cut him a break. "The details can wait for another day, if ever. But I gotta know one thing."

Danny scowled. "Really?"

"Really. What the hell were you thinking?"

Danny searched for the right words. "I was keepin' my options open."

"What options?"

"Like what I said before."

Arky wasn't satisfied. "You said a lot of things before. Like what options?"

"Like if we get stuck here and I have to make a life."

"Make a life?" Arky repeated derisively. "What kinda life?"

"I dunno," Danny hedged. "Playin' ball."

"And?"

"Screw that. I'm done talkin' about her." Danny hit the eject button he knew he could count on. "I found our Jongler."

"What?" Arky blurted.

"His name is Rufus Jongler."

"Rufus?"

"Yeah. When I found him, he was playing a cor anglais."

Arky was practically in Danny's face. "Did it have a spider carved on the end of it?" Danny nodded; Arky threw a fist pump. "That's it!" But his triumph was instantly undercut by suspicion. "Wait a minute, was he playing to send you back?"

"Dunno," Danny said with a shrug. "Whatever, it didn't work."

His vague answer sounded like a half-truth. "Where is he?" Arky demanded.

"Last I saw him, he was headed up White Oak Road."

"You asked where he was camped this time, right?"

"He didn't give me a chance," Danny explained. "All he said was something about him guiding his mule and the cor anglais guiding him."

"Why didn't you follow him?"

"Ark, it was follow him or come back here. I figured mission one was getting us outta here tonight, then we can go Jongler hunting tomorrow."

Arky realized he had a point. "When I find that cagey ol' bastard, I'm gonna break the spider stick over his head."

A voice sounded over the churn of the rapids. "Jongler!"

Arky and Danny turned to see Talcott coming toward him.

Talcott stopped on the bank and glared down at Arky. "I've been looking all over for you. General Gibbon specifically asked for you to carry a message. Get your ass up to his HQ on the double quick."

As Arky ran up the hillside, he was pumped with adrenaline from Danny's discovery of Rufus Jongler and the cor anglais. But it didn't wash away the bile of Danny's moronic choices and the resentment of having to play messenger boy for a few more hours before they escaped.

The old camp on the hill looked like a ghost town. The company streets were empty. The only thing left, besides piles of refuse, were row after row of what looked like log pens after the canvas tents that had capped them had been struck, and the regiments had moved down to the river. The one remaining tent, rising from the loneliness like a white elephant, was Gibbon's field headquarters.

As Arky approached the tent, the two chairs sitting out front were empty. There were several saddled horses hitched to a rail. He heard voices coming from inside the tent. They were interrupted by someone shouting. "How the hell can I know a damn thing if the telegraph's down and the road to Chancellorsville is so clogged with troops Hooker's couriers can't get here?" Arky recognized Gibbon's Southern drawl.

In the silence that followed, Arky announced himself outside the tent.

"Enter," a voice ordered.

Arky obeyed. Inside the tent, Gibbon stood over a table of maps. Several staff officers sat around the table, looking helpless. Standing off to the side was the barrel-chested lieutenant.

The lieutenant turned to Gibbon. "Your mounted courier is here, sir."

Arky blinked with confusion. "I'm a foot courier, sir, not a mounted."

Gibbon snatched up a pen and thrust it into an inkwell. "If you can run, you can ride." He grabbed a sheet of stationary and began writing on it.

"Actually, sir," Arky pointed out, "I can't."

Gibbon didn't look up. "In my division, there's only one soldier who says, 'I can't.'"

The lieutenant finished the maxim he'd heard a hundred times. "A dead one."

As Arky fought the temptation to say *If you put me on a horse, I* will *be a dead one*, Gibbon finished writing and thrust the sheet of paper at the lieutenant. "Get him on his way."

After grabbing the order, the lieutenant escorted Arky out of the tent, and pulled him toward a tethered horse.

"I mean it, Lieutenant," Arky pleaded. "The only horse I've ever ridden was a pony at a birthday party."

"Well, it's no party where you're going," the lieutenant said. "You're riding to Hooker's headquarters in Chancellorsville. Gibbon wants to know the major general's intentions for his two brigades." Reaching the horse, the lieutenant stuck the sheet of paper between his teeth, lifted Arky and swung him into the saddle.

Arky clutched the saddle horn. "I don't know how to get there."

The lieutenant plucked the paper from his mouth and folded it. "Follow the stream of troops heading upriver and crossing at US Ford, then ride west to Chancellorsville." He thrust the folded paper at Arky. "If anyone tries to stop you, show 'em this."

Before Arky could protest, the lieutenant whacked the horse on the rump; it took off like a shot. Arky clung to the horn with one hand, crumbling the folded paper against it. With his free hand, he grabbed at the bouncing reins and struggled to stay on.

41

White Ball

When Arky's horse reached the camp perimeter and the trio of sentries posted there, the only thing Arky had accomplished, besides not getting thrown off, was getting a hand on the reins. Not that whatever he did with them slowed the horse. As it galloped toward the guards, with Arky flopping in the saddle like a rag doll, the guards yelled at him to stop. When he didn't, they raised their rifles and shouted, "What's the password?"

Arky screamed, "I don't know how to ride!"

As the runaway horse barreled past them, the soldiers doubled over in laughter. One of them yelled after Arky. "That's not the password, but we believe ya just the same!"

By the time Arky reached the stream of troops marching north, the horse had slowed to a trot. While Arky joggled up and down, he managed to get his feet in the stirrup, and get some weight off his sore butt. It also gave him the chance to finally open the folded sheet of paper, and read Gibbon's order. "Free passage to whomever holds this. Gen. John Gibbon."

As soon as he read it, Arky's pain vanished. The forced trip to Chancellorsville had delivered a prize and a new plan. After he crossed the river, delivered Gibbon's request for orders to Hooker, collected the response, and delivered it back to Gibbon, Arky and Danny wouldn't need to wait till night to bribe their way to safety with a baseball. They had "free passage" anywhere, allowing them to find Rufus Jongler, and go home!

Anticipating their escape muted the laughter and jests thrown at him as he rode past the marching soldiers. Arky looked more drunk in the saddle than any mounted courier they'd ever seen.

Riverbank, Sunset

Cambell and Dabney combed through the dog tents of the 34th New York and quietly informed all the Herkimer ballplayers to make their way to a group of trees hugging the riverbank.

Dabney found Danny, who had begun to worry about Arky. His courier duties didn't usually take him away from camp for so long. When Danny asked Dabney what the secret meeting was about, he wouldn't say; Dabney had been sworn to silence. Danny agreed to go, but only if Dabney stayed by their tent and fetched Danny if Arky returned.

Gathered under the trees, Cambell told the Herkimers that the extra baseball game he had mentioned during their victory dinner was on. When he announced that the "Blue an' Gray Championship" would pit the Yankees' best nine against the rebels' best nine and would be played on the other side of the river after midnight under the brilliance of the full moon, it was met with stunned silence.

Danny was as shocked as anyone. As the wild notion sunk in, the Herkimers erupted with exclamations and questions. They thought Cambell was a lunatic, and the game was a suicide mission.

Some had more practical concerns. "How'd you arrange the time and place?"

Cambell had a ready answer. "Captain Jacko an' I had a meeting. All we had ta do was count on generals Lee an' Hooker ta keep the fightin' somewhere else."

"Even when the moon's full, it ain't no sun," another player pointed out. "How we gonna play baseball in the dark of night?"

Cambell reached into his jacket pocket and pulled up a baseball. It was unlike any ball the men had ever seen. It was *white*. He held up the ball. "With the bright moon hittin' it," Cambell said, "it'll be as easy as seein' a firefly."

Danny flashed on Rufus Jongler telling him about his vision of a baseball glowing like the moon.

As Cambell tucked the ball back in his pocket, Piper weighed in. "Bein' Army of the Potomac champs is plenty good for me. The only reason I'm crossin' the river is to kill rebels, not to play with 'em."

Cambell nodded. "Yer right about one thing. Bein' the best nine on this side o' the river put a polish on us. An' tamorrow, we're most likely crossin' the river an' tryin' ta take Fredericksburg again. We tried it in December an' paid a dear price, didn't we? Many o' our mates fell beside us, never ta rise from the frozen brown grass. But now we're seein' a new spring. Green grass is poppin' up, an' risin' from the graves of our brothers." He bent over and plucked a handful of willow-green grass. "An' as sure as I'm standin' here, I can hear their voices in the new grass. I hear our dead mates askin', 'What are ya fightin for?'" He held the grass close. "'The same as always,' I tell 'em. 'Ta preserve the Union.' 'But tell me this,' the voices ask again, '*why* are ya still fightin'?'"

Cambell's eyes returned to the faces of his players. "I've only got one answer for the voices in the grass. I did more than sign up ta fight the war. I signed up on the chance o' bein' a hero, o' makin' history. An' right now, the stars an' the moon have come tagether ta give us jus' that. The chance ta cross the river in the middle o' the night. Ta play a ball game against the rebels. Ta claim a victory like no other. A victory that'll become a rallying cry on the battle lines tamorrow, the next day, an' everyday till the war is done." He lifted his handful of grass, released it, and let it flutter down. "If tomorrow is our day ta die. We'll be more than voices whisperin' in the grass. We'll be heroes. We'll be legend."

The mesmerized players didn't move. The only sound was the murmur of the rapids.

"Are ya with me or no?" Cambell asked.

The players answered with a booming, "Huzzah!"

All but two.

Piper watched with contempt as the players repeated their cry. "Huzzah!"

Danny knew that as soon as Arky got back, and night fell, they'd be heading in the opposite direction of a crazy Blue and Gray Championship on the other side of the river. They'd be heading away from the battle, and home.

Danny's absorbed silence wasn't missed by Cambell.

42

Left or Right

US Ford, Dusk

Arky drew close to where the great snake of Union troops, artillery and wagons crawling upriver bent left and crossed the pontoon bridge spanning the river. Despite the falling darkness, the scene was illuminated by a huge full moon rising above the forest on the Yankee side of the river.

Having adjusted to the rhythm of riding a horse and settling into the saddle, Arky was now being spared the gibes and laughter of marching soldiers as he continued riding by them. Not that he was comfortable.

Arky's biggest fear had risen from the horizon across the river. The flashes and sounds of a new battle raged from the direction Arky would be riding after crossing the river. Unlike the soldiers he rode past, he knew what it was from his visit to the Chancellorsville Battlefield Visitor Center: General Stonewall Jackson making his surprise attack on the Union army's right flank north of Chancellorsville. Arky felt like he was about to ride into it, like one of those storm chasers driving right at a tornado.

As Arky approached the turn onto the bridge that would take him toward the raging battle, a thought hit him. If he didn't turn left, and turned right, he could desert sooner than later. He would be riding away from the battle, and if he got stopped by Yankee troops on the Union side of the river, he had his free-passage note for cover. There was only one downside. Danny was waiting for him back in camp. The only way to get him was to go to Chancellorsville and back.

A moment after Arky turned his horse toward the pontoon bridge, he heard a faint sound. He reined his horse to a stop at the foot of the bridge. He strained to hear over the clop, clatter and creak of horses pulling supply wagons across the wooden-planked bridge. He heard some kind of music. The more he heard it, the more he was certain what it was. A cor anglais. *It could be another hallucination*, he told himself.

He weighed the decision. Ride toward the roaring chaos of battle at Chancellorsville and find Hooker, or find the source of the music that would send them home?

Arky wheeled his horse, rode away from the bridge, and followed the music pulling him into the forest.

As the sounds of the marching army faded behind him, and the music grew clearer, came the biggest surprise. It wasn't *any* music being played on a cor anglais. It was the solo from Dvorak's *New World Symphony.*

Arky pulled his horse to a stop. The slow, sustained notes seemed eternal next to his pounding heart. What they signaled made his heart race. Dvorak's 9th Symphony, *From the New World*, had been written in 1893, thirty years in the future. There was only one person who could be playing it. His mother.

43

Father Daughter Dance

THE SAME MUSIC filled the attic office in the Jongler-Jinkses' house. On the computer screen, Octavia was playing the Dvorak solo.

Besides the haunting music, and the bittersweet sight of his wife playing it, Howard held the old, B/W photo of Octavia, in Victorian dress, holding the cor anglais. It was like a postcard from the past, looking out at him, telling him she would be home soon.

As the music ended, and the screen went dark, Iris stepped through the open door of the attic office. She held a tray of food.

Her father looked absently up at her. Whiskers stubbled his face. His hair pointed to every corner of the room.

"Dad," Iris insisted, "you have to eat something."

"I will," he answered as if the problem was trivial.

She put the tray on the desk. "You've been telling me that since yesterday."

"Iris, I listen to my body. If it doesn't sing for its supper"—he patted his stomach—"I don't feed it." He turned to the computer to play the video again.

"Dad—"

"However"—he raised a finger—"I'll eat something if you'll do something for me."

She blinked. "What?"

He looked up at her. "Have you answered Matt yet?"

She was taken aback. "Answered him about what?"

"Whether you're going to the prom with him or not."

Her embarrassment only grew. "How do you know about that?"

Howard laughed. "Just because my wife and children are driving me crazy, doesn't mean I'm going deaf." As he used the mouse to click the play button, he intoned, "'If music be the food of love, play on.'"

Back in her room, Iris picked up the cell phone on her desk and nervously dialed Matt's number. She nearly hit the call button before she realized she was holding Arky's phone. She whacked herself in the forehead. "I'm losing it!"

Getting her own phone, she called Matt and got his voice mail. While his outgoing message played, she imagined that at this very second, he was asking another girl to the prom. After the beep, she blurted, "Yes, yes, yes! Let's go to the prom!" The declaration left her speechless. Before she said something *really* stupid, she hung up.

44

Benders

Riverbank, Night

WITH THE BRIGHT moon rising higher in the sky, Danny began to panic. Arky had been gone for hours. He should've been back. Danny struggled not to imagine the worst. Then there was another possibility. Arky had slipped through the camp perimeter, deserted on his own, and begun the Jongler hunt early. *Maybe that's his revenge*, Danny thought, *for me falling for his greaty-great grandma. I mean, it's not like Arky's ever been into leave-no-man-behind. He's always been leave*-everyone-*behind.*

Danny tried to take a break from worrying and ate some cold beans and hardtack. Swallowing had never felt so hard. It was like he'd forgotten how.

A voice punctured his bubble. "I know that look."

Danny glanced up to find Cambell.

The sergeant gave him a sympathetic smile. "Every soldier gets it before the first time he sees the elephant: scared shiteless." He sat down. "But, in yer case Danny-boy, is it scared shiteless o' minié balls flyin' at ya, or baseballs doin' the same?"

"I'm not scared of either," Danny said, trying to sound cool, and not let anything slip about his plans. "I just don't get how the entire team's gonna sneak outta here"—he raised a hand to the cramped scene of tents and soldiers—"and cross the river without anyone noticing."

"I'll tell ya how." Cambell kept his voice low. "When I heard we're gonna throw a bridge across the river at dawn an' attack

Fredericksburg, I volunteered ta put tagether a stormin' party ta go across in the night, establish a bridgehead on the other side, an' protect the engineers layin' the bridge against snipers."

Danny put it together. "And your stormin' party are the Herkimers?"

Cambell grinned. "Right. We'll get the game in when the moon is highest, an' be on the other side ta protect the engineers 'fore anyone knows a bat was swung." He leaned in close. "An' if ya don't come along, ya know what you'll be missin'?"

Danny was tempted to say it wouldn't be his first night game, but didn't. "What?"

"Yer chance ta get yer pound o' flesh outta Jacko."

It caught Danny by surprise. He tried to cover. "I've got nuthin against Jacko."

Cambell cocked his head. "Then I guess ya don't mind a man stealin' yer girl."

The painful reminder was eclipsed by curiosity. "How do you know about that?"

"Dabney knows the servants up at the Conways," Cambell explained. "They don't miss much."

Danny realized that the sergeant probably knew everything.

Cambell let the silence stretch. "It's a fight I'd like ta see," he finally said. "You an' Jacko goin' at each other."

"It would be short," Danny scoffed. "He's missing a fist."

"Aye, but the match would be even if ya were pitchin' to 'im."

The thought rolled pictures in Danny's head: Thomas Jinks swinging wildly at every pitch—Thomas stomping away from the plate—Liza crying tears of regret. Danny tossed the fantasy aside and got back to reality. "I know why you're workin' me."

Cambell arched an eyebrow. "Oh, ya do? Why's that?"

"'Cause you don't have me, and you don't have Piper. You don't have a pitcher."

"Not true. Piper had a change o' heart. He's back in."

Piper's flip-flop from rebel slayer to ballplayer was a surprise. "Why?"

"He had a premonition he's gonna die tamorrow," Cambell explained. "He reckons he'll be remembered longer as a ballplayer who played in a legendary game, than a soldier who fell in the field."

It made Danny think about death, and if he and Arky were destined to die in their own century or the one they'd come to. "What about you, Sarge?" Danny asked. "Are you scared of dyin'?"

Cambell chuffed a laugh. "No reason ta be scared o' dyin' itself. That's comin' whether we like it or not. I'm scared o' dyin' bad. O' not dyin' in a blaze o' glory." He patted Danny on the shoulder. "I'll leave ya ta think on the game. Ya still got time."

Cambell stood and took in the dome of stars, and the moon, growing brighter the higher it rose. "Tell me this, Danny-boy. Have ya ever wondered who the first pitcher was?"

Danny shook his head at the weird question. "No."

The sergeant spread his arms. "The first great hurler was the Creator himself. An' what do ya think he throws?"

"No idea."

Cambell spread his arms to the heavens. "Nothin' but *benders*. He throws the moon 'round the earth, the planets 'round the sun, an' the solar system 'round the Milky Way." Cambell looked down at Danny with a roguish grin. "An' you, with yer bender of a pitch, you've got a touch o' the Creator in ya. I'd hate ta see what'll happen ta us without our little creator at the pitching point."

Despite the flattery, the weird talk made Danny wonder if Cambell had been drinking.

45

Reunion

WITH THE MOONLIGHT cutting through the treetops in thick shafts of light, Arky had no problem guiding his horse through the woods. But he had lost the music. All he had to go on was the direction he had heard the music coming from. He didn't understand why she had stopped playing. He stopped now and again and shouted, "Mom!"

No answer came back.

After calling into the maze of trees and moonlight several times, he began to think the music had been another hallucination.

Just as Arky was about to give up, it sounded again. *Daa-da-daaa, daa-da-daaa*—the opening notes of Dvorak's cor anglais solo.

He kicked the horse and trotted toward the sound. The music kept beckoning.

Flickering in the play of darkness and moonlight, he spotted a campfire.

He raced toward it as the music swelled to a pause. Before reaching the fire, he saw a covered wagon and a mule grazing nearby.

The intrusion of a galloping horse killed the music.

Arky reined the horse to a stop at the edge of the campsite. Churning with exhilaration and disappointment, Arky recognized the cor anglais player—the peddler, Rufus Jongler, standing by the fire.

They stared at each other until Arky blurted, "How do you know that music?"

"The same woman who taught me 'Goin' Home,'" Rufus replied, "taught me the lovely solo that inspired the song."

"My mother, Octavia Jongler!"

"Yes," Rufus said with a nod, "that's the name she gave me."

"What did you do with her?" Arky demanded.

"I presume"—he lifted the curved woodwind in his hand—"the cor anglais sent her home."

"She didn't *get* home!"

"Oh," Rufus said, surprised, "then her voyage wasn't over."

"Meaning you blew her somewhere else."

Rufus answered with a sympathetic look. "I wish I could tell you where."

His ignorance and placid acceptance infuriated Arky. "If you knew she was a Jongler, and you knew *I* was a Jongler, why the hell did you sell me and Danny to the army?"

"At the time of your arrival, I didn't know you were a Jongler, if I had—"

"You should've known!" Arky shouted.

"Perhaps," Rufus acknowledged with a shrug, "but no Jongler is perfect."

"No, you're a perfect asshole! You showed up at the baseball game on a horse, playing the cor anglais, and then you vanished. What was *that* about?"

"Hmm." Rufus cocked his head. "I don't own a horse."

Arky couldn't tell if he was lying or if it really had been a vision. It didn't matter. He was sick of useless answers. Arky pointed to the grazing mule. "You gotta get on that thing and come with me."

Rufus answered with a curious look. "Where are we going?"

"To get Danny, and you're gonna send us home."

"Now?"

"We're getting thrown into the Second Battle of Fredericksburg at dawn!" Arky yelled. "Do you wanna be the Jongler who gets remembered for killing his voyagers?"

Rufus looked aghast. "Of course not." He raised the instrument. "I can play it for you now." He wetted the reed. "Should I?"

Arky fought the temptation. After all, he didn't know if Danny had told him the truth about whether or not Rufus had been playing the cor anglais when Danny had found him, or if Danny had *asked* him to play it. But, despite Danny's train wreck of screw-ups, one thing stopped Arky. If he got home and Danny didn't, he'd never hear the end of it from Iris. She would hound him to death.

"No." Arky pointed at the mule. "Saddle that thing up. We're going to Danny."

Rufus moved to Arky on the horse and took him in with kind eyes. "Arky, I know you think I'm an ignorant old fool. But I know a thing or two"—he held up the cor anglais—"about this blessing and curse on the Jongler clan. And I promise you, when you return with Danny, I'll be waiting right here."

Arky kicked himself for not bringing a weapon. He could have force-marched Rufus back to the Union camp. He glared at him. "Why should I trust you?"

Rufus's whiskers bent with a smile. "We're family, Arky. If you can't trust family, whom can you trust?"

Arky resented the cliché from a man who'd withheld his identity for so long. But it's not like you can pick and choose your ancestors, especially when he's the one holding your ticket home. "I'll be back in less than an hour with Danny," Arky declared. "Put more wood on that fire so we can find you."

He turned his horse, prodded it, and trotted back toward the river and the road leading back to Falmouth.

46

Into the Fog

Riverbank, Midnight

THE BRIGHT MOON illuminated tendrils of mist rising off the river and weaving a blanket of fog over the Rappahannock. From the western hills came the sputter of musketry and rumble of cannons. Light flashes preceded streaks of molten fire from burning shells arcing above the horizon. Chancellorsville was still hurling the sparks of war.

Danny was sick with worry. He had moved among the men of the 34th New York and asked if they'd seen or heard anything about Arky. None of them had seen him since sunset, when he'd been sent on courier duty. Even Talcott was concerned and told Danny it wouldn't be the first time a soldier had deserted without telling his best friend. It tightened the growing knot in Danny's stomach. *Maybe his courier duties had put him in the sights of a rebel sniper,* or *he'd been swept into the battle across the river.*

Fighting his worst-case fears, Danny tried to will Arky's appearance from the moonlit sprawl of men catching their last sleep before battle. If Arky appeared, everything would be easy. They'd desert together, find Rufus Jongler, have him play the cor anglais, and their long and bizarre dream would be over.

To avoid his darkest fears, Danny reached into his pocket, and pulled out their ticket past the Union perimeter: the championship ball bannering their victory and signed by the Herkimers. As he turned the ball in his hand, his name appeared in the moonlight. Seeing his signature in white ink reminded him of those eight balls you ask a question of, turn, and the ball floats up an answer.

Staring at his name, Danny Bender, released a tumble of thoughts. *What if the game's really played? What if Cambell's right, and the Blue and Gray Championship becomes a legend in the history of baseball? But if the game does make it into the history books, it'll have an asterisk. "The only Herkimer who didn't play, Danny Bender, deserted the same night."*

Danny silenced the nagging thoughts by reviewing his options. *Wait for Arky. If he doesn't come, there's three choices. Desert without him, or cross the bridge in the morning and fight, or be a ballplayer first and then join the fight.*

The rattle of armed soldiers moving through camp pulled Danny's eyes up. He saw a small group, carrying rifles, heading upriver. Danny stood to get a better look.

The Herkimers, with Cambell in the lead, stopped and looked at Danny. They silently waited for him to join them.

Danny spotted Piper in the group. He would be the one pitching to the Alabama Brawlers, to Thomas Jinks.

Cambell called to him. "What's it gonna be, Danny-boy? Do we have our bender or not?"

Danny looked to the rising hillside—where Arky should have appeared hours ago. Nothing moved in the pearly moonlight.

He turned back to the Herkimers. They waited for an answer. The vision of an asterisk next to his name in the record book of history, and baseball, was the only sign he needed. He pushed the dark baseball into his pocket, turned, and grabbed his rifle.

Cambell led the dozen Herkimers up the riverbank past Falmouth. Just above the small town, a wooded island split the river. It would hide the first half of their crossing. After the island, the thickening fog would provide the cover they needed to reach the rebel shore.

They waded across the narrow channel toward the island.

Piper was the last to wade in. He gradually slowed to separate himself from the others. Silently, he watched the other Herkimers wade to the island and then step into its thick woods. When they could no longer be seen, or turn back and see him, Piper turned, and waded back to the Union shore.

Having picked their way across the island, the Herkimers reached the other side of it. They hung back in the trees and took in the scene. The fight near Chancellorsville had fizzled out. Silence had returned; the fireworks of battle had been replaced by the flicker of campfires from General's Wilcox's brigade up in the hills.

The fog shrouding the river and the opposite bank exceeded Cambell's expectations. It was so thick, the brilliant moon gilded it with a silver skin.

Cambell whispered an order for silence. It was the rebel pickets, with their midnight chatter, who would give away *their* positions on the other side, not the silent, stealthy Yankees. The sergeant led the Herkimers into the shallow water.

Following, Danny slowly shuffled through the water to keep the sound of his steps masked by the chatter of the rapids. What he couldn't quiet were his nerves. They felt like power lines humming through him. What emerged from the curling fog made them *buzz*. Wraithlike rebels seemed to loom out of the swirling mist, making Danny's thumb dance on his rifle musket from stock to hammer, then back again, stock to hammer. The only thing stopping him from yanking the hammer back and firing at one of the fleeting ghosts was the stone silence of his fellow soldiers.

47

Betrayal

IN THE LAST stretch to Falmouth, Arky kept trying to kick the horse into a run. It refused and would only canter.

Approaching the sentries guarding the road into camp, he heard them yell as they raised their rifles, "What's the password?"

Arky hoped the guards hadn't changed. "The same as before, 'I don't know how to ride'!"

The soldiers whooped with recognition and delight as Arky rode past them. One shouted after him, "It's a lie! Yer lookin' like a trooper!"

Riding through Falmouth, Arky rehearsed the plan in his mind: collect Danny, use the excuse of delivering Hooker's "message" to Gibbon's HQ to get them a ways up the hill before veering off to White Oak Road, use Danny's championship baseball and/or Arky's free-passage note to get them past the guards, then use the roads Arky knew from his courier runs to get them back to the forest upriver and Rufus Jongler.

Arriving in the river camp, Arky was surprised to find the dog tents struck and several thousand troops assembled. Their bayonets glistened in the moonlight like a field of silver wheat. The irony didn't escape him. A harvest was coming all right, of death.

When he found the 34th New York, Arky's foreboding vanished the moment he swung from the saddle and hit the ground. In all his years of cross-country running, he had never felt anything like the pain that seared his legs and butt. He felt like he was carrying a medicine ball of barbwire between his legs.

He sucked it up and moved among the soldiers, looking for Danny. The men either dozed or watched the engineers assembling the long pontoon boats that would, one by one, stretch a bridge across the water for them to cross at dawn.

His search for Danny took a turn when he found Piper and asked him if he'd seen Danny. Piper told him that Cambell and the rest of the Herkimer ballplayers had already crossed the river as a forward skirmishing party.

"Danny couldn't have gone with him," Arky declared as the hair prickled on his neck.

"He did," Piper said. "I saw it with my own eyes. It wasn't enough for 'em to take the army championship, they wanna take Freddy'sburg too."

Arky was stunned. He didn't believe it; he didn't believe Piper. The corporal had carried a grudge against him and Danny ever since their first night at mess and had hated Danny ever since Danny had taken away his pitching duties. Arky checked with another soldier. The soldier confirmed it: Danny had left with the Herkimer players.

Something inside Arky snapped. He had done everything in his power to help Danny. All he'd gotten were lies and betrayal. No excuse—a broken heart, or the insane delusion of Danny thinking he could "make a life" in 1863—made sense of Danny going on the suicide mission of playing baseball with a bunch of rebels.

Surprisingly, the rage Arky expected to consume him didn't. He only felt cold calculation. Danny had made his choice. It made Arky's simple.

A few moments later, Arky was back on his horse to supposedly return it to Gibbon and deliver whatever message he'd gotten from General Hooker. As soon as Arky was halfway up the hill, he turned toward Falmouth. With his free-passage note, he would soon be on his way back to Rufus Jongler.

Down in camp, as Piper still gloated over the shock he'd given Arky, the quiet was broken by galloping horses. Soldiers turned to see what the fracas was.

In the moonlight, a dozen cavalry troopers charged into the clearing between the thick ranks of soldiers on the riverbank and the hill rising toward the abandoned camp. The troopers reined their horses to a stop. At the forefront was General Barlow, identifiable by the brightly checkered shirt under his open jacket. He barked an order for the 34th New York's commanding officer to step forward.

The regiment's commander made his way through the gauntlet of soldiers and identified himself as Colonel Laflin. Barlow ordered Laflin to assemble the New York Herkimers baseball team.

Laflin explained that the players had volunteered to cross the river as forward skirmishers to protect the engineers throwing the bridge.

"They're not protecting anything!" Barlow shouted. "It was a ruse to play a baseball game!"

Laflin held back a smile at the absurdity of the claim. "Baseball in the middle of the night? If you ask me, General, it sounds unnatural."

Laughter erupted from the troops.

"Silence!" Barlow bellowed. When they obeyed, he barked, "It's more than unnatural, it's treason!" The red-faced general yanked a letter from his coat. "Thanks to one decent soldier in your lot, it's been exposed!"

Piper enjoyed a sneering smile at the sight of the letter he'd sent Barlow as soon as he'd learned about Cambell's wild scheme of a Blue and Gray Championship.

A figure on a horse, coming down the hill, weighed in over the murmur that passed through the regiment. "That sounds like the excitable voice of my good friend, General Barlow." The speaker was General Gibbon.

Barlow whipped his horse around to Gibbon, still ambling down the hill. "Did you hear what I said?"

"I did," Gibbon replied, "along with the rebels on the other side." He garnered a laugh as he approached Barlow, whose face had darkened with rage. "Now, General," Gibbon continued, "I appreciate your concern for the loyalty of my men, but shouldn't you be more concerned with the condition of your own men of the Eleventh Corps, especially given their collapse this afternoon and their humiliation by Stonewall Jackson?" As Barlow turned purple, Gibbon didn't wait for an answer. "Now take your cowboys and leave my soldiers to rest. Come sunrise, we've got a war to fight."

Gibbon turned his horse and started back up the hill.

The soldiers waited breathlessly to see if Barlow would draw his revolver and shoot Gibbon in the back. The fear dissipated as Barlow reined his horse and conferred with his troopers. The watching soldiers relaxed and mumbled their approval of Barlow's comeuppance.

With the incident over, Piper slipped over to Barlow and his troopers. He shared something quickly and quietly with the hotheaded general.

It made Barlow stiffen in his saddle. His face hardened with renewed resolve. He hurled a last blast at the soldiers. "Those who desert their duty to fraternize with the enemy can't escape justice!" He wheeled his horse and spurred it into a gallop upriver. His troopers thundered after him.

48

Engaging the Enemy

Floodplain, Rebel Side of the River

HAVING EMERGED FROM the fog blanketing the river, Cambell and the Herkimers moved silently through a honeycomb of mist and moonlight.

Danny couldn't believe they hadn't heard or run into any rebel pickets. They either weren't there or were waiting in ambush. Glancing to his left, he spotted shapes in a patch of fog. As the misty screen thinned, the shapes filled in. A group of rebel soldiers, rifles stacked, waiting in a silent tableau.

At first, Danny thought it was another phantom image conjured by the fog and his adrenaline-jacked body. But the vision didn't dissipate; it grew more distinct. He quick-checked the Herkimers to his right. Their eyes were front, blind to the threat. He slowly got down, flat on the ground, and positioned his rifle. He pulled the hammer to full cock. It clicked.

The nearest Herkimer, Cambell, snapped to the sound, and the sight of the rebels. At the same instant, one of the rebels turned and saw the Yankee on the ground, ready to fire. The rebel shouted an alarm; they lunged for their stacked weapons.

Cambell sprang forward, stomping on Danny's rifle barrel as a shot rang out. The ground spit a burst of dirt. Cambell thrust his rifle aloft. "Hold fire!"

With the Herkimers training their weapons on the rebels, and the rebels shouldering rifles to do the same, one of the rebels shouted the same. "Hold fire!"

Danny recognized him. It was Jacko, Thomas Jinks, captain of the Alabama Brawlers. Strangely, he was wearing a rebel uniform.

"Are you here to play ball," Thomas demanded angrily, "or start a bloodbath?"

"Recover," Cambell ordered, and the Herkimers lowered their weapons. "My apologies, Jacko. My hurler"—he gave Danny a kick—"is all jubus."

Danny got to his feet. "I thought—"

"Don't think," Cambell scolded. "Yer here ta pitch." He looked back to Thomas. "Where are we?"

Thomas's expression relaxed and he spread his arms. "Where scouts should be, in the outfield."

As the Herkimers and Brawlers moved through the meadow, whatever worries they'd had about the fog obscuring play dissipated along with the vanishing mists. The only sign the broad meadow had been a bowl of fog an hour earlier was the dew on the grassy field. The green expanse shone in the light of the full moon at its zenith. The Brawlers had already laid out the infield with makeshift bases and a home plate.

Cambell finally commented on Thomas's rebel uniform. "General Lee must be desperate if he's now takin' one-handed men."

Thomas came right back. "Lee's not desperate for anything after cuttin' off Hooker's right flank." The Brawlers enjoyed a laugh over the collapse of the Yankees' right wing just hours before at Chancellorsville before Thomas explained, "I joined up to push you spoilers outta the river valley and stop my girl on the other side from throwin' you Billy Yanks anymore fancy parties."

Cambell laughed. "Ya heard about that, did ya?"

Thomas threw Danny a look. "I don't miss much."

The insinuation, and the unwanted reminder of Liza, made Danny want to say how Thomas would also not miss a bullet or piece of shrapnel to the head before the war was over. But Danny checked himself. He was saving his revenge for the game.

Before the bat toss, the Herkimers finally noticed Piper was missing. Cambell took it in stride. "It's not a game for cowards," he said, then assigned one of the reserves to Piper's position in right field.

The Brawlers agreed to play by the rules Cambell proposed: overhand pitching and no plugging. Thomas won the bat toss; he picked the Brawlers to bat first. If the game was suddenly called because of war, it might give them the extra at bat.

"Get out there," Cambell said to Danny as he handed him the white ball. "An' show 'em yer best stuff. It's time ta treat 'em ta the bender."

As the game began, Cambell's prediction proved true. The white ball caught the moonlight like a mini comet. No one was more awed by it than Danny. It's what Rufus Jongler had seen in his vision.

Danny started by throwing good stuff, mixing up his speeds and location, and throwing sinkers, sliders and changeups that his teammates all called "benders." But the first three innings delivered just as many surprises.

Between practice and the games Danny had played in 1863, he'd gotten used to lots of errors because of the wild bounces the ball took on the rough fields. Playing by moonlight should have forced more errors, but it was the opposite. The moonlight was so bright it seemed to wrap the white ball in an aura of light. The eerie luminescence seemed to tighten the fielders' focus and improve their defensive play.

The second surprise came from off the field. After the *crack* of ball-on-bat penetrated a nearby woodland, figures began to appear from the trees. They were men, women and children coming from their slave quarters on a nearby plantation. Watching from a safe distance, the slaves stood like silent specters taking in the bizarre sight of rebels and Yankees, sworn enemies in the fight over their enslavement, playing a boy's game in the moonlight.

The last surprise was neither awe inspiring or eerie. It annoyed Danny. For baseball players who'd never seen the kind of speed and movement he put on the ball, the Brawlers were getting a little bit of wood on his pitches. They were pop-ups and weak grounds, but they were still making contact.

In the top of the 4th inning, with the Herkimers holding a 5–0 lead, he found out why. The Brawlers got a man on base with a bloop single, bringing Thomas to bat. In his first at bat, Danny had enjoyed the satisfaction of striking Thomas out on a sinker that left him clueless. But this time, with his one-armed swing, Thomas sliced a shot to right field. By the time the right fielder ran it down, and threw it in, Thomas had driven in the Brawlers' first run, and had a stand-up triple.

Thomas grinned at Danny from third base. "Liza told me about your pitchin'," he said. "We've been practicin' up for it."

Danny flushed with anger. Not only had she stabbed him in the heart, she'd betrayed him. It made him wish they were playing the plugging rule. If he got the chance, when Thomas tried to run home, he could drill him with a rocket.

Seeing Danny's reaction, Cambell weighed in from his position at third. "No worries, Danny-boy, we'll answer with our bats."

49

Going Solo

WHILE ARKY HAD easily gotten past the guards at the camp perimeter, finding Rufus Jongler's campsite in the forest again proved more troublesome.

Between the moon guiding his way and finally spotting the campfire, Arky rode into the site. Rufus sat on a barrel by the fire but no longer had the cor anglais. Arky dismounted.

Rufus ignored the funny way he walked. "Where's Danny?"

"He's not coming," Arky answered bluntly.

"What happened?"

"He'd rather play baseball than go home."

Rufus only responded, "Hmm," then said, "so you want to go alone."

"No, I wanted to go home with Danny," Arky corrected. "But I've lost him to 1863. Get the cor anglais, and let's do this."

Rufus nodded. "Sure." He fetched the cor anglais, still assembled, from his wagon, brought it back to the fire, and sat on his barrel. "I've been thinking a lot about your mother."

Arky frowned at the random thought. "What about her?"

"That she didn't make it home."

"We know that," Arky said impatiently. "What are you saying?"

"What if the cor anglais sends you chasing after her?"

The thought had never occurred to Arky. He brushed it off. "Whatever. It'd be better than getting killed here."

"True," Rufus acknowledged, then wet the reed with his lips. "As per your request, 'Goin' Home.'" He began the yearning Dvorak solo. *Daa-da-daaa, daa-da-daaa...*

Arky listened, watched, and waited.

When Rufus felt the keys begin to feel light and his fingertips follow the awakening pressure from the keys, he threw Arky a wink.

Arky heard the music begin to change from the melody he'd heard his mother and Iris play dozens of times. Hearing the shift, knowing the cor anglais was coming to life, filled Arky with nervous anticipation.

As the music grew more frenetic, and the cor anglais took full possession of Rufus, the first strand of mist snaked from the instrument's bell.

Arky greeted it with a tight smile. He didn't move as the white diaphanous serpent coiled around him.

50

Horizon Event

IRIS HAD GOTTEN out of her car with her oboe case, and was headed to the school's media center for orchestra rehearsal, when she got a text. It was from Matt. It was his answer to her "Yes, yes, yes!" phone message. "GOOD, GOOD, GOOD!" he had texted in all caps. Iris thrust her phone in the air and shouted, "Ha!"

Minutes later, she was playing her oboe with the orchestra as they rehearsed the third movement of Brahms's *Symphony No. 1.* The music teacher had already stopped the rehearsal twice in the movement's trio section because Iris was off on the entrance to her oboe solo. Starting into the lead-in to the solo again, Iris finally chased away all her Matt-distractions and nailed her entrance.

As she played, and the orchestra answered her phrases, the scene in front of her—the music teacher conducting the orchestra—started to bubble and distort like something you see in old movies: the hot bulb in a film projector melting the film.

Iris fought the urge to panic. She knew it was a synesthesia vision, but she dreaded any vision in rehearsal or performance. She feared it would turn so bizarre and intense that she'd forget it was a vision and do something crazy like jump up and run out of the room like a total nutjob.

As she played on, the bubbling white consumed the room. Iris calmed herself with the hope that it would turn into a vision of Matt. Instead, the field of white softened, became blurry. It wasn't liquid anymore, it was mist. As soon as she realized it, the twisting mists condensed into a cocoonlike egg. Recognition dawned. It was one of the misty cocoons created by the cor anglais.

She yanked her oboe away, jumped up, and ran out of the media center.

Driving home, all Iris could think of was how it had been the most clear and literal horizon event she'd ever seen. She was certain that someone—Danny, Arky, their mother—was in that misty pod and coming back from the past.

When she got home, Iris raced through all the rooms, including the attic office, looking for who might have come home. No one was there, not even her father. She called him on her cell.

Howard answered. "Hey, Iris, what's up?"

Compared to the last time she'd seen him—binge-watching the video of Octavia like a zombie—he sounded too chipper. "Where are you?" she asked.

He told her he'd had an inspiration and was at Bender Excavation. He was helping Ray pour the last concrete slab in the new wheelchair access ramp to the office. Iris could hear Mr. Bender in the background. "I also told Ray that we heard from the boys on their fishing trip," Howard added.

"You didn't!" Iris blurted.

"Yep," Howard announced. "And that they're on their way home."

"Dad, stop!" Iris shouted, then lowered her voice in case Mr. Bender was close enough to hear her on the phone. "You gotta come home, now."

"Sure," Howard said. "Soon as we finish the ramp."

Iris heard the line go dead.

"Shit!"

She stood there, frozen, unsure if she should call a crisis hotline and have her dad taken away in a straitjacket, or if she should assemble the cor anglais and be ready and able to bury Danny's memory of the past if he was the one coming home first.

51

Delay of Game

ARKY CAME TO. He was lying on his back. The last thing he remembered was the high wild note of the cor anglais and the blinding flash of light.

He blinked his new surroundings into focus. A brilliant full moon shone down at him.

He jumped up. He was in the woods. His head snapped right and left, looking for anything to signal twenty-first century and Belleplain.

A distant *crack* grabbed his attention. He ran toward the sound. Reaching the edge of the woods and the field beyond, he saw a sight that stopped him dead. Soldiers—Yankees and rebels—playing baseball.

He was staggered by what Rufus and the damned cor anglais had done. The only space and time he'd been launched across was the Rappahannock River to the insane ball game being played in the shadow of war.

Arky blew an f-bomb.

Compounding his torment was the action on the moon-washed field. The Yankee pitcher wound up and released a submarine pitch. It was Danny. Just as jarring was the batter who swung at it. He swung with one arm, missing the pitch. Thomas Jinks.

"Strike one!" several Herkimers in the field cried.

Arky started from the woods and into left field. There was only way he could make sense of him being there; the cor anglais was torturing him for trying to leave Danny behind. One couldn't leave without the other. Time travel had turned him and Danny into Siamese twins.

Danny delivered another pitch. Again, Thomas slashed at it and missed.

"Strike two!" echoed across the field.

A haunting feeling suddenly stopped Arky in his tracks. It was déjà vu. He'd been there before, in this meadow, but it had been different. The epiphany came in a flash. It was the meadow his father had taken him to after the battle reenactment on Marye's Heights. But where there had been small houses, there were now trees. It was the same meadow where there had been a predawn skirmish on May 3 killing all the soldiers but one—Thomas Jinks, left for dead with a terrible head wound.

The premonition of the massacre fired Arky's legs. He sprinted forward.

The rebel soldier waiting to bat after Thomas was the first to see the Yankee soldier racing toward them. He dropped his bat, grabbed a stacked rifle, and sounded the alarm. "Yankee comin'!"

Other Brawlers grabbed rifles, shouldered them, and waited for more soldiers to rush from the woods behind the Yankee leading the charge.

Having turned to the threat, Cambell was the first to recognize Arky. "Hold fire!" he shouted as he quickly moved between Arky and the rebels about to release a hail of bullets. "It's our ball boy!"

Seeing the intruder was unarmed and leading no charge, the Brawlers lowered their weapons.

Arky dodged past Cambell to Danny. "We gotta go, now!" he shouted.

Danny gaped at him in disbelief. "Where the hell have you been?"

"Tryin' to get us outta here! We gotta go!"

Danny waved a hand at Thomas, still in the batter's box. "I'm about to strike him out."

"This place is gonna turn into a slaughter!" Arky yelled.

"Yeah," Danny concurred, "after I take down Jacko and we double our score."

Two reserves for the Herkimers grabbed Arky and started hauling him off the field. "C'mon, ball boy," one said, "time for you to get on duty."

"Danny!" Arky implored. "I don't know how, but it's comin'! It's a death trap!"

"Shut that lunatic up," Cambell ordered.

Arky kept shouting as one of the reserves wrenched his arms behind his back. "Remember my dad's story about Thomas!" were the last words Arky got out before the other reserve split Arky's mouth with a gag, garbling his protests.

"Take it easy on 'im," Danny told the reserves. "He's harmless." Arky's last outburst stuck in Danny's mind. He remembered the daguerreotype of Thomas Jinks—the gouge of a scar on his head—that he'd survived a bloody skirmish.

Cambell's voice broke through. "C'mon, Danny-boy. Finish Jacko so we can get ta the ninth, an' end this thing."

Danny turned back to Thomas, waiting at the plate. Danny told himself, *One more strike, finish Thomas, then I'll talk to Arky.*

Striking Thomas out would also put Danny on top in their grudge match, which, so far, was even. In the six times they'd faced each other, Danny had two strikeouts and a groundout to his credit. Thomas had a triple, a single, and a home run that he'd gotten away with because the centerfielder couldn't find the ball in the weeds. Their personal score was tighter than the game score. The Herkimers held a three-run lead, 10–7, with the 9th inning one out away.

With a two-strike cushion, Danny felt a sensation he'd been waiting on for the entire game: the serene calm of his déjà vu ball—to see the pitch in his mind's eye and throw exactly what he saw.

Danny saw his pitch—heat, inside, to jam Thomas—and threw it.

Thomas backed away, not falling for it.

Danny saw another pitch—slider, down and away to make him reach—and hurled it.

Again, Thomas didn't swing.

"C'mon, Bender," Cambell urged. "Put 'im away."

Danny checked Thomas and fingered the ball across the seams for a fastball.

Something made him glance toward Arky beyond the third-base line. He was still being held by the two reserves; his eyes were wide with fear. Then Danny noticed a strange movement. Beyond them was a small group of slaves. They were doing the oddest thing. They were slowly backing away, as if they wanted to disappear, unnoticed, into the trees.

It sent a ripple through Danny's calm. He blinked it away, returned his gaze to Thomas, and waited for the next pitch to roll in his mind's eye.

His focus was broken by Arky's strangled voice protesting through his gag. Danny's eyes slid to Arky just as Arky wrenched one of his arms free and desperately pointed to the rim of hills protecting the meadow like a distant backstop.

Danny looked to where he was pointing.

On the brow of the hill, lit by the moon, was the silhouette of men on horseback, about a dozen.

Following Arky's and Danny's lead, the other Herkimers lifted their eyes to the ridge. The Brawlers turned, including Thomas.

In a silence that seemingly stretched forever, they all understood. Their game had been discovered. By rebels or Yankees it didn't matter. It didn't look like the silhouetted troopers had come to watch.

An image spun in front of Danny like a whirling ghost. A fastball rising high and inside—Rafael Santiero taking the shot to the temple.

Danny quick-checked Arky again. With his captors frozen by the troopers, Arky wrestled with the gag in his mouth. Danny knew exactly what he was thinking because he was thinking the same. He wasn't there for a baseball game. He wasn't there to take his revenge on Thomas Jinks. He was there to *save* him.

Arky jerked the gag away. "Throw it!"

Danny bent into his windup, powered through, and released as he shouted, "Thomas!"

Turning to the sound, Thomas's forehead met the rising fastball. He dropped in a heap.

The lead rider on the hill raised his saber and bellowed, "Charge!" The troopers bolted down the hill. Their drawn sabers shimmered in the moonlight, along with the checkered shirt of General Barlow leading the assault.

Danny was frozen by the sight of Thomas's limp form on the ground. He felt the same nausea he'd felt when he'd hit Rafael. Someone grabbed his arm. It was Arky.

"Run!" Arky screamed, as they both turned and sprinted toward the river.

Yankees and rebels alike scrambled for rifles. It was too late. Barlow and his troopers rushed into them and began their butchery, not caring whether they were rebel or Yankee. They were all traitors.

As the moon dropped toward the western hills and first light began to gray the sky, Arky and Danny reached the riverbank. They stopped at a row of trees cresting the bank and struggled for breath. Wincing from the burning in their lungs, they heard a sound. Their eyes shot to it.

A man was struggling toward them, staggering and weaving from his bloody wounds. As he stumbled forward, they recognized him.

"Sarge!" Danny yelled. He lunged forward to help Cambell.

Cambell accepted the help with a bloody grin. "Not ta worry, lads. Nothin' a good whiskey won't mend."

Danny ignored his bravado. "We gotta get you across before you bleed out."

Cambell's eyes shifted to the babble of the river and its sheen in the dawn light. "Aye, but it's lookin' more like an ocean ta me."

A new sound came across the floodplain: pounding hooves.

Cambell pushed away from Danny and fell against a tree. "Get down below the riverbank, an' don't come out till the world is silent."

Danny moved to help him. "Go!" Cambell ordered as he reached behind his back, pulled up a sidearm, and mustered a cocksure look. "They don't stand a chance."

Arky grabbed Danny and pulled him below the crest of the riverbank. They found an undercut, like a curling wave, that provided a hollow to hide them.

As the galloping hooves rumbled closer, Danny started to rise. "I gotta help 'im."

"No!" Arky grabbed Danny and pulled him down. "You did what you came here to do!"

Between the riffle of the river and the thunder of horses, a new sound arose: a harmonica playing "Yankee Doodle."

Danny's face twisted. "He tricked me!"

"Shut up!" Arky beseeched as the sound of the horses approached and pulled up.

The harmonica stopped, replaced by Cambell's voice. "Sergeant George Cambell, o' the Thirty-Fourth New York, at yer service, sir. On this bonny mornin', I had every intention o' reportin' the first Union victory o' the day, if ya spoilers hadn't jumped in—"

The *slash* of steel on flesh silenced him.

Arky slapped his hand over Danny's gasping mouth.

The horses thundered away.

52

Jongler's Playlist

DAWN DELIVERED THE thump of cannons and the renewed battle at Chancellorsville. The crackle of muskets downriver signaled that the attack on Fredericksburg had begun.

Arky and Danny stumbled through shallow rapids toward the opposite bank. Arky knew they weren't out of danger. There was still a chance Barlow might spot them if he and his troopers crossed back over the river. It wasn't the only fear clutching Arky's chest. *Was Thomas Jinks still alive?* The only way to know was to get back to their hometime. If Thomas, with his bloody head wound, had *not* been left for dead by Barlow's men—the way history was supposed to unfold—and he was dead, Arky and Danny might start for home, but only Danny would make it. The ray of hope that history was still on track was Cambell's death on the riverbank. Arky now understood the truth behind something his father had told him. The burial cross that had been placed by the river, with a harmonica nailed to it, marked the grave of George Cambell.

While Arky was trying to keep his head, Danny had lost part of his heart. He was devastated by Cambell's death. He couldn't escape the image of the sergeant's contorted body lying face down in the grass, with the revolver stuck under the back of his belt—the revolver he had never intended to use. As Danny slipped and staggered through the rapids, there was only one consolation to cling to. Cambell's last action was the ultimate act of a soldier—not to kill, but to save and sacrifice.

The boys scrambled out of the water and onto the riverbank. Arky led Danny through the woods, still harboring patches of mist, with the hope of finding Rufus's campsite. They soon spotted a road through the trees.

Reaching it, Arky assumed it was the same road he'd ridden upriver the night before to the pontoon bridge. In the dim light, his belief was confirmed by the trampled dirt from thousands of troops that had marched over it, the wagon ruts, and the trail of clothing and gear soldiers had tossed aside to lighten their loads.

Hearing the thunder of hooves, they shrank back into the woods.

A squadron of Union cavalry galloped by, heading upriver to cross over it, and join the battle at Chancellorsville.

The boys waited for silence before reemerging from the brush. With sunrise brightening the treetops, Arky tried to orient himself. He was fairly certain Rufus's camp was further upriver and deeper in the woods. Another sound broke the silence.

Around a wooded corner, from the direction the troopers had gone, came the rattle of a wagon and a voice singing: "Goin' home, goin' home, I'm a goin' home."

Danny started to dart for cover, but Arky stopped him. "It's him."

The singing continued, "Quietlike, some still day, I'm jes' goin' home." The canvas-covered wagon appeared, pulled by a mule. Rufus Jongler drove it, singing on.

Mother's there 'spectin' me,
Father's waitin' too;
Lots o' folks gather'd there,
All the friends I knew.

Arky wondered if the lyrics were literally true.

It's not far, jes' close by,
Through an open door;
Work all done, care laid by,
Goin' to fear no more.

Reaching them, Rufus reined his mule to a stop, and greeted them with a smile. "Good to see you two together again."

Arky was in no mood for pleasantries. "We've been through hell!"

Rufus waggled his head. "Some say hell is of our own making."

"Then my sister's the devil," Arky snapped. "She sent us here, and now you gotta send us back, all the way back, or do you have some other torture planned?"

Rufus's eyes shifted to Danny. "Who won the ball game, Yanks or Rebs?"

While Arky was thrown by Rufus's knowledge of the game, Danny showed nothing. "Everyone lost," he answered.

"Prophetic," Rufus said with a nod.

His stalling riled Arky. "How 'bout you skip the woo-woo bullshit and get out the cor anglais?"

"All right," Rufus agreed. "But I can't let you go without extending my congratulations."

"For what?" Arky demanded. "Surviving?"

Ignoring Arky, Rufus studied Danny's steely expression and his stillness. He turned back to Arky. "Your time voyager resembles a young man altered by his journey."

"He's not *my* time voyager," Arky protested. "He's yours."

"When you're a Jongler," Rufus replied, "it's all in the family."

Before Arky could retort, Rufus shot up a hand and craned to hear something.

Arky and Danny heard nothing but morning birdsong.

Rufus ordered them into the wagon. Hearing the urgency in his voice, they climbed into the back of the covered wagon. Rufus reined his mule, pulling the wagon to the side of the road. Reaching under his seat, he pulled out a familiar wooden music case.

Inside the wagon, Arky noticed the crates of Jongler's Rejuva-Nation. At the front of the wagon, he was glad to see Rufus assembling the cor anglais. Arky sat on one of the crates and turned back to Danny, doing the same. "Here we go."

Danny didn't respond. He was still being buffeted by a hurricane of feelings and thoughts. As much as he wanted to go home, he felt like he was deserting another.

Arky suddenly remembered the note in his pocket: the free-passage note from General Gibbon. He pulled it out and looked at it. Despite thinking a signed order by a Union general was the best gift he could ever give his father, it wasn't worth the risk of smuggling it to the present. Arriving home in an authentic Yankee uniform was bad enough. Arky crumbled the sheet of paper and tossed it on the wagon's plank floor. "If you've got anything in your pockets," he told Danny, "leave it here."

Danny patted one of his pockets, as Rufus starting playing the cor anglais at the front of the wagon.

Arky turned to the opening phrase of *The New World* solo. *Daa-da-daaa, daa-da-daaa...*" He turned back to Danny.

Danny, holding the metal frame housing his tintype, studied his picture.

"You gotta leave that," Arky said.

Danny looked up.

Arky didn't like what he saw. "What you get in 1863, stays in 1863."

Danny answered with a rueful smile. "Easier said than done."

"It's proof you were here," Arky urged. "We don't want that."

Danny shrugged. "It's just a picture."

As the cor anglais music began to shift from the yearning melody to erratic and atonal, Arky realized he had little time. "You can't take it."

"People will think I Photo-Shopped it, or had it taken—"

Arky grabbed for the tintype. Danny yanked it back. Arky dove forward, knocking Danny off the crate. They sprawled on the wagon floor, fighting for the tintype. Danny tried to scoot away with the case still in his hand.

"Give it!" Arky yelled as he grabbed Danny by the front of his jacket.

When Danny refused, Arky slammed him backward. Danny's head banged hard against the top edge of the wagon's tailgate.

Danny saw stars and everything went black.

Arky snatched the metal case from Danny's hand and flung it behind him. As it slid across the floor toward the front of the wagon, a serpentine of mist slithered past it.

Rufus was in the grip of the cor anglais. It ruled his fingers and worked his lungs. His eyes were the only thing he seemed to control, shining with ecstasy as the wild music played. Ribbons of mist poured from the instrument's bell and curled into the wagon.

Down the road, around a bend, a squadron of Union cavalry rode. The captain leading the cantering horsemen heard the strains of music. He raised an arm and brought the squadron to a stop. They all listened, puzzled by the alien music. Not recognizing it as a bugle call he knew, the captain spurred his horse, and led his squadron forward.

At the wagon, the cor anglais playing Rufus reached a crescendo of a last screaming note. A double flash of light exploded from the wagon, knocking the reed from his mouth.

The silence was filled by pounding hooves. The troopers on horseback galloped around the corner.

Rufus clutched the cor anglais and heaved for breath.

As the cavalrymen thundered by, they hardly gave Rufus a glance. They had no time for a deranged-looking musician clutching some kind of woodwind instrument. They only answered to the song of battle.

Catching his breath, Rufus turned. His time voyagers were gone. He spotted something on the wagon's floor. It was a metal photo case. In it was a tintype of Daniel Bender, holding a bat.

Rufus smiled at the sight. Just like the lovely music Octavia Jongler had shared with him, it was always nice when one of his time voyagers left a memento.

Part III

Ensemble

1

Hometime

IRIS WAS ON double duty. She had the wooden music case in the car in case someone returned from the past and she was driving to Bender Excavation to extract her father from the present danger of divulging something to Ray Bender.

In the Jongler-Jinkses' garage, the old Bender Excavation van was still parked nose in first. With the garage doors shut, late-day sun poured through the glass panels in the top of the doors. The light illuminated what had been spray-painted on the van's side panel: You Can Run but Not Hide.

The van jerked with the *squeak* of rusty springs.

Inside the van, Arky and Danny sprawled on the floor. Still wearing their dirty Union uniforms, the boys looked dazed.

Blinking to awareness, Arky swung his arm into the van's side panel. The *clang* of metal was the sweetest sound he'd ever heard. He snapped up to sitting. His eyes locked on the glass windows in the van's rear doors. "We're back!"

Danny was slower to sit up. He winced as he felt the knot on the back of his head. Reaching into his jacket pocket, he found it empty. "I hope you're happy."

"I'm so friggin' happy, I don't feel like myself!" Arky yelled and kicked open the rear doors.

"I meant about my tintype," Danny explained. "It didn't make it."

"It's where it belongs." Arky scooted out the back and recognized the inside of his garage. "All right, Iris, you finally did something right!" He turned to see Danny climbing over the console into the driver's seat. "Whoa! Where you going?"

"I gotta know if Rafael's okay."

"You can't go anywhere in a uniform," Arky protested.

"Why not? It's where I've been."

"If you get seen in that and start blabbing about being in the Civil War, you'll be wearing a straitjacket," Arky warned. "We need new threads"—a giddy chuckle escaped him—"or they'll put us on major meds."

Danny opened the driver's side door, giving Arky the assurance he needed. He jumped on the van's back bumper and looked out the glass panels in the garage door. He was relieved not to see his dad's Subaru sedan—seeing him too soon would be a nightmare—but not seeing the Subaru wagon was a disappointment. Getting Iris, the cor anglais, and Danny together ASAP was mission number one.

Arky herded Danny through the door leading into the house and pushed him toward his father's bedroom to find clothes that would fit Danny.

On the way, Arky jerked Danny to a stop in the hall. They both stared at the daguerreotype of Thomas Jinks, with his left wrist tucked in his Confederate uniform, and the scar jagging into his hairline. "Me and Iris wouldn't be here," Arky said, "if Thomas Jinks wasn't on our wall." Arky had no idea how time voyagers could or couldn't change history. He just knew he was still alive. "You saved him with that pitch."

"Yeah," Danny nodded. "But it doesn't help Rafael."

In Howard's bedroom, Danny raided the closet for some clothes that would fit. As well as jeans and a shirt, Danny grabbed a sport coat.

"You, in a jacket?" Arky questioned.

Danny shrugged. "Kinda got used to wearing one."

They went upstairs to change out of their uniforms in Arky's room.

It gave Arky the chance to pop into Iris's room and grab the case with the cor anglais from under the bed. Surprised to find the case missing, it gave him hope. Maybe Iris knew they were coming, and she was armed and ready to push their memories so deep that the Civil War would go back to gathering dust in history books.

Rid of their telltale uniforms, they headed back downstairs. Going through the kitchen, Arky stalled by throwing open the fridge. "Oh no!" he proclaimed, "nothing but hardtack and cold beans!"

He got a chuckle, and Danny to remember they hadn't eaten in over 150 years. Hitting the fridge for fried chicken and soda also bought Arky some time. He yanked the portable phone from its cradle and speed-dialed Iris. As the call went through, he chased after Danny, scarfing down a piece of chicken and heading to the garage.

Iris was driving down the road toward Bender's when her cell phone rang. Seeing the call was from home confused her. Her dad had to still be at Bender's. She pulled over and took the call. "Hello."

"Me and Danny are heading to the hospital," Arky announced.

"Arky!" Iris shouted.

"Have you got the spider stick?" Arky demanded.

"Yes!"

"Then get your ass to the hospital."

Hearing the line go dead, Iris threw her cell on the seat and did a U-turn.

Arky raced after Danny into the garage. Luckily, Danny had trouble finding the button to open the garage door. It gave Arky enough time to get into the passenger side of the old van before Danny cranked the engine and shot the vehicle into the sunlight.

As Danny drove like a maniac, Arky white-knuckled the dash. "We survived the Civil War, for Christ's sake; could you please not kill us a couple miles from home?"

With his eyes fixed on the road, Danny didn't respond. Coming to a stop sign, he brought the van to a hard stop.

The jolt dislodged something that slid from under Arky's seat. He looked down and saw a cell phone. As Danny surged the van forward, Arky picked up the phone and recognized the Navy SEALs cover. He pressed Danny's phone on.

When it booted up, Arky tapped the calendar icon. "Holy shit."

"What?"

"We've only been gone four days."

Danny took it in. "Maybe nineteenth-century time is different than twenty-first-century time."

The comment threw Arky. The same thing had happened with Matt when he had gone back to 1907—present time and past time ran on different clocks—but it wasn't something Danny would know. "How'd you know that?" Arky asked.

"Maybe time isn't much different than pitches," Danny said. "It comes at you at different speeds."

"Say what?"

Danny felt the pull of a smile and a pang in his chest. "It's like Sarge told me. When God created the universe, galaxies and solar systems, he was throwin' curveballs, sliders, and sinkers. I bet God throws an off-speed changeup too."

Arky was impressed by Danny's insight. He suddenly sounded like he might have a future in physics. *Nah*, Arky told himself, *there's no way Danny changed that much.*

Moments later, the van screeched to a halt in front of the emergency room entrance to the hospital. Danny jumped out and rushed inside. Arky hustled after him.

Danny and Arky followed signs to the ICU. On the way, they bumped into a candy striper they knew from school. She gave them Rafael's room number. They found the room, and pushed inside.

It was vacant.

Danny stared at the tightly made bed, empty, waiting for another patient. His insides welled with dread and fear. "He's dead."

"We don't know that," Arky pulled Danny out of the room. "C'mon."

An inquiry at the nearest nursing station delivered the news. Rafael had been taken out of his drug-induced coma. His head trauma had improved enough for him to be discharged.

The fear clutching Danny let go.

Exiting the hospital, they got a surprise. The van had been towed.

2

Reunion

Before Arky could finish dialing Iris, a Subaru wagon rushed toward him and Danny. Iris was behind the wheel.

Reaching them, she jumped out, and locked Danny in a hug. "I thought I'd never see you again!" She ran to her brother. "Arky!"

He threw up his hands. "Touch me, and I will beat the crap out of you."

She threw her arms wide. "Have at it, then wheel me into the emergency room!"

"Your ass-kicking can wait. We've got stuff to do." Arky gestured at Danny. "You ride shotgun."

"Right," Iris said, still beaming at her brother. "You drive; I'll ride in the back."

As Danny got in the car, Arky checked the back. A beach towel lay over the curved and distinctive shape of the cor anglais. Arky was relieved Iris had the foresight to assemble it. He went sotto voce to her. "We're going to Rafael's house. On the way, play it and hope it does its thing."

"You think it'll bury your memory, too?" Iris whispered back.

Arky reached for the driver's door. "I sure as hell hope so."

The prospect fired a thought. "What about Mom?" Iris asked. "What did you find out?"

The car's moon roof powered open. Danny shot a hand through the opening. "C'mon, let's roll."

Ignoring her question, Arky slid behind the wheel.

As they drove, the sun had begun to set.

From the back seat, Iris grilled them about their journey to the Civil War. Danny answered her questions while Arky shot his sister looks in the rearview mirror. He couldn't believe she was stalling, not firing up the cor anglais, and doing what it was supposed to do: bury their memories of time travel below the realm of consciousness.

Since Arky hadn't answered her question, Iris put it to Danny. "What about our mom?" she asked. "Was she in the Civil War, too?"

Arky's impatience jumped to anger. "Would you shut up?"

The lightbulb went off in Danny's head. "Whoa! That's where your mom's been all this time? In the past?" He turned to Arky. "You never told me that."

"We don't know where she is," Arky insisted.

Iris could barely contain her excitement. "Dad found a picture of her matching the vision I had of Mom. She's dressed Victorian style."

Seeing Danny oozing curiosity, Arky threw Iris a scrap to hopefully shut her up. "Mom was in 1863 but only passing through to somewhere else."

Iris almost jumped into the front seat. "Did you see her?"

"No."

"Then how did you know?"

"A guy named Rufus Jongler told me."

"We have his picture!" Iris exclaimed. As excited as she was, she stopped herself from mentioning Danny's tintype.

"Good," Arky snarled. "I look forward to burning it."

Danny turned back to Iris. "I'd like to see that picture of Rufus." He reached into his pocket. "It's not the only thing that made it from 1863." He pulled up the signed, Army of the Potomac Championship baseball.

Arky almost drove off the road. "You had that all the time?"

Danny grinned. "The tintype was a sac fly. It was all about advancing this."

"You're a prick."

"You're easily fooled." Danny chuckled with self-satisfaction as he handed the ball to Iris. "When I show this to Major-League scouts, they're gonna flip."

"No," Arky declared, "they're gonna show you to the nuthouse."

Iris took in the dark brown ball with its bleached signatures. "Wow."

Arky's patience was gone. "Get your fingers on something else," he hurled at Iris.

Danny took the ball back from her and rolled it in his fingers, admiring it.

Iris slid the towel off the cor anglais.

Trying to keep Danny distracted, Arky asked, "What are you gonna do when we get to Rafael's house?"

"You'll see," Danny answered.

Iris began to play the Dvorak solo. *Daa-da-daaa…*

Danny jumped at the sound and whipped around. "What are you doing?"

"It's something that's gotta be done," Arky told him.

Danny tried to open the door, but Arky was ahead of him, hitting the lock button.

As the music shifted from classical to otherworldly sounds, Iris's fingers and lungs submitted to the powers of the cor anglais. The first strand of mist snaked from the instrument's bell and curled into the front seat. Danny recoiled from the mist in recognition. He'd seen them twice before. "I don't wanna go anywhere else!"

"Don't worry," Arky assured him, "we're not going anywhere" He pulled the car over on a street lined with modest houses. "It's the icing on the time-travel cake."

Danny looked terrified as several mists coiled around him.

"And it's the icing that *hides* the cake," Arky added as he reached for one of the serpentine mists to ensnare him. But the ropey mist turned away and joined the white coils enveloping Danny.

As the cor anglais continued its wild music, Arky gaped at the cloud swallowing Danny. "What about me?"

Iris had no will to answer.

The misty cocoon enshrouding Danny turned into a scrim of images flickering to life and fading away: Danny hurling a rock across a river—Danny swinging a bat, blasting a lofted pitch—Liza, dressed in a hoop skirt, turning back to Danny—a bottle of Jongler's Rejuva-Nation—Danny throwing a submarine pitch—Liza, dressed as a boy, flipping a baseball to Danny—a bottle of tonic exploding against a door—Rufus Jongler, holding the cor anglais, looking down from his mule—a giant full moon shining in the night sky. As a scene of Yankees and rebels playing baseball under the moon receded into the mist, and the last note from the cor anglais faded to silence, the misty cocoon dissipated like fog melted by the sun.

Arky stared at Danny, still there, looking hypnotically ahead.

Gasping for breath, Iris pulled the reed away.

"Hey, Cap," Arky said, "do you know where you are?"

Danny turned with a frown. "Where else would I be? There's no wishing your way outta this town." He looked around. "Why'd you pull over?" He pointed through the windshield. "Rafael's house is a block up."

"Right," Arky said, as he wondered how much Danny remembered and realized something had killed the car's engine. He turned the key. The starter sputtered and died.

Danny tried to open the door, still locked. "Open it," he ordered as he pushed back in his seat. Tapping his head on the headrest, he winced and touched the knot on the back of his head.

Arky kept trying to confirm what should have happened. "Do you remember getting that bump?"

Danny didn't answer as he clambered from his seat and up through the moon roof.

Iris pushed the cor anglais down out of sight. "Where are you going?"

"Like I said"—Danny pushed himself up and out of the car—"to see Rafael."

As Danny jumped down from the car and jogged down the street, Arky wheeled on Iris. "What's going on?"

She answered with an innocent shrug. "I didn't know the cor anglais could disable cars."

"Not that! Did it bury his memory or not? And what about me?"

"Maybe because you're a Jongler," she suggested, "you remember everything."

"Great," Arky snapped, hitting the unlock button, "I'm stuck with PTSD for life." Getting out, Arky ordered, "We gotta get the baseball from him before he remembers what it is or does something really stupid and shows it to Dad." Arky started after Danny.

Iris put off telling Arky that their dad knew everything, and that she was going to the prom with Matt. All that could wait for as long as possible. She put the cor anglais on the floor, covered it with the towel, and hurried after Arky.

As Danny ran ahead, a teenager on his porch spotted him. It was one of the guys who had fish-slimed Danny's van and had chased him after Danny had beaned Rafael. The kid pulled out his cell phone.

Reaching Rafael's house, Danny knocked on the screen door.

The front door opened. Rafael stared through the screen at the surprise visitor.

Danny noticed the dark spill of bruising on the left side of Rafael's face. "I'm glad to see you, man."

"Sure you are," Rafael said with a scowl. "Killin' me might've have spoiled your shot at the bigs."

Danny wasn't thrown by the bitterness in his voice. "Are you okay?"

"I'll play ball again, if that's what you're wondering."

The relief washing through Danny pushed a smile. "I'm glad to hear that."

"What do you want?" Rafael asked bluntly.

Danny thought the answer was just wanting to know Rafael was all right, until his hand brushed against the baseball in his jacket pocket. He didn't know why it was there, but it gave him an idea. "I've got something I wanna show you."

"What?" Rafael asked impatiently.

"A new pitch."

Rafael chuckled derisively. "After the last one, there's no way I wanna see another." He started to shut the door.

"Wait, Rafael, I don't blame ya for hatin' me." Rafael hesitated and Danny kept going. "But this pitch is totally different. I've even got a name for it." He chuckled as words kept popping out of him. "Believe it or not, it's called a 'bender.'"

"Ha-ha," Rafael deadpanned.

"C'mon," Danny urged, "grab a bat, and let's take a ride. It's gonna be worth it."

Rafael wasn't sold. "Where are we going?"

"You'll see." Danny grinned. "Trust me, you're gonna love this pitch."

Moments later, Rafael drove his car out of the driveway. Danny was in the passenger seat.

Arky and Iris made it to the house in time to see them drive away.

"Where are they going?" Iris asked.

Arky watched the car with a worried look. "Not a clue."

3

Going Yard

WITH THE SUNSET painting a backdrop to City High's baseball field, home of the Banditos, Danny and Rafael walked from his car in the empty parking lot onto the field. Danny carried a black wooden bat.

As they moved to the area around home plate, Rafael asked, "What the hell are we doing here?"

Danny held the bat out to Rafael. "We've got something to finish."

Rafael didn't take it. "You sure it's not me?"

Danny shook his head. "Absolutely." He offered the bat again.

Rafael reluctantly took it, and Danny started toward the mound. "What's this 'bender' pitch do?" Rafael asked.

Danny turned with a grin and kept walking. "Takes people back in time."

It wasn't just curiosity eroding Rafael's fear; it was Danny's sense of confidence and calm. Rafael stepped into the batter's box.

Danny pulled the ball from his pocket. He was immediately thrown by the look of the ball: dark brown, strange stitching, and with lots of white writing on it. He rolled it in his fingers, reading some of the writing.

"You gonna throw it?" Rafael asked. "Or turn it into a crystal ball?"

Danny looked up. The plate seemed so far away. While he couldn't recall where he'd found the weird ball, he had a vivid memory of when he had last stood on the Banditos' mound. "Bottom of the eighth," he announced. "Three–two, Cyclones lead. You got a man on second with two outs." He pointed at Rafael. "One ball, no strikes."

"I don't remember it all," Rafael said, "but it sounds about right."

Arky and Iris, having followed them the few blocks to the school, hung back in the shadows of the third-base stands.

"What's he doing?" Iris whispered.

Arky answered quietly. "Shut up, and watch."

Danny felt the familiar press of his right foot against the rubber. He lifted his gaze to Rafael.

Rafael crouched in his stance.

Danny's stomach ballooned as he flashed back to the sickening memory of the riser catching Rafael's temple and dropping him. He shook it off, like shaking off a sign. He fingered the ball into position. Another flashback hit him: an even stranger vision of some kind of soldier, at home plate, turning his head into a rising fastball and dropping with the same rag-doll helplessness. Danny violently shook his head.

Rafael straightened up. "I'm not liking this."

"No-no," Danny assured him. "I'm fine, just a little nervous."

"You're nervous?" Rafael came back. "I'm scared shitless."

It got a laugh from Danny. He heaved a breath. "I'm good if you're good."

Rafael retook his stance. Danny bent into his bowlike delivery, reached down low, powered through, and released a fastball over the heart of the plate. Rafael unleashed his swing and crushed a towering shot into centerfield.

Rafael watched it with a flood of relief and pride.

"You still gotta run!" Danny scolded.

Rafael ran toward first as Danny went announcer. "Santeiro sends a blast to center." The ball sailed over the centerfield fence. "That ball is yard! The tying run crosses the plate and here comes the game changer, Rafael Santeiro!"

Arky grabbed the chance he'd been waiting for. He raced from the shadows toward centerfield.

Danny saw him but kept announcing as Rafael rounded third. "The Bandito fans go apeshit! The Banditos take the lead. End of ball game. The Banditos win!"

Rafael stepped on home and turned to Danny. "What about the ninth inning?"

Danny glanced toward the darkening sunset. "Game called 'cause of darkness."

In the shadows, Iris texted her father.

Having jumped the fence and fetched the ball, Arky ran back toward Iris.

Danny called to him. "Hey, ball boy, I want that back!"

Arky didn't like being called "ball boy," but more troubling was whether Danny's memory of 1863 had been buried completely or not. Arky jogged toward the mound. The good news was that Arky didn't have to scrape Danny's name off the ball. It had been blotted over by a smudge of black paint from the bat.

Reaching the mound, Arky flipped Danny the ball. "All yours. You remember where you got it?"

Danny's brow knitted. "No."

"We found it in a junk shop when we went fishing."

Danny's confusion grew. "We didn't go fishing."

"Yes, we did," Arky insisted. As Rafael joined them on the mound, Arky expanded on the lie by turning to Rafael. "He probably doesn't remember 'cause he fell in the boat and cracked the back of his head." He turned back to Danny. "It's why we came back before the weekend. You should get checked for a concussion."

In the dimming light, three other figures had appeared in the stands back of home plate. It was Hector and his two friends; they'd been waiting for Danny's return. They all held baseball bats.

Hector called to Danny on the field. "Hey, Pescado, you've got some cojones comin' back here."

Danny answered. "Had to finish the game. Congrats on the win, four–three." As Hector and his friends exchanged looks, Danny added, "But if you ever mess with my ride again—"

Rafael finished for him. "You'll have to answer to me." He grabbed Danny's arm, and pulled him toward the third-base stands. Arky followed and picked up Iris along the way.

Iris pulled Arky back from out of earshot of Danny and Rafael. "What about his name on the ball?"

"Taken care of," Arky confided.

As the four of them reached the parking lot, Howard's Subaru raced toward them.

Arky called to Danny. "You should come with us."

Danny shook his head. "Nope. Rafael and I have one more thing to do."

The two of them got in Rafael's car and drove away as the Subaru jerked to a stop. Howard jumped out.

Iris couldn't wait any longer. "Arky," she confided, "Dad knows everything."

Arky shot her a shocked look.

"You're back!" Howard wrapped Arky in a bear hug. "I saw Danny, too! Thank God!"

"Geez, Dad." Arky squirmed. "Spare the ribs."

Still clutching him, Howard asked Iris, "Is Mom back too?"

Iris met his eyes, dancing with excitement and hope. "No, but she's on the horizon." Answering his disappointment, she added, "And Arky discovered that Mom passed through 1863."

Howard pushed back from Arky, holding him at arm's length. "She did?"

Arky threw Iris a baffled look. "What are you talking about? I went fishing, not Mom hunting."

"You told me all about it on the way here," Iris protested. "About how Mom taught Rufus Jongler 'Goin' Home' and the Dvorak solo."

Arky kept playing clueless. "What are you saying? Mom left us to become a music teacher?"

"Iris," Howard interjected, trying to understand. "Did you play the cor anglais already?"

"Yeah," she answered, "but it didn't work on Arky, and he knows it!"

As Arky got in the back of the Subaru, he raised his arm, and smelled his pit. "How 'bout we get outta here? I'm in bad need of a shower."

4

Busted

As Rafael and Danny drove, Danny read out loud everything written on the old baseball, from "1863—Army of the Potomac Championship—34th New York—16, 77th New York—14" to the signatures of the long-forgotten players.

"You gotta Google it when you get home," Rafael said, "and see if it was a real game or the ball is just a fake."

"Yeah, I will," Danny replied.

Rafael got back to a more immediate concern. "Shouldn't I be taking you to the hospital so you can get your head checked out?"

"It can wait," Danny said. "I've got something else to show you."

With Howard driving and Iris in the front seat, she told him how she'd played the cor anglais in the Subaru wagon and buried only Danny's memory of time travel.

When Howard turned back for confirmation, Arky shrugged unknowingly. "Dad, if she's gonna have one of her whacky visions, it was a good thing I was driving."

Stopping at the stalled Subaru near Rafael's house, Iris jumped out and collected the cor anglais hidden under the towel in the backseat.

As she got back in the front seat of the sedan with the cor anglais, Arky had already anticipated his strategy. "Funny place to leave your cor anglais," he said.

She turned to him. "So you admit you know about the cor anglais."

"Of course, I do," he acknowledged. "You showed it to me months ago."

"If I showed it to you months ago," Iris challenged, "why didn't I show it to Dad?"

"I don't know," Arky answered with a skeptical frown. "Something about some girly secret between you and Mom."

"You're lying!" Iris yelled. "You know everything! You went to the Civil War with Danny, and you're the only one who knows everything about it!"

"The Civil War?" Arky echoed. "Isn't Dad the expert on that?"

"Ahhhhhh!" Iris screamed.

"All right, all right," Howard cautioned. "Let's calm down."

Iris collected herself, turned back to Arky, and went into prosecutor mode. "Okay, smartass, how did Danny end up wearing Dad's coat? You guys probably came back in Union uniforms, then swapped 'em out for clothes at our house."

"Iris," Arky explained patiently, "we hadn't changed clothes in over three days of fishing. We smelled like sewer rats, and there's no way we were going to take all those germs into the hospital to visit Rafael."

She hit him with another fact. "Danny's van was in our garage the whole time you say you were fishing. How did you get out of town and back?"

Arky raised his thumbs. "Two thumbs up, Sis. It's called hitchhiking."

"And what about the old baseball in Danny's jacket?" she demanded.

Arky looked perplexed. "Okay, what about it?"

"It's a Civil War baseball," she told their dad, then snapped back to Arky. "It's real, and Danny brought it back with him."

"Yeah, it's a real baseball," Arky admitted. "We found it in a junk shop. I tried to tell Danny it was a fake, but he had to buy it. And it's good thing. Otherwise, he wouldn't have had a ball to finish the Cyclones-Banditos game." He finished his summation with a smile for Iris's benefit.

Before she exploded again, a muffled text alert sounded from her pocket. Arky recognized the alert. It was from Matt.

Iris quickly dug in her pocket, snatched out Arky's phone, and tried to erase a text string. Her finger was almost on "Delete" when Arky snatched the phone from her.

He checked the latest text from Matt. It read, "Leave no man behind. If you do, he'll take your sister to the prom."

"What the—" Arky exclaimed before he checked his anger. He scrolled through the message string, reading all of Iris's faux-Arky texts with Matt.

For the rest of the ride home, Arky faced the toughest test of his false amnesia. He was torn between two urges: wanting to barf at Matt thinking his sister was "Hot, hot, hot!" and throwing the phone at Iris so hard she'd go down like Thomas Jinks.

But Arky knew going ballistic on Iris in front of their dad might lead to questions he didn't want to face. Why did he lose his phone? When did he last have it? Did he remember what happened at Bender Excavation before he and Danny got blown to 1863? So far, Iris hadn't been smart enough to hit him with questions that might blow his cover. In his brilliant way, Arky was content to stay ahead of the less-than-brilliant.

As soon as Howard pulled the car into the garage, Arky jumped out and went inside.

Howard turned to Iris. "I know it's a dumb question, but what's the use of time travel if you don't remember when and where you go?"

Iris was still furious at Arky. "I'm telling you, Dad, he's faking it. He remembered everything about it until you showed up."

Howard pondered her answer. "If you ask me, whether he remembers or not isn't the most important thing. What matters is that he and Danny are home." He turned to her with beleaguered hope. "And Mom might be right behind them."

5

Déjà Vu

On the green roof topping the mall, a breeze rustled the tall prairie grass spanning the roof. A full moon, climbing in the darkening sky, burnished the waving grass.

Danny and Rafael walked to the parapet at the edge of the roof. The parking lot and a scattering of cars glowed under the light poles. The fishing pond shimmered.

Rafael had followed Danny's lead long enough. "What are we doing here?"

"Looking for a sign," Danny answered.

"What sign?"

Danny pulled the old baseball from his jacket pocket. "If I throw it, and it makes the pond, we both make it to the big leagues. If it doesn't, we don't."

Rafael chuckled. "Hate to tell you, but your arm almost sealed my fate once. I don't wanna test it again."

Danny wagged his head. "You got a point."

"I don't need a sign," Rafael said. "I know we're gonna make it. Keep the ball; it's too cool to lose. Besides, it might help you remember what you've been doing the last few days."

Danny raised the ball and held it against the big moon. A ring of light encircled the ball. It filled him with a strange sense, like a déjà vu. A question crossed his mind. "Do you ever wonder who threw the first curveball?"

Rafael scoffed at the random thought. "Not really. Who was it?"

Danny kept rolling with his déjà vu. "The guy in the sky. He threw the planets around the sun and the moon around the earth."

Rafael stared at Danny, unsure if he was different because they hadn't been friends for years or if he was different from something else. Rafael responded. "Sounds like Sky-Guy isn't a very good pitcher."

Danny lowered the ball. "Why not?"

"You can't just throw curveballs. You gotta mix it up."

It pulled a chuckle from Danny. "Sky-Guy mixes it up."

"How so?"

"He made people—nuthin but screwballs."

6

Twin Tangle

As Iris and Howard went into the house, they heard the TV coming up from the basement den. Iris handed the cor anglais to her father and asked him to take it to her bedroom. After he started up the stairs, Iris went down to the den.

She found Arky sprawled on the couch, watching ESPN. He looked as kicked back as if he really had gone fishing. She realized screaming at him wouldn't work. She told herself to be as cool, calculating and devious as he was. "I thought you said you needed a shower," she began.

"What's the point?" he asked not taking his eyes off the TV. "No shower's gonna wash off the stank of you and Matt having a thing."

She prickled at his grossness but refused the bait. "Why are you doing this?"

Arky flipped a hand at the TV. "I'm catching up on my sports. It was only a few days"—he shot Iris a teasing grin—"but it feels like a hundred and fifty years."

"I mean, why are you lying to Dad about where you went?"

Arky yanked out his cell phone. "You're one to talk. If I'm Deceit, you're Deception. You texted so many lies I'm gonna have to find an exorcism app for this thing."

"I was covering up for you and Danny," she explained.

"I read the texts," he shot back, "and what's between the lines. Now I get why you blew me away with Danny. So you could weave a spell over Matt."

"Yeah, that was my plan," she said scornfully. "It's all about me."

Arky sat up. "Okay, Sis, cards on the table. You know I love pissing you off, but it's not why I'm faking the memory thing."

"What is it then?"

"Dad's gotta think I'm clueless."

"Why?"

He muted the TV. "If I told Dad what happened in 1863, and the real story of how our great-great-great-great-grandfather got left for dead on the battlefield, he wouldn't be able to handle it."

Her eyes widened. "You didn't tell me about that."

"For good reason."

Iris fought getting sidetracked. "Dad has handled Mom being gone for a year and a half. Why can't he handle what happened to Thomas Jinks?"

"Because Dad's a Civil War wonk and History Cop. He'd never be able to stop himself from writing about it and setting the record straight."

"What's wrong with that?"

Arky gave her a disparaging look. "You really don't think this stuff through, do you?"

"Stop being a dick, and tell me what you mean."

"There's a ton of reasons Dad needs to know as little as possible. One, if I told him exactly how Thomas Jinks got left for dead, he'd publish it, and people would want to know his primary source. His answer would be, 'Ah, a couple of kids who time traveled there.' How do you think that would go over in academic world? Two, if Dad thought he could ramp up his Civil War research by actually going there, he'd start racking up time-travel points till he was in the Million-Mile-Million-Year Club. Three, the Pandora's box of time travel has been opened wide enough to launch Matt, Danny, and me to the past, and it's only a matter of time before someone gets killed, like Danny and I almost did. That is, if Mom hasn't been killed already."

"I know she hasn't," Iris insisted.

"A vision of Mom isn't real," Arky countered. "It's a *vision*."

"You found out she passed through 1863," Iris pushed back. "That's a solid clue."

"As solid as a crumb on a trail."

"It's more than we've ever had before."

Arky released a sigh and met his sister's eyes. "Bottom line, we lost Mom to the cor anglais before she even disappeared. I don't want the cor anglais taking Dad too."

"Me neither," she agreed.

"There's one more thing I haven't told you," Arky said. "Our little trip to 1863 almost got you and me unborn."

She pulled back. "What?"

"Danny almost screwed up the marriage between Thomas Jinks and our great-great-great-great grandmother, Elizabeth Conway."

Iris's eyes widened. "You met her too?"

"Yeah. And now I know where you got the crazy gene."

Iris was more fascinated than offended. "But I *did* get the crazy gene. We did get born, and everything worked out."

Arky fell back into the couch, exhausted by their differences. "Yeah, it's working out great. I'm in a family where now *everyone* knows about the time-travel spider stick. How fantastic."

"Wait!" she exclaimed, struck by a memory. "There's stuff in Mom's computer explaining why Danny couldn't have screwed up our family tree and us being born."

Arky eye-rolled. "I can't wait."

"It's called the 'Grandfather Paradox' and the 'Novikov Principle.'"

7

Desperate Measures

When Howard had carried the cor anglais up to Iris's bedroom, the narrow stairwell leading up to the attic office had caught his eye and pulled him up to the attic.

Having opened Octavia's *The Book of Twins: Sphere of Science* on the computer, he now sat at the desk. The cor anglais lay on the desk in front of him.

As rain began to drum on the roof, he picked up the old photo of Octavia in Victorian attire and holding the cor anglais. He gazed at it with a winsome smile.

Taking the computer mouse, he moved the curser on the screen and clicked open the "*Tempus Ludendi*" file. When Octavia's image, holding the cor anglais, came up, he clicked the play icon.

In the basement, Arky had listened to Iris's descriptions of the Grandfather Paradox and the Novikov Principle. When she was done, he gave her a put-upon look. "Thanks for the lecture on how we can and can't change history, but you know, Iris, wouldn't you be better off blowing on your oboe and practicing for your Oberlin callback, than blowing bullshit theories on time travel?"

"I didn't make 'em up," Iris retorted. "They're on Mom's computer."

"Good for them, but right now I'm tapped. Fact is, if you really wanna get into the whacky weeds on this, I haven't slept for centuries. All I wanna do is forget that we're cursed with the last name of Jongler and chill in front of the TV." Keying the remote, he turned the TV sound back on to a commercial. He changed the channel. What he saw pushed him deeper into the couch: a rerun of Ken Burns's *Civil War*. "Great"—he threw a look to the ceiling—"it's stalking me."

"Maybe it's a sign that the only brilliant college essay you're going to write," Iris said, "is about your experience in the Civil War."

Channel surfing, Arky groused, "Writing an essay about time travel would get me into a school all right: Asylum U."

The chime of a doorbell sounded.

In the soundproof attic, on the computer, Octavia was now playing the cor anglais solo. *Daa-da-daaa, Daa-da-daaa...*

After the first few measures, Howard noticed the strangest thing. The volume seemed to be increasing. At first, he thought it was his emotions playing tricks on him. But then he noticed something stranger. The keys of the cor anglais, lying on the desk, were *moving* in sync with the keys Octavia was fingering in the video. The increase in volume wasn't coming from the computer; it was coming from the cor anglais.

8

Double Trouble

On the front stoop of the Jongler-Jinkses' house, Matt stood under the protection of the eave from the pouring rain. He rang the doorbell again. Behind him, in the street, his pickup was parked in the deluge.

Iris opened the door to find Matt, glazed with rain. She was startled to see him. "Hey!" was all she could manage.

"Hey," Matt echoed. "I heard Arky was back." He kicked himself for messing up the sequence he'd rehearsed. "And I wanted to thank you for wanting to go to the prom with me."

"No, thank you!" Iris blurted.

Matt gave her a beseeching gesture. "Are you gonna invite me in?"

In the nanosecond before she answered, she spied something more shocking than Matt's surprise visit. In the reflection of the side window flanking the door, she saw a rope of mist curling down from the living room ceiling.

Her vocal chords fired—"Shit!"—followed by her arm slamming the door.

On the stoop, Matt went deer in the headlights.

Iris shouted through the door. "Don't take that the wrong way! I'll tell Arky you came over, but he was so wiped he went to bed! Tomorrow!"

"Okay," Matt muttered. "Tomorrow." It wasn't exactly the encounter he'd imagined seeing her the first time after she'd said yes to the prom. *But*, he mused as he slogged back to his pickup, *that's the thing about girls. The second you think you have them figured, you're wrong.*

In the attic, Howard was saucer eyed by the sight before him.

While the video of Octavia playing the cor anglais had ended, the cor anglais on the desk was far from silent or still. The keys clattered as the woodwind played wild music and pumped twisting mists from the spider-clad bell.

Having only witnessed this once before, when Iris and the cor anglais had produced the racing ropes of mist that had sent Arky and Danny to the past, Howard was shocked by a new twist. The mists not only disappeared through the floor, some coiled around the room. It filled him with expectation: the mists in the room, snaking around and above him, were for *him*. If Octavia wasn't coming to him, he was going to her.

In the basement, the first ribbon of mist snaked down from the ceiling several feet behind Arky, as he watched the Major League ball game he'd found on TV.

The sound of someone pounding up the stairs to the second floor pulled his eyes upward. He thought about going to investigate, but he was too zonked, and he couldn't imagine anything else happening on a day that was surely maxed out on drama.

Another strand of mist roped down from above, alongside the first. Their leading heads disappeared behind the couch, pulling thickening bodies down from the ceiling.

Arky's eyes drooped.

The misty heads rose behind his shoulders, hesitated, then shot around his neck.

His eyes snapped open; his mouth opened to scream. Nothing emerged. His throat was in the vice of the serpentine mists.

Iris charged up the last steps and threw open the door to the attic office.

She was hit by multiple shocks: the unworldly music of the cor anglais—the ancient woodwind on the desk playing itself—her wild-eyed father, with outstretched arms, offering himself to the tangle of mists swirling in the room, but leaving him untouched.

Before Iris could lunge forward, grab the instrument, and try to stop it, the serpentine mists stopped, recoiled, and rushed at her. They whipped around her like white stoles.

As many times as Iris had wished for the mists to ensnare her, to wrap her in a cocoon, and launch her into the past, she couldn't stop herself from shouting, "But I'm going to the prom!"

Appendix A

From Dr. Octavia Jongler's *The Book of Twins: Sphere of Science*

The Grandfather Paradox and The Novikov Principle

The Grandfather Paradox is the nightmare of time travel. You go back in time, kill your grandfather before he sires your father, and thus eliminate your birth from the future. And because you were never born, you cease to exist upon your grandfather's death.

The Novikov Principle counters the Grandfather Paradox. It argues that just as you can't unbreak an egg, you cannot change the past in a way that would radically change the future. In the past, you may alter the *how* of an outcome, but not the outcome itself. You may go back in time and stop John Wilkes Booth from shooting Abraham Lincoln, but you won't be able to stop Lincoln's untimely death by another means.

Appendix B

Civil War Fact and Fiction

Characters

SGT. GEORGE CAMBELL was a real Union soldier in the 34th New York Volunteer Infantry. From the regiment's roster report, only this is known about him:

> CAMBELL, GEORGE H. – Age, __ years. Enlisted, May 1, 1861, at Herkimer, to serve two years; mustered in as sergeant, Co. G, June 15, 1861; no further record.

There was a black manservant named Dabney who worked for a Union soldier at Falmouth. Dabney's wife, a laundress working for a Confederate general in Fredericksburg, really did hang garments to signal the movements of rebel troops. It was called the "clothesline telegraph."

While General Francis Barlow's action to end the Blue and Gray Championship is conjecture, he was infamous for his harsh and merciless discipline. Civil War soldiers who fled from battle were threatened with death and sometimes shot by their officers.

One character in the book lives in the ether between fact and fiction: Henry Fleming, the young soldier who challenges Danny to throw a rock across the Rappahannock. If you want to know more, web search "Henry Fleming" and you will find where he "lives."

Music

Dvorak's 9th Symphony, *From the New World* (a.k.a *The New World Symphony*) was premiered by the New York Philharmonic in 1893 at Carnegie Hall in New York City. The English horn solo from the second movement, the Largo, became the melody for "Goin' Home," written in 1922 by one of Dvorak's students, William Arms Fisher.

The "lemon peel" ball of the 1860s was slightly larger and softer than a modern baseball. Its dark leather, readily available, made it easier to see against a daytime sky.

Baseball

Jim Creighton

CREIGHTON WAS BASEBALL'S first superstar. In an era when pitchers were expected to deliver a hittable pitch, Creighton was the first to challenge hitters with speed, even while throwing underhand. Playing for the New York Excelsiors from 1860 to 1862, he became the game's best pitcher *and* batter. In October 1862, Creighton swung so hard at a home-run blast that he ruptured something internally and died four days later. He was only twenty-one. He is buried in Brooklyn, New York, under a monumental gravestone.

Besides the "baseball fever" that swept through the Union and Confederate camps on opposite sides of the Rappahannock in the spring of 1863, that summer also sparked the imagination of the boy who invented the curveball.

Candy Cummings

In the summer of 1863, a fourteen-year-old named Billy Cumming and his pals were on a beach in Brooklyn, New York, throwing clamshells out over the water. Billy noticed how the shells curved through the air. He thought it would be a "good joke" on his buddies if he could do the same with a baseball. It took him four years of experimenting and playing for Brooklyn baseball clubs to perfect his "curveball." On October 7, 1867, pitching for the Brooklyn Excelsiors, he debuted the curveball, baffling batters. His curveball turned him into a winning pitcher and earned him the name "Candy" Cumming. At the time, "candy" was a superlative meaning the best in anything.

If you'd like to know more about New York baseball versus Massachusetts baseball in the mid-eighteen hundreds, check out http://vbba.org/rules-and-customs/ for the New York game and http://www.baseballchronology.com/baseball/History/Massachusetts-Game.asp for the Massachusetts game.

The War

The Confederate army, under the command of Robert E. Lee, enjoyed their last major success in the Battle of Chancellorsville and the Second Battle of Fredericksburg. After driving the Union army into retreat, Lee attempted to invade the North. In the first days of July 1863, he was stopped at Gettysburg, Pennsylvania. At Gettysburg, Lee's army suffered losses from which it would never recover. It turned the war's tide, and the Confederate cause slowly unraveled until Lee surrendered in April 1865.

More fact versus fiction can be found at blowbacktrilogy.com.

Blowback Trilogy Continued

Poor Arky! He just got home, and now he's being trampolined to another spacetime by the dreaded "spider stick." Thrilled Iris! She finally gets to experience the wonders, woes, and wackiness of time travel.

Where do they land in the next and final book, *Blowback '94*?

SPOILER ALERT!

What century might it be? Hint: Arky almost takes a round trip.

That's right, 1894. But *where* they go couldn't be more different than the Civil War. They arrive in Paris, 1894, in the midst of the infamous Moulin Rouge, a veritable menagerie of human eccentricity running wild in the City of Lights. Toulouse Lautrec, Edward Degas, Jane Avril, and a parade of bizarre characters are waiting for Iris and Arky with open arms and life-changing adventures. The greatest of them all, of course, will be how and where the twins find their mother, Dr. Octavia Jongler.

Now, if you're wondering—given all the football in *Blowback '07*, and the baseball in *'63*—what could the sport be in 1890s Paris? Hmm, perhaps there's more than one. One that you would never guess in a million centuries, and one that may be the ultimate exercise for the heart: love.

We can only promise this: *Blowback '94* will take you to the heart of the Jongler family legend and bring the Blowback Trilogy to a time-shattering finale.

Acknowledgements

A WRITER IS like a sculptor who works in clay: a master of adding on. An editor is like a sculptor in stone: a master of taking away.

In other words, I owe a great debt to my editor, Gerri Brioso, a.k.a my literary exterminator, character assassin, and dialogue jihadi. She knows where all the bodies—whether they be chapters, characters, or lines—are buried. For the Civil War part of *'63*, she knocked off more generals than Sherman on his march through the South.

So, while it pains me to thank Gerri for her brutality, it gives me great pleasure to thank her for her brilliance in helping shape the *Blowback* stories. All writers should be so blessed to have such a taskmaster in storytelling.

I owe a round of thanks (and drinks) to my coterie of golf buddies, who put up with me interrupting their sports talk on yesterday's game with obscure sports trivia from another century. A special fist bump to Gary Malbin for his excellent story notes and for being my "math consigliere" of manuscripts. Another to John Morrison for teaching me about the intricacies of pitching and why Bruce Springsteen matters.

A special thanks to my twin brother Torsten Muehl for his wonderful drawings of the Jongler cor anglais, the 1863 map, and scheming with me for the first time since we were kids.

Lastly, I owe thirty years of gratitude to my beloved wife, who still doesn't mind living with a guy with more imaginary friends than she can shake a stick at. At least my IFs don't mess up the house. Knock on wood.

About the Author

Brian Meehl is the award-winning author of six novels, including the vampire comedies *Suck It Up* and *Suck It Up and Die*. He enjoyed a successful career writing for television, winning three Emmys, and performing Muppets on *Sesame Street*, and in Jim Henson films, including *The Dark Crystal*. Brian welcomes visitors to his websites, blowbacktrilogy.com and brianmeehl.com.